Side Stories
A.D. Harvey

Published by
Mandrake of Oxford
PO Box 250
OXFORD
OX1 1AP (UK)

Also by A.D.Harvey and published by Mandrake
Mind-Sprung

Contents

Author's Note

These stories are arranged not in the order they were written but in the order I would prefer them to be read. Three of them were written in the course of a single uncomfortable night in Leeds, after a telephone conversation with the anthologist Michel Parry followed by a Chinese take-away that gave me food-poisoning: of these 'The Last of the Daubeney-Fitzalans' appeared in Michel's collection *The Rivals of Frankenstein* (Corgi, 1977) and was subsequently translated into German, Italian and Japanese, 'Second Chance' went through numerous re-writes before publication in its present form on the Internet and 'The Man with the Living Brain' provided the germ of the idea for my novel *Warriors of the Rainbow* (Bloomsbury, 2000) but is printed here for the first time in its original form. 'Gamlingay Churchyard' also dates from the late 1970s. 'Like the *OGPU* and the *Stasis*' was originally written in 1990, at a time when it still seemed just possible that the Green Movement would result in interesting new departures. 'Bitch' and 'The Orgasm Files' also date from the 1990s: 'The Orgasm Files' is a conflation of two stories published in the soon-afterwards-defunct *Journal of Erotica*, thereby entitling me to think of myself as a 'sex-worker', nowadays regarded as a more respectable occupation than 'unemployed academic'. 'Doris Lessing's "One off the Short List" and Leo Bellingham's "In for the Kill" ', was a spoof article published in *Critical Survey* vol.5 no.1 (1993): the Lessing story is to be found of course in collections of her short fiction but 'In for the Kill' has, I believe, the distinction of being the first and perhaps only published short story that exists only in the excerpts given in a scholarly article. The character Jennifer Manley is modelled on the artist Jennifer Lewis, whom I first met on a bus in 1986 – I only ever spoke to her in the presence of other people – and who was murdered in St Vincent in 2012: the poem at the end of the volume was written for her about 1996. 'The Last Days of Shakespeare' appeared in *Contemporary Review* for April 1991: it is not a spoof but shows how scholarly analysis and invention might indeed drift quite close to one another. 'Tess and Thomas Hardy,' an earlier version of which appeared in *Thomas Hardy Yearbook* for 2000, shows how they might even overlap in a fashion guaranteed to annoy various people. To annoy these people even more I reprint my two best literary spoofs, relating to Dickens (*The Dickensian* no. 458 Winter 2002) and Hans Christian Andersen (*Times Literary Supplement* 21 February 2014), and also provide a short note that might partly explain my motives (other than sheer boredom) for writing spoofs in the first place. Most of the other pieces here date from after 2002. 'Isabella Jefferson Gets Laid' is a revision of a passage in my novel *Oxford: the Novel* (Brewin, 2012). Readers will no doubt notice my frequent return to certain themes and images, and I include a couple of autobiographical pieces that may elucidate certain of my preoccupations.

Three Wishes

Oliver had been living in London for some months but was still wondering how to find himself a girl.

The best looking ones always seemed to be at the far end of the platform of the Underground when the train came into the station. The window of his living room faced approximately in the direction of the West End, and his street's location on one of London's forgotten, bricked-over hills enabled him to gaze out over an immense geometrical wasteland of chimneys, television aerials and roofs, each one of the latter conceivably sheltering Miss Perfect Ecstasy 2003 if only he knew how to meet her. He tried answering small ads in *Time Out*, even got a couple of responses, and progressed as far as an embarrassing rendezvous in a pub in Camden Town, from which he would have escaped via the lavatory window if only he had been able to open it. He tried going on political demos in support of postmen and nurses and troop withdrawals. For a couple of weeks, inspired by a chance collision of supermarket trollies, one of them propelled by a schoolgirl with cherry-coloured Dr Martens and a deliciously lopsided grin, he explored the possibilities of various branches of Safeway and Sainsbury's. He even tried going to dances at the University of London Union.

And then, one morning, after wandering for two or three depressed hours through some of the least known back streets of Shoreditch, he found himself standing beside a canal. It was overlooked by the endlessly repeating windows of a group of tower blocks but he knew that if he threw himself in amongst the rusting prams in the canal, no stunningly pretty girls' club swimming champion would dive from a ninth floor balcony to his rescue. He contemplated throwing himself in anyway.

'Don't do it,' said a voice. 'You can help me instead.'

The obvious response would have been: How did you know what I was thinking? But Oliver did not ask, because the voice which had spoken to him came directly from a puddle on the towpath. He looked closer. It wasn't exactly a puddle: one of the flagstones of the pathway was missing and the resulting gap was brimful of water:

water so dark and opaque and unreflecting that it was as if he was peering into the depths of the ocean, as if the towpath was nothing more than duck boarding over the middle of the Atlantic. And as he stood staring down at the square of water, its surface plopped suddenly and the voice said: 'You see that round slightly bluish pebble by your foot?'

'Yes,' said Oliver. (We'll skip providing a description about his astonishment, as it was beyond words.)

'Pick it up.'

Oliver picked it up. Something told him it would be colossally heavy, in terrifying disproportion to its small size, but it turned out to be as light as polystyrene.

'Now drop it in me.'

'Why?' asked Oliver.

'Because if you do I'll grant you three wishes.'

'Three wishes?

The square of water at his feet plopped impatiently.

'Three wishes. They'll really work, too.'

Oliver held out the pebble and let it drop. It disappeared into the depthless water without even a ripple, though just as Oliver thought to himself, why, there wasn't even a ripple, the surface of the water plopped again and the voice – a surprisingly *dry* voice – said:

'So what's your first wish?'

'I wish I was incredibly good-looking.'

'You are'. The voice made it sound so simple. 'And your second wish?'

'I wish I had an incredibly beautiful girl friend.'

'You'll meet her later today. And the third wish?'

Oliver decided he would like to see if his first two wishes came true before he asked for anything else.

'Can I save it for later?'

'If you like, but careful what you wish for,' said the voice: but suddenly there was no longer any water in the space between the flagstones, only a shadowy muddy hole that smelt of someone else's fart.

Oliver looked around but there was nobody in sight: only the tower blocks rearing against the sun like a close-up of tombstones.

On the way home Oliver had an idea, from glimpses of his reflection half-caught in shop windows, that there was something odd about his appearance. He noticed people looking at him too, especially teenage girls. As soon as he got home he inspected himself in his bathroom mirror. His features were the same, they were still his nose and his lips, but they had been subtly re-arranged and reordered and there was now no doubt about it, remarkably handsome. His hair seemed blonder and wavier too, like in a hair-conditioner advert, and his clothes sat on him with a new stylishness.

More than somewhat bemused he stepped into the next room. The most heart-rendingly beautiful girl he had seen in his whole life was standing by the table, leafing through a copy of *Socialist Worker*.

'Richard?' she said, with a radiant expression of hope.

'My name's Oliver.'

The girl looked away for a moment, her delicious larkspur-coloured eyes filling suddenly with tears, but when he put his arms around her she dropped the copy of *Socialist Worker* and stuck an eel-like tongue in his mouth.

She was called Samantha. During the next few weeks he found himself permanently amazed at how lovely she was: her breathtaking profile on the pillow beside him when he woke in the morning, the More-Than-Miss-World body in the bathroom before breakfast, the incredible unselfconscious elegance with which she stood in a doorway or nibbled a Yorkie bar or scratched her elbow. When he went outside the flat with her he felt like Prince Camaralzaman in the *Arabian Nights* or King Arthur promenading with Guinevere through the streets of Camelot: people would come out of the shops to stare, and when the traffic halted for them at zebra crossings it would only start up again when they had passed out of sight round the next corner. On the other hand, shop assistants were often rude to them, to show they weren't impressed, and men in pubs were always trying to pick fights with him.

Sometimes girls came up to Oliver with various pretexts to speak to him. As soon as they realized Samantha was with him they would withdraw, looking as if they had drunk tea with salt in it. He remembered the voice at the canal towpath telling him to be careful what he wished for.

'Who's Richard?' he asked her, on their fourth day together.

'Oh, he was a boy I once knew,' said Samantha, giving him a Barbie Doll smile. 'When I was ten, would you believe it. We were going to get married, only we had to wait till we were sixteen. Then he moved with his parents to another town and I've never seen him since.'

The curious thing was that he didn't really want her. Hormones called to hormones, but only at the GCSE biology text book level. It was like having it off with Jennifer Aniston. Sometimes he felt like telling her, 'Look, the girl I had in mind isn't like you at all, she's got different hair, isn't so tall and –' but that wouldn't have been true, Samantha was so exquisitely right that no other curve of throat or thigh, no other way of standing, no other colouring, could have been righter. It was simply that . . . . He didn't know what it was. He began to lie awake at night, thinking about his third wish.

One thing he couldn't understand about Samantha was where she had come from. She had told him about this Richard kid when she was ten, but there was definitely something odd about her just turning up in his living room, without friends, without antecedents, and with only the clothes she stood up in. Finally he asked her how it was that she had stepped so suddenly into his life.

'You won't believe this,' she said, 'I was really depressed and lonely, I mean it was so bad I even tried placing a small ad in *Time Out* – you know Ugly Duckling seeks Hans Christian Andersen to help her become Beautiful Swan –'

'I saw that one.'

'Hoping that Richard, – did you write in?'

'No, I thought it a bit soppy.'

'So apparently did everybody else. I got no replies at all. Then one day I was coming home from a demo against the reintroduction of the Poll Tax, all on my tod as usual, and I stopped at a little old fashioned cabbagy-smelling corner shop, and bought one of those cardboard cartons of Ribena, you know, the ones that come with a green plastic straw with an articulated bend and have a little hole covered in silver foil. This time, when I poked the straw into the hole there was nothing inside the carton, though it felt full, and when I took the straw out and tried to squint into the hole, you won't believe this, but a voice inside, definitely from inside but coming from a long way away as if from infinity, offered me three wishes if I would drop the carton in the litter bin at the point in Holloway Road where the buildings towards Archway have the appearance of a skull.'

'Three wishes?'

'Three wishes. The voice said I should be careful what I wished for, but I thought, golly, and wished to be incredibly beautiful because I thought that might make a difference to my life. And then I wished for a smashing boyfriend.'

'And there we both were.'

'Yes.' She smiled at him, her wonderful larkspur-coloured eyes laughing and wistful at one and the same time, and it was impossible to believe she had ever not been unbelievably pretty. 'There we both were.'

'And you held on to your third wish for later?'

'No. My third wish was ….' She hesitated. 'My first two wishes I thought were too personal, so I wanted to wish for something bigger than my own life that would help other people. So I wished for a revolution.'

'A revolution?' Oliver laughed. 'But there hasn't been the least sign of one.'

'Perhaps we'll have to wait a bit.'

That night, as so often, he awoke after a couple of hours' uneasy sleep and lay pondering the question of what he was going to do with *his* third wish. It was a question that would not go away. He wanted to sleep, but it nagged at him like an exposed nerve in a broken tooth. His Third Wish.

For a few moments he seemed to doze, and then he woke again with a start. In the distance, on the other side of the city, but quite distinctly, there was the sound of artillery fire. Every thirty seconds or so orange flashes lit up the drawn curtains. There was a machine gun firing some streets away and, once, a shout from the pavement just below their window and the sound of running foot-steps. He waited for the police sirens, perhaps the braying of ambulances, but there were none of the customary noises of law and order coming to the rescue. Suddenly there was a detonation that shook the whole house. He had an idea it came from the police station on the other side of the park.

Samantha continued to breathe regularly but shifted her position in her sleep so that her rump was against the palm of his hand.

'Richard,' she whispered, still asleep.

From the Archives
of Gaia Nova

If it wasn't genuine it was the most accomplished forgery Z54FF6 CLINT had seen in all his two decades as an archivist. The document consisted of five sheets of paper or paper substitute bearing the dates, successively, December 31. 1799, December 31st 1899, 31 Dec. 1999, 31-12-2099 and 31-12-199. The paper/paper substitute, though wonderfully preserved, seemed genuinely of the vintages attributed to it — respectively late eighteenth, late nineteenth, late twentieth, late twenty-first and late twenty-second century. The hand-writing on each sheet had a curious family resemblance — on the paper dated December 31.1799 the double ss's were written fs and the double ll's had the second l shorter than the first, otherwise the script was similar to that on the next two sheets; the fourth and fifth pages in the series were written in the squarish, simplified block capitals that had been adopted once writing by hand had come to be taught only for use in unforeseen contingencies, but retained an indefinable likeness to the older writing in the anglings of the junctions of vertical and horizontal lines.

December 31.1799

The political convulsions of the last ten years, the overthrow of the power of the House of Austria in the Italian Peninsula and in Flanders, of Dutch sovereign independence, of Polish nationhood, and above all of the family that has ruled France for eight centuries, has caused some to talk of the imminent second coming of the Messiah, others to speak of continent-wide conspiracy of Freemasons, yet others of the subversion of morality or the triumph of a new communal order. To me, who recall the tar-daubed heads of executed Scots insurgents displayed on spikes at either end of London Bridge after the risings in favour of the Chevalier de Saint George, and was at the Arsenal to greet Gustave III the morning he promulgated the restoration of monarchical authority in Sweden, the course of recent events seems perfectly familiar: almost tediously so from the universally mistaken insistence that any of it is novel. Previous centuries have seen the trial and judicial murder of consecrated kings, the dictatorial rule of fortunate but self-deluded generals, the machinations of international loan speculators, the exile or proscription of entire social classes, and the arrogant misapplication of lessons purportedly learnt from Greek and Roman history. My grandfather has told me how he saw Charles I step out on to the scaffold in Whitehall and I myself, on my last visit to Paris, saw Louis Capet, formerly known as *Sa Majesté Très Chrétienne Louis XVI*, kneeling at the guillotine, not far from where, thirty-six years earlier, I had watched Damiens being slowly torn asunder by four terrified horses following his attempt on the life of Louis XVI's grandfather, Louis XV. The one or two turns of public affairs for which I recall no exact precedent, the short-lived republican government composed entirely of university professors at Naples, the project of turning an entire unpopulated continent into a prison in the southern ocean, are not in themselves of much importance to those who are not professors, or convicts, or Kangooroos, or Neapolitans.

December 31st, 1899

It's been a century that began hard and cruel but turned out better than might have been expected. Its greatness was in the early, cruellest years. Jefferson, whose house-guest I was both in Washington and in Virginia, used to say that the English bombardment of Copenhagen, together with the crimes of Napoleon Bonaparte, made that period one of the three epochs in human history, along with the Macedonian and Roman imperial eras, signalized by the total extinction of national morality; yet as I write these has not been a war in western European for nearly thirty years and they tell me that even private murder is less frequent than in former times.

I saw Charlotte Durance two days ago, at the Café Royal with Edward Cassavetes: the first time I had set eyes on her in twelve years. That astonishingly skimmed milk and strawberry juice complexion of hers, which even I had thought was the most exquisite I had ever seen, has not so much faded as dried out, and that glow which had suffused her whole face and bosom, in fact her whole being, like the radiance of a young girl when she first has her monthly flowers, has entirely vanished — like the light from one of Edison's electric bulbs when it is switched off. She comported herself with an aplomb that amounted almost to sexual swagger but one could detect in her a kind of fidgety impatience, almost desperation, as if even she had realized a couple of seasons ago that she had very little time left for this sort of game. I observed a row of tiny vertical lines on her upper lip, which in ten years will be the puckered lip of an old lady. I forget how long ago it is that I used to tell myself that I would never ever get used to seeing girls first encountered in the glory of blossoming womanhood fade, grow fat, heavy-footed, stale-scented and then bent, raucous, balding and vindictive. But of course I saw the process repeated so many times, over so many generations, that eventually I taught myself not to seek any connection between the dew-fresh miss of one decade, the thickening matron of the next, the grandmama of a couple of decades after that. Charlotte Durance, by virtue of having drawn my attention (seized my imagination is not too strong an expression) more forcibly and more entirely than any other woman since — how many years? — reminded me of how appalling I once used to find this pell-mell progression of ripeness and decay. I suppose that's the most worthwhile observation I have to record as this only-almost-glorious century draws to its end.

31 Dec. 1999.

The end of the century again. The end of the millennium. Neither means much: the latter even less than the former.

I remember the coming of canal navigation and the railways, of power-weaving and electro-magnetism: consequently I am not likely to be overly impressed by the microchips and miniaturized computers and mobile phones of the last decade. The vast acceleration of the speed at which facts can be sorted and communicated only emphasizes the perennial difficulty of, in the first place, formulating facts that are objectively significant and, in the second place, deciding what constructive use to make of them. The century began with the first transmission of radio signals and, as Lord Rutherford predicted at the dinner I arranged in his honour at the Reform Club, at one level it was a century dominated by radio in its audio and televisual forms: but except perhaps in accelerating a decadence in musical and literary art that was in any case rendered inevitable by the spread of mass education, what difference did any of this new science make? The machine-processed syllables of the first men speaking from the surface of the moon were a lesser thrill for me than three breathily mis-pronounced words whispered in my ear by Justina af Geijerstam as we crossed Brooklyn Bridge that same evening.

As for biotechnology —

The fireworks are beginning.

31-12-2099

The massacres of the 21st Century have exceeded even these of the 20th Century. In the 20th Century the millennium-old struggle between the Individual and the Collective — the Principle of the Individual, the Principle of the Collective, two different kinds of Will — flared up. The Age of Individualism, it was sometimes called: yet the collectives of Fascism and Nazism were defeated, shattered into fragments, not by Individualism but by even more collected collectives. In the 21st Century the collectives have put all idea of the Individual to rout. People have become valued simply in proportion to the degree of their resemblance to everyone else. Late 20th Century fantasies about biological cloning have given way to the reality of a kind of social-behaviourist cloning. Faces, skin colour, the shape of eyes and mouths, the width of cheekbones, the length and angle of noses, remain infinite in variety and combination but the minds behind the faces are bewilderingly the same, as are the trisex garments people wear and the endlessly repeated avenues of apartment blocks in which they are kennelled. It was inevitable that I, with my unique perspective, should feel the unimportant sameness and predictability and evanescence — the absolute *forgettableness* — of even the most transcendantly stereotypical avatars of this mass culture, but these was something chilling in the discovery that each one of these countless sleep-walking millions now have the same casual indifference to one another.

31-12-2199

Of course they had sailed round the world, sailed to Cape Horn and to Australia and to Hudson Bay, sailed north into the three-month's day of the Barents Sea, years before I was born. All I saw for myself was a progressive speeding up of travel, so that instead of being bored waiting to arrive people were bored at having nowhere to go after they arrived. An exponential leap in achievable speeds enabled, first the moon landings and the Mars probes of the 20th Century, then in the 22nd Century the expeditions to Mars and Titan. Then the encounter with the thousand-year total ecosystem spaceship with 81 colonists on board, the 18th generation since they were launched from their home planet in the Antares sector.

They televised a trans-space video of them. Perhaps I wouldn't have recognized her amongst all the centuries of women who have passed before me if a chance resemblance between the sneering smile of the colonists' captain and the sneering smile of Edward Cassavetes had not pointed my memory to the right city in the right decade. The navigation officer of the spaceship, a woman of twenty-one or twenty-two, who had recently miscarried and was awaiting confirmation of a second pregnancy, was Justina af Geijerstam.

After so many years of avoiding the boredom of travel, I am to fly out to Titan the day after tomorrow, the first working day of the new century.

Z54FF6 CLINT replaced the papers in their capsule. 'That must have been about the time the rings of Saturn imploded and wiped out all organic life on Titan,' he reflected, pressing the R-button to send the capsule back to the 87th basement level vault.

The New Keats

In the age of the Internet and the iPod it is a moot question whether the standard prose narrative, if it survives at all, will become longer — like those thick romantic sagas the secretaries on their way to work on the Tube always seem to be buried in — or shorter, like:-

Oxford (or perhaps Cambridge) undergraduates. A rejected lover bombards his cold-hearted beloved with poems. After impatiently scanning the first three or four she begins to realize that they're actually very good. By the seventh or eighth she's beginning to think he might be a poetic genius. By the tenth she's beginning to think she perhaps ought to encourage his next desperate attempt to date her as he is definitely the only real star around worth hitching her star to — also the break-up of her previous relationship, with the Secretary of the Union, means that there's well, a vacancy — and then she hears the news : he's killed himself.

She keeps his poems of course. She even takes them out now and then and rereads them. More and more her rejection of him and his suicide seem the great tragedy of her early adulthood. If only. . . . Meanwhile his work slowly and subterraneously establishes a reputation amongst the critics. Eventually a slim volume of his 'Collected Poems' is published, rapturously reviewed, made the theme of two television documentaries, etc. The twenty-first century's John Keats has been discovered. What would it have been like to have had an affaire with, what would it have been like to be *married* to, someone like that? But the dozen poems she has been hoarding aren't even in the 'Collected Poems'. She rather fancies they are even better than the ones that have been printed, and though they are *very* private and personal, written for her eyes alone, she realizes of course that they belong to *every* lover of poetry. She sends photocopies to one of the new 'experts' in the dead poet's *oeuvre* who have taken over his fame.

No response. After an anxious month of waiting she sends a reminder and receives the photocopies back by return with a curt cover note: 'Good try. These are all by Auden, Yeats, Meredith etc. I have written in the name of the real author on each poem.'

The Prime Minister's Ghost

A haunting is a disturbing business, and it frequently happens that the disturbance is not limited to the appearance of the ghost itself. A curious instance of this occurred some years ago to a distant cousin of my wife's, W.A.G Platt, of — College in the University of Oxford. Dr Platt (I have heard him insist upon his title) enjoyed world renown in one of those fields of academic research in which lack of competition is not perceived as lack of scholarly significance. His annotated bibliography *Lord Grenville 1759-1834* had commanded wide sales, relatively speaking of course – it is not to be expected that a bibliography of a long-dead British prime minister should sell as well as a cookery book by a living prime minister's wife – and he had obtained from the prestigious Oxford University Press a contract for the preparation of Lord Grenville's literary works, which include the once celebrated *Letters of Sulpicius* (the last of which, however, was written by his elder brother Thomas Grenville, the bibliophile) and his *Essay on the Supposed Advantages of a Sinking Fund*. Dr Platt, who was unmarried, was living in his college rooms, working on his Grenville edition, during the Christmas vacation when our story opens. At this season the colleges are virtually deserted, even the wickets being closed to discourage inquisitive tourists, and the general dampness of the Oxford winter, together with the mists rising from the circumambient tributaries of the Thames, encourage a retreat, not merely into cosy, book-lined rooms behind closed doors, but into the recesses of the mind. At whatever hour of the day one ventures forth, one is oppressed by the gloom of impending and premature nightfall, and the penetrating chill of the damp air makes it impossible to step out on to the street without desiring the immediate refuge of a blazing fire, toasted crumpets, and as much light as will serve to read a book by. It was in these peaceful, isolated but perhaps somewhat melancholy circumstances that Dr Platt received, along with the usual spatter of undesired Christmas cards, a letter in an unfamiliar but elegant hand-writing, sent from an address in, or rather near, Lostwithiel in Cornwall.

It must be premised that Lord Grenville, like other prime

ministers of his day, did not achieve the purple by his own unassisted efforts. His rise to the premiership was facilitated by more than the usual advantages; his father himself had been prime minister and as such had contributed notably to the rupture with the American colonies; his wife was a considerable heiress; after his brother-in-law had contrived to be shot dead in a duel he found himself in possession of two country houses, as well as a dark and inconvenient mansion in London; the letter which Dr Platt received was written by the present occupant of the larger of Lord Grenville's two country houses, Treconnoc, near Lostwithiel. Now it so happened that all Lord Grenville's papers, and all personal mementoes of his residence at Treconnoc, had long since been removed to other places – the papers to the British Library in London – and Dr Platt had never visited Treconnoc. He was now, in this unsolicited letter invited to do so. Even more unexpected than the invitation was the information which accompanied it: Dr Platt, world renowned expert on Lord Grenville, was invited to visit Lord Grenville's former country seat because it was currently being haunted by Lord Grenville's ghost.

The writer of this letter did not in fact go so far as to assert that the apparition he had twice seen in an upstairs corridor was Lord Grenville. He merely stated that he had taken the liberty of writing to Dr Platt because of Dr Platt's reputation as an expert on Lord Grenville: the apparition might be that of Lord Grenville: it was certainly dressed in the leather knee-breeches and stock and large-buttoned coat of Lord Grenville's period, and the hair was, as far as had been ascertainable in the shadows of the corridor, and in the confusion of encountering a ghost, tied at the nape of the neck with a black ribbon in the fashion of those days. The writer of the letter also mentioned the wart on the spectre's cheek and the intent, perplexed expression in the eyes which seemed to require a constant effort to focus on any point beyond the formidable nose. This certainly sounded like the physiognomy of Lord Grenville, as presented in William Owen's portrait at Christ Church.

Dr Platt's first response on reading the letter was embarrassment. He had been studying the life and career of Lord Grenville for twenty years and this was the first he had ever heard that Lord Grenville's ghost still walked. Moreover, he was one of those agnostics who do not absolutely believe that there are no such things as ghosts but who resolutely doubt that anybody they have met, or are likely to meet, has ever seen an authentic specimen of the genus. He reread the letter. After twenty years of studying Lord Grenville it was slightly shameful that he had never once been to Treconnoc, from which house many of Lord Grenville's most important letters had been dated. Also the truth was he was feeling somewhat jaded in the Christmastide vacuum of a university town. A visit to Treconnoc might, professionally speaking, be a waste of time, but it would provide a welcome change of scene. He immediately wrote to his Treconnoc correspondent, stating that he would arrive on the second day of the New Year.

Having survived Christmas, New Year's Eve, and the train journey to Lostwithiel, Dr Platt duly arrived at Treconnoc House on the evening of January 2nd 19 —. Not much was visible in the darkness apart from a number of large square windows of Georgian style, illuminated on either side of the principal entrance, and a darkened wing to one side. His host, a remote descendant of Lord Grenville's sister, was a dim, spare individual whose facial resemblance to a hare suggested a long and misguided process of in-breeding. As it was already late they merely exchanged conventional politenesses over a whisky and soda. Discussion of the haunting was reserved for the morning.

Dr Platt's bed was not merely unfamiliar, but also uncomfortably soft and yielding, and the wind blew strongly outside, rattling the windows and occasionally giving rise to a disagreeable moaning noise somewhere in the region of the chimneys. Dr Platt once or twice rose from the too yielding bed, which seemed constantly on the point of enveloping him altogether, and looked out through the curtains. The first time he saw an almost full moon, surrounded by a gruesomely pale halo, tossing amongst the ragged wind-driven clouds, but the next time he peered out it was no longer visible. He reflected that there were various features of the house which might well disconcert an overwrought imagination. Eventually he fell asleep.

After breakfast the following morning his host showed him the house. Part of the structure that Lord Grenville had known had been demolished in the same year as his death, and much of the furniture dated from after his time. There had also been extensive alterations in the lay-out of the garden, and such trees as had existed in Lord Grenville's time were now much older and of course much larger than they had been in the 1800s. Consequently one had only the most misleading indications of the views and vistas outside and the colour schemes and furniture arrangements indoors with which Lord Grenville had been familiar. Yet Dr Platt was agreeably reminded of his early days as a student of Grenvilliana, when having examined one side of a voluminous correspondence between Lord Grenville and a supporter in one archive collection he had moved on to another town and another archive deposit to look at letters written in answer to the ones he had just read, with a constantly renewed sense of Lord Grenville as a flesh and blood individual, a man who had actually trod the earth, wrestled with quill pens and intractable ink, and waited impatiently for the daily post. It is so easy, even for historians, to feel that historical characters truly exist only in history books, as figments of the collective imaginations of those who write about them. Going over this old and rather impersonal house, he had a sense of renewed insight, of contact, almost of *rapport*.

After this revival of awareness of the former real-life existence of Lord Grenville, his host's account of the ghost was the merest anti-climax. The older part of the house was truly old. In an upstairs gallery which must have dated from the sixteenth century, Mr Foster, his host, had twice encountered the inexplicable figure, hurrying with a rather waddling gait, from one end of the gallery to a point halfway along. On both occasions the apparition had disappeared in a blink at precisely the same place, which Mr Foster indicated. The direction from which the figure appeared seemed to have led formerly to the wing of the house demolished in 1834. The point where the apparition had twice disappeared had nothing about it to suggest a solution or explanation. They rolled back the carpet: the elm boards of the floor were in good condition but dated at least from the seventeenth century. The panelling on both sides of the room at this point was possibly more recent, but still earlier than the period of Lord Grenville's birth. It was true that, on examining the adjacent windows, they found themselves in agreement that the walls would have been thick enough to contain some sort of cupboard or enclosure or even a secret staircase, but a good two hours, rapping at panels convinced Dr Platt that there were no concealed hollow places.

Dr Platt suggested that the servants could move a camp bed into the gallery, and expressed himself ready to pass the remaining nights of his visit there. Otherwise, as he pointed out, 'It might be months before anyone is on the spot at the moment the ghost appears.'

His host paused for fully a minute before responding: 'Then you don't believe that ghosts deliberately seek out the individuals to whom they appear?'

'No,' said Dr Platt, more than ever agnostic on the subject of ghosts. 'Why would they?'

From that night on he slept in the gallery. The size of the room, and perhaps its different position in the house from his previous lodging, seemed to magnify the groanings and clickings of the wind against the roofs and he often woke to find the floor alive with bright silver rectangles of moonlight flooding through the un-curtained windows: but nothing appeared that he would have cared to designate a ghost.

Mr Foster was a man of education and cultivation, both of which had been largely wasted on him. He seemed to lack the will-power to do more than idle through days each one of which was as much as possible identical to those preceding it. He had at one time read extensively and travelled as far south as Naples and as far east as Székesfehérvár, but these efforts had left him with insufficient energy to voice more than a couple of sentences regarding anything he had ever read or seen. It was a wonder to Dr Platt that he had been capable of the effort of writing to him about the ghost; indeed it seemed that the ghost was the sole topic that could rouse him from his almost preternatural lethargy: on this subject alone he seemed as if under some sort of obligation or compulsion to exert himself, and even here he was devoid of enthusiasm or vigour. Being incapable of sustaining conversation, he was not an easy man to learn to know. Dr Platt's questioning in the course of the first three or four days of his visit elicited little more than the fact that, prior to the first manifestation in his own home, Mr Foster had never had the slightest interest in the supernatural.

As already hinted hauntings, or reports of hauntings, can be disturbing in more than one way. I'm afraid that as the brief sky-less days passed, sandwiched between long darknesses, and Lord Grenville's ghost continued invisible or otherwise engaged, Dr Platt began to be disturbed by the suspicion that he had been the victim of a hoax. Now you may recall that though Dr Platt was indisputably the doyen of Grenville studies he was not in fact the only scholar to have devoted time and energy to this subject. The notorious H.D. Arnold, the veritable black sheep of the historical profession, was also a Grenvillite. In a career the versatility of which had dizzied rather than dazzled H. D. Arnold had tackled many research topics and Lord Grenville had been one of them; in fact his Cambridge Ph.D. dissertation, with which various scandalous circumstances were associated that are too notorious to require further ventilation, had dealt with the Grenville connection in parliament. Having been, quite properly, blacklisted by the Historical Federation Dr Arnold had sought a paltry revenge by engineering a series of hoaxes on the organization. The last of these had been a couple of years previously, and as Arnold remained blacklisted and unemployed, there was no reason to suppose he had repented of his malice. He might however, have shifted his target: and Dr Platt had the uncomfortable impression the bullseye at which Dr Arnold was currently aiming was the back of his head. He was sufficiently exercised with this possibility to slip into Lostwithiel one afternoon and to ring Professor Dick Glass of the Historical Federation from the post office.

'I wouldn't be at all surprised if Daff Arnold was behind it,' said Professor Glass. 'We've had word that he was cooking up something of the sort.'

'But what I can't understand is how he managed to set it up,' said Dr Platt. 'Apart from the alleged ghost everything here is absolutely genuine. Mr Foster is in *Burke's Landed Gentry* – I checked before I came. The house. It would cost a fortune to hire such a house, and poor Arnold of course is quite penniless.'

'Poor Arnold, as you call him, has always in the past worked his little tricks on the principle of the simpler the better. It will be painfully obvious how he arranged matters once it's too late. What I can't understand is what he hopes to gain from this sort of malicious nonsense.'

Afterwards Dr Platt was never able to rid himself of the idea that his telephone call to Professor Glass somehow precipitated the next stage of the drama. That night he went to bed in the haunted gallery as usual. The wind outside moaned and hummed as usual, and the now waning moon cast patches of silver light through the windows. Dr Platt slept fitfully and about 2 a.m. woke to a strong sense that something had changed in the room. He sat up in the camp bed and saw something that hadn't been there earlier by the wall halfway down the gallery, though in the meagre light from the uncurtained windows it was impossible to distinguish what kind of object it was.

Dr Platt did not feel in the least afraid. It was not for nothing he had served as Senior Dean of his college for almost a decade. He rose from his camp bed and walked barefoot down the gallery toward the object. As he approached he saw that it was a low door, about five foot high, set in the panelling between two window embrasures. It was a door which opened outwards: it stood open at this moment and therefore projected at right angles about two feet into the room, resembling at a distance a chest of drawers or a small wardrobe placed in a spot that had been empty when Dr Platt had gone to bed.

Coming level with the door, and already wishing that he had more light, Dr Platt was able to distinguish a narrow spiral staircase leading upwards from immediately within the doorway, with a faint radiance from above illuminating the uppermost steps as they turned out of view. Dr Platt immediately entered the doorway and climbed the stairs. Afterwards he had the clearest recollection of the chill of the stone steps under his bare feet.

The spiral stairs came out in the corner of a small attic room. When Dr Platt saw that there was someone in the room he remained standing half a dozen steps from the top with only his head and shoulders projecting level with the room.

In was a small chamber apparently without windows. The walls were lined with cupboards. In the middle of the room was a large table. On the table were several papers, and some large leather-bound volumes resembling cash registers, a candelabrum holding four candles which provided sufficient illumination for the whole room, and a naked baby girl, very young judging by its small size and the sparse quantity of hair on its head, and apparently dead. Sitting on a Chippendale chair pulled up to the table was a figure with its back to Dr Platt. Dr Platt's first impression was that it was his host, Mr Foster, dressed in eighteenth-century costume, as for a masquerade. Apart from the period of the costume – a long dark blue coat, leather breeches, stockings – there was nothing about his figure to suggest the portly and ponderous Lord Grenville. The figure was slim, almost boyish, and far more erect than the elderly Mr Foster. From the rear it had one notable peculiarity. An immensely thick plait of blondish hair hung from the back of his head down to the vicinity of the seat of the chair on which the figure was sitting. Dr Platt could see the bow of narrow black ribbon securing the plait dangling through the open back of the chair. In pictures of Fredrick the Great one can see an equally long plait, which the Prussian monarch helped establish as a military fashion in the second half of the eighteenth century. But this was not a thin waxed soldier's queue, but an inconvenient mass of hair. No civilian, or at least no English civilian, had ever worn such a colossal pigtail. Then slowly, the figure turned, revealing a soft, unformed face, huge eyes apparently swimming with tears. Supposing that his presence had been detected, Dr Platt decided to advance boldly into the room, but he forgot that he was standing on a spiral staircase. As he attempted to move forward he tripped on a step and fell forward, and the next thing he knew he was lying on the floor of the gallery below, beside the camp bed.

Lighting a candle, he investigated the wall where he had found the door. He rapped on the panelling, as he had rapped several days previously. There was simply no sign or trace of any door. He was obliged to conclude that he had been dreaming, and had fallen out of bed.

But the more he thought about the dream the more disturbed he became. The figure had given the distinct impression of being nothing other than a girl dressed as a man: not a girl who habitually dressed as a man, but a girl who normally appeared as girl with long flowing hair which could not be disguised when she dressed as a man. Now, by a process of association, a girl dressed, on some extraordinary occasion, as a boy suggested the idea of a boy who normally dressed as a girl, but now and again resumed male attire.

This in turn reminded Dr Platt of one of the more ludicrous theories that had been circulated by the unfortunate Dr Arnold. This hypothesis was that the Hon. Ann Pitt, whom Lord Grenville had married in 1792, was a man. It was true that Lady Grenville's father and brother, the first and second Lord Camelford, had both been memorably eccentric whereas all that was known about Lady Grenville was that she was an unexceptionable wife, fond of gardening and a great help and comfort to her husband. In short, suspiciously unlike her closest male relations in character. It was also true that the Grenvilles had no children: on the other hand remarkably few of Lord Grenville's male connections had had children and whatever the precise medical reason Lady Grenville's childlessness was as likely to be her husband's fault as her own. And yet, as much as he feared and disliked Dr Arnold, Dr Platt had to acknowledge that he occasionally manifested a remarkable insight into past events, an almost intuitive sense of what was possible or feasible. In view of Dr Arnold's theory it seemed very unwise to dismiss the possibility that the figure at the table was Lady Grenville, or rather the ghost of Lady Grenville. Where the dead baby on the table fitted in he scarcely dared wonder.

When morning came he hastened to inform his host of what he had seen, or thought he'd seen. Mr Foster sat hunched over his boiled egg, murmuring 'Remarkable, quite remarkable.' Dr Platt had the feeling, as when he had telephoned Professor Glass, that it was useless to expect guidance from anybody else. He would simply have to see this through on his own.

'I'm convinced there is a secret doorway in the gallery where you've seen the ghost disappear,' he said firmly. 'The reason why we haven't been able to detect it by tapping is probably that it's been carefully bricked up.'

'The panelling...?' Mr Foster suggested in his feeblest manner.

'The panelling –' Dr Platt almost struck his head in a gesture of vexation. He was not an architectural historian but he should have seen this obvious point. 'It's probably the panelling that was in the originally in the wing of the house demolished in 1834. Naturally when they demolished the wing they salvaged various items of interest. The demolition probably occasioned a considerable amount of rebuilding and reconstruction in the older part of the house and in any case much of the original panelling in the older part of the house was probably in poor condition. It would have been perfectly normal therefore to take out the panelling from the demolished section and use it to re-panel parts of the surviving structure. If so there is no door in the panelling because when the door was in use the panelling was somewhere else.'

'Remarkable,' said Mr Foster. 'Quite remarkable.'

'My advice, Mr Foster, is to have your carpenter take down the panelling so we can see what is behind.'

'Do you really think so?' said Mr Foster, visibly shrinking into himself. 'Quite remarkable.' He seemed to flicker like a candle about to go out. 'Perhaps you would be so good as to point out the section of the panelling to the carpenter. Parry will ask the carpenter to step up, if you would mention it to him.'

Parry was the butler. He seemed to find it quite normal to take instructions from his master's guests. As Mr Foster stood, quite speechless, in the background during Dr Platt's conversation both with Parry and the carpenter, his mere presence had the effect of giving Dr Platt's request the force of orders.

With the help of the stable boys, the carpenter draped sheets over the furniture in the gallery and, with a great deal of dust and some unnecessary splintering of wood, began to remove the section of panelling where the door seemed to have been. Behind the wood was a wall of aged brickwork, covered with traces of plaster and a great many cobwebs, and sure enough a doorway, old enough but still evidently more recent than the wall itself, judging by the condition of the oak beam which formed the upper edge of the opening. The whole doorway was blocked with large yellow bricks held in perfectly preserved mortar. A pick-axe and sledge hammer were brought forward, and after a considerable addition to the dust which now filled almost the whole length of the gallery, sufficient space was opened to reveal a spiral staircase.

'Quite remarkable,' said Mr Foster.

By the time a couple of lanterns had been brought up from the pantry, a large hole had been made to admit Dr Platt. A faint natural light was visible at the top of the stairs. Followed by Mr Foster and the carpenter, he ascended to the room he had been in the night before.

It was exactly as he remembered it, except that no one sat at the table, and the surface of the table had nothing on it other than a thick coating of grime. Light entered the otherwise windowless chamber through a narrow sky-light in the ceiling. Dr Platt guessed that above the dirt-encrusted glass there was probably a glazed opening along the ridge of the roof, concealed amongst the slates and not visible from ground level.

The cupboards lining the walls were not locked but most of them were empty. In one of them however was a quantity of archaic electrical equipment, dating apparently from the era of Galvani and Volta. Dr Platt recalled that, as an undergraduate at Oxford, the future Lord Grenville had won the Chancellor's Prize for Latin Verse for a poem on 'Vis Electrica', beginning:

Ante oculos foede rerum Natura jacebat

Oppressa obscuri densa caligine saecli

Later Lord Grenville had been elected a Fellow of the Royal Society though, as was customary in those days, this had been more on account of his social position than his scientific attainments. Here, however was seeming evidence that he had not given up his youthful enthusiasm for electricity.

Not being an expert on eighteenth-century electrical science Dr Platt nearly missed the most curious item amongst the equipment. This was a stack of boards, each about twenty inches by twelve inches and each furnished with a number of buckles and straps, the leather of which was now rigid with age. These were evidently boards for strapping down living specimens during experiments. The size of the boards suggested an animal such as a cat, a small dog or a newly born piglet, but the arrangement and size of the straps intended for the limbs indicated that the destined specimens were not four-footed creatures of which the legs were naturally positioned below the trunk of the body. The configuration might have suited a monkey, but Dr Platt judged the straps intended for the limbs would have been too loose to restrain a monkey. He remembered the dead baby he had seen, or dreamt of seeing, the night before.

He recalled that, in the eighteenth century, before any practical application of electricity had been discovered, savants had been particularly interested in the effects of electrical currents on animal tissue. Frogs were decapitated, and their legs made to move by means of electrodes. In Mary Shelly's novel *Frankenstein*, published when Lord Grenville was 59, it is not clear what provided Frankenstein with the means of instilling life into the monster he had constructed out of bits and pieces stolen from the graveyard, but Mary Shelley was certainly cognizant of the electrical experiments of the day. And here, incredible though it was, was evidence that Lord and Lady Grenville, at much the same period were carrying out similar experiments, though not with a body reconstructed piecemeal as was the case in *Frankenstein* but rather – this was sheer speculation of course but it seemed the most plausible explanation – with the bodies of new-born babies who had died within a few days of birth and had been buried in neighbouring church yards. This then was the explanation of the long periods Lord Grenville and his wife had spent in isolation at Treconnoc, even when his presence in London was urgently required by the turn of events in public life. This then had been Lord and Lady Grenville's response to their childlessness, though it complicated rather than elucidated the question of whether this childlessness was the result of masculine deficiency in the husband or of some bizarre secret regarding the gender of the person he was supposedly married to.

That night Dr Platt slept in the room where he had passed his first night in Treconnoc. The dust raised by their explorations had rendered it impossible for him to continue sleeping in the gallery: and though he did not care to admit it he was reluctant to pass the night with no barrier between himself and the sinister chamber that had been revealed. It was a relatively quiet night for it had begun to snow steadily, and he slept well. He was woken by Parry at about eight in the morning.

'If you could come, sir.' said Parry. There was a certain reserve in his manner which Dr Platt had not observed previously. 'It's Mr Foster. I've already sent for the doctor, as I take it yours is not a medical title.'

Mr Foster was lying on his side in the gallery, still dressed in the clothes he had worn the night before. He was about three yards from the hole in the wall leading up to the spiral staircase. His eyes were open. Persons who die of fright are traditionally alleged to retain an expression of inexpressible terror on their faces, but Mr Foster had either not died of fright or else the muscles of his face had relaxed subsequently. His features showed merely that vague absence of expression which the features of dead persons customarily have.

The local medical practitioner arrived just as Dr Platt was dressing.

'Heart failure,' the medical man announced as soon as Dr Platt joined him in the gallery.

'What brought it on, would you say?'

'Old age. He was seventy-six. Dicky ticker. He had a mild heart attack last year. I told him the next one would probably be the end of him.'

'But why *here?*'

'It was his house, wasn't it? Why one room is rather than another? Though it does happen that people become markedly restless an hour or so before a heart attack.'

'I mean, you don't think he *saw* anything?'

'Look here,' said the doctor, who had evidently had a word with Parry concerning Dr Platt's presence at the house. 'Either he had heart failure because he was an old man whose heart had failed, or he had heart failure because he'd seen a ghost. Do you believe in ghosts? I don't, and neither does the coroner. You feel there ought to be an inquest? Can you arrange for the ghost to be at the inquest? If you can't the coroner would prefer not to have his time wasted. I feel the same way. I propose to make out the usual death certificate.'

Mr Foster's solicitor arrived shortly after the doctor left. Parry spoke to him briefly in the hall and then came through to the breakfast room to ask Dr Platt if he would be so good as to join the solicitor in the library.

'Ahem,' said the solicitor. 'A rather unfortunate end to what has perhaps not been an un-agreeable visit. We hope to bury Mr Foster, as per instructions in his will, at the parish church the day after tomorrow, or the next day. If you propose to stay for the funeral, I'm sure you wouldn't mind putting up at a hotel in Lostwithiel for a couple of days? Mr Foster has left everything to a distant cousin, almost his only surviving relative, in New Zealand. It'll be some weeks, I imagine, before this cousin will be able to get here and in the meantime the house and estate will have to be run on a minimal routine basis which, I'm afraid, means regular servants only, no visitors, no guests. Unless of course you think I should wire the gentleman in New Zealand to ask if you should stay on?'

'Of course not,' said Dr Platt irritably. 'I suppose at least Parry can get me a taxi to the station.'

As I suggested at the commencement of this narrative, in the case of a haunting it is often not just the appearance of the ghost which creates disturbance. Poor Dr Platt is still by no means certain he *did* see a ghost, but he is convinced there is some extraordinary and macabre mystery with regard to the secret chamber, and some incredible and probably quite horrible circumstances in the relationship of Lord Grenville and his childless wife. The trouble is, he feels quite out of his depth with this sort of thing, and though he would hardly acknowledge that the disreputable Dr Arnold was a better scholar than himself, he cannot help supposing that a man of Dr Arnold's peculiar talents might be better equipped to elucidate dark mysteries of this sort. On the other hand Dr Platt, as a respectable and respected scholar, does not care to leak useful professional information to persons of Dr Arnold's type and whereas Lord Grenville, Foreign Secretary 1791-1801, prime minister 1806-1807, leader of the opposition 1807-1812, Chancellor of Oxford University 1809-1834, is a safe and respectable subject on which a scholar could base a reputable career, Lord Grenville as husband of a transvestite, forerunner of Frankenstein and haunter of subsequent generations is quite a different cup of tea, more suitable to the kind of popular, coffee-table historian Dr Arnold would evidently have liked to be. On the whole he has found it expedient to keep quiet about what he saw at Treconnoc, in case any hint of it reached the prominent ears of Dr Arnold. There might be a good story in the Grenville marriage, but Dr Platt is proud of the fact that he is not a story teller but a historian, and scrupulously aware of his obligations to the profession. The truth of the matter is that not all facts about the past are useful to the historian.

Dreams

He took a cocktail specially prepared for him by Mike Vörösmarty consisting of hashish, codeine, toadstool extracts and Viagra and dreamt on three successive nights of being married to one of the three girls whom in earlier days he had successively loved and been successively rejected by.

In his first night's dream Pauline ignored him when he came home from the college where he worked, shouted at the kids, and talked to her sister on the phone for an hour. That night, when he reached for her in bed, she said, 'Oh, all right then,' and spread her legs without raising her knees. She kept her eyes closed during sex except that, when he lifted himself up on his arms in press-up position as he approached his climax, she suddenly looked up at him and gave him the beginnings of a smile of what might have been encouragement, or pity. Afterwards her first words were, 'I've got to go to Marks and Spencer tomorrow to get underwear for the children. Do you need anything while I'm there?' He said, 'I've just had a so-called major erotic experience with you, and you talk of Marks and Spencer.' She said – rather cleverly for her – 'Marks and Spencer are just as much part of marriage as sex is.'

She had been *victrix ludorum* in her final year at the school in Chelmsford they both went to, with a teenage boy's muscly-looking arms and, as far as he could tell from furtive scrutiny across the playground plus imagination, conical little all-but-collar-bone-high boobs which a boy in the year above informed him were almost firmer than her arse, though of course she couldn't clench them. A face like a nymph by J. W. Waterhouse and a Burne-Jones body. And a Jackson Pollock brain. He had realized at the time that she was fairly stupid, but he had kept telling himself that if only he could get to know her better he would find there was a lot more to her. Now, in his dream, he *had* got to know her better, and it had turned out that there was even less. And unsympathetic too: from somewhere there came a recollection of wrestling with the waist button of a girl's brand-new jeans and her voice exclaiming, 'You're useless!' (This was odd, as he had only ever seen her at school, in a pleated skirt in winter, school uniform frock in summer, and once or twice in gym kit, showing long sun-reflecting thighs that seemed to narrow at the tops; but it was definitely *her* voice, *her* tone.)

In the second night's dream Emma raised her eyebrows by way of greeting when he came home from college, shouted at Jacob, their six-year-old, and talked to her sister on the phone for an hour. That night, when he reached for her in bed, she wrapped her arms round him, crossed her ankles over his calves and stared up at him fiercely throughout, as if willing herself to believe in the absolutely vital significance of what they were doing with each other's body. She humped back too, but didn't make as much noise as she had done in the days before their marriage, let alone cry out 'Fuck me!' as she had done on occasion in earlier times. Afterwards she said, 'You don't play with my breasts as much as you used to before I had Jacob.'

'Somehow they've never seemed quite the same to me since I saw him burping after he suckled you,' he said diplomatically. In fact she was now a bigger woman below the waist than above it and motherhood and two career-related abortions had caused what had been emphatically hemispherical hand-fillers to morph into popped balloons.

In his dream the golden radiance from the open door of the toilet as he went along the landing for a post-coital pee suggested that Christ in Glory was waiting for him there – but on checking it turned out that they had simply left the light on in there for Jacob's benefit.

'Who was that you were talking about to your sister when I came home?' he asked her when he returned to bed.

'Chris Hampton.'

Chris Hampton. When they had started out together Chris Hampton had just made the headlines as the country's youngest Member of Parliament, having been returned in a by-election that week, and Emma had announced in a contrivedly casual voice, 'I lived with him for most of my second year at Oxford.'

'What do you mean *lived with*?' he had asked.

'You know, lived in the same house, slept in the same bed, did things in the same bathroom at the same time. Shared the same Kleenex after sex.'

Now, in his dream, he asked, 'Chris Hampton? That chap you went out with at Oxford?' '*What!*' Emma almost shrieked. 'Where have you been dreaming? It really pisses you off that my boyfriend but three before you has become prime minister.'

Prime minister? *Prime minister?* He couldn't believe it. Surely Chris Hampton had faded from public view after being caught fiddling his expenses. Was this reversing of relationships changing everything else?

And where was all this coming from? In another part of the dream Emma was telling him his erect penis looked improvised and extra-terrestrial, like something from a 1950s sci fi movie or from a diorama of life on the ocean bed: and he was pretty certain he would have remembered if anyone had ever said anything like that to him in real life.

On the third night he dreamt of Bella, the most brilliant undergraduate of her day, famous for reading out the day's crop of marriage proposals at breakfast in college (on the days she had breakfast in college), afterwards the failed White Hope of Middle English studies and last heard of as a lecturer at a provincial university. He dreamt he was lying next to her in bed after the customary exchange of marital fluids, her cold little hand in his, and he was saying to her, 'I thought it would be so marvellous with you, paradisical, a kind of sustained delirium of bliss, a non-stop excitement with a constant sense of rising to a crescendo rather than sinking in a diminuendo, a sense of being always just on the point of discovering yet another wonderful thing about you. Why has it turned out so fucking banal? *Is* happiness banal?' And in his dream she responded tearfully, 'I've always known I've never really made you happy. You've never really loved me, not the way I loved you. I've been feeling for years now that I've never really been able to develop as a person because the man I've been living with couldn't love me.'

He was puzzled. Had he missed something? Surely the whole point of these dreams was that they were the women *he* had loved to desperation, who hadn't wanted *him*.

He woke up on that third morning, as on the previous two, alone in bed. He had a quick shower, made himself breakfast, read for half an hour and went to the bus-stop.

There was a girl he had never seen before waiting there, gobsmack gorgeous, black, dread-locked, somehow simultaneously pouting both boobs and pubes, with that irresistible combination of a sweet face and a pissed-off expression. Perhaps it was the vividness of the last three nights' dreams, but it was suddenly like being sixteen all over again, trying to burst out of a small-town existence so circumscribed that the most exciting thing anyone had ever done was go to Frinton, and suddenly experiencing not merely love at first sight but falling in love for the very first time.

'Hi,' he said.

He noticed she had amazingly long, slightly curving lashes. The arm-holes of her skimpy tank top revealed not just the shoulder straps of her bra but also the side edges of her black bra cups.

'Fuck off,' she said, not even bothering to turn away.

He obsessed over her all the way to college, wondering (not for the first time) if he was destined never to experience *reciprocated* love at first sight. It occurred to him that the breathless, stomach-clenched feeling he had was not the sensation of falling in love for the first time, because he was too old for that, but the sensation of falling in love for the *last* time. He wondered when he would see her again, and remembered how, somehow, it had never been the often anti-climactic encounters with the loved one, but the gap between encounters which had nurtured the intolerable yearnings he had felt on previous occasions.

Of course he was not now the innocent he had been back in the days of first love. The girl at the bus-stop had had strikingly beautiful hands and he had a sudden jolting vision of those long, slim, milk-chocolate-coloured fingers curling around his pale apricot-coloured erection as she – Hold on! That bit about his penis looking like a diorama of life on the sea bed – could that be from the *future?*

As soon as he got to college, he rang Mike Vörösmarty. It was a land-line number: Mike was an old-fashioned kind of chap and his rants against the obtrusiveness of mobile phones sometimes lasted up to two hours.

A woman answered the phone. He did not recognize her voice so he asked, 'Could I speak to Mike Vörösmarty, please.'

'Not another!' she said. Though her voice was unfamiliar she had the same mid-Essex accent as Pauline had had when she was fifteen. 'I've been getting a lot of phone calls for this Mike Whatever-his-name-is this past week, but I've had this number for thirty-one years and I've never heard of him, not till all these phone calls. The last person who wanted him said it might be something to do with alternative universes or something, but all I can say is *please don't ring this number again!*'

And she broke the connection.

Love and Loss at the Bottom of the Garden

Max Morris opened the French windows of his work room and stepped down to the terrace. Behind him the lamp on his desk shone on book shelves crowded with the home and foreign editions of his seven best-selling future shock novels. In front of him the moonlit lawn stretched down to the belt of trees which separated his property from the road along which, according to the Rector, Charles I had retreated with the remnants of his army after the Battle of Naseby. Overhead were the moon and the stars: all around the night-time hush of rural Oxfordshire.

Inside him: a feeling of dissatisfaction, almost of loss.

Here he was, a success beyond his luridest dreams, and he had almost no personal contact with anyone. He didn't even know who his readers were or what effect his books had on them – his agent dealt with all fan and crank mail.

He crossed the lawn and followed the path through the trees to the gate that opened on to the road. From the verge he could look out over the countryside, pick out the lights of far-off farms where the people whom by day he thought of as unimportant failures bedded down for the night with those they loved.

As he latched the gate behind him he caught a movement with the corner of his eye. Wheeled back off the road in the shadow of the low branches just to his right was a motorbike, no, a motorcycle and sidecar combination. The rider of the motorcycle, still astride, was watching him. The passenger in the sidecar was gaping up at the stars, head held at an awkward angle. Both rider and passenger were young women, Max registered: and at almost the same instant he saw that the passenger was not craning to see something amongst the constellations, but was dead.

'It's *you*,' said the woman on the motorcycle. She was wearing a silver one-piece suit of motor-cycling leathers. She had removed her helmet and her hair, braided in a single thick plait, was the colour of old gold in the moonlight. She was impossibly beautiful. She was about twenty.

And there was only one thing he could say in reply, because here she was, the distillation of every fantasy he had ever had.

He said: 'It's *you.*'

'I recognize you from your dust jackets. Oh gosh. Your books – they've been our main inspiration. My favourite's *The Conquest of Now,* but all of them are important. I think they must be the single biggest influence on Freedom Fighters the world over.' She was staring at his face as if she counted on finding ultimate revelation there. 'Not just your insights into how societies are held together and torn apart, but your vision of – in our group it was what brought us together in the first place.'

'They're just....' They're just my whole life, he thought bitterly, or what I've had in place of a life. 'They're just *books.*'

'Yes. We've done it because you've written it.'

'I would have done it too – but I was always the clumsiest, most cack-handed boy in my class at school. Always the last to be picked when they chose teams.' His voice tailed away, as if exhausted by the vacuity of the excuse, but even as he was mumbling *chose teams,* the girl broke in passionately:

'What you were doing was far more important. Your books gave us the standard we try to live up to. And me, I've let you down – the mission bungled, Marianne dead, even if that was *her* fault, and now I've got to go to ground for at least three weeks till the maximum-scale search for me is scaled down – the one person in all the world I've wanted to talk to, and I've only got time to say, sorry, I screwed up.'

Pushing with her foot, she eased the motorcycle combination forward from under the trees. The motorcycle was like the automatic pistol he could now see strapped to her right thigh – same cold gleam, same design values, same used look. Her hand closed on the throttle.

Her face reminded him of Sir Edwin Arnold's lines:

> [her] lifted countenance
> Glowed with the burning passion of a love
> Unquenchable, the ardour of a hope
> Boundless, insatiate. . . .

The curve of her upper lip said: Kiss me.

'Wait –' he said.

In the distance there were police sirens. She twisted her head, not towards him but away from the sirens, to hear them better. They were moving further off.

'I've got to hide up. Bury Marianne somewhere and simply vanish.'

'You could stay here.'

'But your work –'

'My work –' It had always been his ambition to write a one-thousand page novel, a prose epic that would indicate, through all the cobwebs of human nature, the prime issue of man's relationship with his ego, with eternity, with morality (as a datum, not as individual laws to flout or equivocate with), his own sense of guilt, beauty, truth – 'You can help me.'

'Could I? Could I?' Her eyes shone. 'It'd be amazing to be around you for a while, there's so many things I want to talk to you about. And I'm not a bad cook, I know how to type, and if you're between girlfriends at the moment I guess I'm OK in bed – leastways the only one who's ever complained turned out to be a plain-clothes cop from the Special Branch.'

'If you don't mind my being so clumsy and walking into doors and only waking up behind a keyboard.'

Her face was radiant.

'Oh, gosh, it would be so exciting – Oh, shit, act normal'

She pulled the motorcycle and combination back out of sight amongst the low branches just as, with a screech of brakes, a set of dazzling headlamps swung around the corner a hundred yards down the road, temporarily blinding him. He felt rather than saw the car slew to a halt inches away from his knees.

'Police. Have you seen a woman in a silver biker's suit on a motorcycle and sidecar combination?' Blinking, still dazzled, he could just make out three men in the car, and there was a second car coming to a halt close behind, both nearside windows sliding down as he glanced towards it.

'No. No-one's passed in the last minute.' Max indicated the

footpath to the house his seven best-sellers had bought. 'I've only just now stepped out for a breath of air.'

'Have you heard anything? Anything unusual?'

'Nothing.' A particularly deft touch occurred to him. 'There might have been a siren somewhere a couple of minutes ago. That's fairly unusual round here.' It was amazing to think that the girl was concealed less than two yards away. Without intending to he glanced in the direction of her hiding place, hoping she was listening and admiring.

His blood froze. Less than two yards away, sticking out from between the leaves, was the front of her front tyre.

'What's happening?' he asked, stepping forward to block the policemen's view. He wondered how long it would take her to realize there was no actual connection between his books and what he was in himself – but perhaps with her they would find the connection. 'Has there – ?'

'There was a serious incident in Banbury about one hour ago,' intoned the policeman in the front passenger seat of the first car: a hard faced Neanderthal with a shaven head.

Feeling more than a little theatrical Max turned to look in the direction of Banbury, managing to get his body right in front of the protruding motorbike wheel, but bending one of the concealing branches out of posit –

A jumbo-jet taking off right on top of him – it was something like that. A demented winking from the rear window of the second car, a buffeting of the air next to his left shoulder and a deafening racket in his face that lasted only five seconds or so but continued to fill his ears after it had ceased. Shredded leaves and twigs pattered down on his shoes, followed by a blonde head and a silver-clad arm spilling from the shadows on to the grass verge at his feet. Her motionless face was beautiful in the moonlight. Her upturned eyes, no longer focussed, no longer shining, looked away from him towards the muzzle of Heckler & Koch sub-machine gun that poked from the window of the second police car.

'Clumsy sort of chappie, aren't you?' said the policeman in the passenger seat of the car beside him. 'For a moment I thought you were going to step right into the line of fire.'

Gamlingay Churchyard

He had always been fascinated by country churchyards. He enjoyed the triumphant irrelevance of the churches themselves, the remorseless encroachment of couch grass and weeds, the wind sniffing indifferently at the trees. Only occasionally would he look at the inscriptions on the tombstones. The repetition of birth dates and death dates, names that were sometimes quaint but were usually commonplace, the coy euphemisms for dying – 'Fell Asleep', 'Passed Away', 'Entered Into Rest', 'Departed This Life', and the stereotyped vanity of the sentiments – 'Not Dead, But Gone Before' – 'Resurrecturis' – 'He Liveth For Evermore' – 'With God' – 'Requiescat In Pace' – seemed to him less the distillation of the lives of autonomous individuals than the merged and blended notes of some vastly complex harmony; a harmony of which the central theme was not the insistence on human death and decay, but rather the multitidinousness of that death and decay. It was the vast numberlessness of those who were dead which possessed such a hold on his imagination.

Nevertheless he did read the inscriptions of a few tombstones, if only to vary his enjoyment, and one afternoon in the village of Gamlingay in Cambridgeshire, in a somewhat arid graveyard excessively mowed and pruned like the esplanade of a fashionable seaside resort, he saw for the first time an inscription which held his attention. It said:

ELIZABETH FARRAR

1880-1972

EMILY FARRAR

1918-1919

He had not wandered in rural burial grounds for twenty years without learning that married women's tombstones invariably bore some indication of their married state, either a reference to their husband, or to a father possessing a different surname. Elizabeth Farrar, he could only assume, had not been married. Emily Farrar must have been an illegitimate daughter. A thousand times before he had read the shorthand of lives stretched decades beyond the Biblical span, or abbreviated to a few delusively promising months or years. The juxtaposition of these two opposite fates on the same unimaginative and already weatherstained marble cross was curious, but that was not the reason why he paused there, staring down at Elizabeth Farrar's grave while cars passed and repassed in the road beyond the churchyard wall.

Elizabeth Farrar had been thirty-eight when she had had her bastard child – rather old to be snared unawares by the mysteries of her own body – and it had been fifty-three years before the death of that same child had been publicly commemorated. Together those thirty-eight years and those fifty-three years made up a story he could not forget. The year of the child's birth provided a partial explanation, of course: 1918, the fourth year of that great war of which the memorials recur throughout Europe, in the hushed squares of remote villages, in city parks, and in mainline railway stations, inevitable and predictable like the innumerable outlets of a vast underground reservoir. It may have been that Elizabeth Farrar had had a war-time romance with a soldier. Perhaps he was killed at Fourth Ypres, perhaps he had been in Allenby's army at Armageddon and had died fighting the Turks, or had succumbed to typhus at Salonika. It may have been that she was an evening's random adventure while he was on leave, a youngish middle-aged woman fortunately available to provide a brief escape from the pent-up desperation of months in the trenches. Probably he was no more than a boy himself, with no wife of his own to go home to, boasting somewhat of his battle experience but not willing to go into any details of what he had lived through; while she for her part, all dolled up for her Saturday night out with the brave lads in uniform, was too incurious to ask about the life at the Front, and never knew that the sound of his own breath panting as he had intercourse with her, thrusting into her under her bundled petticoats, reminded him of how he had to gasp for breath after sprinting under fire between shell holes. Probably he would have only learnt her name was Elizabeth a few minutes before, and never even knew the Farrar bit. But perhaps it had not been a soldier in the shadows behind a public-house, but a matter of dingy hotel rooms and a country-town businessman, one of the suet-faced men who only did averagely well in the war, married and moderately respectable, with a bogus-frank gaze that never quite met her eyes and a middle-aged odour of cigars and eau de cologne and mothballs: the kind of man who referred to his furtive seductions as 'being a bit of a gay dog on the side'.

But whoever the father, the war and the war-time upheaval of people and ideals must certainly have had something to do with her having a child; and then the father was killed, or died, or went back to the safer banality of married life. Elizabeth Farrar, already middle-aged, already long since resigned to loneliness, suddenly found herself with a baby all her own, with no one to claim a share of it and no one to take it from her. It could not but have changed her life completely. Perhaps she was ostracized by her acquaintances and had to move to a place where she was unknown. Perhaps she was penniless and had to work long hours, sewing sleeves or taking in washing. Nevertheless to have discovered motherhood at that relatively late age, when she had already given up the idea of ever being married or a parent like other women, must have been a miracle for her. And like all moments of grace, it came prematurely to an end. The postwar influenza epidemic, or encephalitis, or measles, or a routine tenement building outbreak of meningitis, took the child, and with it the mother's last chance of fulfilment and acceptance. She returned to being a dreary, lonely, self-sufficient spinster growing old on her own, pottering about a small garden, alternately feeding and shooing away stray cats, listening without much conviction to the stage by stage decline and fall of the British Empire on her wireless, and watching her neighbours from her front-room window. She never forgot her little girl however – how could she have done? – and when she died, after fifty-three years of remembering, she left it in her will that they should put up the child's name on the gravestone with her own.

All this was speculation however, and it worried him that he could never know for sure what had happened. He made enquiries with the verger, of course, an old man himself, whose memories must have stretched back as far as those of anyone who was still living in the village, but the verger could only report that Miss Farrar had come to Gamlingay in the early 1950s and that no-one knew anything about her. He thought of asking the verger if he remembered the name of her solicitor, but it seemed too much trouble in a case of transient curiosity, and so he left the village knowing almost nothing more than what was engraved on the cross. His curiosity was more than transient, however; he was unable to shift the recollection of those few neatly chiselled letters from his mind. It disturbed him that he would never know the true circumstances for sure, however much he weighed probabilities: neither the identity of the father, nor the circumstances of their liaison, nor even the truth about the child's death. For all he knew she might have been a notorious prostitute who had schemed to provide for her retirement by trapping some especially eligible client into marriage by bearing his child: not quite in the King Edward VII's mistresses league but she would have had a past full of eminent enough lovers, or gallants (probably never even thought of them as customers) who had wined and dined her in the private rooms of second-rate French cuisine restaurants and laughingly thrust banknotes into the low-cut front of her dress; but those past successes would not have prevented the father of her child being called away on urgent business for an indefinite period when he detected the swelling of her stomach. Or she might have been one of those formidable free-thinking Edwardian ladies living most of her life in suburban domesticity with some forgotten radical prophet of the period, in a relationship fully as staid and stifling as legal wedlock; friends perhaps of Marie Stopes, or even George Bernard Shaw and the Webbs, but money in the bank account too, and cousins in shipping and the Indian Civil Service, and a distant no-nonsense demeanour towards the butcher's delivery boy and towards those of their neighbours who had been brash enough to hint their curiosity, or even their disapproval. Fifty other possibilities or variations of possibilities occurred to him.

It was in the graveyard at Alwinton, Northumberland that he discovered the solution to this multiplying of hypotheses. This time it was not a marble cross, like Elizabeth Farrar's, but a plain upright headstone with a rounded upper edge. It said:

SARAH HUMPHREYS

1880-1972

CATHERINE JANE HUMPHREYS

1918-1919

He realised then that the human intellect cannot create, it can only remember; it was impossible for him to think of any set of events which had not actually taken place. Each and every one of his hypotheses concerning Elizabeth Farrar had been correct; everything he had thought might have happened had happened; it had only been the names he had confused.

Second Chance

At First Rosalind seemed to like talking to Mark. It was an instance of the age-old mind-body problem, he told himself knowingly: she's only interested in my mind and I'm only interested in her body. This was not quite true of course: though Rosalind was probably the most eye-catching woman undergraduate at Oxford, she was also one of the brightest, and as far as Mark was concerned her combination of brains and good looks was pretty much what Oxford was meant to be all about.

She talked to him about her work (they were both reading Modern History) about Life, and about herself. He told her of his ambition to write at least one great novel, a great English novel that would trump all those sycophantically praised transatlantic attempts to write the Great American Novel, an English equivalent to *War and Peace*. . . . they talked of possible scenarios. She told him about her sister Juliet, who was her identical twin. 'She's up at Cambridge, at Newnham: it would have been far too complicated if we had both come to Oxford. Even our parents can't quite tell us apart.' She told him how she and Juliet had sometimes gone out on one another's dates and the boys they had been seeing hadn't even guessed – 'But for Heaven's sake don't put *that* in your novel!'

And then, perhaps inevitably, she began to change towards him, became cooler and more distant. It was the usual situation: when one was not interested in a person, one paid too little attention, and when one *was* interested one paid too much. He was falling in love with her, she was aware of it, and she was embarrassed. He had always fancied her of course: she was archetypal ice-cold blonde, leggy, athletic (somewhere between a Renaissance Diana and a Nordic Valkyrie), not unaware of male admiration, but thoroughly bored by it. Though she had grown accustomed to the idea that Mark liked looking at her, she seemed to shrink away from the additional, much more challenging, claims of his total infatuation. At first it was a case of her refusing to have tea with him when he ran across her in the library, and of being in too much of a hurry to linger in conversation when they met in the street. He dropped in on her in her room at college: she said she was just about to go out. He sent her a facetious note: she didn't reply. Finally, catching up with her after a lecture, he asked what the matter was. 'Nothing's the matter,' she said vindictively, and turned on her heel.

It had overtaken him quite suddenly and unexpectedly. Unable to help himself, as if pursued by a kind of doom, he found himself head over heels in love, his every waking moment flood-lit by images of her. He could hear her name in that special sound the wind makes in autumn as it scrapes dead leaves against the gravel of paths. A blonde head glimpsed further down the street, or just turning into the gateway of one of the colleges, would make his chest tighten, as if there were no other blonde heads in Oxford. A paragraph in one of his books about debaucheries of eighteenth-century politicians would conjure up a collage of Hogarthian scenes centring on a countess who was Rosalind in an earlier incarnation; and he was tortured by the unvoiceable fear that one day he would see her as the Page Three girl in *The Sun*.

Whenever their paths crossed between lectures or on the street she would acknowledge him coldly or look to one side. He would stand, watching her stride away from him, his heart pierced by the arrogant slender shapeliness of her legs, by the way the blonde hair swirled on her shoulders as she moved. His mind constantly revolved on ways in which they could return to their former comfortable footing of easy friendship: he even had the ridiculously banal idea of pushing her out of the path of a runaway bus or diving in to rescue her from drowning in the river. But easy friendship would no longer have been enough in any case, it would simply have meant exchanging the torment of proximity for the torment of total exclusion. He cried out within himself against the destiny which had arranged that they should be up at Oxford at the same time. The memory of how well they had got on together only a few short weeks previously seemed to mock him with an illusion of lost opportunities. Somehow they had started out together at the wrong speed, she had so quickly grown accustomed to him as a friend that it prevented her from seeing him as a lover. If only things had been ever so slightly different at the very beginning, on the first two or three occasions that they had spoken together. If only they could return to those first times, if only he had known then how he would feel – but there was no returning. Life moves only forward: there could only ever be one beginning.

There could only ever be one beginning – or could there . . . . ? Fate had played a strange trick when it had selected the girl Mark was to fall in love with. Part of the uniqueness of Rosalind was that she was *not* unique. There was her genetic double, her identical twin sister at Cambridge: 'It would have been far too complicated if we'd both come to Oxford. Even our parents can't quite tell us apart.' He remembered how Rosalind had told him how she and her twin had sometimes gone on one another's dates. The idea that began to form in his mind was fantastic, obscene, even insane: he didn't care. He was too desperate to care.

It was a three hour cross-country coach ride to Cambridge. Winter was coming: the trees were almost bare, the shadows beneath them were orange with fallen leaves, and he himself felt turned to ice. Not just his heart, but his brain too, seemed frozen: he could not even begin to think what he was going to do in Cambridge or why.

He still had no idea what he intended to do by the time he was threading the Cambridge back streets which led to Juliet's college. It was only a last minute inspiration, literally at the gates of Newnham College, which caused him to turn aside and head for the faculty libraries which clustered against the freezing wind on the other side of the street. A last minute inspiration: a stroke of genius: the guiding finger of an inscrutable and obscurely purposed destiny: he didn't know. All he knew, as he hovered at the entrance of the History Faculty Library, was that the blonde head bent over a book ten yards from where he stood was as rivetingly familiar as if he had been thinking of it, and looking at it, every waking moment for the past numberless weeks. The hair was cut a little shorter than Rosalind's, but the bend of the neck, the line of the cheek and chin were unbelievably identical: the clothes deliciously unfamiliar, the clothes sense and personal style exactly Rosalind's. Even her handwriting, as he paused beside the girl's desk, was the handwriting written on his heart in Oxford.

'Rosalind,' he said. 'What on earth are you doing here?'

The girl snatched her eyes up from the book, startled but laughing.

'I'm not Rosalind, I'm her twin!' she exclaimed delightedly, in Rosalind's voice.

He explained he was on a visit from Oxford, knew Rosalind slightly, had not known she had a twin sister. He asked if there was somewhere they could have tea.

Over tea they talked like in a French film, interrupting each other, laughing at each other's jokes and at their own, comparing tutors, comparing Oxford and Cambridge, the Isis and the Cam, the High and King's parade, comparing, contrasting, recounting, questioning, teasing. Mark felt as if electrically charged by all the social energies that had been pent up in him during the past weeks of desolation. They sat so long over their tea that by the time they stood up it was time for dinner. They went together to a restaurant in the centre of Cambridge, near the market. Even while they ate they were interrupting each other continually, with an exhilaration which, for Mark at least, seemed presage an inevitable disaster. Only as he was walking Juliet back to her college did she fall silent.

It was a wonderful evening, crisp and cloudless. All those stars above, unique pinpoints of light in an eternity of darkness: for once it seemed credible that they had the power to arrange and order the lives of people on earth. They leaned on the parapet of a bridge over the Cam, Juliet was not looking at the stars but at him. He kissed her.

'Where are you staying tonight?' she asked after a while.

'I hadn't arranged anything.'

'I suppose you could sleep on my floor.'

Once they were in her room they kissed again. 'I could see you were checking out if I had all the standard bits,' she remarked. After that it never really was a question of his sleeping on the floor. Her college bed was very narrow for two, as college beds designably are, but for most of the night either he was on top of her or she was on top of him.

They arranged to see each other again in Oxford. Those were her last words to him when he left for the coach station in the morning: 'See you in Oxford.'

During the endless coach journey through the early winter countryside he dozed feverishly, remembering her kisses, the way she had looked at him, the touch of her skin, that chip in her tooth, her hair. It had been a couple of days since he had seen Rosalind: she could have had her hair cut shorter since he had last seen her, bought some new clothes. No, that was ridiculous. But the way Juliet – if it was Juliet – had more or less thrown herself at him as soon as they met, exactly as if she had been waiting all her life for their meeting: and the sudden way, weeks previously, that Rosalind had turned away from being so friendly to being so cold and distant: there was some mystery there too. Perhaps not two separate mysteries but a single connected one. Supposing Rosalind had been angry with him for some reason, supposing he had failed somehow to respond in the required way, supposing, once she had seemed to reject him, she didn't quite know how to renew their friendship. He could hear her voice – Juliet's voice too – telling how they had gone on one another's dates and the boys in question hadn't even guessed. A complex sense of betrayal which had been lingering like a shadow at the back of his mind gave way to a glorious confident certainty.

Eventually the coach reached Oxford. He headed straight for Rosalind's college.

Perhaps, in the beginning, she hadn't wanted to get bogged down with him in one of those long-running Oxford twosomes (and one night stands with close friends were always awkward). That morning, in Cambridge, the open-eyed was she had looked at him – exactly as if she was seeing him, not for the first time, but in an entirely new way. It had been something bigger than he could comprehend.

The corridor where Rosalind lived. The identical doors. Rosalind's door. He knocked. Inevitably, as in all real life dramas, there was an anti-climax: no answer. Not in.

One of her friends came out of a room further down the corridor. Her eyes were red and puffy, as if she too had had an interesting night.

'Do you know where Rosalind is?' he asked.

'Hadn't you heard?' the girl said stiffly, as if unable to believe the sound of her own voice. 'She was in a crash last night, coming back from Cambridge with her sister in a friend's car.' The girl had been crying. 'They're both dead.'

The Last of the
Daubeny-Fitzalans

'They were a queer family, the Daubeny-FitzAlans,' the vicar mused. 'Amateur scientists amongst other things. They do say that for three or four generations, father and son and grandson, they were experimenting with the generation of life, trying to discover a means to convert chemical compounds into living tissue.'

'Did they succeed?'

'Of course not.' The vicar sniffed contemptuously. 'There were the usual rumours that they built a strange man-like creature, but of course there was no truth in it.'

'I can just imagine it,' I said, looking across the valley at the gloomy many-roofed Tudor mansion, and trying to shut out of my mind the loud noises of shovelling and banging from the parish church behind us, where they were digging up the floor of the chancel. 'A long workshop on the first floor, with dark panelled walls, test tubes and retorts, and homunculi in jars lined up in rows on shelves –'

'Homunculi?' queried the vicar.

'Little man-like creatures. That's the kind of thing these alchemist fellows tried to bring to life.'

'Yes, of course. It's just rather odd that the idea should have occurred to you in this connection. You see the Daubeny-FitzAlans were homunculi themselves. I don't mean they were brought to life in their own laboratory, just that smallness ran in the family. They were all pygmies, from generation to generation, each generation smaller than the one before. Except for the last of them, Sir Forbes Daubeny-FitzAlan. He was a giant. They have some of his dress-suits in the County Museum – he must have been seven foot four inches at least. He had to import horses from Flanders to ride. The only native horses that could carry his weight were cart-horses, which were of course totally unsuitable for a man of his birth and wealth. They say the strongest chairs used to break under him and that when he died, it took twelve men to carry the coffin out of the house.'

'Twelve?'

'So they say.' The vicar pulled a gold watch from his waistcoat. 'They should have got to his coffin by now,' he said, inclining his head towards the church behind us.

It was a Norman church, the only one in anything like its original state in the county, and it was being restored. That was why they were digging up the chancel floor: to strengthen the foundations.

We moved towards the south porch. The vicar continued with his two-hundred-year-old gossip. Like most country clergymen he was a devoted student of his parish's history.

'He was rather a mystery man, Sir Forbes Daubeny-FitzAlan,' he said. 'There was not even any mention of there being a baby at the time of the death of his mother, Lady Amelia Daubeny-FitzAlan. Not that anyone in the village or in any of the neighbouring great houses even knew a tenth of what was going on in Daubeny Hall. No-one even knew the boy existed till he was already full-grown. Incredible, isn't it? He was educated at home, probably by his father or by one of his father's assistants, and never left the neighbourhood during his entire life. He became a Justice of the Peace of course, when his father died and he inherited the baronetcy, but he never served on the bench, none of the family did.'

'What became of him?'

'He died of some perfectly loathsome disease. He must have been about fifty. Apparently he always suffered from some kind of eczema but it became worse and worse, till it seemed his flesh was actually decomposing on him as he walked about his house and grounds. That's why he never married, I suppose. No-one would have wanted him, even with his money. And perhaps he wasn't interested either; there was never any local talk of his tampering with the farm girls.'

We entered the church. At the further end a number of workmen were grouped under a scaffold. Beside them were several very old coffins. None of them were longer than five feet.

'This one makes up for all the rest,' said the foreman as we approached. We peered over the edge of the dank-smelling hole. The last remaining coffin was over eight feet long and broad in proportion. A harness had been fastened around it; the workmen were about to start hoisting it out.

There were six of them and there was a complicated pulley system which helped take much of the weight, but even so it was fully five minutes before they had lifted the coffin clear of the hole. It was a good solid job, of oak, smeared with cobwebs and mould, but with the silver handles and name-plate still in good condition.

'Lord, it's heavy,' said the foreman.

'Perhaps there's a lead lining,' I suggested. I turned to the vicar. 'Are you going to open it?'

'Certainly not.' He seemed almost scandalized by the idea. 'We shall remove these coffins to a partially empty tomb in the churchyard for the duration of the restoration work, and then replace them. To do anything else would be most improper.'

I was just about to say, as delicately as I could, that this was a great pity, as I would have dearly liked to have seen a giant's bones, when the harnessing gave way on the massive coffin and it fell to the floor. I don't think the wood was particularly rotten; it must have been the way it fell with its corner striking the flagstones first. It split, right down its whole length, and the bones I had wanted to see came tumbling out.

They were enormous. They were obviously extremely heavy, too, for they did not clatter and bounce the way dried bones normally do when thrown down, but merely thudded immovably on to the flagstones. The other peculiar thing about them was their colour. They were almost black. At first, I thought this blackness was caused by the dried and darkened skin having shrunk over the bones, but a second glance told me that they were completely bare. And it was a very distinctive blackish colour, more like very dark green.

I think we all realized at about the same time what that dark green colour meant.

Sir Forbes Daubeny-FitzAlan's bones were solid brass.

The Book

While the Rev. Arthur Llewellyn spoke to the archdeacon on the telephone I moved down to the other end of his study so as to avoid the appearance of sitting in on their private conversation. Not that what they had to say to each other interested me in the least: church business. Withdrawing my attention I idly glanced through some of the books which were piled carelessly on the tables and on most of the chairs of the overcrowded room. I had just picked up a volume entitled *999 Ways of Passing the Time* when Llewellyn finally put down the telephone receiver.

'What's that you've got there?' he called rather tetchily.

'*999 Ways of Passing the Time*', I said. It was a cheap pre-war publication on thick, poor quality paper, bound in faded orange cloth. Rather an odd book for a country clergyman to have in his library.

'I didn't think it was down there,' he said, mystified. 'I'm sure I'd put it in the bookshelf over here. Do you know, Thomason, I could swear that book is moving around the room of its own accord. I bought it with the others a few days ago, a job lot including some interesting sermons. Not my kind of book at all, I haven't even bothered to look at it yet, but it came with the others. But ever since I've had it, I've been putting it down in one place and finding it turn up somewhere else.'

'Most peculiar,' I said. It was the kind of book which had been very popular between the wars: *1001 Household Hints* or *500 Games for Children and Grown Ups* sort of thing. One still occasionally found tattered copies of such publications at jumble sales, but most of them had been thrown in the bin years ago.

A few days later, Llewellyn telephoned me. 'You know that book, Thomason,' he said, '*999 Ways of Passing the Time*. It seems to be following me around the house. It's even turned up in rooms where I could have sworn I've never taken it.'

'You probably keep mixing it up with a pile of other books,' I suggested. 'Or perhaps the maid is reading it and keeps moving it around.'

'No, the maid never reads anything, I'm quite sure. I tell you,

Thomason, it's getting on my nerves. I feel myself going quite cold whenever my eye falls on that wretched volume, and I'm almost afraid to pick it up.'

A strange predicament for a man who had devoted his whole life to books, I reflected: that was the first thought that came into my head.

'And another thing, Thomason,' Llewellyn went on. 'I feel a most extraordinary reluctance to look inside the book. I've actually glanced through it a couple of times and read the odd sentence, nothing more. It seems just what you'd expect, childish games, advice on how to prepare charades, that sort of thing. But every time I open it I feel my heart in my mouth and I breathe a sigh of relief when I put it aside.'

'Perhaps you should read it more systematically,' I suggested, wondering whether Llewellyn was losing his mind, and not knowing what else to say to him on the spur of the moment. 'If there is some mystery connected with the book, you won't find it out by looking at the cover or by flipping through it and reading the odd sentence at random.'

'I suppose not,' Llewellyn agreed. 'But as I said, I feel a strange unwillingness to look inside the wretched thing. The more it haunts me, the more reluctant I am to open it and see what it says inside.'

He then turned the conversation to some other topic and after a few minutes more, rang off.

I visited Llewellyn a couple of days later. He seemed pale and restless, as if he had been having uneasy nights. He did not refer to *999 Ways of Passing the Time*, but he was constantly glancing around as if expecting it to appear miraculously on his desk or on a nearby chair, and finally I asked him: 'Have you had a proper look at that book yet?'

'Not yet,' he said, pretending nonchalance. 'Various other things to do, you know. Fact is I've been putting it off. But I mean to sit down and read it from cover to cover tonight.'

'If you wish I can call round,' I said. 'About ten thirty. You can tell me what you discover. If anything.'

'Good idea,' he said, and seemed immensely relieved by my suggestion.

He accompanied me to the front door and I repeated my offer of returning that evening. I feel a little guilty about this; I don't know whether, if I had returned that evening, it would have made any difference to what happened. As it was my car broke down on the way home and I was not able to get the garageman to repair it till the following morning. As soon as the car was fixed I drove out to see Llewellyn.

They were just taking his body to ambulance when I arrived.

When the maid had come in that morning, she had found him dead in his study.

She insisted on taking me to the study to show me where and how she had found the body. She had already told her story to the police, the doctor and the ambulance men but she seemed to think it improved with the retelling.

'There he was,' she said, 'sitting bolt upright, fully dressed, staring at that book open in front of him, as if he was still reading it, but stone dead.'

I paid no attention to her. Instead I was looking at the book she was pointing to. It was a cheap, pre-war publication, on thick, poor quality paper, bound in faded orange cloth.

It was entitled *1000 Ways of Passing the Time*.

Where Two Rivers Join

Actually she had been rather boring. A kindergarten teacher, she spoke rather good English (like at least half the population of Sweden) but had no intellectual interests or curiosity about anything that might interest him. In any other country there might have seemed something romantic, or touchingly hare-brained, or whorish, in a nice-looking girl on her way home from a visit to her mother stopping to give a hitch-hiking male a lift, assisting him to buy a week's food at a road-side supermarket, spending the night with him in a tent, and solemnly and level-eyedly promising to rejoin him the following weekend. In backwoods Sweden though, having sexual intercourse out in the open, or in a tent at 6 a.m., seemed to be something females over sixteen regarded as a matter of course, if not actually obligatory, and as for shagging a total stranger, though he didn't suppose she made a habit of it, since kindergarten teachers in the back parts of Sweden would rarely get to meet total strangers, she seemed to think there was nothing unusual about it. In the car her frank, direct, tomboyish manner and her focus on the road and the steering wheel (gripped high up on each side in the instructor-approved way) contained no hint of flirtation or sexual promise, and it was not much different when quite a bit later, without even a perfunctory preliminary cuddle, they undressed and lay down together. The ensuing half hour was as comfortably co-ordinated as if it was not their first coupling but their fiftieth, and so uncomplicated as almost to suggest, if that was all there was to sex, why on earth had one ever made such a big thing of it.

They were together a whole week after she came back from her five-day shift at the kindergarten. 'It is a holiday,' she explained: the isolated camping site she had found for him was separated by so many kilometres of forest from human habitation that what the rest of the Sweden was doing seemed irrelevant and he never discovered if it was a holiday she had arranged for herself at the kindergarten or if everyone else in the country was on holiday too. He asked why she didn't have a regular boyfriend and she answered that in fact she had: 'He is in America for a year. But I don't know if we will still be together when he comes back.' She never mentioned him again. For a week she sun-bathed nude, swam in the river nude, had desultory lilting nude conversations on her mobile phone, took turns at gathering firewood and cooking (partially dressed), plaited and unplaited her hair, smiled occasionally, made banal remarks in eighty-per-cent correct English, went walking with him in the woods, and humped back obligingly whenever they had sex (always missionary position). At the end of the week she dropped him on the main road beyond the small town/large village where she worked and they exchanged e-mail addresses and telephone numbers. And that was it.

Her name was Helena. As the years passed he found it increasingly difficult to remember that, or even what she looked like. Blonde hair, initially in a single plait hanging forward over her collar bone, later often loose. About five seven. Square shoulders. Routinely pretty features. Remarkably few moles on her body. The usual squeezable bits, very nearly girlie mag standard perhaps, but all he really remembered about them was the mere fact that they had been there, or at least that they assuredly hadn't been absent and unclasped. What his memory did dwell on, and to an increasing extent, was the five days he had had to wait for her between their first meeting and first embraces and her return from her working week at the kindergarten.

The first day after she had left for her job—day one of his five day wait—had been as near normal as it could be in an unfamiliar location and in unfamiliar circumstances. The location itself was hauntingly beautiful, with a pristine quality as if, since the dawn of time, only an incredibly small number of people had ever ventured there before. There was a flat-topped crag about twenty feet above water level, overlooking the confluence of two broad rivers, with wooded hills pressing in on all sides. The rivers, though fast-flowing, were so wide that together they formed what at first glance seemed to be a considerable lake. A rocky track, in places like a flight of rough-hewn steps, wound alongside the crag down to the water's edge, and just behind the crag there was a stand of pines arranged in a semi-circle as if waiting for an important visitor, and beyond them larch and spruce scattered down a gentle slope that ended in an artificial ride of grass, perhaps intended as a fire-break, with more

larch and spruce and long narrow vistas beyond. His tent was pitched
under the pines. It was the end of June and the sky was unchangingly
turquoise, the wind sometimes busy in the trees overhead, sometimes
dying away to a faint stirring like the muffled ticking of a clock a
great distance away. He spent the first day alone exploring the vicinity
and taking photographs, while that strange anaesthetizing shock that
follows an unexpected sexual encounter, or a fight, or an accidental
injury, wore off comfortably and the issue of taking on a new personal
factor in his life presented itself with diminishing insistence, each
time it recurred to him somehow failing to engage his interest. Ditto
the recollection of the squeezable bits, of almost girlie mag standard,
that he had palmed and juggled the night before and again early that
morning. During the long evening –the quality of the light changed,
as if just before sunset, around 8.45 p.m. though the sun did not
actually set till two hours later – he began to be convinced that Helena
would not be coming back and he felt an agreeable melancholy at
the thought. Somehow the notion of waiting hopelessly and in vain
in the wilderness for a girl he was never going to see again was more
romantically appealing than the prospect of embracing her once more.

   This mood was intensified, almost as it were solidified, during
the following days. There was nothing to do but sit around, day-
dream (not usually about Helena) and swat the occasional queen
ant-sized mosquito, but he was not in the least bored. The beauty of
his surroundings grew on him, became imbued with an elusive
significance. He relished the sense of isolation, of remoteness from
humanity. The air, especially when he first stepped out of his tent in
the early morning, was like champagne. There were no sounds other
than the suck and murmur of the river, the soughing of the wind in
the trees and the occasional scuttling of small creatures in the
undergrowth, more frequent during the hush of the protracted
evenings and brief darkness but always friendly and unthreatening.
Now and then snatches of birdsong. Once a deer appeared, poised
for retreat between the trunks of two pines, as beautiful and almost
as unexpected as a unicorn, staring at him with opal eyes before
shrinking back into the greenery. Occasionally he saw a vapour trail
overhead, the bit furthest from the barely visible plane oddly ridged
like a white bicycle wheel track across an azure sky. The fact that he

was waiting for a more than averagely good-looking stranger who was (or possibly was not) coming to join him in this idyllic spot somehow underlined, gave a curious poignancy to, his sense of isolation and remoteness. She began to appear more beautiful, more implausibly magical, in retrospect – in retrospect, in parenthesis, in theory – but that gave him no particular sense of impatience or longing, simply added to the enchantment of waiting. It was like a dream, and it was this dream element that stayed with him most insistently in the years that followed.

It was the longest continuous period of happiness, of exhilaration at being alive, that he had ever experienced. It was a constant high, with perhaps just one single moment that was more of a high than all the rest, when about 10 p.m. on the fifth evening Helena's blue SUV rolled into view through the trees, twigs and cones crackling under the big tyres, and his heart lifted as the driver-side door opened and a naked golden leg emerged, reaching down tentatively for the ground; and then his heart sank to normal as with a '*Hej!*' of greeting the rest of her debauched from the vehicle, in a sporty orange blouse and white shorts, smiling and tanned against the stationary evening sun, and inescapably prosaic and matter of fact.

As the spell of those five days of unrepeatable beauty developed an increasing significance for him over the years there also clarified in his mind, as a kind of minor detail, the notion that it was a kind of flaw in the perfection of it that it should be associated with, framed in, the anti-climax of his brief, comfortable not-even-an-adventure with Helena. If only the pretty girl element had involved the great love of his life, or at least unforgettable rather than merely routine sex. In the end it had been simply one more of the *almosts* of his life, another of those two-thirds or three-quarters of a day-dream come true, minus the last fraction required to make it extra-special. Still, this was only a minor aspect. The five days of waiting stood on their own, quite separate and distinct from Helena at the problem-free beginning and anti-climactic end; it was somehow the waiting itself, the sense of horizonless expectation, of the imminence of something unique, that haunted his memory. Sometimes he even fantasized that he had been waiting for a girl encountered for a bare two minutes in the queue going down the gangway of the ferry at Gothenburg, with only just enough time for a hurried explanation of where they could meet up the following week, or a girl he'd been in love with in a five-year-old way, in his first two years at school, or passionately fancied at nine and had not seen since. It was as if he had been on the brink of discovering a new destiny and had failed to recognize it, not because of Helena herself, but because he had not waited long enough. As time passed more and more his thoughts turned to finding the place again and waiting a bit longer.

He might never have actually done it if he had not been in Stockholm one June, on business, and found himself at a loose end for some days. He was staying with a business contact, and one morning noticed the camping equipment belonging to the son of his host, ready for use at the back of a closet . . . . Without allowing himself time to think about it he told them at breakfast that he would like to go camping, and thirty hours later he was back at the confluence of the rivers, this time with a hired car.

Nothing seemed to have changed. Within a couple of heartbeats it was as if he had never left, as if all the years between the dream and the present had rolled away. Even the hearth they had made, in a gap between two rocks at the edge of the trees, was still there. It seemed to have been used quite recently, for the charred fragments of wood that had been left when the fire had last burnt out did not look as if they had passed even a single winter under snow and ice: but he told himself he had no experience or expertise regarding changes in appearance over time of burnt sticks from woodland camp fires in sub-arctic Sweden, and that for all he really knew these were the remains of their last camp fire from all those years ago. They certainly looked oddly familiar, though it was hard to believe his mind could have retained a distinct mental image of any particular camp fire's charred wood for such a long time.

As he stood there wondering he had a strange sensation of being observed, or perhaps not so much observed as involved: the feeling that something marvellous was about to happen in this place was stronger than he had ever felt when there before. Fighting against an impulse to hurry he gathered twigs and fallen branches, screwed up a couple of pages of that morning's *Dagens Nyheter* which he had discarded on the back seat of the hired car, applied a match and watched the smoke begin to rise in a lavender-coloured veil against the backdrop of trees, as it had used to all those years previously.

He closed his eyes, remembering, opened them again. The quiet crackling of the igniting branches seemed to be echoed by another crackling behind him: there was a crunch of tyres on pine cones, and the clunk of an engine being switched off, and he turned to see a blue SUV, half in sunlight, half in shadow beneath the pines. The door opened and then slammed closed. It was a blonde girl, about five foot seven, square-shouldered. Hair in a single plait hanging forward over the lapel of her short-sleeved blouse.

'*Hej!*' she said.

Numb Night in N16

Stoke Newington. Just after midnight, probably. Date: about a year before the date on the reverse side of the title page.

Nick was on his way home after a late-night session at Peter Moretti's. Adrian had been there, insisting that the man who had sold Peter that white powder should be charged under the Trade Descriptions Act. Novocain and cheap speed – two per cent of coke, if you were lucky, to give it flavour. They had done the knives too, first time in years. Peter even had the traditional fox-hunter's bugle for snorting up the acrid smoke from the match-head-sized piece of dope squeezed between red-hot kitchen knives. Straight through the back of your throat into the brain cells ordinary lagers couldn't reach.

Still seriously mind-warped, he took a short-cut between the allotments and the backs of the neighbours' houses, along a narrow lane between back-yard gates and iron railings. He was just coming level with the Turkish Working Men's Caff's back windows (they were his next door neighbours) and was counting the syllables of a haiku –

> We want to laugh and lark
> in Eden
> before we pass into the dark –

when a man stepped out in front of him, not as tall as he was, wiry-looking, dressed in denims and a red woolly ski hat, holding a knife in an awkward way that might denote esoteric expertise.

'Gimme your money, your wallet,' the man hissed.

As if in a dream Nick went for his knife hand, tripped him with his left toe, knelt on his kidneys. It took half a second but it was one of those seconds that lasted twenty minutes. As soon as the man hit the ground he shot sideways like an eel but Nick had already shifted the aim of his descending knee and scored a groin's eye. Next the head-lock – after that it would be a question of whether simply to go through the mugger's pockets or do a Charles Bronson on him. Her. Nick held in his hand irrefutable evidence that his assailant was a woman.

'Just a friendly fight, officer,' Nick said, throwing the mugger from him with an expansive flourish and smiling perkily up at the two policemen with chequer-boarded caps who had suddenly appeared three places forward from where the ring-side seats should have been. He stood up, dusting his trousers. 'Just coming home from a stroll with the lady. A small spat became a pushing game. One of those, you know, wrestling matches.'

The girl was supposed to look as if she had an intense dislike of being interrupted by the police while, you know, wrestling. Instead she looked as if she had at intense dislike of men who thought it funny to discover that what they were squeezing was, you know, her left tit. Fortunately the two looks were very similar.

'Well, that's warmed me up,' she murmured in a choked voice, pulling off her woolly hat, releasing hair to her shoulders. 'It's cold isn't it? Can we . . . .

'Any means of identification?

Nick handed over his bus-pass holder, which also contained a British Library pass describing him as Dr N. F. Woodward and a Bank of Scotland card, ditto. 'Clara here is one of my pupils.' Not a bad performance considering how many brain cells he had fried that evening.

'Live near here?'

'This house here. The front door is just round the corner.'

'Show us.

Nick took his attacker's fingers, which gave a boyish minimum of a return squeeze and then lay rough but passive in his hand. The four of them walked around the corner, Nick looking up bug-eyed at the lights of a Boeing 747 flying overhead, like a Spanish galleon only faster. Better get this over quick before his knees fell off. 'Here,' he said, opening the gate, dropping the girl's hand, resolutely mounting the step to the door. 'Is there anything else?'

'No, sir, that'll be fine,' said policeman Number One – or was he Number One Million and One? He was surrounded by a penumbra of sounds from other policemen jabbering at him over the radio, like speeded up walkmen, apparently a different voice in each ear-phone. A car alarm went off in the next street: he didn't even flinch.

Nick unlocked his front door.

'Good night then.' he said, stepping aside to allow Clara to pass in before him. In a minute he was going to collapse in giggles.

'Good night, sir.'

'Good night,' said the girl unnecessarily from the doormat, in a voice inflected too high. Even if she was not really called Clara, she was making a good job of pretending she was.

Overhead, a police helicopter began circling as he closed the front door on the two chequered caps.

'I live upstairs,' he said quietly. 'You'd better go up.'

She followed him up to the top of the house, to a front room with a leafy three-piece suite that clashed with the fitted carpet and a view over the park and the main road from Islington. He switched the light on.

As he had suspected, she was beautiful. No, that was the dope talking, but she was definitely a lot better-looking than the usual run of people who assaulted him. One of those well-scrubbed, well-chiselled choir-boy faces, good skin, sweet sulky mouth, nose like Kate Moss's only much nicer, fawn's eyes that were looking at him warily. A small fly was orbiting her head.

Words came up on a screen behind his eyes:

'If I immortalize your name in rhyme,
I asked her, 'would you give yourself to me?'
She answered from the other side of time,
'Immortal means for all eternity,
So why not wait a thousand years and see?

What was her name anyway? Was it really Clara?

He said, 'I guess the pigs'll hang around for twenty minutes or so, lurking, listening to their radios. Changing a suppository perhaps.'

He was really zonked: once the immediate crisis was past the adrenalin had gone phut and he was completely brain-dead. Adrian had been right – that zombie-like power of movement was from cheap speed, and he had just used up the last milligram. 'I'm going to crash out.'

'Oh, shit.' she said. 'Look, can I stay?'

'There's the sofa, shortie. I'll give you a couple of blankets. And a pillow. Sorry it smells. There's sheets if you want them.'

'You got anything to eat?'

'Yoghurt, chocolate. Bread. Orange juice. You can't cook.'

'I already know I can't. Hey. Show me.'

He showed her what was in the fridge.

'Take it,' he said. 'I'm crashing out.'

He got to his bedroom and fell on his bed. Probably should have tried to get her to fall on the bed with him:

> It's often rather like a game of chess,
> Unless you make your move you'll never know.
> 'Let's make love,' you say; she says, 'Let's undress.
> And do it properly,' or 'I must go
> To the loo first,' or — fretfully by fifth girl
> Fucked — 'This is childish,' as she elbowed free
> And hurdled to the window, hair awhirl
> To pull the curtains lest the neighbours see:
> Even the classic, 'Maybe I'll just slip
> Into something more comfy,' or newspeak
> Pill-checks like 'Are you safe?' or bar-girl flip
> Demurrals like, 'God, not again this week,'
> Followed by, as you clutch another crutch
> A breathless, 'Do you always talk so much?'

After two hours or so he woke up, half-way human, needing a pee.

He could still hear a helicopter outside, circling over the park.

Someone was in his kitchen.

Oh, it was the girl.

'I wanted another yoghurt,' she said. She had taken her clothes off except for a T-shirt, and she noticed him looking at her bare legs. 'Got any dope?'

'Why?'

'Why do you think? To roll a joint with. To roll the smoothest and best-joined joint you —'

'No.' The fly had stopped circling her head and was now whizzing around inside his skull, crashing into things. 'No,' he said again.

'Look, I'm sorry I tried to mug you. And I've eaten all your caramel eggs, and this is your last yoghurt. All the same I thought, you know, a joint to round it off would make it perfect.'

He weakened. Probably something to do with the fading mark of a love-bite low down on the side of her throat.

'All right.'

He gave her his stash, large-size papers, one of those cards mini-cab services keep thrusting through your letter-box, and watched her roll the spliff. She was right, it was smooth and tapering and elegant, like her fingers, like her wrists and fore-arms, Her thighs were tapering and elegant too but instead of being smooth had a delicate blonde fuzz that said, 'Don't stroke me unless you're Justin Bieber.'

'Tell you what,' she said, 'We'll smoke it in your bed so you won't keep looking at my legs.'

They smoked it in his bed, passing it back and forth, making cocktail party conversation about his being a university teacher, and taking it in turns to brush ash off each other's front. The spliff seemed to spend more time going from hand to hand than being toked. When he finally stubbed it out they continued moving in ballet-like unison, nose to nose – he was so stoned he managed to bump his head against hers – mouth to mouth – he hadn't realized he was such an expert kisser – right hand to left whatsit – amazing how co-ordinated he was, considering – duvet to floor – like a kind of haiku.

> Duvet to floor
> that left whatsit is her left boob again
> bed-springs shout.

'I suppose those policemen think we're doing this anyway,' she said.

Things became rhythmical:

> I too once groped as good as their Page Threes;
> Goggling globoid grabbable grapefruit that
> Seemed far uniquer than the conjoined twat,
> Though I confess my fondest fantasies
> Focussed in those days on the stand-up sort
> Pert pyramidal isosceles cones,
> Not pendulous like penthouse entry phones

But trampoline-tightened, uptilted, taut. . . .
So many – not enough – parading wanton
Plump-pointed pairs before my inward eye:
Can 'Round their waists!!' be Father Time's reply
If one now asks, '*Ou sont les mamelles d'antan?*'

'Ho! Ho!' said the bed-springs, with a couple of beats between *Ho!*'s, as in a sardonic pretend laugh. 'Ha! Ha!,' said Clara, at about the same speed, each *Ha!* half a beat behind each *Ho!*

He was still too stoned to be quite sure which of her holes he had had his finger in.

Afterwards she ate half a box of jellied fruit and told him her name wasn't Clara, but Angie.

'And I'm Nick.'

'How do you do?'

They shook hands.

After that they were having it off again and Angie was making noises, crescendo, like a small girl – a histrionically whiney small girl – having her hair combed out by a peremptory mother, when she suddenly stopped bouncing and said, 'Shit: my knife.'

'Your what?' he said slowing down.

'My knife, I left it in the lane, back of the house. Someone will – Shit. Oh, go on, there's no need to stop.'

But when, twenty oinks from the bed-springs later, he rolled off her, she said as if on cue: 'My knife, you wouldn't go and look for it would you?'

'Why me? Why not you? It's your knife.'

'I'm so, you know, comfy and warm here.'

'So am I.'

'My leg's gone to sleep from having all your weight on it just now.'

'If I go down, do you promise to show yourself to me at the window?'

'O.K.'

'I mean, stand in front of the window just as you are now so I can see you.'

'I will, I will. But really and truly, I'm worried someone's found my knife.'

He struggled back into his clothes and went downstairs, head reeling. All stories are basically shaggy dog stories. His dick didn't fit in his underpants any more.

He searched around in the lane at the back of the house. The knife was lying in deep shadow against the step of one of the backyard gates. A lock knife, imitation bone handle, but handsome and strongly made. He turned to locate his bedroom window. She wasn't there yet, the bitch. He needed another pee. Something to do while he waited. The police helicopter seemed to be flying lower, but even if they were watching him they wouldn't be able to do anything about it. He undid his zip, fumbled tender meat, and let zeeeee. Oh, good, his curtain was twitching, being drawn aside, and there she was, thirty yards distant, framed in his window, the light behind her. After a moment she turned sideways on so that the light fell on the gravity-tweaked cones of her tits.

She wouldn't be able to see him where he stood in darkness but he waved his knife at the window, still peeing. This was it, dick in hand, the woman you had just shagged flashing at you from your own bedroom window. This was what they called pissing towards paradise. There was a sudden, brilliant golden aura – wow, it was more like doing acid than being on dope, perhaps she had managed: to slip him something. He chortled out loud – and it was then that the police helicopter crashed into the house.

At the End of the Lane

With thanks to Agnes Neubert.

She washed her hair on alternate days, and always left a trail of water in the bathroom like a mermaid, scattered her panties round the bedroom, never asked his permission before using his razor to shave her armpits, and tended to give unnecessary instructions during sex. In other respects she corresponded exactly to the blueprint of the ideal companion which he had dreamt up as a student, when the idea of living his life as a full-time author had first taken on detail in his fantasies. She was almost invariably good-tempered, and most of the time ready to fall in with anything he proposed, without boring him with proposals to do the opposite. She did not distract him with pre-cornflakes conversation if she found him crouched bare-arsed at his work table checking synonyms in his thesaurus first thing in the morning. She also read every book he suggested and if he ever ran out of suggestions she picked out for herself books he had as not yet got round to mentioning, including those he had written himself. She seemed to remember every incident in every book she had read too, though increasingly her remarks struck him as not so much incisive as insipid. Perhaps that was the problem with his student blueprint: it hadn't paid much attention to what was going on in the dream companion's head. When he had first known her, in the days of her £600 a week heroin habit, she had used to say, 'One day I'm going to write it all down, what it's really like, what it really feels like to be a junkie,' but since she had come off she had never referred to her addiction (except one evening when, à propos of nothing in particular but with a would-be significant glance at him she remarked, 'Something's missing') and she made no sign of embarking on a considered autobiographical project. Perhaps this was just as well. Sometimes she would sit amongst the cow-pats and the whirring grasshoppers in the field that ran down to the stream below the cottage, birdsong in the background, and sketch the *Wind in the Willows* countryside and the grand massifs of late summer cumulus with the slightly constrained air of one resuming a duty – she had returned to her ballet exercises in apparently the same spirit – but when the stretching out of the shadows brought her indoors, scratching her midge-bites, barely visible parallel hairs bleached white on forearms and temples, the squiggles on the paper she complacently exhibited to him consisted mainly of unfinished lines.

He wondered if he should get her to write something about her wholesome, hockey-playing, hanging-out-in-hamburger bars, hand-fending, pre-hypodermic teens (the Chelmsford version of *American Graffiti*), on the theory that it was not the dramatic externals but the capture and fixing of subjective states that made literature; but in the end he decided her literary ambitions merely belonged to the aspect of their relationship where she was still saying things simply to impress him.

Punctually at twelve noon, and when he also did an afternoon writing stint, no less punctually at four, she would bounce into his work room – sometimes do a cartwheel from door to table, for she could never resist the chance to show off – swoop to the left into an open eyed kiss of varying daily tonguiness, swoop to the right to prop herself against the back of the authorial chair with a *noli me tangere* expression and let him read bits of his latest chapter to her while the wood pigeons hoo-hoo'd hoarsely beyond the French windows, and rooks cawed in the middle distance like an echo of childhood.

'You're my muse,' he would tell her, whereat she would smile ironically; but she had indignantly repudiated his suggestion that she should present herself each noon wearing only a bunch of poppies from the wheat-field next door. 'People used to *pay* to look at me with no clothes on!' she had said, with even more of a ringing note than usual in her always clear emphatic voice, and gave the back of his chair a vigorous push that almost tipped him out of it. The fact was that memories of their previous existence in London cast a shadow even at the end of the bramble-lined lane that led to the cottage. He kept thinking of the evening only a few months back when he had called at the squat in Tufnell Park where she had been living and had found her in the middle of fixing. The syringe sticking wince-makingly out of her slender forearm and the man's neck-tie which she had knotted above her elbow as a tourniquet had by then become familiar, but there was still something shocking in the cosy way she was fending off her two pet kittens from the tumbler of water she needed for her syringe, addressing them as 'darling' in a cooing voice, while the syringe dangled from her arm. She looked as if she was posing for a Benetton advert illustrating how completely un-hygienic it was possible for a lifestyle to be. Adding to the effect was an out-of-character nightie she was inexplicably wearing – the kind of nightie a 1950s-vintage travelling salesman might give to a barmaid as an inducement to do something naughty – lace-fringed and with a neck-line that plunged to her navel and showed the inside angles of her unsupported breasts. In the un-shaded electric light of her basement her cleavage looked coarse-pored, and surprisingly saggy, so that physically as well as morally there was an aura about her of human identity in an advanced stage of disintegration, and he had suddenly thought: 'I can't go on, she's not worth it, I'm not sure I even fancy her.'

But he had gone on. She had been his tragic princess: he had been a modern Sir Galahad hacking his way with the bright sword of his will-power and dreams through the encompassing thicket of a society in the process of dissolution. She had seemed so essentially unattainable in those days, too, though not exactly in the style of Courtly Love: she had had enough of men, she said, and on a couple of occasions spoke sardonically of 'cirrhosis of the lover' (presumably a borrowed phrase, she was not clever at putting words together like that). She didn't even like him looking at her: 'Stop looking at me if I was bits,' she said once. 'I'm not bits, I'm *me*.' The chief relationship in her life, excluding all others – he sometimes thought, embraced as a substitute for all others – had been the heroin that was destroying her before his eyes. The whole horrible business, with all its disheartening worse-than-anticipated details, the lies, the broken promises, the word-perfect excuses, the whingeing about dealers who weren't in or who over-cut the gear, the sinking feeling in his gut (as if the ground had fallen away beneath his feet leaving him nowhere to stand) when she had mentioned, as if he already knew and presumably approved of the fact, that she sometimes 'went back' (hostess's euphemism for going back to a hotel for sex and a bigger tip) with men met at the night clubs where she worked, had given an almost unbearable urgency to his feelings that was now no longer there.

He was reflecting on this one evening while they were sitting together reading. It had been a windy, restless day (the Equinox, he had informed her – to which she had responded teasingly, 'You always know how old everything is, don't you?'), and whenever he had looked out of the window during the hour before sunset he had been oppressed by the sense of unseen people struggling to materialize amongst the waving trees; now, with a moon so bright that it seemed in front rather than behind the racing clouds, these unseen presences seemed stronger and more insistent as the gusts of wind alternately crescendoed and dwindled overhead amongst the chimney stacks. She was sitting sideways in an armchair across the room from him, knees up to the level of her shoulders, one of his own books steadied against her slanted legs and partially hidden from him by a curtain of flaxen hair as she bent over his words. She was still as physically graceful as she had always been, without the poignant contrast of the uncharacteristic clumsiness she had used to exhibit with cups of coffee directly after a fix, but the physical novelty of her and a lot of the chemistry had been siphoned away by a spring and summer of vigorous 11 p.m and 7 a.m humping. (He had asked her once whether she had been so active with men from the clubs whom she had gone back with and she had said, 'That wasn't sex, it wasn't *me* they wanted, just someone who would lay on her back and let them get on with it.') All that was left, he realized, was a smiley blonde, with 3-D tits and a dancer's countable ribs, who had had to grab at heroin as an alibi when she had woken up to the fact that being top girl in the gang at sixteen was no guarantee of being top girl in the gang at twenty-one.

She noticed his eyes on her and looked up from her – his – book with a familiar round-eyed, questioning expression – almost the same expression he told himself resentfully, that she always had before a fix, when she was going through her routine of energetically wind-milling her tourniqueted arm to bring up the veins. For a moment he thought she was going to tell him to stop staring at him – she only liked being looked at when she was showing off. Instead she said, 'I don't think I've ever been so happy.'

Just like that, as if trying it for size.

'You've never said anything like that before.'

'I kind of thought I might be showing it,' she said, with a tone and look that combined mild reproach with a kind of smugness.

Outside, beneath the tossing and creaking trees by their front gate, a fox barked, a single unearthly *arf*, a little like the call of a rook, but higher-pitched. Once a fox had followed her in the lane during her period.

'Did you hear that? It's probably your fox again,' he said, because he didn't know what else to say. And he went to the window and looked out, but of course saw only tree-tops swaying in the darkness, and the moon and the clouds.

Next day, when she came to his work room at twelve noon, she didn't kiss him but instead presented him with a seven-page story she'd written out in her very legible semi-italic handwriting.

It was about a girl called Natasha. Every evening Natasha returned home from the office where she worked, depressed and humiliated by her experiences during the day, the pettinesses she had overheard, the two-facedness, the lack of idealism. Once she stood in a queue behind an attractive young couple, obviously newly-weds: and there was something in the man's coolly witty responses to his brand-new wife which suggested he was using her to rehearse the witticisms he would try later on his male workmates. On another occasion Natasha noticed an overdressed woman of the BMW class throw a coin at the feet of a beggar, in a manner that proclaimed, 'Considering how much I pay in taxes and rates to keep the streets clean, I shouldn't really need to give anything to charity, yet here I am, tender-hearted me, feeding the five thousand.' On the crowded bus home Natasha stood behind a man who was reading her favourite book, through the shifty sidelong glances he intermittently directed at the bust of the pretty shop-assistant standing next to him indicated how far he was from responding to what the book was about. Such little incidents built up in her, and when she got home she would often throw off all her clothes, start her favourite music on the player, raise her arms like a just watered flower, and simply dance: dance and dance to herself, round and round, from one corner of the room to the other, letting the music flow all over her, sucking in the notes and letting them flow all through her and carry her away until she dropped breathless and exhausted on her bed, with all the bad memories of the day, all the hurt she felt purged away, drawn out of her and dispersed in the air along with the fading notes of melody.

Sometimes Natasha would walk in the wood at the end of the street, for she also found comfort amongst the trees, one or two in particular reminded her of the beeches that had been in her garden as a child; she could lean against them, and found herself drawing strength and calmness from knowing they had experienced more than one generation. One afternoon there was a man walking among the trees and they struck up a conversation. Afterwards Natasha could not quite remember what they had talked about, only that there had been an instant connection, an instant rapport, as if they had known and liked each other all their lives. She went back to the man's flat for tea and discovered that he lived right opposite her window: and there was something in the way he glanced across at her window told her that he knew it was her window and that he knew her from having watched her dancing to herself evening after evening.

That evening when she was once more alone in her room and had switched on her favourite music, she discovered she was no longer able to dance to herself.

That was the story he read.

The only word for it was embarrassing – and not simply because of the absence of talent it showed. It was the evocation of the inner world of an adolescent who seemed to have no connection with the ex-junkie who boasted of having gone on the pill for Chelmsford's leading jazz pianist at sixteen and of being a bit of a nymphomaniac at seventeen – 'I used to sleep with all sorts of men I thought I ought to fancy, which I guess wasn't the best way to find out I didn't. Like with smack later on, once I started I couldn't stop'– and had left home at eighteen to become a go-go dancer before moving on via topless bars to the kind of night club where the hostesses cost less than the champagne. 'I had to go back with this German guy,' she explained one day having turned up two hours late to a breakfast date. That was how he had found out. 'I couldn't have done it without the heroin,' she said, 'though without the heroin I wouldn't have needed to.' And now she had written a story that could have been by a girl two-thirds her age.

It would have been too obvious, especially after all the times he had held forth to her on the problematic relationship of authors and fictional characters, to have asked if *she* was Natasha, or if she had ever made a habit of dancing round her bed with no clothes on. As for asking if she liked the idea of being secretly watched while dancing in the nude, she had told him that the main reason why she had given up go-go dancing was that she couldn't stick the way men gawked at her while she gyrated in a sequined bikini, and the only time he had ever had a proper look at her in the past few months was in the shower or while bonking her.

That evening he asked her:

'At the end of the story, the reason why she can't dance any more, is it that she feels disgusted to learn that the man she had liked so much has all the time been spying on her in her most private moments or is it – because you make her out to be sensitive and perhaps even too quick to see the ugly side of things, but you don't show her being at all angry with the man – is it that she suddenly sees that she's been dancing for him without realizing it, dancing not just to clean her mind but dancing to send a message to someone like him, and now she knows the message has got across?'

'Both,' she said, very positively.

But he didn't believe she knew. All the same the sheer ham-handedness of her story gave it something that his own writing had always seemed to lack: not just the awkwardness of sincerity but an almost painful sense of real life and real feelings that were not trimmed and smoothed by a practised wordsmith but poured out onto the paper unrehearsed in the order they were felt. Her story seemed to have a kind of genuineness his own writing never seemed to achieve, simply in the way its artlessness grated.

He looked across at her. She was once more deep in her book, evidentially happy enough to wait until he was ready enough to discuss her story further, or perhaps content not to discuss it at all. Her little-girl way of sitting sideways in the armchair, flaxen hair falling obliquely across her face almost to the tip of her nose, was one of his favourite: one of the ways he used to think he would always remember her, along with memories of her pirouetting (for once unselfconsciously) on borrowed roller-skates in the middle of the Great Court at Somerset House and spread-eagled naked on his bed (a few hours after the pirouette) looking up at him from the pillow with eyes so solemn they seemed to squint, and asking him to be gentle with her –'Be gentle with me'– her voice husky but off-hand, as if this was part of a set routine (but all her set routines were new to him in those days). He had used to wonder, almost obsessively, if the men she met in clubs had heard the same words and seen the same squinty-eyed solemn expression when in hotel room after hotel room they had climbed on top of her – seen too the same ironical little smile when she took their money as he used to see when she accepted another 'loan' from him. How many had there been? He'd asked once, but she had merely replied, 'I don't know, I didn't keep count' – and he had a sudden vision of the pages of her too legible manuscript, now minus paperclip, spread across her upper body, tilted this way and that by the splay of her breasts and the jut of her dancer's xylophone ribs, and creased and crumpled by a man's thicker body pressing down against hers.

'You're not bored here, are you?' he asked kneeling down beside her chair.

'Well I am a bit, but I don't know if I'm ready to go back to London yet. And you're the only person I can talk to.'

(Not that she ever said anything very significant.)

'We could stay here over Christmas if you wanted,' he said. He felt nothing inside; nothing beyond an awareness of being still cut off from her by an unbridgeable void as wide as the Grand Canyon, as vertiginous as a £100-a-day habit and £200-a-night whoring, reaching out for her across a widening abyss, each of them on lone promontories of continents drifting apart. Outside by the sycamore at the end of the lawn the fox was barking again. It was getting on for eleven o'clock. Bed time. He began undoing the buttons of her blouse.

Like the *OGPU* and the *Stasis*

The Green Revolution had made little outward difference to the Halloran household. As Eugene H. Halloran Ph.D. shaved the wind pump whirred busily beyond the bathroom window – they had had the wind pump and the solar energy panels long before the Revolution, back in the days before the thirty month waiting list for the kits – and the raised voices of his normative two children, bickering unattractively on the staircase, mingled with the more distant kitchen sounds made by Dorothy Knox Halloran, B.A. (Swarthmore) as she prepared the family muesli. These were a-day-like-any-other sounds, it was 7.45 a.m., his customary shaving time for the last fifteen years, and there was the same cosy stale feeling that he had had at the same hour every day during semester when he had been preparing to go to work at the State Campus, where he had been Associate Professor of Political Science. The only thing that looked and felt different was that, having shaved and slipped on his shirt, before putting on his jacket he strapped a thin leather harness over his shoulders and across his back: a thin leather harness from which there dangled a holstered Glock pistol.

Well, that *was* a difference. He'd certainly never carried a heater when he had gone to the university every day: in fact in those days he had never in his life even once fired a pistol, only, very occasionally, under protest, an acquaintance's sporting rifle. But in those days he had been an Associate Professor of Political Science, a theoretical analyst and analytic theoretician of state and communal violence. That had been before the Revolution. Since the Revolution things had changed: he had become Assistant Chief of Police.

And, just as in the old days he had pondered, as he moved about the bathroom, on the problems likely to be waiting for him when he arrived at the Faculty Building – what the Head of Department might have to say, which students would be loitering in the corridor hoping for a private word, what letters were in the mail – so now his mind drifted familiarly over the day ahead of him at police headquarters.

Really, old Kaldermann, the Head of Department at Pol. Sci., had been far more of a pain in the sphincter than Gurney, his present chief. It wasn't just that, in the old days, while waiting for tenure, Kaldermann had had him to a certain extent under his thumb (and made him feel it) whereas Gurney, a policeman 'of the old school' – that was putting it mildly – inherited from the old regime, was being kept in office only so long as he, Halloran, felt he had anything to learn from him about running a police department and only until such a time as he, Halloran, decided he was ready to take over the top job. Within his ideological limitations, Gurney was good at his job: Kaldermann had not been.

It was the same after every Revolution: it was necessary for the security, stability and survival of the new order that it should take over much of the apparatus of the old, even the most controversial and unpopular parts of the apparatus like the police. The Bolsheviks had done this after 1917, recruiting the *Cheka,* the later *OGPU,* from members of the Tsarist *Okhrana:* again, under Soviet influence, the East German *Stasis* had been recruited from amongst those members of the *Gestapo* who had survived the Nazi collapse. A type like Kaldermann would never have been smart enough to recognize the necessity of this: a sly, devious, procrastinating tyrant in his Department, he was a fanatic for principle, idealism and uncompromising rejection of expediency in his public utterances. They had had to pension him off last year: ludicrously, he had continued to insist, despite all that the country was going through, that one of the duties of the academic was to offer a critical perspective on current events.

At this point in his reverie Halloran tried to flush the toilet. No water.

'Another sabotage case come in,' Gurney said, when Halloran looked into the chief's office precisely fifty-five minutes later. Gurney: big chin, narrow eyes: a casting director's idea of a senior police officer: the eyes (blue) more intent, alert, narrowed even than usual: not just the policeman's customary pig/wolf gaze, not just the almost-supplanted-soon-to-be-ex-boss watching his designated successor's every amateurish move: these sabotage attempts were political, aimed explicitly or implicitly against the regime which was about to take Gurney's career away from him, the regime that had wielded the alchemical power which had transformed a former Associate Professor of Political Science into a policeman.

Politics: police: same Greek root. So what the hell, as Gurney would have said. But for the first time in his life, Halloran could see, Gurney was developing political antennae.

Interesting crime, sabotage.

'I'll check it out,' said Halloran comfortably. Being a university teacher was at least as good a training for getting the right casual inflection into one's voice as being a flatfoot. 'All right if I take O'Casey?'

'He's a good man, O'Casey,' Gurney said, his voice a little out of pitch. The way in which Halloran, without even a pretence of concealment, was working his way systematically through the personnel of the department was bound to make Gurney nervous; Halloran had already noted the signs. And Gurney knew he knew, and now, to cover up that instant of self-betrayal in his voice, put on one of his occasional displays of urbane sophistication: one educated professional to another. 'Keeps his eyes open and doesn't jump to conclusions, that man. Yes, he's limited. No doubt about it, he's finding it difficult to adjust to new ways, new circumstances, but he's one hundred per cent straight, almost you could say, pure. He believes in the word "duty". If ever he seems confused, seems to falter, just mention the word "duty".'

'I'll remember that. Duty to what, incidentally?'

Gurney was by no means out of his element in this show he was putting on.

'Duty to what?' he echoed. 'Man, I said he's *limited.* That means he knows the word "duty", but doesn't know that duty is something owed to something.'

They both laughed, almost an authentic faculty common room laugh only they were both carrying semi-automatics and Halloran could never quite suppress the idea that Gurney might suddenly pull his out and shoot him plumb between the eyes.

At that moment Jane Jonas, the prettiest damn cop in the county, sidled in with a file. Halloran looked at her – all the cops looked at Jonas. Sometimes it wasn't so easy to be the regular tunnel-visioned family man you were supposed to be in the Movement. He saw that Gurney noticed his looking and was smiling almost invisibly to himself. Smart bastard, thought Halloran. Plumb between the eyes.

'I'll leave you guys to it,' he said, and left Gurney's office.

He picked up the details of this latest sabotage incident at the desk, and read them over while waiting for O'Casey to be winkled out of wherever he was hiding himself. As he read he was thinking: wouldn't do for it to get round headquarters that he fancied policewoman Jonas. Even if everyone else did. She was a red-neck in any case, even if she did have a figure like the Venus de Milo: like the rest of the police department she was one of God's Own Country's natural Fascists, for whom, up till a couple of years back, Ecology had been a kind of swear word. He shook his head, tried to concentrate. This sabotage case: it was the new wind-pump station up at the lake again: telephone wires cut, a shot-gun fired at the watchmen's cabin, some superficial damage apparently with an axe, the usual graffiti: 'Greens suck', 'Nuke energy for ever'.

Just as O'Casey came in the sergeant at the desk called Halloran to the phone.

'It's *The Free Enterprise*,' she said.

The Free Enterprise was – still – the name of the local paper. It had been on the agenda to order a change of name, at the party section meeting about a week ago, but they had not got that far down the agenda by the time the meeting had broken up: about the fourth time this had happened.

'Halloran', he snapped in his best chief-of-police voice.

'Morning. Hammerschmidt.' The editor himself. 'Just turned up an unsolicited contribution that might interest you. Like poetry?'

'Crazy about it. Read it out, if it isn't too long'.

'A dozen lines. Here goes:

> Beautiful rose-pink mushroom cloud
> Burning war out of our world
> Cheap power
> Power without smoke and smog and wires
> Power without gallows and gibbets and glass
> On every roof

> Or stupid Dutch primitive windmills
> Submarines cruising under the polar ice
> All that power
> The biggest thing man ever made
> A poem ten billion times bigger than Shakespeare
> No wonder the little green people
> Want to bury it under wholegrain flour.

That's it. Like it?'

'Love it. Can you send someone round with it? The original. Oh, and don't bother to print it. Anything on it to identify the author? Is it typed?'

'A poem in praise of technology, but no, it isn't typed. Fountain pen – well, that may be because they've stopped making ballpoints – very legible teenage girlie hand-writing.'

'Send it round. And thanks for thinking of us, we're grateful.'

'And we're *careful*. Bye for now.'

* * *

'Odd colour paint,' said O'Casey.

Halloran thought this a typically crass remark. They were up at the wind-pump station, surveying the previous evening's graffiti. All around them, at a slightly lower level, were densely wooded hills, with the town visible as a scattering of sun-lit white cubes framed between two of the higher hills on their left. There was yeast in the air. Halloran tried to interest himself in the question of paint.

'I suppose eventually they'll run out,' he mused. 'They're not making paint any more, causes too much pollution.'

'These people will find something else to use. Hey, Professor, I'd been about due to paint my house when, you know, the new government took over. It's pretty well shabby. I'd been looking forward to maybe touching it up when I next had time off. You mean there just isn't going to be any more paint?'

'They're working on it,' said Halloran reassuringly, 'They've got scientists working on environment-friendly paint. It'll be every bit as good as the paint we had in the old days and – this is worth remembering – less than half the price.'

'Well, I'm glad to hear that. You mean lots of things that are short now will come back cheaper? Or is it only paint that will be cheaper?'

'No, lots of things. You see the ingredients will be mostly local, and cheaper because not imported, and things will be made to last longer so people won't have to keep spending on replacing them.'

He paused to examine another rash of daubed slogans. 'Greens suck' and this time a new one: 'Let Big Brother do your thinking for you'. That was a bit more ambitious, though of course sarcasm always impressed intellectuals like himself more than it did most people. Here was another formulation: 'Remember all the time you used to waste choosing who to vote for? Now Big Brother does it for you.' This indication of a certain political sophistication behind the vandalism annoyed him more than the physical damage: also he felt embarrassed because O'Casey had had to see it. People like O'Casey who weren't desperately bright had to be protected from ideas that might confuse them.

'I guess some people just don't like being told what to think,' O'Casey remarked, having spelt out the Big Brother slogans.

'Nobody's trying to control ideas and discussion,' said Halloran with elaborate patience. 'Everybody's agreed that something had to be done to save us from ecological catastrophe.'

'Oh well, sure,' said O'Casey. 'Only some people is like mules, push 'em one way and they'll dam' well make sure they go the other. Mind you, they'll go the right way of their own accord, most times, if you give them their head, sooner or later. Mules I mean, not people.'

'People perhaps don't have as much common sense as mules. And what do you do with your mule anyhow if you're in a hurry and it wants to head the wrong way?'

O'Casey shrugged.

'Well, like you say, Professor, people aren't mules.'

* * *

'The kids are doing their homework,' said Dorothy, but as he stooped to kiss her she turned even more impatiently than usual so that his lips bruised themselves on her cheek-bone. 'There's something you'd better look at.' She handed him a sheet of writing paper. 'I found it when I was tidying Diane's room this afternoon. She hasn't said anything yet, but maybe she's already noticed it's gone.'

It was a poem, written out neatly on a sheet of the unlined recycled paper they used nowadays in the schools. The writing was largish, regular, slightly squarish, without individuality: probably that of a teenage girl.

> Down with Windmills
> Time was when power came from out of town
> Humming cross-country on elegant pylons
> (You see them now rusting in field corners
> Being cut up for scrap because there are
> No more iron mines)
> You just plugged in, switched on, sat back
> Television, ice-box, oven, air-conditioner
> (If anything stopped
> You phoned the electrician
> Because in those days phones worked)
> Now nothing works
> Only stupid primitive windmills
> Creaking all night long
> To power our last light bulb
> (The last light bulb factory
> Is to become a museum)

Halloran felt himself go cold all over, as if ice cubes were being poured down his spine. He hadn't checked at police headquarters to make sure *The Free Enterprise* had sent over the poem they had received. 'Very legible teenage girlie handwriting' was what Hammerschmidt had said. Even if this was not the same very legible teenage girlie handwriting, it was definitely the same windmill-obsessed poet. In his daughter's bedroom: his own child caught up in this shit. He knew suddenly what his older colleagues had gone through in the Clinton-Bush era when they had discovered their kids were involved with heroin and crack: the feeling of outrage, powerlessness and, right at the heart of what should have been love for one's own, resentment, even hatred, of the unknowable and unacceptable.

'Diane,' he called from the door of the living room. For some time they had been developing one of those customary, unappealing father-teenage daughter relationships, growing apart. Only a couple of years ago they had cuddled together practically every day, their goodnight kiss often mouth to mouth, but nowadays he dared not even put his arm round his daughter's waist, and he hadn't seen her naked since – But it was only now, as he watched her coming across the room walking a woman's walk (something about the unconscious/self-conscious way she simultaneously held in and held out her chest) a partly questioning but mainly bored expression on her unformed face, it was only now that he saw her as a separate, entirely autonomous, even threatening individuality.

Even threatening. It had been no joke, in the old days, having a junkie as a daughter, people immediately concluded you had failed as a parent, as a citizen, as a human being, it was the kind of thing which, without being openly discussed, could tip the scales against one in a job appointment or promotion. But things were different now, in many ways worse, or at least less tolerant of personal failure, especially with regard to the family, which had emerged as one of the key platforms of the Movement: and this wasn't a matter of illegal drugs but of political subversion – and him a member of the regional committee and, even if only unofficially, political head of the police.

'Honey,' he said, holding out the sheet of paper but ready to snatch it back, 'Who gave you this poem?'

She recognized it but made no attempt to grab it.

'Sugar,' she said.

'Honey, we're arresting people for this kind of thing.'

'It used to be a free country,' she said, in a familiar childhood whine, though what she said was marginally more interesting than usual, especially if one was a former Professor of Political Science. 'Freedom of Expression is guaranteed in the Constitution.'

'So was the right to carry a gun, with which to murder thy neighbours,' he said, before he quite remembered that he was carrying a gun himself. 'This isn't the first one of these poems we've seen, Diane. Do we have to come to the High School tomorrow, search everybody's lunch box and notebooks, waste a lot of time, maybe break a few heads if some of your friend choose to be uncooperative, or can we perhaps handle it, you know, a bit discreetly?'

'Gee, dad, you're such a pain in the neck. What's *discreetly* for Jesussake? A nice discreet drive in your fancy official car and collect the body from the game wardens the following week?'

'Diane!' he exploded, but then checked himself. It rather sounded as if she had heard something about what had happened at Thionville a couple of weeks previously: better say nothing that might serve to confirm a dangerous rumour. 'Diane, you know I'm one of the people in charge of the police round here and I'd *never* permit such a thing to happen. But there's a lot of stupid, malicious people out there, people living in the twentieth century, who don't like what we're trying to do for this country. People who are trying to undermine us at every turn. There was another sabotage attempt up at the wind-pump station last night. Criminal damage. People might have been killed.'

'Oh, I know, dad. I mean, how do you know it was anybody at school? Guess you have us followed all the time anyway. Guess there's no point in trying to hide anything from you. I mean, yes, I got it at school, jeez. It was meant to be a *secret* and, I mean, it's kinda a friend of mine, I'd be getting a friend into trouble, she didn't mean anything by it. She didn't even *write* the stupid poem.'

'But she probably knows who did and I have to know who or what is behind this.'

'Well, I guess she *does* know. Oh, dad, why on earth did you have to become a policeman? Three-quarters of the guys at school keep away from me already.' She began to weep. 'And now everyone else will too. Oh dad, can't we keep all this a secret?'

She didn't look so pretty when she cried, but it gave Halloran a not unpleasant sense of his own ruthlessness and readiness to insist on principle.

'Sure we can keep it a secret,' he said. 'All I need to do is ask the girl a couple of questions. You could ask her to come here. She can stay to supper. I mean, we *like* to see your friends here. But I've got to ask her a couple of questions and I'll have to do it the hard way –

that's hard for me too – if it can't be done easy. A couple of questions in private and no follow-up, no report, no names, no record. Otherwise it's five police cruisers in her driveway and we'll be coming in with fire-axes and pump guns whether she's at home or not.'

He said this only half as a joke – he was still not quite able to strike an assured note when speaking of police action as an insider – but fortunately Diane took it the right way and even managed a smile through her tears.

'Oh God, dad. You're sure it's just a couple of questions? I mean it's so *embarrassing* for me.'

* * *

It was a fact that in recent months he had often used his work with the police as an excuse to come home late. Nothing had been discussed, but it was pretty much over between himself and Dorothy: even the regular Sunday morning bout she still insisted on 'for my natural hormone balance' was pretty much a chore for both of them. This was a bit awkward as the Greens had made something of a cult of the family. And of course, he still loved her, he supposed, knowing he owed her more than he had ever confessed. He had been the one who had always spoken up at meetings in the old days, he had always been the one who had formulated the ideas and the critiques, drafted the discussion papers, written the fly-sheets and the letters to newspapers: but it had always been Dorothy who had given the conviction, the clarity, the certainly. If it hadn't been for her he would probably never have got off his butt. But he had: and now she seemed even more discontented than before the Revolution. He no longer cared: but somehow he seemed to be staying away longer hours at police headquarters.

But this evening he was home dead on six. Diane was in the living room, playing the Bob Dylan re-releases that Egger had given him (for technical reasons they still hadn't reached the shops). They sounded scratchy, though whether that was the quality or a problem with the aging player, Halloran didn't know. At first he thought Diane was alone in the room but as he advanced from the door he saw another girl who was uncurling herself from his favourite arm-chair, preparatory to standing up.

'Dad, this is Nancy.'

His first reaction was astonishment, and a kind of pain. She was the most beautiful girl he had ever seen in his life. Long silky blonde hair framed a heart-shaped jewel of a face, with huge northern blue eyes, long thick lashes, full, rather pale lips pulling back in a smile from dentifrice-ad teeth. She glowed with the radiance that comes simply from being very young. She shook hands vigorously, like a boy who is still uncertain how much macho pressure to exert in a handclasp.

He found himself checking out her body surreptitiously as they sat down. It was as perfect as her face. She was presumably sixteen, the same age as Diane, and her bits and pieces must have arrived where they were a couple of years ago. She moved them about with assurance, but it was more the assurance of the High School athlete then of the professional beauty. Still, she was as regularly, text-bookishly beautiful as a girl in a Pirelli calendar, in the days when they still had Pirelli calendars: it would almost have been boring, if it had not been for something vulnerable and ardent and sweet and incredibly individual in her face. Halloran found himself hoping against hope that he was going to be able to help this wonderful child, going to be able to save her from the trouble her so called friends were involving her in.

'I'll just see if mom wants help in the kitchen,' said Diane, her voice tricky, higher-pitched than normal. She paused to turn down the CD-player as she went out.

They looked at each other. Nancy had a very fair skin, one could see her colour coming and going in her cheeks and in her clear elegant slender throat. She half began to laugh, embarrassedly, and Halloran thought it could not have been long since she had grown out of pre-teen giggling.

'I'm sorry, Professor Halloran,' she said. 'I know there's nothing to laugh about.'

'No, relax,' he told her. 'This is strictly off the record. Consider yourself a friend of the family.'

'Well, I guess I've been a bit stupid.'

'Everybody's stupid once in a while. Anyhow, maybe you've been lucky. My daughter likes you and I like my daughter. You're the people we're doing all this for, the people who are going to make the future. Believe it or not, I'd have much rather stuck to being a professor.'

'I've a cousin who was one of your students before . . . . ' She meant, before the Revolution, but only Movement people found it easy to use that word. 'He always said what a really sympathetic guy you were.'

'I hope I am. We're doing this out of *love*, do you get me, trying to save the whole damn world from what was happening to it. Maybe we've been too late. And then there's certain sectors, interests, organized groups that will stop at nothing to discredit our movement: the big business cartels, the corporate engineers, fellows who in the old days could have bought and sold me and you and your father a hundred times over. It's no surprise that they're against us. But it's the millions of little people who don't understand, who don't try to understand, that really worry us. Do you think we've been trying to change things too quickly?'

'It's difficult to understand. We hear all about things at school, but it seems it's not really supposed to be discussed. It was the same at my last school – we, my folks, only came to this area about six months ago, before that we lived in St Louis. Well, even I can remember how much more news there was in the papers in the old days. But I guess we all appreciate that something had to be done before it was too late. That's why I feel so stupid.'

She pronounced it st*oo*pid.

'Why do you feel so stupid?' he asked,

'Oh, you know, sir.' He liked the old-fashioned way she called him *sir*. 'Copying out those poems and all. It was only a kind of joke. Kind of a reaction, I guess, after all the Ecology pep-talk at school, kind of letting off steam. I guess you want to know about the guy who actually *wrote* these poems. Well, he's kind of a friend, there's no harm in him. Do you think you can get to speak to him and talk things over with him the way we're talking now?'

'Well, I'd certainly like to check him out.'

'I mean you're not going to arrest him?'

'Not if all he's done is write poems.'

'They're not even very good poems, are they? It was kind of a joke. I've been thinking, sir, I could fix it so you could meet.'

'I'd be very grateful.'

'How would it be if he came here, sir?'

Halloran nearly said *fine* but recollected himself in time. It wouldn't look good if he ended up arresting people who had paid social calls to his house. It was only the guess of this young lady with the thirteen-year-old face and the twenty-year-old body that her friend had done nothing but write poems. Better keep family and work separate.

'Well, I think I'd prefer neutral ground,' he said.

'That's even better,' said Nancy, almost enthusiastically. 'I'd fixed to see him Saturday, up at an abandoned mill four miles up the valley. Monson's they call it.'

'Sure, I know it. Used to drive up there when the road was still usable by cars. Nice view.'

'It's kind of a favourite place of mine too, sir.'

'What time's this meeting then?'

'Ten-thirty.' Nancy looked suddenly depressed. 'I'm sure Tom doesn't know anything about sabotage and all. You're really not going to arrest him, are you?'

'I'll try not to.'

Diane came in just then with a bowl of salad and the both pivoted to see who it was: and Halloran found himself giving Nancy's arse a once over as she turned.

* * *

'Hi!' It was Nancy, alone. The weather that day was hot, for it was almost summer, and she carried a windcheater slung over her shoulder and wore a sleeveless blouse and Levi's. With her slim child's arms and her pony tail swaying frantically as she came towards him, and the vulnerable curve of her neck and nape where her hair was swept up into her pony tail, she looked about fourteen. But very beautiful. It was as if the miracle of beauty had come into his life and the quality of the light in the whole world had changed, and yet it was a kind of delicious secret for only he could see it.

'Hi,' he said. He had walked up from the main road and was sweating. He took his own jacket off, remembering too late his shoulder holster and Glock.

'I always wear it now,' he said, laughing self-consciously. 'To begin with it used to give me a sore patch on the side and shoulder.'

Her smile tugged at his insides.

'Gee, I was wondering, how on earth did you come to be a policeman?'

'Well, you know, in the old days the police as an institution were about the most reactionary group there was: lots of problems with the minorities, civil rights activists, student protesters. We couldn't allow them to carry on as they were.' They sat down on a flat rock and he talked, she listened, her big blue eyes locked on his. He found he liked talking to her. He had missed talking to young people, but it was more than that. He felt that pang again. Christ, if only he was not too late to save her from being seriously involved with the people who were working to wreck the new society. She was so beautiful, and so young! Her whole life in front of her. And she asked intelligent, interested questions. There was one problem though. Her friend hadn't shown up. Maybe she was *too* interested. Maybe he was being set up.

He stood up casually, as if to stretch his legs, and moved a couple of yards to a point where he could see the whole length of the mill's derelict facade at the same time as being able to keep his eye on the track up from the road. Be casual. Don't look round too much, but make sure you have a good field of vision and see everything in it.

He turned slowly, deliberately.

Froze.

Nancy was suddenly no longer there.

Gun in hand, safety catch off, he sprang to the corner of the mill. No sign of her. As quietly as he could he moved along the side of the mill. At the back he might be able to climb up amongst the trees and shrub on the hillside behind the mill, and see if anyone was approaching. It was obvious he had been led into a trap: but the bastards had yet to catch him in it.

At the corner of the mill he caught a slight, unidentifiable grating sound. He sprang clear of the building, pistol at the ready, facing down the back of the mill.

The hillside had been cut away slightly, and faced with a three-foot high course of brickwork. There was an alleyway between this embankment and the back wall of the mill: probably serving for drainage in wet weather but now choked with dead leaves. At the top of the embankment, about three yards from him, Nancy was squatting, Levi's pulled down about her ankles, taking a pee.

'Oh God, no', she breathed. The muzzle of his pistol pointed directly at her suddenly ashen face. 'Please Professor Halloran, don't, please don't.'

He kept his gun pointing at her as he advanced. The certainty that this was a trap almost suffocated him. Nancy stood up, not covering herself, her Levi's concertina'd about the ankles of perfectly-shaped, creamy-skinned legs. The neat triangle of fur below the hem of her blouse was only slightly darker than her blonde hair: he had time to wonder if it was quite professional to notice such a detail.

'Please, Professor Halloran, please,' she repeated. 'You don't have to do it this way. I mean I like you. I'll do *anything* you want only don't shoot me. I don't want to die. I'll go to bed with you. You don't have to worry. I'm a virgin. You don't have to worry about AIDS.'

'Shut up!' He pulled her down into the space between the embankment and the wall of the mill, and crouched beside her, scanning the hillside. Leaves swaying gently in the breeze against the sunlight gave a momentary impression of hostile movement, but no, there was nothing up there. But there had to be. He snatched a glance at Nancy. She had floundered amongst the dead leaves on her hands and knees but now she was rearranging herself into a more comfortable squatting position. Her Levi's and panties were still around her ankles. What was it she had said? 'You don't have to do it this way.' Oh God, she thought he was going to rape her. Tears of mortification sprang to his eyes. Desperately he turned his attention back to the hillside.

But there really was no-one else there: a soft breeze swaying and clicking amongst the branches, a wood warbler singing in one of the trees, answered by another bird somewhere behind them: a dog barking a huge distance away, pigeons cooing on the roof of the factory. Unbearably ashamed, he looked at Nancy.

She was standing beside him. And laughing.

'God, Professor, you really thought there was some guy out there with a gun, didn't you?'

'Well, what about you then?' In his frustration he could only try pitifully to answer jeer by jeer. 'Saying you were willing to go to bed with me so long as I didn't shoot you.'

She looked suddenly solemn. There were still tears on her eyelashes, giving her an odd, almost feral expression.

'Well, I meant that,' she said defiantly. 'I *want* you to go to bed with me.' She leaned forward and kissed him hard on the lips. 'See?'

He didn't see at all, but she was so beautiful, and he had been so afraid, and as he reached out to clasp her, her naked bottom was so smooth and warm and alive under his hands. All he managed to say between kisses was: 'We shouldn't be doing this.'

'Not here at any rate. My folks are away for a couple of days. There's nobody at my place.'

This should have been his cue to say *But Nancy you're in my daughter's class at school.* But he didn't.

'It's all a bit sudden,' he said.

'It's kind of sudden for me too, Professor. I want you to know something. I've never had a man see me naked before.'

'You don't have to invite me home just because of that.'

'It isn't just because of that. I've been really stupid. I got you to come here because I wasn't sure I could trust you, I wanted to see if you really would come all alone the way you promised. You see, there isn't any Tom, sir. *I* wrote the poems.'

'*You* did?'

'As a kinda joke. I wanted to meet you.' She kissed him again. 'I guess I'm just weird. Someone pointed you out — "That's Diane's dad, he's kinda head of the secret police ? " '

'I'm not — there's no secret police. Just the ordinary police.'

'Whatever. I don't care. I like you better as a professor anyhow.'

She stood up, began to pull up her Levis, then stopped. 'Hey, do you mind if I finish my pee?'

* * *

Fifty-five minutes later, at Nancy's place:

'So that's what everyone keeps going on about', Nancy was saying, extricating herself from the asymmetrical sprawl of elbows knees and heels in which they had been entangled. 'I guess I never realized it would be so. . . .' Finally she managed to sit up. 'Wow, but I've got to go and pee *a-gain.*'

She was only a child: there was something so vulnerable in the contrast and combination of her thin child's arms and her precociously large breasts, which bounced in heart-rending counterpoint to her swinging pony tail as she loped towards the door.

I've got so much power, he told himself: mustn't abuse it. Always neat, his clothes were stacked on a chair, his holstered pistol hanging from the back. Nancy's clothes were more generously distributed: her Levi's, which had come off first, were on the floor just beside the door, her bra which had come off last still beside the pillow: and yet despite this significant scatter of garments, and his own aching presence in the narrow bed, it was still, poignantly, an early-teenage girl's room: a few pre-Revolution posters, a guitar with a string missing, school files. Tears came to Halloran's eyes. I've so much power, he thought again.

He stood up, and standing to one side of the window, as in an old TV movie, he looked down the drive. Nothing moved. He found his watch amongst the stack of clothes on the chair. People would be wondering where he was. He wondered if there was time to ball her again. God, he ought to be ashamed of himself, with a kid like that. No, the fact was it gave him a guilty relish. He looked round, taking in all the sweet details of her room.

Something under the desk seemed out of place. It looked like a blueprint of some kind. He fished it out.

It was a plan of the windpower station in the next county that had burnt down two months previously.

His ears caught the sound of a door opening on the other side of the landing. He hurried back to the bed.

Her smile as she (literally) bounced back into the room was so sweet, he couldn't bear to believe what he had to believe.

'Move over, muscle man,' she called gaily.

He moved over.

'Hey, you're not going to put all this in a report are you?'

'Of course not.' Or was he? It looked as if there might be more to report than he had bargained for.

'I suppose I shouldn't say this to you since you're a kind of a cop' – Nancy seemed suddenly to be in a chatty mood – 'but I hate being checked up on. I hate being bossed around. It's really boring at school, the way they're always telling us what to think, what to believe. I mean, most of us believe it already. And sometimes it's not what they say, but the way they say it, like they *enjoy* giving orders and making us have the same ideas as they have.'

'It's a bit like Christianity,' he said, pushing the fact of that blueprint to the back of his mind, seeking comfort in the accustomed flow of words. 'To begin with, when the Christians were few and powerless, people laughed at them and even joined in persecuting them. Well, we Greens weren't actually locked up or crucified upside down or thrown to the lions but we were certainly laughed at a lot. Then Christianity became the official religion and eventually everybody was obliged to believe it. And got into trouble if they didn't. Half the beauty of it had been that the faithful believed *in spite of* the government: it wasn't at all the same when the government told them to believe it. Well, that was a long time ago, and we hope we've learnt a few lessons from the past. The way we see it, Ecology just isn't going to become an official religion, with a Spanish Inquisition and heretics burnt at the stake. No more McCarthyism.'

'You mean, people'll be able to stand up and criticize if they want?'

'That's what I mean.'

'So why were you so upset by those poems I wrote?'

Suddenly he was angry, almost desperate.

'Don't you see? It's an emergency. We need *time,* and we have to do so much so quickly. It's like wartime. Before you and I were born, when this country was fighting the takeover of the world by Hitler and his Nazis, one of the first things that had to be done was to lock up people who thought differently from the rest about what Hitler stood for. We defended freedom by taking freedom away from its enemies. Sometimes, as Rousseau said, people have to be forced to be free. As a temporary measure, of course.'

With a womanly though inexperienced gesture Nancy took his head in her arms. With his face between her breasts he heard her voice saying 'I know honey, I know, I'll help you.' He could hear her heart beating.

* * *

'I think I'm on to something,' said O'Casey. 'You know I thought the paint was an odd colour? Well, I had half an idea I recognized it. So I checked, and it *was* familiar. It's the same paint as they were using to paint the Lowell house the day the State of Emergency was declared.'

'That was the day Lowell was arrested and executed.'

'Yeah, I guess executed is what you have to call it. Maybe his son wouldn't call it that. Well, after that they stopped painting the house. And his son – well I guess he just took off, hid out somewhere. Well, you know Mr Lowell wasn't the kind of guy who went down to the neighbourhood store every day that he was painting the house and bought the paint one can at a time.'

'You mean – ?' But Halloran saw exactly what he meant. Lowell had been the richest man in the county: the paint would have been specially ordered, without thought of expense, and more than enough would have been got in for the whole job, which meant that when the work was abandoned there would have been plenty of paint left. And as O'Casey hinted, Lowell's son might well have been somewhat fired up about his father being liquidated. But what O'Casey presumably did not know was that it had been Robert R. Lowell Junior's idea to liquidate his father. The younger Lowell had been active in the Militant Wing. Now he was out of town not because he was on the run but because he had some sort of job in Washington.

Some sort of job in Washington: Halloran suddenly felt hollow, and very old. It wasn't the kind of thing that was discussed, even within the Movement, but it was pretty widely known what kind of jobs people from the Militant Wing had taken over in Washington: Federal Bureau of Investigation, Secret Service, Homeland Security. There was every reason to suppose that what O'Casey seemed to be suggesting was on the right track and that Robert R. Lowell Jr. was behind the sabotage and vandalism – but not for the obvious, ostensible reasons. The most obvious explanation was that he himself, Eugene H. Halloran Ph.D., was under surveillance: they had created a crisis just to see how he responded. Pointless to ask why. He had once thought of giving a seminar course on the mentality of secret police organizations. The really important question was how Nancy was involved.

How? Or was it more a question of *if?* That radiant face, the swinging pony tail, the part-sun-tanned body spreadeagled for him on the narrow bed. Christ, she was only sixteen . . . . 'Keep this under your hat,' he told O'Casey. 'You've given me an idea.'

* * *

Despite the shadows of doubt already forming over their relationship, escaping from Dorothy to Nancy was like passing from an airless, dry-rotted community hall to a spring meadow where all the sweetest-smelling flowers of the botany textbook bloomed side by side under blue sky, silver clouds and yellow sun. But there was a danger in this. It was only when turning in his unmarked car up the drive to Nancy's house, later that afternoon, that it occurred to him that perhaps one of the neighbours would recognize his vehicle. He was an important person, nowadays, let's face it, and there were very few other vehicles left on the road in any case. Getting out of the car before Nancy's front door, he made a casual 360-degree turn to check how many neighbours' windows overlooked him. Only one: and the afternoon sun was shining directly on it so it was not possible to see if anyone was behind the glass staring out. Too bad: but he was almost as new to the world of surveillance as he was to adultery, and it made him nervous.

Nancy was standing at the front door, grinning, radiant, pouting her boobs. But when, closing the door behind him with one hand, he tried to kiss her she turned her face, giving him only a cool cheek, and then pushed him gently away.

'Gee, I'm glad to see you', she said breathlessly. 'I've been so worried I've been lying awake all night thinking about you.'

'About me?'

'About us.' She grabbed his hand and pulled down to sit beside her on the stairs. 'I'm so confused, honey. You know, I've never done anything like this before, and besides the fact is I just don't understand the general situation as well as you do.'

'What do you mean? What's happened?'

'Honey, you know what happened!' She giggled. 'I guess we were both carried away. Perhaps I'm oversexed or something and you're – well, you're you. But then I remembered what they've been telling us at school.'

'What's school got to do with us?'

'Some professor you are!' She produced a school file that had been lying behind them on a higher step, and opened it at a printed document. 'I suppose you've seen this before?'

He had and he hadn't. It was immaculately laser-printed on the cheapest, grainiest recycled paper, a typical example of the information and exhortation sheets circulated by official organizations since the Revolution. He hadn't looked closely at one for months. The layout and type face and the cartoon of a fat man in an Uncle Sam top hat with a missile in his pocket, a huge cigar belching smoke in his mouth and a copy of *Playboy* in his fist, were all unfamiliar. On the other hand he recognized the text because he had written it. Having a ready pen and not wishing to isolate himself too much in police work and thereby cut himself off from the mainstream of reconstructive activities, he had continued to write educative material for the Movement whenever he had time.

He wondered for a second whether Nancy somehow knew he had written it but of course that was impossible, no record was ever kept of who wrote what – their ideas were common property – and if any changes had to be made they were made by whoever required the change. Not that his drafts were normally altered, he had always had something of a knack of thinking the same way as the rest of the group.

The paper was, essentially, a manifesto against sexual self-indulgence. It began: 'Sex is beautiful. And like other things of beauty it has been taken over and commercialized, shredded down to yet another area of exploitation and corruption and angst in the old society we are now trying to escape from.' He didn't have to re-read it, he remembered the phrases: 'There's nothing wrong with being good-looking. There's nothing wrong with taking pride in one's appearance, or in the neatness of one's clothes. There's something wrong with looking like a plasticized bionic model in a trashy mass-produced magazine. We're all individuals.' Nevertheless he pretended to read it, deciding that it was safer to pretend he had never seen it before. '. . . . it's not just a problem of producing unwanted unloved babies in this already over-crowded world of ours . . . . the culture of the throwaway boy-or-girl-friend is like the culture of clothes fashions that change every four months, like the built-in obsolescence of cars.' Well, it was a bit glib, to say the least, but that had been one of the weaker passages. '. . . . pills to prevent pregnancy, lotions to suppress the smell of one's private parts, programs of injections to cure sexually transmitted diseases, pep-pills to cheer one up after abortions all represent ways in which Big Business and the Technology of Waste have invaded the most precious private areas of our lives . . . . Without deeper feelings that can only be developed with time sex is one of the most selfish things there is, the same self-obsessed selfishness without regard for others that littered our streets with expensive wrappings while half the world starved and the ozone layer eroded over our heads. . . . Sex is beautiful. Self-indulgence is ugly, unworthy of a human being. Maturity means being able to distinguish between the two, being able to control oneself, and to help others control themselves.'

Jeez, he thought. Can she really have taken this seriously? Well, he had taken it seriously enough when he had written it, but that had been before . . . . He'd better go warily.

'So you think . . . . ' he began tentatively.

'I don't know what to think. Yesterday it seemed so *right* in bed with you. But you're *married*, you've already got the big permanent relationship of your life. And I'm only sixteen, if I start balling regularly now, how many men am I going to ball before I finally settle down? It's kind of fun, I can see why they want to stop people doing it. I wouldn't like to get, you know, addicted to it, what with all the risk.'

'But like it says, Nancy, we're all individuals, and it's a question of personal maturity. You're incredibly mature for your age, and I don't mean only physically, and this is written, as you see, as a kind of general statement, while in fact we're not generalizations, we're individuals with individual needs and circumstances.'

This must have been the wrong thing to say, for Nancy began to cry.

'Oh God, I want you, I want you more than I've ever wanted anything in all my life,' she gasped between sobs. 'For a moment it seemed so natural, so *beautiful*. But that's the trap, don't you see? In reality it's wrong, so self-indulgent, against everything people believe in now.'

After a while he found the most effective way to still her crying was by kissing her, and matters may have proceeded directly to their logical, if self-indulgent, conclusion if they had been situated anywhere other than on an uncomfortable staircase. When Halloran had got most of her buttons undone he could not think what to do next, but Nancy came to his rescue, saying with sudden decisiveness, 'I guess it's not going to make any difference if I ball you one more time.'

As they were going up the stairs to her room, she asked:

'Would you leave your wife for me?'

'I'd do anything. You're right, my marriage is a sham. We were talking about separating when the Revolution came. Then divorce kind of went out of fashion.'

'But it's still legal?'

'It's not encouraged. But it's not against the law to move out and move in with someone you really and truly love.'

As he said this, he realized that the problem was having somewhere to move into. House-building had declined enormously since the Revolution – it was unbelievable how much pollution was caused by cement factories – and a *lot* of people were on waiting lists to be rehoused. And what if Nancy got pregnant before they found somewhere? He remembered suddenly that there were two hundredweight of impounded condoms in the cellars at police headquarters: but for the moment Nancy seemed to know what she was doing –

The whole business of the blueprint of the windpower station completely slipped his mind, and only came back to him later when he was already back on the road and it was too late to change lanes and return to Nancy's.

* * *

'When are you going to do something about this rag?' Dorothy Halloran asked him, waving a copy of *The Free Enterprise* at him.

'Honey, something's come up,' he said wearily. 'I'm a bit preoccupied. What's wrong with *The Free Enterprise* this time?'

'Well, will you just *look?*'

He looked: an article on the new style trade in antiques and curios. Disposable wrappers were becoming collectors' items: top prices were being paid for unbroken containers, especially the type that had originally cost as much or more than the item contained, such as the nastier type of Christmas gift or souvenir from the old days. At the top end of this part of the market was furniture made out of expensive wood painted to look like plastic.

'Pretty tasteless,' he commented. 'But then the antique trade always was about the tastelessness of so-called good taste.'

'*Tasteless!*' shrilled Dorothy. 'It's simply *vicious*. It's time *The Free Enterprise* was closed down. There's hundreds of idealistic kids out there who'd love to run an alternative newspaper that was genuinely sympathetic to what we're trying to do.'

One of the most idealistic of them had been threshing around in bed under him only an hour previously.

'Those kids, they couldn't run an ice-cream parlour on a summer's Sunday morning.' he said patiently. 'Anyway, Hammerschmidt's been cooperative, more co-operative than perhaps we expected, and we need to win over his kind of people, not alienate them.'

'Compromise. You can't compromise with the devil. The whole movement's being corrupted by compromise, abdicating its true objectives out of a cowardly surrender to what people call common sense, or fair play, or awareness of public mood. It's sickening.'

'Honey, I've got to draft a report.'

He went to his old work room. Dorothy was so out of touch. Basically it was their flexibility that distinguished them from earlier revolutions: and Dorothy simply wasn't flexible enough. A wife like that could hold a man back. Nancy, on the other hand: where Dorothy had too much personality, Nancy was sweet, but, not to put too fine a point on it, too young to have much personality, or at least (as was definitely not the case with other women he had known) only enough to complement her body.

That blueprint of the windpower station was worrying, though.

One indisputable plus from his involvement with Nancy was that it had made him think a bit more clearly about the libertarian aspect of the Revolution. It was beginning to seem to him now that they were on the wrong tack, pursuing a wrong strategy, politically speaking. Well, perhaps with his specialist academic background he saw a bit further into things than the others.

One couldn't make a revolution without breaking eggs, and heads: the question was how many. One had to avoid as far as possible flying in the face of people's prejudices. If it was impossible to avoid antagonism, the unnecessary changes had to be sacrificed to the necessary, to reduce the antagonism as far as possible. It seemed to him now that the coercive, confrontational, Big Brother aspect of the Revolution had gone too far, uselessly, unnecessarily far. A movement whose key theme was self-discipline, self-denial, mutual responsibility had become a business of external discipline, institutional restrictions, paternalism. It was the Big Brother aspect, much more than the shortages of baby clothes, light bulbs, fast food, that was causing resentment. The sooner the Movement faced up to this problem the better.

It was a question, in a sense, of broadening the popular base of the Revolution. Put in those terms, what he proposed was largely cosmetic. It was not – ought not to be – a question of the regional committees turning over their responsibility and leadership to a mob of hippies and old-style neighbourhood politicians. The real location of power, in the hands of those who had proven they fully understood the problems and the requirements of the situation, would have to remain the same. But more people would have to be involved, be given the sense of sharing in the direction of the new order. This meant the whole *style* of the relationship between Movement and the Mass would have to be altered.

Having wound a piece of grey recycled notepaper into his typewriter, he began to sketch out some of his ideas.

* * *

'I hear you're dating a High School cheer leader,' said Gurney, when he looked into the Chief's office the following morning.

Nancy. So he *was* under surveillance. Halloran recovered himself quickly.

'I thought cheer leaders had been abolished,' he said, 'as an overly commercialized intrusion into the school community.'

'Well, that's how my informant described her.'

Dirty old man, thought Halloran. But there was a similarity of the eyes, Gurney's northern blue eyes and Nancy's northern blue eyes. What kind of a name was Gurney anyway, wondered Halloran: and Nancy's? – Oh cripes, some cop he was: he didn't know Nancy's last name.

'So what's her name, this cheer leader?' he asked Gurney.

'Hunter. Nancy Hunter.'

He went to his desk. No choice now: he was going to have to make a report about Nancy. Following up a lead. Obtaining the suspect's confidence. He ordered up the file on the windpower station in the next county that had burnt down two months before he met Nancy. The file contained:–

a photocopy of the floor plan of the station
a ten page summary
2 witness statements
2 personal dossiers relating to the two sworn witnesses
an inventory
6 photographs
a signed cover note, neatly typed down to the signature

Nancy   Gurney Hunter.

That's right, a signed cover note neatly typed down to the signature Nancy Gurney Hunter.

Using a special code number possessed only by members of the regional committee, he called up the police service file of Nancy Gurney Hunter. Whose file photo showed his Nancy. Aged 21. Widow. It was a long time since he had thought that it must show if a girl wasn't a virgin, but there must have been signs he should have picked up that she was older than her mid-teens. But it wasn't the deception or the personal betrayal: it was the political consequences that most concerned him. Essentially this was a conspiracy of rightist police leaders like Gurney who were using *agent provocateur* tactics against Green Movement officials in exposed positions of responsibility. True it would usefully bring to light at least two hostile agents, but even if they handled the case in secret (and took measures to suppress any rumours) it would be difficult to make his part in it seem creditable. Balling a suspect was bad enough: balling a suspect he thought was a sixteen-year-old was beyond the pale. As far as opinion in the regional committee was concerned it would be touch and go whether he would be allowed to remain even as *assistant* police boss. Basically he was finished as far as the Green Movement was concerned: and Dorothy would throw him out and there was no chance of getting his old university job back, and without a home and a job, in a country with thirty million unemployed – it would be less disagreeable simply to be liquidated. But the important point was the damage it would do to the Movement. It was playing directly into the hands of their worst enemies, to provide them with instances of personal opportunism and unprofessionalism. They were bound to make a public issue of it. It was really painful for Halloran to realize that his own actions, his own stupidity, were to result in the kind of squalid commercial scandal that would work against everything he had ever believed in.

He still believed he had a hell of a lot to offer the Movement. Inevitably all that would be sacrificed.

It wasn't his private feelings – but it was her fault really of course. Perhaps it was what she had wanted all along. Those poems. He had ended by liking them for her sake:

Creaking all night long
To power our last light bulb

He wondered why she should get away with it.

The whole case could be closed quite easily.

In a sense it was a question of choosing between Nancy and the Revolution. Between loving her (and he did) and the duty of responsibility.

He recalled momentarily the paper he had been writing last night. Theorizing. Overshadowing all the possible theorizing was the sheer problem of seizing, maintaining and exercising power.

He drove to Nancy's, forced her to kneel and held his gun to her head.

'Yeah, I'm a cop', she said. 'I was nineteen when the Revolution came. My husband was in the police – killed in the counter-insurgency period in Pennsylvania. Gurney is my uncle. He said, this is a big thing, but it isn't so big the rules of right and wrong will change. Just the context.'

'It was a set up. Kind of thing Tsarists would do. We're making the same mistake as in 1918, recruiting the Tsarist *Okhrana* as the best qualified to man the *Cheka* and *OGPU*.'

'I don't know what you're talking about, you pathetic man. I wish I could show you what I'm going to write about you in my report.'

So she wasn't so professional.

'You've reported to Gurney?'

'I don't report to him. He's not my boss, so I don't tell him anything. OK he made me, encouraged me, to be a cop, but we stick to channels. He wouldn't have it any other way.'

'So it's a trap. The Stalinists are taking over.' The Glock was heavy in his hand and the muzzle began to droop. 'It's the continuity of the *Okhrana* and the *Cheka/OGPU* all over again.'

Nancy's face was transfigured. 'I don't care. There'll always be people like you – and always people to stand up against them.'

He raised his gun as she spoke.

A gentle, even pressure on the trigger, like on the practice range.

A red star spreading on her shirt.

Fingers reaching as if to pull out the bullet. Her forearms were suntanned and she wore a bracelet of emerald coloured plastic.

It was the first time he had ever fired the Glock except at a cardboard target.

It was quite startling how it made one's ears ring to shoot without ear-protectors.

The Penis and the Poet

He had had a certain amount of success in previous relationships, with erotic – or even positively obscene – verses which he had presented to the lady in question either by way of introduction or after brief acquaintance. He missed the opportunity to use his best *haiku*:

> I want to greet the Millennium
> Looking down at you as I come

but shortly afterwards met a lewd Jamaican girl who only did foreplay – what she called 'making out'. She had a habit of coming to the front door of her rooming house wearing only panties and her response to:

> My nuts went numb
> When I saw you plumb
> Stretched out on your tum
> Flexing your bum
> And you said,
> 'Hey dude
> I'm in a cocktail mood:
> Make mine two-thirds rum
> And the rest hot come.'

had been to hand him her panties and allow him to digitate her from behind on the way upstairs. (On the other hand the *Erotic Review* thought the poem was terrible.) Then there was the pissed-off-looking teenager in a hooded track-suit top he used to see on the bus. She looked like the kind of girl who would say 'Fuck Off' when a simple 'No' would have served, but he finally plucked up courage to give her:

> On your way home from disco bar or rink
> Or outward bound to meet friends for a drink
> You boarded the bus I sat bored on

The red bus that was our only link
        Hoodie in Pink

I'd worked till late at Durward, Schlep and Grinkk
And was in the act of massaging the kink
In my neck that came from long hours
At a computer pretending to think
        Hoodie in Pink

You looked straight through me without a blink
Looked the dead opposite of a wink
Looked back along the line of my look
In a way that made my manhood shrink
        Hoodie in Pink

In a way that made my heart clunk-clink
And my throat tighten and my stomach twink
And my brain start boiling with thoughts
Of giving you champagne, sports cars and mink
        Hoodie in Pink

But because I knew there wasn't a chink
Or chance you'd play chicken on the brink
Of listening to me
At my stop from the bus I did slink
        Hoodie in Pink

It turned out she was in fact twenty-two, and nothing like as formidably cross-grained as she looked, having an unexpected 'Gosh-I-like-you' smile that turned off and on as if with a switch, each time exactly the same brightness and width as the time before. Sex with her was a bit repetitive too, reminding him of using the carjack on an old Peugot he'd once owned – every time he pushed home her knees came up higher. Reflecting that the old-fashioned literary convention of four dots and the more recent practice in novels by ex-literary agents of sliding over sex scenes with no more than a nonchalant allusion of muffled cries and colliding hips was in direct opposition to the possibility that the real truth – or *a* real truth – of an individual's personality is revealed in their love making, this being the reason why essentially sex is private, he moved on to a blouse-

busting blonde from Bletchley he met in Harrods called Honoria –
stress on first and third syllable to rhyme with gonorrhoea – who was
amused by:

> Did you dream of me last night
> And did your dream give you a fright?
> Not even at arousal's height
> Did I intend to nip and bite
> Those bits of you, translucent white
> Now packed and bodiced out of sight
> That set my fantasies alight :
> Those tooth marks arranged like a kite
> That show up on your aluminium-bright
> Flesh, well, I admit I had no right
> Even in sleep to clinch so tight,
> Like Tyson in a title fight,
> And forage till you were, well, quite –
> What's that? You *didn't* dream of me last night?

With her he achieved a personal HMBC best – that is rapid progress
through the sequence of Hand-holding, Mouth-mashing, Buttocks-
kneading and Crutch-fumbling, what in some instances had taken
him two weeks in her case only needing two minutes – but he was a
little put off, once her knickers were discarded, by the way she humped
back, completely out of sync with his thrusts, as if she been told to
hump back but hadn't figured out how, and she wept when he gave
her:

> Good morning, Miss
> I want to kiss
> Your clitoris
> And taste your piss
> And dried-in spill
> From last night's bliss.

He didn't get even as far as hand-in-bra-and-hunt-the-nipple
with the cashier at Tesco to whom he gave:

Princess of the check-out till
Mona Lisa of the fidgeting queue –
As I unload my tins I wonder, will
You like this poem I write for you?
While werewives wait for me to pay
With shopaholics pushing them behind
Will you ask how's life today?
Or just pretend you're going blind?

Perhaps it wasn't obscene enough. Not that obscenity, or the lack of
it, seemed to be a factor either way. A classics graduate from
Cambridge called Chloe with a rather prissy little mouth was revealed
as a walking refutation of the fallacy that size of mouth indicated
size of fanny when she made him stay overnight to try a sexual
position guaranteed to give multiple orgasms, which she had read
about in *PiV*, yet all he had written for her was:

Did Heloise's hand feel moist
When Abelard had held it for an hour?
Did Beatrice wear stays to hoist
Her bubbies higher and use flour
To blanch her arms? And is it true
That Juliet's upper lip looked blue?
Beatrice and Juliet are dust
Dispersed throughout the planet: You
With wind-blown hair and Miss World bust
Are here and now, turned out brand new
To fire my twenty-first century lust.

On their next date however, having made him demonstrate how many
times he could get it up in a single night, she told him the poem
wasn't dirty enough for *Erotic Review*, and when he tried to introduce
a more tender note into the relationship by giving her:

I want to have fun in your fanny
I want to crow in your crack

I want to crease up in your cranny
And to bubble over your back
And I want this before you're a granny
Bag-ladying in a soiled mac.

Her response was, 'So you think I'm going to shag my way down through the strata of society till I end up as a bag lady? Fuck you!' And the relationship finally foundered when she spilt the contents of her handbag in the street one evening and remarked, when he helped her to retrieve everything, 'What would I do without you?' – he had responded, 'Use a vibrator, I guess.' (He had never been able to take girls who were even slightly knock-kneed seriously.)

A completely monoglot and aphrodisiacally stupid Italian girl, in London to write a 40,000 word dissertation on synecdoche in *Finnegan's Wake,* was less of a problem, thanks to his familiarity with the language of Dante:

Una Donna Dimostra La Differenza Tra 'Sapere' E 'Conoscere'

La sua bocca
sapeva di albicocca

Il suo ombelico
sapeva di fico

La sua clitoride
sapeva di formaldeide

Alla Università di Impotenza
È laureata in giurisprudenza

Admittedly she was a bit puzzled by this, but was too fond of lying in his bed with a box of chocolates to make any objections, other than when he wanted her to roll over.

We'll skip the Marxist sculptor (the trouble with girls with exquisite profiles is that one has to hump them face full on) who assured him her pubic hair grew more abundantly when she was shagging regularly and the obliging lady from Human Resources who looked positively radiant (especially her nose, which she'd had forgotten to powder) when he said let's be part of each other's dream, but seemed to think it perfectly normal that he couldn't get his dick into her even with the help of Vaseline. His biggest investment in time and verse was Rosemary. To begin with she seemed to be another case of one-way sexual chemistry. She was long-legged and very slim, though with boobs a size too large for the rest of her, and so high and round that he wondered if they were not falsies: but she was a trainee accountant and an avowed Christian, and he was only able to get a date with her by taking her off balance. 'I know you are a Christian and an accountant,' he told her, 'And I'm a complete moral degenerate with not much money – but how about meeting up one evening?' This made her laugh so much that she had to say yes to avoid seeming narrow-minded and lacking in Christian charity.

On their second date she told him off about the way he looked at her, and at their next meeting he gave her:

> 'Don't look at me as if I was something to eat,'
> You said, when all I wanted was to kiss your feet.
> All the wolf wanted with Red Riding Hood
> Was to show her the red heart of the wood.
> His wanting made her your first heroine –
> Or did it only make you scared to meet
> Anyone who had a chipped-toothed grin?

She read this carefully, folded it up neatly and put it in her hand bag. Then she asked:

'Do you often give girls poems?'

'Quite often, but usually a bit ruder than that.'

'Like for example?'

'Well. . . .'

'Go on, tell me one of your rude poems.'

'Well, you know, something like:

> A human Barbie Doll called Mary,
> As perfect as a Walt Disney fairy

> Met the rightest of Mr. Rights
> But when she took off her tights
> He was shocked to find her crutch hairy.'

Pretending to be disapproving Rosemary punched his arm. She asked:

'Do you see me as a human Barbie Doll?'

'No, you're too. . . .too alive.'

He was slightly surprised that she agreed to meet him again. This time he presented her with:

> The prince not knowing what could be amiss
> Awakened Sleeping Beauty with a kiss
> 'Er- rrugh!' She spluttered, hand on hips
> 'I hate it when men kiss me on the lips.'

She laughed and he said, 'How about it?'

'How about what?'

'A kiss.'

'Do you think I'm Sleeping Beauty?'

'In a way.

'All right, try and wake me up, but *gently* and keep your hands where I can see them.'

In practice she didn't mind his hands going round to her back, even when they moved down from her prominent shoulder blades halfway through their kiss, past the catch of her bra, to her waist and then down to her bottom. He was dying to find out if her boobs would stick out at the same height if she wasn't wearing a bra but when he shifted his hand to the vee-neck of her sweater she caught hold of his wrist.

'You said you wanted me to keep my hands where you could see them,' he protested.

'Yes, I did. And I definitely didn't want them hidden inside my jersey.'

Somehow, they began teasing each other with talk of marriage. She pretended to be seriously interested when he spoke of giving her four sons, to be named Mathew, Mark, Luke and John She invited him back to her place. The girls she shared a flat with were out.

She wore a little gold cross on a chain round her neck. He managed to get the top button of her blouse open on the pretext of looking at it, but that was all she would permit as far as the front of her body was concerned. Somewhat irked, and intending to annoy her, he said, 'I suppose your boobs flop down a bit when you take your bra off.' 'Well, you're never going to find out if they do, are you?' she responded quickly. It quickly transpired, however, that she was one of those girls who was incredibly turned on by having her bottom kneaded. Her kisses became wetter the more he squeezed and she made no protest when his hand moved down from the small of her back, inside her jeans and into her panties. She even did not say anything when he popped open the waist button of her jeans so that he could get his hand in further, only stopping him when he got right in and curled his finger forward and found unexpectedly copious pubic hair and an even more unexpected wetness.

She explained that at eleven she had been the girl who showed her still hairless crack to select boys in her class but that she had definitely reformed since and become a good girl.

On their next date – on what she called neutral ground – he gave her:

> I don't want you to go goo-goo to our tots
> Or look ecstatic when you wipe their bots
> Or give me wifely looks across their cots:-
> The most I want is that you have the hots
> When I twiddle your quim curls into knots.

She pretended to be seriously annoyed, but when parting she gave him a particularly forceful goodnight kiss on – and inside – his mouth: to tease her he said, 'You're not supposed to stick your tongue in someone's mouth when giving a goodnight kiss,' and she responded tartly, 'I was practising a good morning kiss.'

Then, a few days later, she said she wanted him to tell her about all his previous girlfriends. So he gave her another of his rejects from *Erotic Review:*

> Chloe was clever but claws-out competitive,
> Keeping score even when giving head;
> Benedetta was beautiful but deficient in drive,
> Fulfilled by posing bum up on a bed;

Carol was cool but her dozy fixed smile
Reminded me of the front teeth of a gopher,
May had marvelously malleable mammaries
But allowed only finger fucks on the sofa;
Sue spread them more swiftly, but snivelled at anything
From scatology to squirrels squished flat by fast cars;
Laura was loving but relentlessly trivial,
Turned on by Mars Bars and not a bit by the stars.
Christine was creative, but her theories about the body
Under Late Capitalism bored me rigid.
Wendy was well-balanced, a typical Libra,
Compliant in bed, but reptilianly frigid.
Rosemary—

'Apart from yours at the end, I've changed all the names of course,' he said. (Actually he hadn't.)

'Well, really, you don't think I'd sleep with someone who'd write a poem like that do you?'

There was nothing for it.

'Yes,' he said.

But she wouldn't even let him kiss her, not until he had been squeezing her bottom, at first apologetically but latterly with concentrated ardour, for five minutes. When they were friends again he said:

'I'm sorry I gave you that poem. But you asked. And I told you in the beginning I was a complete moral degenerate.'

'Yes, you did. You've always been completely honest, I'll grant you that. The men I meet through the church keep saying they want to marry me: but I don't want to spend the rest of my life with any of them. They kiss me and sometimes they accidentally on purpose put their hand on my bottom but I know they would never dare squeeze my titties, though I know they want to. It's disgusting in a way. Whereas with you, you make absolutely no secret of the fact that you want to squeeze my titties and more, and the reason you ask first isn't so I can tell you whether it's the right thing to do, as a Christian, but simply to let me decide whether to allow it or not. You don't take me for granted – they take it for granted I just want to be a good Christian little wifey.'

'Do you want me to squeeze your titties?'

'Yes. But I'm not going to let you.'

'But you don't mind me squeezing your bum.'

'I've always had this problem with sinful thoughts. You're helping me learn how to resist them.'

'But you seem to enjoy having your bottom squeezed.'

'Of course I do. That's the whole point. If I didn't enjoy it there wouldn't be any progress in making me stronger at resisting giving in to myself.'

'Hmmm. . . You know, in the Middle Ages princesses used to sleep with their knightly lovers, completely naked but with his sword between them to show the purity of their love.'

And he extemporized:

> 'They lay all through the night
> Between them burning bright
> Virtue's sword, a holy sight.'

'That's interesting. Well, I guess we can manage without the sword.'

'I think actually it's a metaphor for an erect penis. Beds were often er. . . . really narrow in those days and they would have to lie really close together. A real sword would have injured them.'

Well, to cut a long story short, they've got two little girls now. Rosemary says it doesn't matter not being married, married couples' children are conceived in sin too, that's why you have Baptism and Christ's sacrifice on the Cross. As for him, he never did succeed in getting his poems into *Erotic Review*, though he's now had a couple published in *Methodist Weekly*, which has a larger circulation.

Bitch

'Where is the bitch?' the photographer asked the group of technicians and studio assistants who were waiting for Roz Zimmer, the half-way famous model.

The photographer was a short-arse – the way his trousers bagged below his knees made it seem as if the bottom six inches of his legs had been sawn off – and tended to throw his weight around to compensate for his lack of height. Nobody seemed in a hurry to answer him. Don Cormic, who had been in love with Roz Zimmer ever since the holograph festival, saw his opportunity and seized it.

'I'll phone her apartment,' he said.

But instead of phoning he hurried down to the street, where his ZYX was parked. Roz Zimmer's apartment was only a few blocks away and within a couple of minutes he was standing outside her door with his foot on her bell.

She let him into the apartment. It had the feel about it of being someone else's home, borrowed for a hurried weekend.

'Of course I didn't forget the bloody photo session,' she said. She was wearing a dressing-gown which she held together at the throat, and he could see that she had been crying. 'It's just that – I was just about to take a shower when Cal phoned up and said it was all over between us.' Cal was her boyfriend. Now, miraculously, her *ex*-boyfriend. 'Just like that. No explanation. No – ' She gulped, and wiped her eyes, allowing the front of her dressing-gown to fall apart. (Don pretended not to notice) 'I mean, no explanation . . . . Hell –' She was standing next to a mirror on which a message was scrawled with her favourite emerald lipstick, and she caught sight of herself as she turned. 'God, I look a mess.' She clutched at the lapels of her dressing-gown again. 'Put some coffee on while I get dressed.'

Don went into the kitchen. He had just located the coffee in one of the cupboards when he heard a strange, wet, rustly, animal noise from across the hall. It was the sound of Roz sobbing. He opened the coffee packet and found a spoon. The noise became louder. Treading softly he went to her bedroom door. She was lying face down on her rumpled bed-clothes, her shoulders heaving.

'Roz.' he said.

She did not answer. He sat cautiously on the edge of her bed and began to stroke her upper arm. After a few moments she stopped crying and rolled over on to her back. She lay there, staring up at him. In the filtered light coming through the window blinds her face was the colour of jade.

'*Why?*' she asked.

Her dark-fringed eyes, flecked like marmalade, were brimming with tears. He leaned forward self-consciously to kiss them away. She permitted this, even draped her long arms round his neck. The next thing he knew was that she had her tongue round his teeth and was pulling him down on top of her. She no longer seemed concerned with holding together the front of her dressing-gown and under it she had on only her panties. He could hardly believe this was really happening.

'I don't want to take advantage,' he said, after they had wrestled Cyclops-eyed, mouth to mouth, for a couple of minutes.

'What's this then?' Roz asked fondly, tweaking the increasingly prominent hardness at the front of his slacks. 'It's because of me, isn't it? Isn't it?'

'It hasn't gone like that deliberately,' he protested helplessly.

'I mean I'm fantastically attractive, aren't I?'

'I – yes – I –' Especially with her dressing-gown hanging open like that. 'I mean –'

'Quick, take it out so I can look.'

His erection was now so enormous that, in spite of his embarrassment, it was a relief (though by no means easy) to unzip his fly.

'Actually, it's bigger than Cal's,' Roz said maliciously. 'And I used to think his was like a, well, like a cucumber. Do you know – no, how could you? – I've never done it with a circumcised man. It'd have served Cal right if I'd been horizontalling with someone when he rang to tell me it was all over between us. Only, put it away now.'

Easier said than done. His swollen tool simply refused to be packed back inside his X-fronts. Roz laughed.

'Here, let me help you,' she said. She put her hand around it, squeezing deliciously, and suddenly they were kissing tongue to tongue again. But this time she didn't have her arms around his neck because her hands were reaching down to her hips, shovelling down her panties.

She made a sharp intake of breath as he slid his six-inches into the wetness below her stylishly barbered quiff of pubic hair. At first only the mouth of her vagina seemed wet – a dryness and tightness higher up impeded him for a moment, then ripened and melted, letting him in all the way. The bed creaked and the mattress seemed to whisper hoarsely as their bodies adjusted to each other's rhythm. From outside came the baritone rattle of freight cars passing a block away: after they had gone all he could hear was the bed and Roz going *nnnnh nnnnnh*.

He could hardly believe this was really happening. Her eyes were closed in a frown of concentration – there were still tears on her lashes – and the noises she was making seemed too relate to something she was doing to herself rather than what he was doing to her, but her eager flesh seemed to rise and curve and fill his hands plumply wherever he grabbed her, and when he tugged at her dressing-gown she shucked it off with a single practised movement, interrupting her self-addressed sex noises to remark, with her ordinary suburban intonation, 'God, I know you always were waiting for a chance to see me in my birthday suit.' And she glanced down at herself with a mixture of complacency and nervousness, as if checking that each one of her long perfectly-sculpted limbs was in place. 'I can hardly believe this is really happening,' he told her. 'You dope,' she said, and then it was back to *nnnnh nnnnnh* and a series of *aaaaahs!* and a long period of silence which he couldn't quite figure out (silence that is except for the squeaking of the bed and the snoring noise made by the mattress as their bouncing alternately compressed and released it, and the minuscule but definitely detectable *schlup schlup* from between her arching thighs as his penis, hugely erect and in 3-D, metronomed in-out, in-out.) Another series of *aaaaahs!* followed by a breathless descendo *oh ahah* a couple of times, and finally a staccato cry like a tape recording of a laugh played backwards and that was it, he had given Roz Zimmer the big O: an orgasm perhaps big enough (he thought for one delirious moment) to send shock waves all the way to Alpha Centauri.

'Was it all right?' he asked.

He wanted her to say, 'You're quite a stud', or something like that, but she merely raised two eyebrows and remarked, 'Typical man, wanting to analyse it afterwards. It's just something I do, you know.' She stretched ostentatiously and pussy-catted briefly against his shoulder before reaching down as if searching for something. 'I haven't shaved my legs this week,' she confided.

'I like you with fuzzy legs,' he said.

Actually he wasn't sure if that was true. She had the most marvellous legs to look at but now that he had got his hands on them he found the long slabs of scrawny muscle off-putting. He preferred the sleeker, tighter muscling of her upper arms, even though they had that female thing of seeming stuck on to her body not quite correctly. He made her crook her elbow and make a fist so that he could feel her bicep.

'Like a little boy's,' he said.

'God, I hope you're not a queer,' she said, extricating herself and reaching across his shoulder to check her bed-side alarm clock.

'I suppose there's no point in going to the studio,' she said. 'Everyone will have gone off home by now. My agent's going to be furious when he finds out I was here in bed screwing someone instead of being photographed. Not that I'll tell him what I was doing of course.' She poked Don suddenly under the ribs, quite painfully. 'God, I'll murder you if you tell anyone at the studio that you've been to bed with me.'

'Of course I won't,' he protested.

Roz wasn't even listening.

'If you do, I'll never speak to you again. Ever,' she said, staring at him with eyes the colour of dawn. It was the last thing that would have occurred to Don, to tell anyone about their unbelievable half-hour together, but he could see that she wasn't even bothering to think what sort of a person he was. 'Well, I suppose I'd better have a shower.'

Was that it? he thought in panic – wham, bang, kapowee, and I'll never speak to you again, ever, if you tell anyone? 'No, hang on,' he said, and tried to kiss her, throwing his legs across hers so that she couldn't leave the bed.

'You're really randy, aren't you,' she said with a smirk, and allowed him to nuzzle the curve of her cheek – the corner of her mouth – the rim of her ear – the side of her throat – her – Her legs opened under his. She gave him a quick appreciative squeeze with her left hand to test his erection: a moment later there came that sharp intake of breath he remembered from the first time.

'I like it slow to begin with,' she said in her normal speaking voice, trying if anything to sound extra-casual, as if she didn't want him to think she hadn't yet figured out the correct male and female roles in sexual intercourse. 'Not too deep, but getting faster and deeper. That's right . . . . faster and deeper . . . . That's good . . . .' *Nnnnnh nnnnnnh*. Her instructions complicated his growing urgency to make love to her as she had never been made love to before. He knew that what was happening – actually he still couldn't quite believe it *was* happening – was the fluke result of catching her alone at a vulnerable moment, but he wanted to convince himself she would let it happen again – and again and again – on a regular basis, and the only way to do that was, now that he had the chance, to give her a fuck she would note down in her little green book as scoring five stars more than the previous record. He tried to project the full force of his love at her, willing her to feel their togetherness, at the same time trying, thrust after thrust, to shove as far as he could up into belly in order to reach – emotionally if not literally and anatomically – her heart, and thereby obtain a real response from her, a task he visualized as something like one of those fairground sideshows where one has to bang a peg hard enough to make a bell ring. For a moment the way she humped back at him, not in time to meet his own thrusts, but a half-stroke later, as if to catch him off-balance as he pulled back, seemed especially intimate, as if in half-ironic response to his own urgency, but then a new fear hit him, that she was barely aware of him as Don Cormic who had been in love with her ever since the holograph festival, that she always humped back desynchronously like that, whoever she was with. That was why she had her eyes shut – not because kissing with one's eyes closed was a sign of true love, as one pretended when one was thirteen, simply that she didn't need, or want to, look at him. When he kissed her she sucked back at him with an aggressiveness that said only that his mouth was not Don Cormic's mouth, but merely a convenient albeit male pair of lips.

Trying to dismiss such ideas from his mind he whispered, 'I've never seen you looking so beautiful.' Her enigmatic smile broadened, became almost seraphic, her lips parting to show the darling little gap between her front teeth, but when he said, 'I can hardly believe this is really happening,' she responded, without opening her eyes, 'Do you always talk so much? I thought it was meant to be non-verbal communication.' He remembered how she had said only a few minutes earlier, 'I'll murder you if you tell anyone at the studio that you've been to bed with me!' and suddenly, even as he rammed himself again and again into her hot wet unseeeable depths, he was filled with resentment and despair, and, inspired by a kind of demon of mischief and revenge, he glued his mouth to the side of that beautiful throat of hers and began to suck hard between his teeth.

Her *nnnnnh nnnnnhs* became *aaaah aaaahs*, building up to a climax like the soundtrack to the removal of a particularly recalcitrant back molar. Then she was there, they were both there. Together.

Then apart. Plop.

They lay side by side for about as long as it takes to count one hundred in a game of hide-and-seek. Don tried not to look at the kiss-shaped bruise that was beginning to show at the side of her throat.

'You know,' Roz said, 'For a moment it felt exactly as if you were giving me a love bite.'

She sat up and found a titanium-mounted hand-mirror.

'*Gaard!* Don't touch me! –' She burst suddenly into a flood of tears, throwing herself face down on her pillow, her slender shoulders heaving.

Gingerly he turned her over, began kissing the tears from her eyes and cheeks, till he noticed how each kiss caused her to give a little quiver, and her sobs to become more like a catching of breath, and lower down, her knees to spread and rise.

'I'll have to keep away from the studio for weeks,' she said, suddenly all arms and legs, and all of them reaching, out for him.

Don, his penis marinated and limp, thought: 'I can't believe this is happening.'

Outside it was a lovely day. The windows of Roz's bed-room,

tinted against Alpha Centauri's harmful omicron rays, emphasized the mauve of the clouds and the orange of the sky.

'Come on, you bastard,' said Roz, hooking all four of her legs round his.

He wished this wasn't really happening. He wished he was on another planet.

The Orgasm Files

Sharon lay passive beneath him, her knees slightly raised on each side of his pistoning thighs, her hips scarcely moving in response to his pump-action thrusts into her. She lay with her head flung back on the pillow, eyes closed, lips slightly parted to show large white front teeth with a slight, curiously attractive little gap between them. One arm rested casually on his heaving shoulders, the other encircled her head against the pillow. She was one of the sexiest-looking women he had ever bedded but he had been pile-driving into her for five minutes now, reaching up into her warm wetness, arching his hips so as to withdraw his penis to the outer lips of her labia to maximize the lengths of his thrusts, and he had not got a single gasp out of her. Between his own panting he could hear that her breathing had scarcely quickened.

He came at last with a delicious hot squirt and rolled off her, and they clung together companionably for a while. Sharon kissed his ear as if appreciatively; impossible to know what she was thinking. *He* was thinking how strange it was that the randiest-looking women, the ones who seemed most frisky and provocative in conversation, were often the most passive and unresponsive in bed.

'What time is it?' Sharon asked.

'Nearly ten-thirty.'

'I've got to go,' Sharon said: she had to make an early start to get to work in the morning and did not like to sleep over.

After she had left he reflected on all her different types of kisses: a brief, chaste peck, slightly moist; the same with a little smacking or *mmmmm* noise; a sudden emphatic ramming of her mouth against his; the same with the addition of a quick blip of her tongue; an approach of her mouth to his but waiting modestly for his lips to make final contact, then opening her mouth gently, tenderly under his; the same with her tongue creeping forward between his lips. She had a nice style in undressing too: not flashy or coquettish, but somehow pausing long enough for him to get a good look when pulling the shoulder straps of her bra down and forward and lifting it away from her boobs, or pushing down her panties: and at the end of the show, *what?* He might have had more response from a shop window dummy bought at a car boot sale. He wondered why it was people so rarely spoke of the difference between how women appeared when they were standing around at a party with a glass in their hand, being chatted up, and how they behaved in a bedroom with one's cock in their hand. There were at least a dozen instances in his own experience of girls who had come on particularly strong and saucy in conversation and had even, at first grope, shown themselves to be Olympic-Standard tongue-wrestling champions, but who had ultimately turned out to be the lie-back-and-think-of-England type. Even as a teenager he had noticed that tongue-wrestling girls who preferred to go upstairs on the bus always seemed to give back less. It was not that he had any reason to believe the old adage that the more like a mouse a girl appeared in social situations, the more like a tigress she would be once you got her on her own with her clothes off. In his limited experience of the shy, inhibited, nervous type, they remained shy, inhibited and nervous even when they had their legs spread; though it generally took more careful negotiation to get them into that position. The women who turned out to be dynamite in bed were generally the ones who were un-distinctive at first glance, neither too much of one thing nor too much of the other; neither too forward and animated nor too shy and retiring.

Of course, there were going to be all sorts of exceptions and explanations fitting individual cases. American women always seemed to feel they were letting the side down if they didn't fake at least three orgasms a night. And there were a couple of girls who had been terribly vivacious everywhere but between the sheets, whom he had got to know well enough to realize their manic animatedness in social situations was basically an act requiring considerable nervous energy, developed to cover an almost paralysing awkwardness and insecurity. Still the fact remained that the most satisfying sex he had ever experienced had been with women who had appeared almost nondescript on first encounter: passably pretty, perhaps, but not in a particularly sexy way (and often with the most disappointing boobs), friendly without being provocative and to all appearances – right up to the final climactic revelation – nor even especially interested in sex.

He wondered if there was some characteristic that distinguished the women who were great in bed from the ones who were as inert as a drowned hamster; some giveaway that, if only one knew how to detect it, would enable one to tell which was which before one had got as far as holding hands. It would save so much time. But the question interested him intellectually too. The idea of discovering a great truth that had been staring everyone in the face for thousands of years had a strange appeal for him.

He decided he would keep a record of his sexual adventures, with special reference to first impressions, first hints of encouragement, and quality of final outcome. He remembered he had once tried to assemble data on the question of whether girls with large mouths had big fannies and girls with small mouths small ones. There hadn't really been a correlation; nor did it seem the case that lanky large-boned ladies tended to have bigger twats than any of the petite little poppets he had been with. He had also investigated boob size/droop in relation to wetness of kisses but there was no match there either. This new line of enquiry would be more than fun; who knows, it might lead to post-industrial society's greatest advances in human understanding.

In due course Sharon faded out of his life. For a couple of weeks he went out with Michelle, one of those blond girls (complete with a little pee-smelling blonde muff) who always wore blue, who complained of her Russian Roulette sex-life and then left him for the drummer in a boy band. After her there was a real bed-spring breaker from Glasgow named Margot, and then Laura, one man away from being a virgin, who had the silkiest pubic hair of any girl he had ever met, and with a smile so open it was positively goofy, and after her. . . . Over the months there were a fair number of them, and he made assiduous notes on them all. How long their nipples took to harden (and how long they stayed hard and perky), how promptly they lubricated, what they did with their legs, whether thy humped back, whether they kept their eyes open or closed, whether they liked sucking his penis or never even put their hand on it. The noises they made.

Then came Tania.

She was a how-long-did-it-take-you-to-fall-from-Heaven

beautiful, with a cute line in back-chat, and a degree of sexual passivity that approached neo-catatonic. It was as if the act of lying down on her back and spreading her thighs caused her to lose consciousness. The biggest thrill in their love-making was when he ran the cold tap over his friction-heated willie in the bathroom afterwards. The un-interestingness of her performance – or non-performance – in bed was ironically highlighted by the circumstances of their first encounter, which was like a fantasy, almost a wet dream.

It had been on a train. Perhaps one should say *two* trains. He had been on his way to visit his aunt in Dorking. (Not much chance of *dorking* anyone there, he had told himself as he left his house.) Shortly after the train pulled out of Waterloo it stopped for no apparent reason. Looking up from his newspaper with a frown of irritation he peered out of the window beside him, but couldn't see anything that could explain the delay.

Another train had stopped parallel to his own, on the next track but one. There were two girls in the compartment opposite. They waved at him teasingly, so he waved back.

He flattened out his newspaper and began to read a profile of the previous week's Britain Lacks Talent final, but out of the corner of his eye he could see that the two girls were still signalling to him, and when he looked up one of them pushed out her lips in a *moue* and blew a kiss. The other girl wasn't bad-looking, but the kiss blower was so pretty that it hurt – hair the same colour as the inside of a lemon, a slight tan that emphasized the brightness of her eyes – blue or grey, he guessed though he was just a little too far away to see – and a ravishing slightly lop-sidedly triangular grin. Young. Built like a boy with boobs.

She and her friend seemed to be giggling insanely, egging each other on. Having caught his attention, the blonde pressed her mouth against the window, as if imprinting a kiss on it.

He waved again. The blonde seemed to be mouthing words to him. It was bound to be nothing more than a cock tease, he told himself, but he stood up and struggled to slide back the top of the window. The blonde, now giggling almost hysterically, moved to open her own window, but just as he was about to call across to her both trains began to move.

'What's your telephone number?' he shouted, but the two trains were already turning apart. Suddenly the girl yanked up her T-shirt. If she had any bra on she yanked that up too. Her twin boobs goggled at him through the carriage window, which remained tantalizingly level with his own. Before he could get a really good look she pressed herself against the glass, producing a blurred effect of whitened, flattened flesh, decorated with two small round smudges of pink. Above them her face seemed to have an expectant, nervous, almost constipated expression as if she were stunned by her own outrageousness. But it was difficult to tell anything for sure at the increasing distance.

Then the railway tracks curved closer together again and the girls' compartment came nearer. He saw her turn her head, calling over her shoulder to her companion, but she didn't cover herself. He could see the arch of her lower ribs as she sucked in her tummy and puffed out her chest to increase the effect of the display, and now she leaned back a little from the window pane so that he could see her tits clearly through the glass – darling cantilevered 34Bs (he estimated) with long eager nipples surrounded by pinky-russet areolas that were all goose-pimply. He was close enough to see that her eyes were green. Then staring levelly at him, she slowly and deliberately pushed her tongue out at him between her pursed lips and darted it back and forth at him, first in slow motion, but with an increasingly rapid tempo and in a manner that could only have been intended to suggest one thing. Then she experimentally leaned her face loser to the window so that only the very tips of her nipples touched the glass. But apparently dissatisfied with the effect, she suddenly pulled her T-shirt right down covering herself and then as quickly pulled it up again.

Then the tracks drew apart one more. 'What's your telephone number?' he shouted again, but her compartment slid out of sight as his own train accelerated rapidly, and within a few moments there was nothing to be seen from his window but the endlessly repeated roofs and chimneys and television aerials of suburbia.

The amazing thing was, they ran into each other at a party only a few weeks later. He saw that she was older than he supposed, though even so not much more than nineteen or twenty. There were no fewer than four men talking to her but he could tell from her mechanical smile, each time identical in width, warmth and number of teeth shown, that she wouldn't mind being rescued. 'Hi,' he said. 'Remember me?' Even more amazing she recognized him immediately, and though she left the party with another man (described in an aside as 'my-soon-to-be-ex-boyfriend') she gave him her telephone number and e-mail address. On their first date he observed, when she was rummaging in her handbag for a tissue, that she was carrying contraceptive pills around with her, as if not sure she would get home for a couple of nights, but it took a second date to get her into bed, and after what happened, or failed to happen, he really wouldn't have bothered with a third date, only he'd heard it was considered bad manners to sleep with somebody only once, and then somehow there was a fourth date, and a fifth. . . . He liked looking at her, he liked talking to her, he liked soaping her in the shower, and he found her sexual unresponsiveness perversely erotic, when he wasn't worrying whether something wasn't wrong with her. Rather to his surprise he found himself settling into a kind of relationship with her.

He even gave her the spare keys to his flat.

But more and more he found himself wondering what it was all for – what was *anything* for – how did one even *know* if one's feelings at the moment of sexual climax were any different from what an animal felt? What was human consciousness anyway? It occurred to him that consciousness – *any* consciousness, not just human consciousness – was simply the complex processing of impressions. With flies, for example, the middle-sized ones that used to circle the light fixtures in his bedroom on summer afternoons, there was a capacity for learning, as after the first couple of fly-swatting sessions they began to fly out of the open window and rest nearby, ready to return, as soon as he entered the room, whereas the tiny flies that were attracted to the week's supply of pineapples in the kitchen never learnt to dodge. And the more evolved the animal, the more elaborate its learning capacity. He wondered if all our mental activity was nothing more than what animal consciousness consisted of at the *homo sapiens* level.

His note-taking on women's behaviour in bed became desultory.

Increasingly his file on Tania consisted only of nude photographs. Perhaps that was his epic mistake. She was bound to wonder what he did with all the photographs; and two weeks before Christmas she found out.

It started off as a day like any other. That evening, remembered ever afterwards as the Night the Earth Moved, he came home from the launderette to find Tania sitting at his kitchen table surrounded by the folders in which he kept his photographs and notes. Including his notes on her.

'You shit,' she said, looking round as he came in. 'You complete and utter shit.'

She had been crying, but now, there was a dry feverish look in her eyes and her pretty face was contorted with hatred. As he stepped forward, uncertain how to deal with this situation, she grabbed a steak knife and slid sideways out of her chair. Everything seemed to be happening in slow motion: he had time to register that she had been using the steak knife to cut the string holding the various folders together; then they were grappling. He hadn't realised how strong she was. He grabbed her wrist but it was as much as he could do to keep the knife away from his throat.

She twisted and elbowed him in the stomach, and as he staggered back the knife blade was glittering right in front of his eyes. But he still had hold of her wrist and he threw his weight against her. She jerked her knee up, but most of the force of the blow was taken by his inner thigh. Most: not all. He pushed himself forward against the pain, lost balance, saw and felt her wrist jerking out of his grasp, the knife blade flashing in the electric light as it arched back, preparatory to the forward lunge that would bury the steel in his Adam's apple. Then Tania cried out as the backward swoop of her hand slammed it against the corner of the kitchen cabinet. The knife fell away from her grasp and clattered on the floor. She clutched at her hand.

'Oh God,' she said. Her knuckles were bleeding. 'What would I have done if I'd killed you?' They looked at each other for a moment and then simultaneously as if on the same cue burst out laughing. To begin with they were laughing with relief, at the sudden release of homicidal tensions, but the laughter of the one seemed to work on the giggles of the other and soon they were clinging to each other in helpless fits, eyes streaming, gasping for breath between uncontrollable guffaws.

And the next thing they knew, they were staggering from the kitchen to the bedroom, pulling each other's clothes off.

As soon as he had got one leg out of her panties he slotted into the wet opening behind her neat thatch of pubic hair as suddenly and as smoothly as a bar of soap shooting from one's clenched fist, and at each one of his thrusts she bounced her hips back at him, her breath coming in rapid sobs which after a minute slowed down and became distinctly-voiced yelps chiming with each of his thrusts, with each of the upward bucks of her pelvis. To begin with she stared up at him, her eyes still wet with tears of both rage and laughter, and looking like big green pools in which he could drown himself. But as the tempo of his thrusting and her bucking increased, she closed her eyes as if to concentrate better. She was still wearing her T-shirt and bra. It didn't seem to matter. All his sensation was concentrated on his bursting loins. His thrusts, and her bucking under him, caused their tangled bodies to slither inch by inch towards the upper end of the bed, till their heads were jammed against the headboard. He tried to ignore the discomfort of having his head squashed at an angle against the wood, ramming into her again and again, but their position finally became too awkward too be ignored. He pulled out of her and shuffled on his knees down to the middle of the bed, dragging her by the elbows after him.

'No, stop a minute,' Tania said, pulling off her top and bra with a single cross-armed movement, accompanied by the sound of ripping silk. There were little beads of sweat at her armpits. She pushed him round till he was lying on his back and climbed astride, plunging her whole body down on his enormously perpendicular penis. He lay there, his hands raised to her pink-nippled breasts, feeling them surge up and down against his touch from palms to fingertips as she rhythmically raised and lowered her body up and down on his sex. Shafts of light coming through the open door gilded her hair, which bounced out wildly at the sides as she moved up and down. Her face was a mask of sweat. He had never seen her more beautiful. Suddenly she began to cry out loudly, as if someone was twisting her wrist: but she was the only one making any movement. Cautiously he began to thrust back up into her, as she thrust down.

Her cries became higher-pitched, the baritone squeaks from the bed, half a beat behind the alto squeaks from her (or *vice versa.*) Then she kind of coughed – and stopped. She had climaxed, and so had he.

As he smiled back up at her he wondered if he still had the phone numbers of Sharon, Michelle, Margot, Laura, Astrid, Elinor and the others. Knowing what he knew now, thanks to Tania, it would be disastrous for his research project if he didn't give them another try.

Fantasy Girl

She had told him she had dropped out of doing her A-levels, which put her at seventeen or eighteen years old. A couple of deft questions about her A-level syllabus – English, History and Psychology – confirmed that despite appearances she wasn't jail-bait. She spent most of their first full day together curled up on his sofa, reading with a childish absorbedness. Occasionally she would look up and ask a question about some matter of fact relating to the book she was reading, as if she was still at school and he was the teacher, except that as she asked her questions she gazed at him with big trusting eyes, as if unable to believe he would not know the answers, and there was no way she could ever have looked at a mere school teacher quite like that – at least not since she was eight; but she never asked him a single question about himself, or about what he was thinking, or what he expected of her. She accepted arrangements he made without query, ate what he put on the table without comment, and said please and thank you in all the right places, as if drilled in an academy for young ladies. When she had got up in the morning she had locked herself in the bathroom, calling 'Bathroom free!' when she emerged, but seemed to take it as a matter of course that he came into the bedroom naked while she was still in her bra and panties.

They had found each other outside King's Cross Station. He had been on his way home from the British Library. She had been standing outside McDonald's, mostly ignored by the early evening crowd: armpit-height teenage boobs, light brown shoulder-length hair fixed behind her ears, a slightly pigeon-toed way of standing, with her bottom cocked out without seeming aware of it. 'Excuse me, could you spare fifty pee?' she said to him. His first response was: this is the most dangerous spot in all of Britain for a young girl to be begging. Then he said, 'I'll buy you a McDonald's if you like.'

'Would you?' She gave him the shy beginning of a delicious grin.

Later when she was more relaxed with him, her smile always had something shy at the beginning of it.

She had told him she had been in London twenty-four hours, had had her bag stolen with her money and change of clothes, had spent the previous night in a shop doorway, too cold and too frightened to sleep.

She hadn't eaten all day. After she had finished a McDonald's, he took her home, made her two grilled cheese sandwiches, gave her one of his shirts to use as a nightie. He showed her his double bed. 'You can either asleep here or on the sofa in the other room.'

'The bed looks more comfortable,' she said, with an amused sidelong look at him, as if she found it funny that he offered her a choice, but in a school-girlish way, completely without any suggestion of sex. 'I've never slept in a double bed before.'

They talked a bit and about 8:30 p.m. she said she was really tired, not having slept the night before, and would he mind if she crashed out. By the time he went to bed himself an hour later – early for him, but he wasn't sure what to expect with her – she was fast asleep, on the far side of the bed, back turned, light brown hair a puddle on her pillow, with part of an ear and cheek just visible.

Next day she read with a steady concentration, as if hiding in her book while she came to terms with her new situation, and in the afternoon they went for a walk in the park opposite his house, and afterwards looked through his collection of postcards together. He had a huge collection of postcards from most of the art galleries in Europe, arranged not on art historian lines, though Art History was how he earnt his living, but in order to tell little stories: Paolo and Francesca, Father Christmas preparing for Christmas present deliveries, Louise O'Murphy at the Court of Louis XV, Tolstoy's *War and Peace* in twenty scenes, a modern girl's adventures in the Big City, and so on; and they sat side by side at his work table with a CD playing, and when she reached across him to move a card that was on his side of the table she pressed against his shoulder and once, for a full minute, put her arm around his shoulder so she could reach across further with her left hand, and made no objection to his hand resting on her thigh. When he glanced sideways at her face next to his he thought she might be expecting to be kissed, but she looked sweetly intent on the postcards, and he didn't want in the world to hurt her, so he took his hand away from her leg.

At other times during the day, in the kitchen and during their walk in the park, if she brushed against him by accident she always apologized.

In the evening they talked about her A-Levels (she thought she might carry on with them at a college in London) and looked at his postcards again. About 9 p.m. she said she was still sleepy and went into the next room to get ready for bed. She came back, bare-legged, wearing the shirt she had borrowed, sleeves rolled up to the elbows, only three buttons fastened, no bra underneath, and stood beside him for a moment.

'Wake me up this time if I'm asleep when you come to bed,' she said, with a bright-eyed, earnest look, touching his shoulder briefly.

He put the postcards away, washed, cleaned his teeth thoroughly, found his always-remember-the-Scout-motto packet of condoms. He still wasn't sure what would happen, only that he didn't want her to go away and leave him, and if she was going to stay . . .

.

She was lying on her tummy reading, book on her pillow, when he came into the bedroom, but put her book aside as soon as she saw him in the doorway and lifted the bed cover aside for him with a welcoming smile.

Their first kiss was a tad anti-climactic, not to say anti-septic: a bit as if they were afraid of each other.

'I was waiting for you to do this last night,' she whispered. 'Or at least this morning.'

'You should have said something.'

'You'd been so lovely to me I was afraid it wouldn't be quite polite to tell you there was something more you ought to be doing.'

She had rolled over on her back. With a feeling of incredulity he shifted over till he was more or less on top of her.

'Ooh, you're heavy,' she said teasingly, but her mouth did not turn away, opening slowly, as if after careful consideration, as his tongue pushed against her lips, and she made no objection when he undid a button of her borrowed shirt, then another. Then the third. Her hand fluttered briefly at the back of his neck. He sat her up, gave her a double-handed both-boobs-together squeeze, and shyly peeled the shirt off her shoulders. She seemed to find this funny.

'Boys always want to know what girls' tits look like, don't they?' she remarked brightly.

But when he reached down to ease off her panties she stopped him.

'You've only known me twenty-four hours,' she said.

'Twenty-eight,' he corrected. *All my life, in my dreams* is what he wanted to say, but somehow didn't dare.

'It's only tonight.'

'You mean – tomorrow . . . .?'

Was she planning on leaving next day?

'I probably would have done it with anybody last night, I was that relieved to find somewhere to stay. But I still feel sort of tense and . . . . well, you'd know if I just let you get on with it and I didn't really enjoy it, wouldn't you? Perhaps you'd hold it against me. It'll be much better if we wait another day.'

'Sorry, I didn't think . . . . mean . . . .'

'You can feel me up a bit if you like, but not down there. Not till tomorrow. It will be better tomorrow, I promise.'

She looked perfectly natural bare-chested, possibly even arching her back a little as if unconsciously wanting her springy teenage bosom to stick out a little bit more. She seemed even younger than when dressed, though practical and level-headed and in charge in a class monitor, vice-captain of the hockey XI kind of way, and he would have felt rather ashamed if her smile had not told him he had no need to be.

Her mouth opened under his when he kissed her again. She leaned back on both hands, shoulders raised towards her ears in a way that made her breasts droop invitingly, but he was afraid to touch them again.

'If you promise to behave I needn't put my shirt back on,' she said, lying down again, smiling up at him from her pillow.

Next day they read, collided lingeringly about the flat, looked at his postcards again, went for walks and sniggered together at the sight of pigeons having it off in the gutter. In the evening she kept her right arm round his shoulder, reaching across him with her left, practically all the time they were looking at the postcards, though this time he did not put his hand on her thigh. It didn't seem necessary, or even appropriate. He felt tender and protective about her and, unexpectedly, somehow knew she felt the same about him. He knew it was absurd, but he felt on his honour with her. But all the time, refusing to stay at the back of his mind, was the thought that when they went to bed she was going to let him fuck her, and he found himself constantly looking at her, at the whiteness of her throat, which soon he would be kissing, at her mouth, at the twin swellings of her bosom, at her long-fingered hand with traces of varnish on the nails, which was now delicately holding postcards by their edges but which, God knows, might soon be grasping his engorged penis to guide it into her teenage quim.

At last it was time for bed. They undressed together, he almost overwhelmed with self-consciousness, she apparently no more embarrassed than if she was stripping off in front of other girls in the school changing room, but with a swift glance down at herself as if to check that her pubes were still in their usual place. Her kisses were more enthusiastic than the night before – not what one might call urgent exactly, there was always something calm and relaxed about her – but definitely wanting him to get on with it, and her legs opened readily when he reached down between them. His erection seemed enormous. He would have to be very gentle with her. Then he remembered he had left his condoms on the mantelpiece of the long-since-blocked-off fireplace, and he had to get out of bed to retrieve them. He had heard that nowadays they were taught how to put them on at school. Perhaps he could ask her to put one on him: he already had the required erection.

But the condoms weren't there.

He had put them ready on the mantelpiece the night before, when they still hadn't even kissed for the first time, thinking, 'just in case.' But they weren't there any more.

He went into the next room to check the place where he usually kept them, in the cabinet above the free-standing bookcase in the corner. Of course they weren't there, because he had definitely taken them out and put them ready on the bedroom mantelpiece. He went back into the bedroom, checked beneath both their pillows, looked on the floor in case they had somehow fallen. She sat up to watch him, slim bare arms clasping bare knees, an expression of increasing amusement on her face.

'I can't find them,' he said desperately. 'I can't find the condoms.'

'Oh well, you can buy some tomorrow.' There was something so wholesome and practical about her that the notion that he had been on the point of causing her to be carried away in a frenzy of sexual arousal seemed not a little ridiculous. 'You'd better come back to bed before you catch a cold. At least we can hold each other a little.'

She snuggled up to him when he got back into bed, even put both her arms around him, which she had never done before, and told him she really liked him. He kissed her breasts and her pubic hair (wirier than he had quite expected – and his kissing her there made her giggle) but he was afraid to do much more in case things became too much for his self-control.

After breakfast next day he was on the point of going to the chemists' when she produced the packet of condoms from the back of the pocket of her jeans. She had hidden them the previous afternoon.

'Very funny,' he said. It was almost impossible to be angry with her, especially when she had that frank, delicious, comradely, complicit grin: but he certainly wasn't feeling as chivalrous about her as he had been the day before. 'And I suppose tonight you are going to tell me it's your period.'

'Well, actually, it feels as if it's due about now. I was going to ask you to lend me something so I could buy some tampax.'

'But if you knew your period was due we didn't need condoms anyway.'

'It was *you* who wanted one,' she said. 'I knew you weren't going to do it without if you had, you know, an infection or something. But I thought you were just being sensible, because they always tell you to wear a condom when you go to bed with someone you don't know very well, just in case.'

'Yes, but why did you hide them?'

'I've never lived with a man before. Well, I was living with my mum and dad, wasn't I? This is a new kind of thing for me. It's not like what some girls do, pulling a boy at a friend's party and sneaking off to the parents' bedroom together, is it? I really want it to work.'

'But you should have trusted me.'

'I *do* trust you. I thought you knew that. It's – I don't trust myself. I feel I know you, even after only three days, but I don't think you really know me. And I still don't quite know how to tell you things that are important to me.'

During the next three days, though she complained of feeling a bit headachy and 'not quite ready for the marathon', she submitted equally to his kisses morning and evening, made no problems about dressing or undressing in front of him, washed her panties and sat around bare-arsed wearing only one of his pullovers while they dried, and once she had changed her overnight tampon, let him come into the shower with her. In the shower she responded to his attentions with cheerful anaphrodisiac remarks like: 'I bet that tastes horrible' (when he kissed her tummy button), 'My tits do that when it's cold too' (when he made her nipples go hard by pinching them gently), 'I wish I was hard all over like you – not your willie, stupid, your arms and legs' (when he ran his hands over her velvety hockey XI muscles). When he asked if she minded that he took so long to soap her bottom, she said, 'It's OK when you do it, but if it was anyone else I'd feel embarrassed.' When they went for walks together she refused to hold his hand – 'It looks soppy and I hate it when one's palms get all sweaty together' – but tucked her arm inside his elbow companionably.

Each morning when he woke and looked across at the puddle of light brown hair and the half-concealed cheek and ear on the other pillow of his as yet unchristened bed, he wondered if he wasn't romanticizing her, romanticizing a relationship that had stalled at the outset – it would not be the first time this had happened to him – but then she would wake too, turn towards him, immediately aware of him and beginning to smile, and a slim white arm would snake out voluptuously from under the covers as if reaching out for him, so it was as if he had no choice but to lean towards her and kiss her passive lips, throat, breastbone, etc.

She began writing a letter to her mother: he kept telling her that her parents must be worried sick about her, and she didn't need to give a return address if she didn't want. She borrowed some paper and wrote diligently for half an hour, then said: 'I'll finish it tomorrow.'

'We can post it in central London,' he said.

On the fourth morning she let him towel her dry after their shower and told him, 'It'll be all right tonight. My period. It'll be over by tonight.' She gave him a radiant smile. 'I know you've got the hots for me.' Later, after breakfast she said, 'Lets get a couple of bottles of wine, you know, make it a party, celebrate.'

They went to an supermarket, bought a couple bottles of rioja since half a bottle each wasn't much of a hit.

Evening came.

'It's nice wine,' she said (evidently not an expert, for it wasn't particularly).

'It'll still be all right tomorrow if you leave some.'

But she liked it so much she drank the best part of both bottles and then crashed out, so that he had to carry her to bed. Undressing her, with her head lolling and her arms and legs limp and unco-operative, was surprisingly unerotic, notably less so than when she was laughing and splashing at him in the shower with her breasts jigging up and down. Taking her bra off made him feel more like a mortician than a lover. He did consider having sex with her while she snored under him but it seemed all wrong, especially for the very first time he made love to her – it wouldn't have been a nice thing to do, and not at all what he wanted with her.

Having covered her up he stood beside the bed staring down at her. Even in a drunken slumber she had the essential characteristic of the kind of girl one falls in love with, that is, every time one saw her she looked prettier than the time before. Suddenly he felt tears in his eyes.

Blowing his nose he went into the next room. The letter she had been writing was folded into the copy of *The Great Gatsby* which she had been reading and had left at the end of the sofa. He glanced at it curiously, then realized it was written, not to her mother, but to a school friend. He sat down and began to read it from the beginning.

Dear Katie,

Well, here I am in London, and I've already scored a boyfriend. Bit older than me, and really into sex, and I must say I'm getting quite a taste for it too. Feels a bit strange after all those years of wondering what my thingummy was there for, and whether I would be any good at it. He says I am! Not that I feel so very different inside really. I'm much more conscious of down there, find I am washing it in the morning with much more interest and sometimes get a twinge there when I bend over or sit down because he's very vigorous (ha ha!) and I always have this feeling it's at the back of his mind too – but I'm still me, and he's still him, and it doesn't matter as much as you might have thought even though I suppose it is half the reason we like each other.

He expected her to be hungover next morning, and to use it as an excuse to put him off yet again, but she perked up after two cups of coffee at breakfast. He decided to confront her about the letter to her friend.

'You'd no right to look at that,' she said, colouring furiously.

'Well, let's pretend I *did* have a right, since you've been pretending and leading me on since you've been here.'

'But it was a letter to my friend. I probably wasn't going to send it anyway. It was like a short story.'

'Like your excuses. Just a story.'

'Well, I *did* have my period, you know I did because you saw the tampax that didn't flush. All right, I admit it, I've been silly. I never told you why I ran away from home. It was my father. He broke the lock on the bathroom door, and wouldn't repair it, and kept coming in while – I don't want to talk about it. It was horrid, and I'm sure my mother knew and didn't say anything. That's the reason I wanted to tell you that you mustn't rush me, but I didn't know how to explain why not. I was afraid you'd get fed up with me if I slept with you, I mean had proper sex with you, and it turned out I wasn't any good, and you'd want me to leave. It wasn't that I didn't like you. I like you a lot.'

'Oh God, what are we going to do? It doesn't look as if it's going to work, you and me, does it?'

'But I *do* want it to work. More than anything. I've never met anyone I wanted to be with as much as I want to be with you. And you want it too, don't you? OK, let's go back to bed now and sort it out. I know it's going to be all right. Or let's have an early night tonight.'

'We were going to go shopping this morning . . . . *Sort it out*, that's not quite how we should be feeling. Let's wait till tonight.'

'I really like you. You do know that, don't you? And you're the most patient, understanding person ever. You don't push and . . . . well, lots of times I'd wished you would just ignore my excuses and get on with it.'

When he went into the bedroom that evening he found her already fast asleep on her side of the bed.

'So what did I expect?' he asked himself. He had a huge anticipatory erection, which made him feel even sillier.

Then she woke up.

'Gosh, it does look funny sticking out like that,' she said. 'Do you think you will get all of it inside me?'

'Yes,' he said, and two minutes later he did.

And once again an hour later, twice the following night, and again the following morning before they got up, and so on.

'I didn't realize people made love so often,' she said after a week.

'They do to begin with, while they're still getting to know each other.' He could have said he was making up for the time she had wasted, but refrained. 'You don't mind, do you?'

'Of course not, darling. Though I wouldn't mind a trip to IKEA for a bed that doesn't squeak.'

A few days later it was Guy Fawkes Night and they went to a fireworks display on Highbury Fields.

Each time a rocket went up she would watch it rising it its trajectory, lifting her face up till she had to crane her neck right back to keep it in view, and all the while going 'whooo-oooo' quite loudly, as if for the benefit of the people around them.

'Why do you keep going "whooo-oooo" like that?' he asked.

'We always did it back home,' she said, linking her arm with his.

Her *whoooo-oooo* reminded him of when they made love and the *wha-wha-aaa* noises she had been making recently, louder than seemed quite justified by the cautiously economic rising and falling movement of her hips under him.

He noticed that they were being observed by a teenage girl standing about ten yards away amongst the other spectators with an older woman who was presumably her mother. The girl – black-haired, eye-linered black-eyed, Morgan Le Fay in a pony tail – was watching them as if trying to figure out what it was about him that got a thirty-five-year-old like him a girlfriend about the same age as herself. Their gaze crossed and he grinned.

She smiled back.

I can't see properly,' he said to the top of the mouse-brown head beside his shoulder. 'Let's move a bit sideways.'

The girl with her mother smiled again, a little more widely, as she saw them moving in tandem closer to where she stood.

The Morning After

As she cleaned the glaze of dried semen off the insides of her upper thighs she reflected that she would not now ever see a unicorn, qualify to be sacrificed to a dragon terrorizing the neighbourhood or be deemed eligible to be included in the reward for a pious youth killed in Jihad.

She stared at her body in the mirror. She didn't look in any way different from the way she had looked at 9.30 p.m. the previous evening.

When they had got back to his place he had said, 'I want to lick you all over.'

'I guess I could handle that so long as I got to keep all my clothes on,' she had said. She had been rather proud of that answer.

'Hey, you didn't lick me all over,' she shouted through the bathroom doorway.

No response from the bedroom. He was probably still asleep. And her clothes were still in there. Not that it mattered: in a bit they could have a shower together. She stuck her tongue out in the mirror and decided that defloration had given her an appetite. She went into the kitchen and opened the door of the fridge.

Her lover's naked body fell out. He wasn't still in the bedroom after all. There was a sprig of parsley between his set lips, and the shiny black handle of a steak knife protruded from the middle of his chest. And as she stood there, paralysed with surprise and horror, she heard the creak of floorboards from the other end of the hall. Someone else was moving about the house. Someone who ?

Clumsy with terror, still naked, she fumbled desperately to get the back door open. She could hear footsteps in the hall now, coming closer, heavy and determined. The door or its latch were stiff but it was moving now. Flinging it open she ran out into the garden.

Outside there was only a daisy-spotted lawn with two neglected rose bushes in a circular patch of garden mould, and a low brick wall separating the property from the surrounding beech woods. Scrambling over the wall – skinning her left knee – she ran between the trees, found a narrow track, ran on, tears of fear and shock half-blinding her, ran with branches reaching out to scratch her bare thighs and twigs snarling her hair and little stones on the path pricking her bare feet, ran until she could run no more, ran until she came to the unicorn.

It was a large, sober-looking white horse with a vertical horn on its nose, standing in a glade of the woods, watching her with long-lashed eyes.

There was no sound of pursuit behind her, and with her heart pounding and her breath coming in agonized gasps she could run no further in any case. And perhaps, with the unicorn, she was safe now, except –

'I'm not supposed to be able to see you,' she panted. 'One's not supposed to be able to see a unicorn if one's not a virgin.'

'I'm not a unicorn,' the creature said, tossing its beautiful mane. 'They just stuck this ridiculous thing on my nose because they wanted me to pretend to be a unicorn in some stupid play they're putting on at the Wimbledon Theatre. And they used super-glue so now I can't get it off.'

She came closer and, despite her terror and sore feet, laughed.

'It looks like a penis,' she said, wondering even as she said this if a single night had made her some sort of expert.

'Well, they couldn't find anything like a narwhal's horn, which is what they were looking for, so they got this plastic thing from a sex shop as the nearest alternative. If you don't like it you'd better get on my back so you don't have to look at it.'

She climbed on, relieved enough to be able to reflect that her poor fanny was getting more wear than in all her previous life altogether, and the horse moved off down a fern-fringed track between the beeches. After a while they came to a series of little clearings with lush grass and bluebells and sunlight falling in widely separated shafts through the leaf-canopy overhead. At least five different species of small bird were singing independently at different points of the compass. She lowered herself down from the horse's back, stretched, arranged her long hair in two gathered tresses to cover her breasts, for even with only a horse to see her it was a bit embarrassing to have no clothes on.

Suddenly something very obvious occurred to her.

'Hold on,' she said. 'If you're a horse, not a unicorn, how come you can talk?'

'The fact is I'm not really a horse either,' said the whatever-it-was. 'I'm a prince. I was turned into this four-footed animal by a wicked fairy. You may have read about it. The only thing that can change me back is if a princess kisses me.'

'But I'm not a princess.'

'You don't actually know that. You might have been swapped at birth. It happens more often than you might think. The only way to know for sure would be to kiss me and see what happens.'

The creature did rather smell like a horse, but she owed it big time for perhaps saving her life, and its long-lashed eyes were rather appealing – blue too, which was unusual in a horse. Re-arranging her hair modestly over her boobs and removing a dead leaf that had caught in her pubic hair, she puckered her mouth and kissed its huge dark lips.

KAPOWEEE !! A flash, no smoke, but a moment in which the sunlight of the forest clearing seemed to have become the light of somewhere a thousand years ago. And suddenly there was no longer a white horse with a plastic penis glued to its nose but a vast, hump-backed, scaley dragon with a twenty-foot tail ending in something like an anchor fluke and eyes like amethysts: three of them.

'Gotcha,' said the dragon. It was the same voice as the horse's, only now with more of a throaty quality and a hiss at the end of phrases that was oddly beguiling. 'You've heard of me. I've been ravaging the district, holding the city to ransom, so long that I've become a legend.'

'What city? I thought this was Stevenage. Oh, you mean the city where they have to choose a virgin every year and deliver it up to, what was it, a kind of sea monster. Are YOU the sea monster?'

'Well, yes, I used to be a sea monster but now I've moved inland.'

She noticed there was no more bird-song amongst the trees, only the distant cawing of crows.

'Well, I'm sorry to disappoint you, but as I've already told you, I'm not a virgin.'

'That bit of the legend is rubbish. Why would I care if any of them were virgins? All I ever did with them was rip them to pieces and gobble them up.'

Curious how little real difference it made losing one's virginity, she thought as the monster reached out a huge seven-fingered claw encrusted with dried blood.

But at that very moment half a dozen men in combat fatigues and balaclavas burst from the cover of the surrounding trees firing sub-machine guns and shouting, 'Paradise will be our reward! Our lives for the life of the Great Satan! Paradise in the arms —'

Why Chaps Should Shave Under the Bedclothes

Having shaved, Ted checked his face in the mirror. There was something odd about the reflection. Not his face, but something on the other side of the room: a door that had opened in the wall behind him with what looked like a dark drop immediately beyond the door frame. He turned, and of course it wasn't there, just the normal white wall with a towel rail that was always on that side of the room. He looked at the mirror again – and again the door with the dark drop inside was open behind him on the other side of the room. He turned and looked, saw the towel rail, and wondered how this optical illusion in the mirror could occur. Well, if one could only see the door as a reflection. . . . Facing the mirror, and holding the reflection of the door fixedly in view so that he could steer by it, he backed cautiously towards the open door, or at least towards its reflection. He had almost reached it – it was still there – another step – it was still there – another step – it was still there, looming over his shoulder – another –

The last thought he had as he fell was – was there any particular reason why he had wanted to step backwards through a doorway into an open shaft?

The Man
with the Living Brain

As you know, brain cells are the only part of the human organism which are unable to reproduce themselves naturally. We are born with most of the brain cells we shall ever have, and throughout our post-adolescent lives they are constantly dying off. By the time we are sixty-five (later in some cases) enough of our brain is extinct to begin impairing our mental activity. Before we reach this stage however, the countless millions of our brain cells are more than enough for our purposes. Even the most brilliant scientist or philosopher is able only partially to utilize the resources of his own brain, and most people carry around with them a vast inaccessible reserve of mental capacity which day by day is dying within them, without their ever realizing the enormous and irreplaceable waste of their intellectual potential.

Nowadays, in a variety of ways, from meditation and drugs to memory courses, people are trying to tap these vast, barely suspected reservoirs inside their own heads. Our approach was completely different. We saw no sense in labouring to extend the powers of a human brain which was actually in the process of dying. We saw no sense in opening up new routes, new horizons within a mind, when they would be constantly choked up and cluttered with each passing day's toll of dead cells. Our idea was to develop a brain which, like any other human organ, could reproduce its own cells. This would have two enormous advantages. It would last much longer; in a healthy human body the brain is the first major organ to fail; our plan was that it should be the last, so that instead of a lifetime's accumulated knowledge and experience being wasted by deterioration, they would become the basis for further accumulation. Secondly, the cell reproduction would be selective; only those parts which were fully used would be completely maintained in trim, and certain parts, which were used a great deal, would be able to grow and to enlarge their capacity.

It took eleven years to develop the necessary biochemistry for brain-cell reproduction and a further six to create a human brain composed of cells capable of reproducing themselves. We had to build it literally cell by cell. It looked like a normal human brain – i.e. roughly like the half of a walnut kernel – but it was not as big as a human brain; it did not need to be because being able to grow and replace itself as it went along, it did not need to start off with all the capacity it would ever require.

We put it in the body of a young medical student who had sustained fatal head injuries in a road accident. We also installed a new heart, one with plastic valves guaranteed to function perfectly for a hundred and forty years instead of the usual seventy, and replaced the pituitary, pineal and thyroid glands, and various other parts of the endocrine system. As a result of these modifications we counted on the host body taking a hundred and twenty years to age the equivalent of twenty five.

It took the Brain – he had a normal Christian name and surname of course but we always called him the Brain – it took the Brain about five years to reach the mental age of sixteen, for though he had an adult body mentally he had to start from scratch. For these five years things went perfectly. We thought then, and still believe now, despite the ultimate failure of the experiment, that to have built a functioning human brain (let alone a *growing* one) was the greatest achievement of science that has ever been recorded. There were millions upon millions of cells, capillaries, circuits, membranes, in that Brain, and not one of them was seriously out of place. True the Brain suffered from headaches in his first year, but thereafter he functioned better than a man with a natural brain.

It was, we estimate, after the Brain's fifth birthday that things started going wrong. We were still monitoring the Brain of course, through innumerable electrodes implanted in his skull, but it was another two years before we realized that matters were not as they should be. There are several theories as to why it took us so long to suspect anything. The most plausible is that the Brain had developed the power to project a force field sufficient to control the monitoring devices with which he was constantly surrounded. Every person emanates a force field (as can be demonstrated with certain types of electro-magnetic-sensitive photography) and in extremely rare cases this force field might be sufficient to bend cutlery or to identify objects in adjacent rooms; during the early 1970s a great deal of publicity was given to people who claimed to have this capacity, of whom the best known was Uri Geller. The Brain apparently developed this power quite quickly, and what is more remarkable, he was able to utilize it with the utmost precision. He was able to read other people's minds (another thing men like Uri Geller claimed they could do) and by that means discovered what kind of readings we expected to find shown on our instruments. He then caused the instruments to show these readings; this was relatively easy in that many of the instruments were extraordinarily sensitive even to changes in atmospheric pressure, though it is remarkable that he was able to cause a hundred and thirty eight separate instruments, all monitoring different things, to malfunction in unison twenty-four hours a day, day in day out for at least two years. As a result of this we were led to believe that his mind was developing in directions parallel to the normal human brain, with the same capacities and the same form of consciousness.

It also appears that the Brain developed a hitherto unprecedented ability to divide his attention. The way in which he was able to control our monitoring devices even while sleeping demonstrates this. Normal brains can, with practice, concentrate on three or four different things at the same time, though only for short periods and with great effort; the Brain however developed a faculty for concentrating while apparently asleep. (Because of his tampering with our monitoring devices we can never know for sure when it was he ceased sleeping and dreaming in the normal sense.) In ordinary humans there are a number of different states in which normal thought processes do not occur; in deep narcosis; in dreaming, when our thoughts lack any form of deliberate direction; in deep meditation, when, though conscious, the mind has been totally cleared of ideas. In all these situations in which the human mind does not, in the most obvious sense of the word, *think*, the Brain was capable of maintaining rational, systematic intellectual activity at some level.

We only began to suspect this was the case when, seven years after the original implanting of the Brain in the host body, a radical change occurred in his sleeping habits. For seven years he had slept ten hours out of the twenty-four. This seemed perfectly normal, for sleep, as well as recuperating the body, is a necessary interval during which the subconscious, through dreams, is able to rehearse, assess, and digest the experiences of the waking hours, and even after seven years the Brain had a great deal of new experience to handle. Then one day, having succeeded in eliminating all subconscious activity whatsoever, or else having perfected the capacity to integrate experience with his subconscious while still wide awake, the Brain gave up sleeping. By keeping his eyes closed for six hours each day, and his ears blocked for another six, he was able to avoid straining them, and the set periods when he was without sight or without hearing were valuable opportunities to improve the performance of his other sense organs; at the same time by remaining fully conscious for 24 hours a day, he was able not only to read enormous quantities, but also to inter-react with his external environment to a much greater extent than if he wasted two fifths of his time in bed.

Throughout all this time he was unfailingly good natured and tolerant. As a person I should say he asked too many questions and gave too little away; though he quickly informed himself concerning the private emotional circumstances of the entire project team, he never once betrayed the least hint of any desire for human involvement. The only real personal idiosyncracy of his I can recollect is that he was very interested in so-called Beef-cake Magazines, the ones that show young men who by means of endless callisthenics and steroids have developed their bodies into muscle-bulging monstrosities. As we understood later, he was amused by the analogy between this kind of body-building, and what he himself was doing with his own mental powers.

Though slightly perplexed by the change in his sleeping habits, and by one or two other very minor circumstances we had observed, we all thought our experiment was going extremely well, till one day, about seven years and ten months after the original implantation of the Brain in his host body, he informed the neuro-physiologist in charge of that shift that he needed a new skull. The rest of us were quickly summoned to the project suite. The Brain, sitting relaxed and fit-looking in a revolving office chair, told us that his skull was too small for his brain to grow any bigger. We would have to make a new skull out of metal, he said; and he suggested that we retained his human facial bones and merely enlarged his cranium above his forehead, above his ears, and back over his neck, so that the enlargement could be disguised under a wig. It was lucky, he said, that we had given him such a broad-shouldered body, so that he would not look deformed.

After five weeks of preparations, we began the operation. The first stage consisted of removing his entire cranium above the hair line. That was as far as we got. I think that, even though anaesthetized, the Brain was still able to read, and probably even to control, our minds, but when we saw what was under the top of his skull, we came to our decision instantly, simultaneously and unanimously, and it was only the work of a second to run a scalpel through four or five of the arteries upon which the Brain's life depended.

The brain we had originally put in had been smaller than the human brain, but of the same shape, with two lobes, like half of the kernel of a walnut. The brain we stared down at, in the same operating theatre, seven years and eleven months later, had six lobes. The original two, slightly contracted and altered in shape but still recognizable, were at the front of the head. What the other four lobes were for we dared not wait to find out.

Dangling Man

I think the worst thing I ever did was when I was a thirteen-year-old schoolgirl. I suppose that under their crumpled-angel exteriors, most schoolgirls are pretty sly and nasty, but they don't usually have the same opportunities to cause disaster as grown-ups: but it just happened that such an opportunity came my way when I was still innocent enough to use it. I was in my second year at St Helena's Boarding School for Young Ladies in —.

— is a sleepy East Anglian sea-side town, with lots of old houses covered in wisteria and honeysuckle, a few pokey shops, bay windows and balconies overlooking a lighthouse, and a line of cannon overlooking the beach. On the outskirts of town are some avenues of new houses that might have been anywhere in the Home Counties, and a bit further out the school, which looked like a sea-front hotel from Atlantic City dropped by accident half a mile inland on a sandy heath – in fact I believe originally that was more or less what it had been – though by night or in fog it aged a thousand years and became something altogether more strange. During the week it was our prison, but on Saturday afternoons, if we were not involved in a hockey or netball match against another school, we were allowed to go into town. All the streets in the middle of town would be filled with girls in green school frocks, walking in threes. It had to be in threes. To be seen outside the school premises on one's own was unthinkable, and couples were not approved of: the Headmistress thought they led to mischief.

One Saturday I was walking along the seafront with two other girls whom for the sake of discretion I shall call Charlotte and Margaret. After a while we noticed that a man who was walking just ahead of us was continually stopping and glancing back in our direction. He seemed a middle-aged sort of man. He moved easily enough but his hair was thinning at the front, and he had a moustache which made him look older than perhaps he was. We wouldn't have looked twice at him if he hadn't so repeatedly glanced back at us. Before long we were giggling amongst ourselves. Charlotte had lost two buttons from the front of her school frock – we were just not quite old enough to mind appearing in public in a slightly dishevelled fashion – and Margaret and I began to tease her about how her low-cut front was attracting attention.

After a while the man walked off, apparently in the direction of the shops and we forgot about him. There was a super two-masted yacht riding the white horses only a few hundred yards out to sea, and we transferred our attention to that. Then I got a stone in my sandal, and I sat down on the steps of the War Memorial whilst the other two wandered on a little way. They were just out of ear shot when a man's voice spoke softly right beside my ear.

'Do you know Miranda Matthews?' the voice asked. It was the man who had been watching us. He was standing right behind me. Closer to, he was quite good-looking, with solemn blue eyes and a rather curious smile, sweet in the middle and bitter at the corners of his mouth, but sometimes the reverse, bitter in the middle, sweet at the corners. One other thing I noticed, he didn't smell of tobacco, like most adults seemed to in those days.

'Do you know Miranda Matthews?' he repeated.

If he had said anything else, I would have run after the others without replying to him, or told him to go away. I knew better than to speak to strange men, especially since it meant instant decapitation, or something very much like it, if any of our teachers saw us. But of course I did know Miranda Matthews. Everyone did. She was in the Lower Sixth. She was a tall, slim girl with masses of chestnut curls and a beautiful elfin face – its charm enhanced rather than subtracted from by a nose that seemed to have an extra end to it, added on in front where it should have stopped – and the most wonderful smile I ever remember seeing on any one. I think all the younger girls at school had a crush on her. I know I did.

'Yes, I do,' I told the man. I was really quite frightened and it was not simply for fear someone might see us: something about the afternoon had changed, the wind off the sea was getting moment by moment stronger, as if building up to a hurricane, whipping up breakers almost all the way to the horizon, and apart from trios of green-uniformed girls in the distance there were no children around – no local children at all, as if all of them had been taken away and murdered by Peter Grimes-like foster parents; but of course I simply had to know what he wanted to find out about Miranda Matthews.

'You don't know where she is, do you?'

'There's a tennis match at school,' I said. 'A couple of the team were ill so she had to play. She isn't really in the team, the tennis team. She's in the school hockey team, though.'

'I know,' he said. 'Give her this.' He crushed something in my hand. 'And don't tell a soul.' He turned very quickly and walked away.

Charlotte and Margaret were coming back. Also I felt someone was watching me from an upper window of the hotel, red brick and half-steepled, at the end of the avenue. I looked down at what I held in my hand. It was a small envelope, sealed and marked 'M.M.'. I slipped it into the pocket of my school frock before the other two had a chance to see that I had anything.

'That man spoke to you, didn't he?' Charlotte said. She was lanky and beginning to come out in acne like measles. She sounded indignant.

'No he didn't,' I said. But of course they had seen him standing next to me. 'Yes. He asked if I spoke French. He's French you see.'

'He doesn't look it,' said Charlotte, gazing after him.

'He doesn't look much of anything,' I replied dismissively. In fact I thought he looked rather nice. And he had given me a note for Miranda! I felt so excited I nearly burst with wanting to tell the others, but of course I couldn't. Though I knew all about Miranda Matthews – or thought I did – I had never spoken to her. I had wanted to of course but I had never dared. She was a Sixth-Former and I was only in the Second Form, and she seemed so far above me that I would have sooner thought of speaking to the Queen than to her. But now that I had the strange man's note to deliver I was obliged to search her out at school, whether I dared to or not.

When I returned to St Helena's with Charlotte and Margaret, the tennis match was still in progress. I sat for a few minutes by the courts, along with some other junior girls, watching Miranda play. She was very good, but I didn't really pay much attention to her style of playing. I suppose you could say I was looking at her with new eyes. She seemed prettier than ever in her neatly pleated tennis dress, very long-legged and flowing in her movements; but whereas I had been accustomed to think of her as much older than I was, I now felt somehow more equal to her. I suppose having the secret note for her gave me a sense of having some kind of power over her, but it was not just that. I realized that the strange man who had spoken to me was very much older than either of us – just as much too old to be Miranda's friend as she was too old to be mine. It made me see for the first time that she was really just a teenager like me.

After the match was over I went to look for her in the room she shared with two other Sixth-Formers. When I finally found her door and knocked. Miranda was all alone. She had just had a shower and was standing barefoot in the middle of the room with a huge turquoise bath towel draped over her shoulders, one leg up on chair, drying the back of her knee.

'Hello, littl'un,' she said to me. 'What can I do for you?'

'A man gave me a note for you this afternoon,' I said. 'At the sea front.'

She went an odd shade of pink, that extended right down into the top edge of her towel, but didn't really look guilty or alarmed or anything like that.

'Well, give it to me,' she said holding out her hand.

I passed it over to her.

'Hold on, littl'un,' she said, tearing open the envelope and scanning the sheet of closely written note paper within. 'Don't go away.'

I waited as calmly as I could. I was still terrified of the two of us being found out. And I was also terribly excited at being all alone in a room with Miranda Matthews.

'You haven't said anything about this to anyone else?' she asked suddenly, swinging that long nose of hers in my direction.

'No, of course not,' I said quickly. 'I wouldn't.'

'It's nothing really, really,' she said. She had needed both hands for the note and envelope, and the two ends of her towel fell away, showing female bits I had previously only seen beginners' sketches of in the showers, but now she dropped the note on the table and went back to drying herself. 'Still, you'd better promise me you won't breathe a word to anyone.'

'I promise, cross my heart and hope to die.'

'Death shouldn't be necessary.' She paused in her towelling and seemed to look at me properly for the first time. Then, quite unexpectedly she gave me an absolutely ravishing smile. 'You're a good kid. What's your name anyway?'

I told her.

'Well, Francesca,' she said. 'You'd better run along now. I'm very grateful to you. And remember, not a word to anyone.

I left, wishing I could have stayed with her longer. The memory of that entrancing smile she had given me remained with me all through the week. So did a recollection, fainter but somehow more disquieting, of the man's expression when he had spoken to me on the sea front – anxious, immensely yearning. It didn't take a genius to figure out what it was all about. They were having a love affair. I thought it must be someone Miranda had met and got dangling after her during the school holidays. Unable to live without her close to him he had evidently followed her to—. It seemed terrifically romantic, and I was bursting to know more of the whole affair.

Of course I didn't really expect that I would learn anything more, but the following Saturday, just before lunch, a girl in my class told me that Miranda Matthews wished to see me.

I had faithfully kept my promise not to tell anyone, and so I wondered what she could want with me. I ran up to her room as quickly as I could.

'Hi, littl'un,' she greeted when she saw it was me at her door. 'I wonder if you could do me a favour.'

'Of course,' I said eagerly. I would have done anything to have her give me that wonderful smile of hers once more.

'We'd better be quick, my roommates will be back in a minute,' she said in a business-like manner. 'I want you to give this note to Alistair – the man who spoke to you last week. Go to the bookshop just along from the Post Office. He'll be there, he owns it. Ask him if he has a toilet. Don't let anyone see you talk to him. I've been picked to play tennis again this afternoon, worse luck, or I'd meet him. And can you come and tell me what he says when you get back?'

'Of course,' I answered my heart sinking. I knew I should get into awful trouble if anyone saw me talking to the man, and worse still, it would be difficult to avoid getting Miranda into trouble too. And though I was dying of curiosity to see the man again, in a strange way I was frightened of him too.

'You'll do it?' said Miranda. 'That's terrific.' She squeezed my arm. 'You're a real brick. Your probably wondering what all this is about aren't you?'

'I am rather.'

'I'll tell you when you get back. Cut along now, and good luck.'

That Saturday I avoided teaming up with Charlotte and Margaret, for I was afraid they would recognize the man if they saw him in the bookshop. I went with two other girls. The bookshop, when I found it, was a sunken little building made to look even smaller by the great white lighthouse rearing up nearby; though its doors and lintels seemed right-angled it had an indefinable look of leaning to one side against a tall-chimneyed, half-timbered teashop, not so much out of affection but to get as far away as possible from the overpowering presence of a newly, and unsympathetically, restored three-storey Georgian mansion on the other side. Both of my companions were keen to look at the books, so we trooped inside. The man from the sea front was standing behind the counter. He smiled as we came in. I could tell from his eyes that he recognized me, but the smile was the sort of coolly polite greeting shopkeepers usually give their customers. As for me, I had been thinking about him all week, and I could not stop myself blushing as he looked at us.

After we had looked over some of his books I said to the other two girls: 'I need to go to the loo. I'd better ask this man if he has one. Wait for me, won't you?'

They said they would. I walked up to the counter, and asked the man if I could use his toilet. 'Of course,' he said, looking more surprised than he needed to. 'I'll show you where it is.'

There was a door at the back of the shop. He ushered me through into a kind of office, leaving the other two girls browsing amongst the Rosemary Sutcliff novels.

'Well?' he asked, when he had closed the door behind us. 'Where's Miranda?'

'She had to play tennis again,' I said. He was better looking than I had remembered him: rather presentable in fact, I could almost imagine myself walking into a crowded ballroom (everyone dressed for some reason in Regency style) with my white-gloved hand on his arm. 'Here's a letter from her.'

'Oh God, she tortures me with her excuses.' He read the note hurriedly. 'There's no time to write a reply. Tell her I'm hers forever. And tell her I'll expect her as usual next week. *Without fail.*' He sat down at an open roll-top desk and buried his face in his hands. I watched him wide-eyed waiting for what he was going to say or do next. After a moment he lowered his hands and stared at me. '*You* wouldn't treat me like this, would you? I mean if it was you?'

'What do you mean?'

'If it was you instead of Miranda.' Suddenly he seized my hand. 'Tell her I miss her desperately. Tell her I want to –' He drew me towards him and brushed a short dry kiss on my cheek. 'Pass that on to Miranda. Now run along. And thanks – thanks more than I can say.'

Back in the shop I felt I was walking on air. I only hoped the others didn't notice. I can't remember what we did for the rest of the afternoon. Walked up and down —'s main shopping street, I suppose, just as one usually did, and inspected the row of cannon and the slate-coloured sea. My mind was totally absorbed with what had passed in the room behind the bookshop. I suddenly realized that I was falling in love with him too. Just like Miranda had. I wondered what I was going to say to her when I returned to school.

When I got to Miranda's room, she was just changing back into her school uniform. I caught a glimpse of a lacy black bra as she did up the buttons of her school frock – we younger girls were only allowed plain white bras, but I suppose it was different for Sixth-Formers. I told her what had happened.

'He said I was to pass the kiss on,' I concluded, wondering if I should attempt to do so, but she indicated with a dismissive gesture that I needn't bother. Sitting down in front of her mirror she began brushing her long, curly, chestnut hair, with long rhythmic sweeps of her forearm, talking to me the while. 'He's not really a bookseller, you know. He says that is just to pay the rent. Really he's a writer. Short stories and things. I've seen some of them. You wouldn't understand half of them, they're very . . . . abstruse.' Her long nose swung, first to the left, then to the right, with each slow brush stroke. 'I'm in love with him, of course. But you knew that, didn't you? It's ridiculous, being cooped up in a silly old school like this. I'm eighteen, I should be able to go out, go to dances – pubs even, if I wanted.'

While we spoke, we could hear the voices of other girls calling to each other on the lawns outside, and occasionally, footsteps hurrying down the passage outside the door. It seemed strange, hearing her talk like this, with the sounds of the school all around us. I found myself saying, 'Well, if you want me to take another message....'

'Would you?' She immediately pulled open a drawer and produced a letter pad and envelopes. I tried not to appear to watch her too closely as she scribbled off five lines: but even from a few feet away there was a resemblance in her writing and my own that gave me an anticipatory qualm. 'When can you give it to him?'

'I'm meeting my mother at the station tomorrow – I can drop it in at the shop on the way there.'

'Would you? You're a darling.'

Well, needless to say I simply *had* to know what she had written: but when, having escaped from her room, I got to the loo and locked myself in a cubicle there was a minor disaster. I was tugging with my recently acquired nail-file at the flap of Miranda's envelope, hoping that the gum (still moist from the beloved's spittle) would separate without the bother of steaming it open with a boiling kettle – where could a Second-Former boil a kettle in a boarding school? – when the edge of the flap suddenly tore. The envelope now looked unmistakably tampered with, and it wasn't even properly open. I couldn't help noticing Miranda's handwriting had exactly the same slant and spacing as my own, and that if I could find another envelope I could easily forge the address on it. 'Here goes, then,' I thought: and ripped the envelope open. My heart and bowels sank again when I read what the most wonderful girl at St Helena's School for Young Ladies had written:

'*Dear Alistair,*

Sorry about the tennis match. We won in straight sets. I didn't muff a serve once though Emma keeps nagging me that servings [sic] my weak point. Looking forward to seeing you next week!!

In haste

Miranda.'

I had been expecting something rather more romantic and, well, more *grown up*. It seemed a waste of time even to go out of my way (and to risk being seen, with consequent ructions) just to deliver such a missive. And I felt for the eager recipient – what a let down for him! I had to forge a new envelope: it suddenly occurred to me that I could also forge a much better letter.

I lay awake in the dormitory till 3a.m. trying to think of something powerfully intimate, touchingly beautiful: something that the bookshop man would be really pleased to get, something that would make it a special day for him. I knew of course I mustn't say *too much*, because then he would want to talk about it with Miranda, perhaps even show her the letter by way of reminding her what she had written to him. It had to be something beautiful and heart-warming and yet possibly referring to any number of things, and therefore not worth specifically referring to when they saw each other again in a few days' time.

During the darkest part of the night I heard footsteps coming and going, and occasionally pausing as if for a confabulation, in a corridor beyond the nearest one, in a place where I knew there wasn't any corridor.

Out of doors a barn owl shrieked. I closed my eyes. Eventually I drifted off to sleep.

The following morning I wrote (after a few dummy runs to adjust my handwriting so it appeared exactly like Miranda's):

Dear Alistair,

Real drag about the tennis match. I would much rather have been with you! Remember what we talked about last time? Well, I think its happening. Had to sometime – I wanted to tell you in person. Frightfully sorry and all that.

In haste

Miranda

Not bad, I thought, considering I produced the definitive version in the middle of a Bible Class in the Geography Room. I considered the omission of the apostrophe in *its*, after the model of Miranda's apostrophe in *serving's*, to be particularly felicitous.

Hoping it would make him happy, I slipped it through the

bookshop's letterbox on the way to the station to meet my mother, who had come down to spend the afternoon with me.

There was a gale that night, with the wind snuffling and shrieking at the chimneys and banging incessantly at the windows; and when the direction changed momentarily the crashing of enormous breakers on the beach half a mile away came to us in our beds. It never occurred to me, however, to suppose that there might be any sort of correspondence or correlation between the disorderly weather and human affairs: not then, at any rate.

Well, I mean, Miranda and the bookshop man must have talked about *something* at their last meeting. How was I to know it had been about something dreadful? Not that I know to this day what it was, though I think from the outcome it must have had to do with her finishing with him, finding a boyfriend of her own age, that sort of thing. I couldn't very well have asked Miranda even if there had been an opportunity: but of course there wasn't one. The police cars arrived, the following morning, soon after Miss Claridge, the Latin Mistress, noticed the bookshop man hanging by a noose, stark naked, from the lime tree nearest the front door of Main School; and after Miranda had spent a couple of hours with the two most important policemen she was collected by her rigid-faced parents and never seen again. I did not even have a last parting sight of her before she disappeared into history, and as for the dangling man's full monty (as they now term it), before they shooed us away from the windows – well, I was far too young then to know about the alleged effects of strangulation on the virile member.

One Night

At the publishers' party
   she was a smiley blonde who knew his name
   from an article in *The New Nerd*.

On the bus back to his abode
   she was a tiddly giggler
   amused by elbow-jabs and alliteration.

In his living room
   she was a silhouette with tilted taut tummy
   in twat-tight trews tut-tutting to his bookshelf.

In the shower next morning
   she was a pump-up rubber doll with five-o-clock
   shadow armpits.
   and two pink pouting points poking at his solar
   plexus sheepishly assuring him:-
   I really (splash) like you but
   I've just (splash) finished with my boyfriend and
   don't want to you know start (splash) straightaway
   organizing my you know life around (splosh)
   another man.

At the front door
   a blonde back of a head wagging a pony tail
   running away from her DNA on three used condoms
   beside the sheet-strewn altar where they had unmade love.

Isabella Jefferson Gets Laid: Oxford 1968

'neither the reality of a single night nor even of a person's entire life can be equated with the full truth about his innermost being.'   Arthur Schnitzler, *Traumnovlle*.

'I haven't been in Trinity since my first year when I made a point of visiting all the older colleges,' she said, going before him lyre-legged up the stairs to his rooms. Her smock was so short that he could have easily thrust a hand up under the hem and squeezed a buttock. Instead he studied her thighs moving in front of his face as he followed her up the winding stairs: seen from behind they were barely wider than her round little calves and there was a surprisingly marked gap between them at the top. He wondered if looking would seem so important once he got round to touching. Did it make much odds how exquisitely contoured the thighs were that you came between? 'For some reason, you're the first Trinity man who's actually asked me to pay a visit. Which landing is it?'

'This one.' He unlocked the door and waited for her to pass in before him. With her high heels the top of her blonde head was just level with his mouth. Perhaps he ought to bow, he thought: but he was uncomfortably aware that most of his more Byronic gestures simply failed to come off. He contented himself with saying, 'Welcome to my palazzo.' He closed the outer door behind him. There was a college rugby club dinner in hall that evening and he did not want any drunken former team-mates bursting in with fire extinguishers.

'Sporting the oak, I see,' she said, with a seemingly inappropriate snigger, almost like that of a dirty minded nine-year-old. 'I'm not sure that I wouldn't feel safer with it open.'

'I'll open it if you like,' he said, looking at her.

'Oh, you can open it in a minute,' she said, and sat down on the sofa, hooking one leg over another, with a swoosh of nylon on nylon.

He went to the arched window to draw the curtains. The moon

had risen over the chapel, on which it shed a weak light, frequently interrupted by passing clouds. There were remote sounds of breaking glass and shouting from the next quadrangle momentarily submerged in the swishing of the curtains as he closed them.

'There's a rugby club dinner in college tonight,' he said, sitting down at the other end of the sofa, trying not to make it obvious that he was unable to keep his eyes off her thighs. He felt like Julian Sorel in *Le Rouge et le Noir,* challenging himself to take hold of Madame de Rênal's hand when the clock struck ten, 'or else I shall go up to my room and blow my brains out.'

Since she was such a verbalizer, perhaps the correct procedure would be to ask, 'Can I kiss you?' Or perhaps, since she was a precisionist in grammar. '*May* I kiss you?' Or – since that was what he really had in mind – 'May I run my hands up and down your legs?' No, a certain amount of mouth contact would be deemed appropriate before one progressed to exploration below the equator: but he wanted not so much to kiss her but to see if she would kiss back. He sidled down the sofa until he was right beside her. One by one the bells of the city began striking the hour. She lowered her eyes as he leaned towards her. It wasn't going to be as straightforward as in *Le Rouge et le Noir* though: the various clocks overlapped so the final chime would be difficult to predict.

'This bit's always embarrassing, isn't it?' she said.

Her false lashes fluttered upwards for a split second, and her eyes seemed huge close to, before she shut them in the approved manner at the moment of contact. He thought he heard her give a tiny gasp – like a gasp of surprise or fear – just before their lips met. He kissed her in the way one picks up a little ornamental horse or miniature elephant of Venetian glass, simply to see how light and smooth it is and because one doesn't know what else to do with it. No lust – in spite of her legs – just curiosity to see what would happen. After three heart beats – he had the impression she was counting – her lips parted to let in his tongue. She tasted of lipstick and iced bun, with a touch of apple. It was as sexy as a schoolgirl's X at the end of a letter. It might have been sexier if she hadn't opened her mouth so wide. Her hands remained immobile in her lap. After another six heartbeats she drew back.

'At least I suppose it is,' she said, presumably carrying on from her previous remark that *This bit's always embarrassing*. 'I've never really snogged anyone before.'

'What about Nigel?'

'Doesn't count. We've never merely really embraced, Nigel and I. The customary preliminaries were always somehow taken for granted. When I first knew him he was going out with my best friend and we could only gaze longingly at each other, and when, in the due course of events, it came to be my turn, the first thing he did was start removing my tights. I realized of course that it was about time I found out what it was all about but there was scarcely time to say to myself, "Odzooks, he means to swive me," before it was "Farewell, sweet virginity." '

She was definitely right about the embarrassment, though: now that he had settled the uncertainty with regard to whether she would permit him to kiss her he had not the slightest idea what to do, say or pretend next. Or what else she was going to permit. Only one way to find out how far he could take it. Their mouths came together again. He tried to put more into it this time, tried to get through to her – to whatever it was in her waiting for him to find: not that he was sure there was anything there. She certainly had none of Stephanie's French-Kissing-Champion-of-the-Fourth-Form expertise, none of that suggestion of long apprenticeship in the back row of the Odeon and in the upstairs rooms at teenage parties; she kept her legs crossed – hardly an encouraging sign – and he had the distinct impression she was having to force herself not to pull back from him. And when he tried to put his arms round her she pushed him off gently and said:

'Good, now we've got that bit over with I can look at your bookshelves.'

But it seemed she was only teasing, for she made no attempt to stand up. Their third kiss was as constrained and measured as those preceding except that towards the end she rested her hand briefly on his shoulder as if steadying herself.

'I suppose it's too late to ask you to watch out for my make-up,' she said. 'I spent ages putting it on and now it must look as if I hadn't bothered.'

Kiss No.4 was still cool and controlled but halfway through her hand came up to the back of his neck as if she intended not to release him when he tried to relinquish her mouth. But when their mouths finally parted she said, 'This is delightful, but I can't stay long. "His erstwhile timid lips grew bold," as Keats phrases it, "And poesied with hers in dewy rhyme." However I've got to get my eight hours sleep every night without fail and I've got an essay to write and need to be in the library at 9.30 a.m. sharp tomorrow.'

If anything kissing her simply reinforced his sense of her elusiveness, but he said, 'You've only been here for five minutes.'

'OK, then it's my turn to put my tongue in your mouth.'

She tried but she wasn't very good at it. Perhaps by way of compensation she began stroking the nape of his neck. He put his hand on top of her crossed knees, tried to separate them. She turned her mouth away to say, 'Nice try, but I'm afraid the Jefferson legs remain resolutely crossed. See any manual of etiquette regarding conduct on first dates.' But her mouth seemed wetter when he found it again, and after this kiss she said, 'Actually it's nicer to kiss a bit first before proceeding to anything more serious.'

He tried to part her knees again during the seventh kiss. This time she grabbed his hand and merely held it out of the way.

'Remember, Queensberry Rules only: nothing below the belt,' she said, disengaging her mouth.

Accommodating himself to this injunction, during the eighth kiss he began fumbling around at the small of her back, trying to figure out if there was some way of getting her bra undone. Because of the one-piece smock she was wearing it was impossible to get his hand to the catch. She evidently surmised what he had in mind for she said, 'Life's very unfair. My sister's bosom is much bigger than mine and she's only sixteen.'

His response (faintly disgruntled) to this was:

'How lucky for her boyfriend.'

'Oh no, hers are still a couple of maiden worlds unconquered.'

Her own Cranach-sized apples being, by implication, not unaccustomed to masculine onslaught, he took this to be some sort of invitation and touched the edge of her left-hand bra cup diffidently, almost reverently, and, when she did not protest, palmed the contents of both bra cups gently upwards, simultaneously poking with his tongue between her teeth in the classic co-ordinated snog-grope, feeling all the while a little as if engaged in an act of violation, telling himself, 'I am one of the select few,– in fact select *two* – to have touched Isabella Jefferson's boobs.' Her bosom was much less forward-thrusting and springy than Stephanie's, so that all he could really identify were her rib cage and the seams of her bra, without much sense of any form or solidity in-between. This seemed to be the right thing to do however for this kiss was the wettest yet and she seemed quite breathless at the end of it. The obvious next step was a bit of hunt-the-nipple. He tried to visualize her pink – or were they fawn? – paps going gratefully hard and pointy at his touch, but despite pushing in centripetally with his fingertips he couldn't identify much of anything through the intervening two layers of thin cloth. It would have been nice to have been able to burrow inside her smock but her neckline was too high for him to thrust his hand past it and inside. Screwing his mouth on to hers again he tried pushing her breasts together to make a cleavage but that too didn't work. It was all very well to fantasize about a girl like Isabella Jefferson moaning with pleasure as his boldly roving hands explored her secondary sexual attributes but when it came down to it, it seemed a bit pointless to squeeze tits that for all practical purposes weren't there. After a final (final?) tweak he let one hand drop to her thigh, but that was no good either, the cool artificialness of the nylon of her tights rasping against his fingers was simply disconcerting.

'I wish you'd take your tights off,' he said.

'I bet you do,' she said, panting a little, and seizing his wrist firmly, she pulled his hand back up to her left breast. 'I don't wish to seem old-fashioned but I'm afraid I must decline. I'm sure you are a most vigorous lover but we have to be sensible. At this stage of the proceedings one would normally withdraw discreetly to the nearest bathroom to insert one's diaphragm but, since this is a first date, not a fifth or sixth when it might perhaps have seemed obligatory, I left mine back at Somerville.'

'I thought you'd be on the Pill,' He was so taken aback by her suddenly talking of diaphragms that he blurted this out without thinking. Then, to cover his confusion he pretended nonchalance and asked: 'Aren't diaphragms a bit out of date?'

'By no means – the very latest formula of spermicidal gel comes with them. And obtaining a diaphragm, though an even more embarrassing procedure in detail, seemed somehow less of an absolute commitment to having one's womb anointed with unseasonable seed several times a week than the Pill.' She was still pressing his hand against her breast, and he was uncomfortably aware of his penis stiffening inside his underpants. 'And what about you? Weren't you a Boy Scout? And even if you weren't, I thought that every average optimistically male undergraduate kept at least one packet of French letters in his writing desk.'

'Evidently I'm less than averagely optimistic.' He certainly hadn't anticipated this turn of the conversation, and experienced an odd little twisting, or sinking, in his stomach at her calm acceptance of the idea of a penis squirting semen up between those delicious creamy thighs of hers.

She gave an almost imperceptible groan, sat up straighter, uncrossed her legs. 'Well, I'm not doing it without. Good old Malthusian Drill and all that. There's no denying that I am turned on by your somewhat impetuous caresses and I suppose it's a good way of getting to know someone better, but I'd rather have a First in Schools than your baby.' This time her dirty little-boyish smirk was half-expected. 'In any case I was counting on remaining celibate for the rest of the term.'

Another wet kiss, with some vigorously inexpert thrusting of her tongue – not so much by way of consolation, he judged, but more an expression of triumph, as if she had scored some sort of competitive point. Then it seemed she changed her mind:

'On the other hand having excited each other to this extent –' (Actually she did not sound in the least excited.) '– it might be undesirable from the psycho-neurological point of view for us each to retire to our chaste beds half a mile apart to masturbate in solitude, and common honesty compels me to admit that I've just had the curse, so it's my safe period.'

'Do you masturbate?'

'I don't make a regular habit of it but it's been known to happen.'

It took another moment for the penny to drop. In spite of the remote Queen's Christmas Message tone of her voice she was telling him that –

'You mean it will be all right if we . . . .'

'I mean it's so silly to go no-no-no like this and then yes-yes-yes. I've tried it, and it doesn't work, at least not the no-no-no bit. And it's not as if we've just met at a party. It was going to happen sooner or later so this is as good a time as any.'

He pulled her to her feet, a leggy Lippo Lippi virgin who presumably wasn't, and after a quick, inconclusive hug they went into his bedroom, her obedient little hand in his.

He had the usual college bed and he apologized for its narrowness.

'I think the general idea is for you to lie on top of me,' she said. 'I hope at least your sheets are clean.'

She withdrew her hand – her fingers were remarkably cold and clammy, almost damp – and sat down on the bed, bouncing experimentally up and down on it a couple of time, then continued:

'Do you think this will be the first ever occurrence of sexual intercourse in this centuries-old chamber, Isabella Jefferson a significant footnote in its history and legend? It's certainly a little demeaning that we women only get to undress in these old gothic rooms if we consent to open our chaste treasure to a male undergraduate's importunate lust.'

No answer to that one; so he pretended to laugh, noticing that as he did so that she had contrived, as if deliberately, to place the bed between them, so that despite visions of stripping her garment by garment like a Barbie Doll he had no choice but to play it casual, as one accustomed to acting out bedroom scenes. Despite the now very visible bulge at his fly he suddenly realized that he was more curious to see her with no clothes on than aroused by the prospect of sticking his willie in her. He began to unbutton his shirt while she, with a somehow self-important gesture, shucked her smock over her head.

'You can put your things on the chest of drawers,' he said.

'I manage perfectly well getting my clothes on in the morning but on occasions like this I never quite know in which order to take them off,' she remarked brightly, boyish little biceps bunching deliciously like freshly peeled hard-boiled eggs as she reached up to smooth back her hair. As if to give him time to catch up, she sat down again on the bed in her tights and flush-fronted bra – thin child's arms, as slender above the elbow as below, thighs with a little groove down the side, and seemingly narrower at the top than where they filled out halfway down, the curve of their undersides as they tapered to the knee like the profile of a Burgundy bottle, her belly, flat enough when she was standing, plumping out now as she sat – and began to inspect herself, tilting her head sideways like a girl on a beach checking her sun-tan, at first with little more than a sense of routine but then, with a quickening of attention, detecting some hitherto unremarked detail, perhaps the beginnings of a spot, or seeing some new significance in her smallpox vaccination or BCG scars, badges of membership of the same diaphragm-dispensing Welfare State as her lovers, and suddenly straightening her arm to bring up the muscle at the back of it into a soft ball, which she massaged as if anticipating in some dismay how his fingers would soon be biting into her flesh at exactly that part of her arm as he clasped her to his manly chest. Catching a glimpse of herself in the mirror she gasped audibly and, taking a tissue from her handbag, jumped to her feet, approached her reflection in the mirror and began determinedly to remove smeared lipstick from around her mouth.

'I'll have to keep my lashes on,' she announced. 'I'll never have time to put them back on again afterwards.'

He had been trying in his haste to take off his shirt without undoing the cuff buttons and by the time he emerged from a tangle of sleeves she had finished blotting her lipstick and was zigzagging her tights down over bean-profiled buttocks with what looked like a carefully rehearsed S-shaped wiggle of her lower body. He could see the dusting of fine silvery hairs on her thighs and shins as her tights came down, and he wondered if he ought to interrupt this stripping off to cop a feel: she noticed him looking and remarked, voice still dead-pan, 'I'm lucky I don't need to shave my legs.' He had no answer to that either. Her stomach was very pale above the top of her low-slung panties; and there was something sly and observing about her tummy button, as if to make up for the way she kept her eyes averted from his face. Actually she seemed as if deliberately ignoring his presence, turning away from him, but only so that she could see herself better in the mirror. She unhooked the back of her bra, arms in full nelson, pointy *art nouveau* elbows indicating north and south. He had fantasized about easing her bra strap down over her thin shoulders but now he had come to it he was having to race to keep up, any idea of synchronizing removal of garments having got lost in the difference between male and female attire. He pulled the lace of his left shoe. She raised her left shoulder. The lace was knotted. He attempted to pick at it with his fingernails. The horizontal creases at the back of each of her knees, together with the thigh tendons above and the two vertical grooves on the topmost part of her calf muscles formed an H like rugby goal posts. The knot was too tight. He tried the right shoe. Her right shoulder bra strap came down over her arm, shoulder blades moving alternately like budding angel's wings. He pulled his right shoelace. Her bra was now dangling from her hand like an eccentric bonnet, (the thin layer of white nylon padding he could see inside the lower part of the cups not perhaps an altogether promising sign), and he glimpsed a radiant kind of half-bulge in the angle beneath a raised arm. His right shoe came off. She turned to face him now, *contrapposto*, weight on right leg, left hand on hip, a twist in her posture reminiscent of Donatello's David, her ribs showing like a greyhound's below little midset isosceles tits. Actually with her proportions altered by the discarding of her clothes they were a bit bigger than he had expected, and not really isosceles: they sagged somewhat though with the nicest possible pendant bagginess, danglers rather than domes, very white and pointing pink tips at right angles to each other, one goggling directly at him, the other aimed away in snub-nosed profile, with just perceptibly more tit below the nipple than above. He hadn't registered before that one of the functions of a bra was to hold the breasts in a parallel position, but he couldn't concentrate on that now because his left shoe was definitely stuck. For one awful moment he thought he was going to find himself unable to remove his shoe and consequently unable to extricate himself from his trousers while the longest legs in the Bodleian library waited patiently to wrap themselves round his. No, the lace was finally coming undone. He looked round at her again, partly to check how far he was falling behind, and partly to have another dekko at he breasts. Girls one thought one knew were always something of a surprise when seen undressed for the first time – though it seemed a general rule that girls with great legs had disappointing tits and vice versa. Isabella's, though turning out to be cuter and slightly more substantial than he had expected from squeezing them – and no doubt he should be grateful she liked him enough to show them to him in the first place – scored nothing like as high on the titometer as Themis-thighed Stephanie's.

'I had pubic hair before the other girls in my class, which made them dreadfully put out as they had just voted me the biggest drip at the convent, but I was the second to last to need a brassiere,' she announced, rotating forty-five degrees away from him as she observed the direction of his gaze, and hunching her shoulders to impede his view; she had not once looked straight at him but from time to time glanced towards his midriff from beneath her false lashes. 'After wondering if my bosoms were ever going to come in the Third Form, and wondering if they would grow a bit more in the Fourth Form, wondering if they were big enough in the Fifth Form and wondering if anyone would care in the Sixth Form, it was something of a relief in one's first year here at Oxford to learn that everybody's more or less flatten out when one is sprawled on one's back with one's boyfriend on top of one.'

Was her incessant prattling a sign of nerves? At any rate she did not seem to expect a reply: he was busy untangling half an erection from his underpants in any case, and wondering whether she was noticing how big (or almost big) it was. Not turning her back this time she stepped out of her panties, with a bob of her head and a sort of curtsey, revealing her next little anti-climax, a small, gingery froth of pubic hair, a vee-shaped mat of welcome, reddish in the way blonde men often have reddish beards, though it was more a moustache than a beard. In its contrast with the altar-candle whiteness of the rest of her body, this school changing-room sprouting was almost shocking: she had always seemed so immaculately packaged he had almost expected a kind of Fabergé fanny instead of a hairy hole like other girls'.

The most exposed he had ever seen her before had been wearing a sleeveless summer frock in honour of a brief heat-wave two weeks previously. The honey-coloured little mole high up on her left arm which he had noticed then seemed intended to match a similar mole on the same horizontal below her left armpit. Eyes even now still lowered, – though seemingly fixed on his chest rather than his groin – she came towards him, a tomboy-boobed Botticelli, and looped her slender ballerina's arms about his neck, raising her elbows unnecessarily high as she did so, as if unable to omit an element of the affected, perhaps the hieratic, from any of her gestures. Her rump under his hands was squidgy like marshmallow and unexpectedly chilly, but after a moment she broke away from him and her two droopy little demihemispheres dipped and went suddenly wedge-shaped as she stooped to draw aside the bed-covers, though as soon as she lay down they projected less than the arch of her lower ribs – more or less as she had just mentioned: he couldn't recall Stephanie's ribs being so prominent.

'What if these were Tom Warton's rooms in the eighteenth century,' she said, adjusting the pillow under her head.

'Whose?'

'Thomas Warton, Oxford's Professor of Poetry in the 1760s, one of the pioneers of literary historiography.'

Presumably there was one way of silencing her donnish burbling, and he was now about to demonstrate it. He lay down beside her cautiously – there was hardly room on the narrow bed for both of them – and tried to kiss her mouth: though she made no objection as he slid himself partly on top of her, she averted her face, as if already having second thoughts and now trying to avoid his lips. He tried instead to nuzzle the fine emery paper stubble in the hollow between her rib cage and out-flung arm, but she brought her elbow across to block him, exclaiming:

'Perdition! All of those years of shaving my armpits with religious regularity when there was nobody to see and now when there is – '

She allowed him however to mouth and mumble both her squashy little breasts in turn, though their halfpenny-sized pink roundels, now slipped to each side as she lay on her back, remained resolutely unerect, apart from a ring of little goose-bumps around the margin of the pigmentation. Stephanie's nipples had popped up when pinched as promptly and pertly as something in a children's pop-up book: instead of points Isabella's were just flattened goose-pimple-ringed round splotches with a tiny, barely perceptible crevice like a miniature letter-box in the middle of each one.

'You're nipples don't seem aroused,' he said after a minute or two of sucking and squeezing each one in turn. 'They're somehow retracted.'

' "Retracted" is nice, but the correct term is "everted". They're usually like that, it doesn't mean they're not exceedingly sensitive. They used to tease me about it at the convent.'

'The nuns?'

'Not the nuns, twit, it was only ever the other girls who saw me without a nightie.' As he foraged and fumbled her calm, almost monotone treble added to his sense of unreality. 'The other girls in my class. But I can assure you they are definitely an erogenous zone. Sometimes when there's a cold wind they stick out like anything and then they're exceedingly long and pointy, but generally the only way to make them show at all is to moisten them with a little saliva and then blow on them gently for a minute or two.'

This seemed far too complicated and clinical, and in any case his exploring hand, now past her crinkly little welcome mat and between her thighs, had found that if her top half seemed not to be sexually aroused, her bottom half, judging by the surprisingly cool wetness that greeted his probing fingers, assuredly was. A liquefaction as startling as that of San Gennaro, though possibly more frequent. The full length of his body was by now on top of hers, and his fumbling at what he hoped was her clitoris caused her suddenly to draw up her knees so that her feet were on either side of his waist in an almost obscenely practical (and unexpectedly practised) plug-in-here position. Good of her to make it so easy to slot into her slit, though he wouldn't now be able to boast, even to himself, of literally having those fabulous legs of hers plaited round his own: not that the fabulousness of her legs now seemed of any importance; and a quick grope of conveniently adjacent thigh and lower leg told him that though agreeably fuzzy they were too stringy, too leathery even to *feel* as nice as her upper arms. No argument, as with Stephanie, about who went on top. He curled his finger tip, hooked it into the moist parting of her flesh. As if on cue she began making little appreciative whimpering noises in the back of her throat, which seemed to gather as he probed and burst out in a little inarticulate cry, *nyeh-nyeh,* wordless but somehow still recognizably in her usual smug tone of voice: no doubt the spontaneous overflow of powerful feelings, as Wordsworth or someone had phrased it. Another finger: she was smaller than Stephanie – he might have guessed she would be a two-finger twat. He was really getting through to her, it seemed, though he was still not sure what he was getting through to. The real point was if, he could do that with just two fingers . . . . Shifting his hand to guide the full length of his huge hammer-hard blood-and-lust engorged cock into her curl-fringed little cranny and up, up, in the general direction of her cold little heart – wondering if his triumphant entry would elicit the same sharp indrawing of breath as he had heard from Stephanie – he made a discovery that was, to say the least, inconvenient at this particular juncture, viz. that his cock wasn't huge and hard at all, but flabby, flaccid, and flexible, a gherkin that had gone soft instead of becoming a cucumber, not even the half erection that had incommoded him earlier, more like 30 per cent stiff at most, which meant 70 per cent limp and useless. He tried to shovel it into her but it wouldn't go. Using one finger as a kind of shoe horn didn't work either, though it made her to cry out again while the two shiny little plateaux of her knees oscillated momentarily on either side of his waist. He began kneading himself desperately with his other hand – his limpness had exactly the same degree of softness and pliability as her sideways-sagging little boobs, a comparison off-putting rather than arousing. Meanwhile her face, just below his mouth, had a rapt, fixed-eyed, almost trance-like expression, like Venus's in Tiepolo's 'Allegory of Venus and Time' in the National Gallery. He noticed blonde down at the side of her face, a small mole he had not observed before just in front of her ear.

'Oh dear,' she remarked suddenly. 'You've got no sense of direction.'

'I want to feel you all around me,' he said.

He tried to concentrate on her vagina as a kind of mystic Inside where few others had been: gooey depths where Truth could be found, or at least *her* Truth: the Truth as far as it went, of her real self that she had kept secret till now: a dark and deliciously deliquescent tunnel up through which one had to force one's way, up through an invisible and indefinable barrier to the meanings hidden in the hot brown muddiness at the very root of her; and all the while he was rubbing himself against her. He wasn't going to fall into her by gravity though, and for all that she was doing everything a convent girl possibly could to offer her opening, for all its slithery moistness, it was clearly designed to operate with a degree of pressure, like a maxi-size flesh-and-blood press-stud, and his great worm Oroubouros remained wiggly, wobbly, weak, wilted, wonky and simply worm-like rather than rampant, resolute and ready to shoot. Every time he tried to cram it – ram it – into her it doubled up and flipped out. It was like standing in a public loo surrounded by members of a rugby club, flies undone and prick pointed at porcelain, trying to wee and nothing coming. Finally, in a panic, he pulled down her left hand, which had fluttered briefly against his bare back and then flopped inertly to her side (right hand ditto, as if she was not sure whether a girl was supposed to put her arms round the man or whether it was the latter who was supposed to do all the touching) and closed her cool clammy fingers around his limpness.

'Is it getting stiffer?'

'I wouldn't know, I'm not used to feeling penises casually.'

Infuriatingly her voice was still perfectly controlled, still with its elocution class modulation, as if she was unaware of, far above, his desperation: but she suddenly placed both her palms on his buttocks, not caressingly but as if in anticipation of guiding him as he thrust into her. To keep her primed he began kissing her face and throat and shoulders, and as he twisted and turned above her he glimpsed in the mirror four sets of toes, hers (with traces of red varnish on the nails) on the outside, soles down on the bottom sheet, his extending soles uppermost beyond the foot of the bed, his legs heaving ludicrously back and forth, hers with their immodestly raised knees modestly immobile. This vision had a sound accompaniment too, his own panting, and an occasional stifled gasp from her, the metronome-like clicking of the bed, an arhythmic susurration which part of his mind identified as the sound of his legs sliding up and down the bottom sheet of the bed with each movement. Faintly in the background he could hear Beethoven on a record-player in the next set of rooms, and the sound of shouting and breaking glass in the quad. Hopefully – somewhat grotesquely – she had begun to hump back at him, not with big athletic bucks like Stephanie but with experimental little jiggles, as if she was having hiccups. She was staring up at him now with intense concentration (Stephanie had kept her eyes closed all through their love-making).

'It's getting stiffer,' he said. 'It's getting stiffer.'

'I can feel it now.' She suddenly mashed her mouth against his in an extraordinarily wet kiss. 'I *like* you,' she said, with sudden emphasis. 'I like you! Yes. Keep going, keep going. Oh, it's your finger.'

He could feel sperm rising hotly and sweetly within his failed, flabby, flaccid tool. '*I want you to come all over me,*' Stephanie had said, her voice more urgent and emphatic than Isabella's ever was, perhaps ever could be. One last boomeranging thrust and, more copiously than might have been expected under the circumstances, millions of aspiring little Paul and Pauline Gibbonses were squirting hotly between their bellies.

'I couldn't get it in,' he said, rolling off her. (That was very Oxford, the compulsion to state the obvious.)

'Never mind,' she said eagerly, as if relieved she could use long words again instead of just making *nyeh-nyeh* noises. 'Penetration is very overrated. It hurt like billio the first time with Nigel. It was the most painful thing that had ever happened to me in all my life, like being impaled on a broomstick. The only thing that enabled me to go through with it was knowing it was a choice between that and a lifetime of celibacy.'

'At least he got it in.'

'What was it the Earl of Chesterfield said? "The pleasure is momentary, the position undignified." He might also have mentioned that it's a complete myth that it's good for the complexion.'

She lay, a Modigliani blonde, if there could be such a thing, with her face turned away from him, legs splayed in an M, calves hanging slackly, addressing her remarks to the bedroom door while his sperm dried on her belly, and he could see no part of her above her skinny shoulders save for the pale gold tumble of hair on his pillow, and the rim of one ear. For a moment he thought she had turned away her face because she was weeping. There was some sort of goo on his fingers which he sniffed surreptitiously, and was reminded a little of mushroom and boiled cabbage. Her. He looked at her vagina's distended lips, like the flower of a cyclamen, closing on each other once more as if never parted, between spread white thighs. More hair between her legs than he had expected: almost more than at the front of her pubes, and with a couple of strands out of place and plastered sweatily cross-ways against her slightly protruding labia. *Lasciate ogni speranza voi chi entrate.* Only he hadn't even entered. Napoleon had told the Comte de Bertrand that the Empress Josephine had the prettiest little cunt imaginable: but that was after he had come in it a few times.

'No peeking,' she said suddenly, drawing her knees together.

To cover this slight awkwardness he leaned over and kissed the tip of her nose with an affectionateness he did not feel, and rubbed her soft flat belly till she began kissing him back with those inexpert wet kisses. Then, because he knew it was expected of him, he stroked her fig-leaf of wiry ginger hair and she reciprocated by reaching down to his shrunk and slime-covered penis and holding it experimentally as if indeed it was the first time she had handled this part of the male anatomy. He looked down at it, encircled by and two shades darker than her snowdrop-coloured fingers, a snot-like thread of semen still dangling from its end. Your pinkie, his mother used to call it censoriously, when drying him after early-evening baths when he was a toddler. His Ithuriel's spear, one touch of which had been meant to reveal truth.

'You mustn't worry,' she said. 'I expect it happens to lots of men.'

'I wanted to give you an orgasm.'

'An orgasm would have been lovely. But I don't think that happens very often the first or second time two people go to bed together. . . . And I like being here with you, just lying here, even if it isn't exactly *Wuthering Heights* . . . . Don't you think just being naked together creates a sense of intimacy?'

'It's hardly the same,' he said, momentarily startled by the fourth-form naivety of this last remark.

There was more shouting in the quad outside, but it seemed remote, unable to affect them. Probably the rugby club. They smiled at each other and he bent over to kiss her intriguingly retracted nipples. He pinched one of them in his teeth, but only gently, and thinking he ought to bite harder to make at least a pretence of passion, but not really wanting to and feeling he needed to excuse his inhibition, he said:

'I mustn't bite too hard or else Nigel will see the marks.'

'He probably wouldn't notice but at this point in time I am not at all sure that he is going to have the opportunity,' she said. 'I thought it was obvious from the last hour that he is now, if only unofficially, an ex.' She swung her legs off the edge of the bed she reached for her panties, her breasts flopping down like purses as she bent forward. 'It's getting late, and I don't want to get locked in. Especially as I was going to write an essay tonight.'

'You're going to write an essay *now*, are you?'

'Before I came up, I thought that when I was at Oxford I should have to work every minute of the day. In the village I come from they're all frightfully impressed that I'm at Oxford, though the fact that I'm an Open Scholar as well doesn't really mean much to them. I used to be terrified that I'd fail to live up to the neighbours' expectations.'

'And have you?' he asked.

'I dare say I've failed to live up to everyone's expectations tonight,' she said, her face hidden from him as she looked down at her pubic hair. 'Do you happen by any chance to have a spare paper handkerchief?'

'Yes,' he said. 'Yes.'

Graduate Sex in the Early Seventies

Twenty-five years before Polly Morris, reviewing one of my books in *Journal of the History of Sexuality*, ticked me off for appearing to believe that women's nipples were 'normally sepia', I discovered how Jackie M., a natural blonde with hair dyed chestnut, had perfectly pink nipples that took on a beige tinge in the cold of my bedroom at 40 Histon Road, Cambridge. Yet one was very ignorant in those days. Jackie, the fourth girl I had had sex with and the first I ever slept with on successive nights, was off-hand when I asked if she was on the pill. 'No; but I'm all right,' she told me. 'I don't always get periods.' She was a third-year at Sussex University, where they were famously expert on such matters, but I asked if she was sure, and she said somewhat huffily: 'It's my responsibility.' She was more than a little put out when, approximately sixty-nine seconds later, I inserted my index finger for a bit of preliminary titillation and discovered what at first I thought was a quantity of cold cream (some of it smeared on her pubic hair too), with a resistant piece of plastic behind it. A diaphragm, no less, inserted a couple of minutes earlier in the bathroom, whither she had gone, she explained, 'to clean my teeth.' Seeing my surprise, she was apologetic. 'Nobody else ever noticed,' she said.

My next girl, 337 miles away in Edinburgh – the first girl I ever went to bed with to have a tattered childhood teddy on her pillow and, though the third to hold my penis, the first actually to put it in her mouth – wouldn't let me have even a peep at her vagina, and said she had never tried to look at it herself, not even with a mirror: yet she was a conspicuously responsive sexual partner, gasping as I entered her – which I subsequently assured myself was a pretty reliable indicator of more than average randiness – and thereafter generally silent but intent, with a trick I found both piquant and endearing of humping back a half-beat after each of my thrusts, as if trying to extract the last bit of sensation as I withdrew. 'Tell me when you come,' she instructed me, the night before she threw me out, 'I want you to come all over me.' She even gave me a love bite on the side of my throat. She was also the first girl – woman – to hook her feet round my spread legs, her ankles across my calves, in the supposedly classic beast-with-two-backs position, which turned out in practice to be less serviceable than it looked in pictures one had seen.

Like Jackie M., she was a final-year student reading history. Although from Somerset she had a typically Celt combination of dark hair, eyes like blue topazes and skin like watered milk, in keeping with which she too had pink areoles though unlike Jackie's paps hers refused to harden when played with and protrude like other people's. She informed me that the only way to make them stick out was to moisten them with spittle and then blow on them gently for four or five minutes. (She also told me that one of her breasts was slightly larger than the other though in spite of cupping, clutching and concertina-ing both of them fairly frequently during the course of the next one hundred and twenty hours I was unable to detect any size difference, and indeed recall them, despite the disappointment of their unpointiness, as pretty much a perfect, standard-defining example of the very-slightly-lolling-two-thirds-of-a-grapefruit variety, though like anyone else's, even less classic examples, they more or less flattened out to the level of her breast-bone once she was on her back.)

Paolo Monelli, in one of the best Italian memoirs of frontline experience during the Great War (*Scarpe al Sole*, translated as *Toes Up*, 1930) wrote of how 'even, the most faithful and humble memory,' distorted the reality of battle: 'The shells fall closer, the actions are enormously exaggerated, the periods of waiting lose their length, the intermediate moments disappear: the falsehoods and rhetoric of others act unconsciously upon us.' It is no different when one attempts to write honestly of ones own sexual experiences: one gives disproportionate attention to genitalia and orgasms, or else to the emotional/romantic aspects: or else one adopts a would-be disarming, perhaps would-be Booker Prize-winning, pose of wine-bar breeziness. After so many years I am not quite sure how much emphasis I ought to give to the feelings of incredulity, violation, surprise and even dismay that I know accompanied my sexual initiation but I am quite positive that I felt none of the 'mixture of power, tenderness and sheer cocky glee. . . . the football fan in the back of your skull, the man with the rattle and the scarf who shouts Yippee and stamps his feet on the terraces' reported in Julian Barnes's *Metroland* (1980). I think it was only during my adventure in Edinburgh that I began to come to terms with how *little* I actually felt, beyond astonishment that another human being actually wanted me to do this to them: and of course there were other things to worry about.

The next girl I spent the night with, in Somerville College, Oxford – a dark brunette with, this time, breasts shaped like those old-fashioned curved baby's feeding bottles, tipped with extra-big blurry-edged brown button-ended nipples – was the first to propose we tried it with her on top rather than in the missionary position. She was the first girl I slept with who seemed openly interested in the technique of sexual intercourse, as technique. Within an hour of picking her up in the Politics and Economics section of the Bodleian Library she was telling me about losing her virginity: 'It must have been very boring for him. I didn't know how to move or anything.' Later on she had had a fling with a man who had asked her to lie quite still, and though she tried and tried she just couldn't. The display of humping and panting she gave me the following night however seemed something of a set routine, neither particularly individual nor personalized, though it was in instructive contrast to the immobility of my next girl, a nymphet- bodied blonde Italian swimming enthusiast with coarse armpit tufts named Caterina G. who was in London writing her *tesi* for her degree at the University of Venice. I remember with Caterina craning my neck to look under my arm and down the length of our sandwiched bodies to see if her hips moved at all as I poked into her. They didn't really: each of my thrusts elicited scarcely more than a quiver. At intervals she would squash her mouth against mine for a more-than-averagely wet sucking kiss or would exclaim, as if to convince herself rather than me, 'I *LIKE* you!' After one routinely mediocre coupling I asked how it had been for her and she responded 'Fantastic.' She was so pretty I had been completely tongue-tied the first time I ever saw her, and had sat all through lunch in the refectory of the University of London Senate House making sheep's eyes at her without daring to speak;

but she was much sexier with her clothes on, for then she was forever hugging and squeezing and pinching and French-kissing me. She once gave me a little lecture about there being two kinds of men, those who made love for themselves and those who made love for the woman. I was the former; only one very special man amongst her (to date) half-dozen lovers was in the latter category. I asked her if she didn't mind having men make love to her only for themselves and she said, with a cold little laugh, 'If I did I wouldn't get anyone.'

In fact the explanation for her under-performance in bed was probably much simpler than her two-kinds-of-men rigmarole: merely that, misreading the wetness of her open-mouthed kisses and the incipient slipperiness of her neat little slit, I had been cramming my salami into her well before she was ready; but apart from her little lecture, and exclamations like, 'Ow' or 'Sweetly' (her mistranslation of *dolcemente*, 'gently'), she never said anything else on the subject. It wasn't till the next girl but one, back in Cambridge, that someone actually grabbed my penis and plugged it into her vagina by way of communicating, with engaging lack of equivocation, that yes, she really was ready for me.

It wasn't just *my* ignorance. A girl I was friendly with but never got beyond holding hands with, who had had two long-term boyfriends, was astonished to learn that men couldn't simply have erections when and as often as they wanted, but ran out for the night after three, four or, exceptionally, five squirts. A St Hilda's girl with whom I failed to get an erection even before the first squirt commented, 'The whore of St Hilda's fails again,' but in spite of confessing to having slept with twenty men during her first term at Oxford refused to comment on my limpness: 'I'm not accustomed to handling penises casually.' The Edinburgh girl too told me she had never examined a penis before, even in the course of an eighteen-month relationship. A Newnham girl who had had six lovers thought condoms made sex easier on the grounds that they 'got in easier because they're oily'.

In those days it was too early in one's career to work out the relationship between normal outward behaviour and being what was called 'good in bed', or the possible significance of some girls keeping their eyes closed in sex while others stared up at one from the pillow, or the distinction between girls who took on sex, with some display of mixed feelings, as part of their teen-and-twenties exploration of life, those who were looking for love, and those who simply happened to be horny, like the girl in Edinburgh, who had all sorts of distinctions between 'affaires' and 'love affairs', told me, 'You can make sex to me, you can't make love to me,' and when I asked (in mid-copulation) if she didn't at least *like* me responded, 'No, I don't like you, that's why this is so good.' (She was a Catholic, kept on referring to herself as being in 'mortal sin' and confessed wistfully, 'I only sleep with people because I don't have faith in life,' but at other times she was quite alarming in her enthusiasm, telling me that I had a big penis and that it made her like me more. 'That's awful,' I said. 'No, it isn't, if you had some good feature people would like you for it . . . . well, perhaps it is awful.' She even admitted that she was always especially randy directly after her period, though an additional factor in taking me into her bed may have been relief at discovering she had not got pregnant as a result of having sex while ovulating two weeks previously.)

Jackie M., on the other hand, the Sussex University third year with the diaphragm and the nipples that turned beige in the cold of my Cambridge bedroom, may have been one of those looking for love. When I asked how many men she had slept with she responded, 'It's childish to keep a score,' but then made a quick count and announced, 'Twenty-one, like my age.' She certainly seemed to have acquired the knack of getting a good night's sleep in a narrow student bed with another student in it, and there was something almost intimidatingly accustomed and rehearsed about the way, when I got on top of her, her two knees would come up level with my waist, angled outwards at 45 degrees so as to open out her fanny as wide as possible. She was game for anything too. She did not take my penis in her mouth or even touch it with her hand, but mentioned that being buggered 'hurt like billio', and when I suggested it she rolled over obligingly and presented her bum so I could try if I wanted to. (I decided I didn't.) She also made no objection when, somewhat miffed by the failure of my manful efforts to extort more from her than an occasional complaisant sigh and diagonal jiggle of her pelvis, I asked her to read aloud to me from George Kitson Clark's manual *Guide*

For Research Students Working On Historical Subjects (issued gratis to all history Ph. D. students at Cambridge) while I was pumping away between her raised knees. Holding the book next to my face, she was able to read from it without a falter. She told me that after her G.C.E. O-levels (in which she had got seven As) she had been off school with anorexia for a year (hence, presumably, her remark about not always having periods) and after we went our separate ways she sent me occasional bulletins from Brighton on how she was putting on weight, partly as a result of nervousness about the approach of Finals. One such bulletin reported, 'Got even fatter – nearly weigh 8 stone which is terrible – seem to be developing a bosom as well which is even worse.' By 'bosom' she probably meant that her previously symmetrically out-curved breasts – what one used to describe as shaped like a champagne glass, though I suppose in fact one meant the type of glass shown in adverts for Babycham or for cocktail olives – were developing a perceptible roundness or overhang on their underside, which actually I quite looked forward to seeing; previously they had barely protruded enough to fit each hand. She was much prouder of her legs, which she claimed were the most photogenic pair at Sussex (though I didn't think they were as beautiful as those of the blonde medievalist I had been in love with at Oxford) and boasted how Peter Burke had referred in a tutorial report on her high skirt-essay ratio, i.e. ratio between shortness of skirts and length of essays. (This was still in the mini-skirt era, of course.) Yet she would never let me have a good dekko at her when naked, simply dabbing scent on her wrists and behind her ears and diving straight into bed as soon as she had stripped off her tights and panties, barely giving me time to register much more – apart from nipple colour – than the fact that though her upper arms were quite podgy I could count all her ribs across the room. She said that 'one night stands are nice,' (*nice* being her invariable term of commendation) and that she never got emotionally involved with the men she slept with, but one evening she asked me why I had invited her to Cambridge. 'Because I wanted to screw you,' I answered. 'Oh,' she said. 'You've damaged my ego.' After that she was very quiet for about half an hour, saying only that she would never fall in love or anything like that, and never marry: then she began to weep, mumbling, 'I hate Sussex . . . . I'm sorry . . .

.' Similarly the Somerville girl who wanted to go on top told me before we set to, 'Be gentle with me, ... be nice to me,' and the following morning jeered at herself and me for 'having fulfilled both our stereotypes,' and then went off to lunch with two male friends whom she consulted as to whether she ought to sleep with me (not mentioning that she already had), triumphantly informing me that evening that they had advised her with great earnestness not to: it was the apparently hard-boiled ones like her who seemed to want approval and moral support the most. Often they had their own private code of rules too. A married woman in Cambridge assured me that I was the first man, apart from her husband, to have given her an orgasm; but then she fell in love with another man and, telling me about it, confessed proudly that he was the first man, apart from her husband, to have given her an orgasm. At the time I wondered why she needed to tell me this.

I am writing all this down now as a kind of experiment in autobiography, an attempt to write about my experiences in a way – with, so to speak, a tone of voice that is exactly appropriate – that exactly reproduces the curiosity and sense of discovery of the time, my surprise at how detached I felt and the extent to which my strongest emotion was my eagerness to register and record sensations, especially visual ones. I find however that even in this I have been untrue to the truth of my subjective states of four decades ago, just as Paolo Monelli found, in his 'still very clear recollections of the lie of the ground, the rocks, the mountain pines, the men, the wounded, the dead, the advancing Germans, the blood flowing from the forehead of corporal-major De Boni', during the fighting between Monte Tondarecar and Castelgomberto on 4 December 1917, that somehow there was no sound-track, only a 'frightful silence', when all the while there must have been a 'tremendous din' of shouts and explosions. My memory has, as it happens, preserved something of the sound-track of my own experiences, the Edinburgh girl's sudden in-drawing of breath as I entered her, the Somerville undergraduate's contralto panting and the squeak-squeak of her college bed, and the married woman's soprano cries, but what I find conspicuously missing from the foregoing account is any reference to whatever physical excitement I may have felt at the time. In the case of Jackie M. and the girl in Edinburgh it must have been considerable, judging by the number of times I spilt my seed in them within the space of a few days. I remember with Jackie, as she hurriedly climbed into bed with me on the second or third night of her brief stay in Cambridge, that I had an anticipatory hard-on even before she reached the bedside, though the truth is she never seemed to me anything like as sexy, once she had given a first demonstration of how little effort was required to get her into bed, as she had the afternoon of our initial encounter in the Round Reading Room of the British Museum (not yet redesignated the British Library), or in the masturbatory fantasies involving all possible orifices that enlivened the two weeks between our first and second meetings. There was much more sexual electricity with the Edinburgh girl, mainly due to a constant friction of personality (rather than the slightly bored consciousness of incompatibility I had with Jackie), but it was predominantly a matter of a sense of impossibility beforehand – though evidently impressed by the fact that I was an Oxford graduate now doing a Ph.D. at Cambridge, her reticent upper-middle class manner made her seem the last person ever to want to suck my cock and tell me how clever it was – and incredulity thereafter, and apart from an unexpected and unintended manifestation on our first night together (which seriously annoyed her as she had been insisting we were not going to have sex) my erections seemed to come only as and when required, and not oftener: one night indeed she had to pester me to renew my love-making when I was more disposed to go to sleep, after an evening of circulating joints with a couple of her friends. I recall the mere fact itself that in my last year as an undergraduate I came in my underpants while groping a girl with whom I only had sex some days later, but after some failures at Oxford the erection aspect of copulation seemed no more than a matter of course. As for emotion, most of these relationships, if one can call them that, were too sudden, too short in duration, for that to be quite possible: on average intercourse took place on the second date.

It was just then becoming fashionable to assert that women had exactly the same attitude to sex as men (i.e. hedonistic, unromantic and basically lecherous) and apart from a couple of occasions already described there was never any mention of feelings. Yet even Caterina

G., the Italian blonde, who put on a convincing act of being one of those who simply took sex in her stride as part of their teen-and-twenties exploration of life, went weepy on me one afternoon. (It was after a condom broke, though I don't think that was precisely the reason for her tears.) There was a French girl too, with unshaved armpits like Caterina but also a slightly off-putting ring of crinkly hairs round her nipples, who took off all her clothes so I could make a better job of feeling her up, but wouldn't let me remove my trousers. She said she had had a boyfriend in Paris who had regarded her as a possession, like his pipe, and she didn't want to be a possession. Then there was Gwynedd from Newcastle University: we were rolling around together on my bed, still fully clothed, when she suddenly announced, 'I don't really want this. I hope you're not going to make me. You could if you wanted, by saying I'm prudish and old-fashioned.' After that I proceeded at a more decorous pace, though only as far as the topmost curls of her pubic hair, while she nuzzled my ear: she said she had been celibate for the past five or six months but, 'I don't like the idea of being one of a procession.' Perhaps, after all, she was one of those looking for love, and had detected with ominous rapidity that she hadn't found it with me. Similarly a Leicester University graduate (name now forgotten) who had recently arrived in Oxford to do a D.Phil. suddenly became indignant when (having at our second meeting deftly unbuttoned the front of her yellow frock and discovered she was not wearing a bra) I asked her what her relationship was with her breasts; 'You're not really interested in me at all, are you?' she remarked, as she threw me out of her room.

She was not the only one to doubt the genuiness of my enthusiasm. 'You don't have to do this if you don't want,' said an American girl as I knelt beside her, fumbling awkwardly with my condom, in the Fellows' garden of Trinity College, in the shadow of the great tower of Cambridge University Library. (It was in this garden, in 1868, that George Eliot discoursed to Frederic Myers on 'the three words which have been used so often as the inspiriting trumpet-calls of men, – the words , *God, Immortality, Duty.*') After I had done what we had come there to do I hung the condom, now with my pathetic quarter-millilitre of juice in it, on a nearby twig. 'It looks kinda dead,' she said. Shortly afterwards we parted and she said she'd enjoyed knowing me. She was from Connecticut, one of those Nordic-looking blondes who always seem to dress in blue, doing her mandatory whistle-stop tour of Europe. I was her mandatory English fuck: she's the girl from that period of my life I afterwards thought of most frequently, but only because I once or twice adopted (and adapted) her name as a literary pseudonym. She probably had the pinkest nipples of them all: very pale Nordic pink and tasting of zinc ointment.

In the Wilderness

Having just completed a laborious volume on the World Wars and brought to a conclusion a decade-long phase of my life when my capacity for sentiment dwelt claustrophobically on scar- and medal-encrusted battlefield heroes, unceasing seepage of blood, statistics of fatality, and killing machines, it seems an appropriate time to reflect on my own solitary confrontation with imminent death.

I was born too late to be swept into the boredom of National Service. I have only once fired a gun, and that was a .410, puniest of farmyard weapons. If I have ever been shot at, my unknown assailant used a silencer, and missed. I have heard bombs explode in various cities. The first, in Oxford during my college-scarf-wearing years, loosened some mortar and cracked a brick on Magdalen Bridge. Another, a decade and a half later, wrecked a shoe shop in Salerno: an incident in a gang war which, at its climax, involved machine-gunnings on the highway outside Salerno at least twice a week. I was generally tucked up in bed when these deeds of derring-do were enacted, merely reading about them next day in *Il Mattino*. It was however not far from Salerno that my one real-life adventure took place.

The coastline of southern Italy is a thousand miles of petrol stations and polluted beaches but inland the countryside is the most cinerama-ishly picturesque in Europe: its neglect by the English and German school teachers who flock annually to Tuscany simply demonstrates how the main objective of holiday-makers is to go to the same place as everyone else. Immediately behind the coastal strip the mountains rise sternly and jaggedly in a complex dog-tooth pattern that stretches right across the peninsula. The Rockies or the Himalayas are vastly higher and huger, but compared to the Italian mountains they are shapeless and poorly arranged, with vast ill-proportioned screes and monotonous skylines that hide the most photogenic peaks. In Italy every mountain seems as if hand-picked for good looks, angled so as to be seen with maximum advantage, and given sufficient individuality to avoid a cumulative effect of repetition or monotony. The two great weaknesses of Italian upland countryside are the birds and the trees. There aren't any: or at least, there are a lot fewer than there might have been. Every Easter Saturday ten million red-blooded Italians form hunting parties and shoot every bird that presents itself. The hills rattle and reverberate all day with the musketry. Consequently even a sparrow is a rare sight in rural Italy. The natural timber has been destroyed too. There are picture-postcard tracts of ancient gnarled chestnut trees in the mountain valleys, but otherwise there is hardly a tree to be seen that is more than a dozen years old. Once they are thick enough to be rigid they are all cut down to make supports for the lemon trees cultivated on the coast. There is of course plenty of barely penetrable undergrowth: few birds, but many lizards, and processions of dung-beetles tumbling in files downhill with their precious pellets of turd, and, once in a blue moon, a glimpse of a poisonous snake, worm-coloured but as thick as a thigh. There are crickets, obviously, and butterflies, and a curious type of grasshopper which, when it leaps to safety spreads turquoise butterfly wings as if metamorphosized by the gods in its moment of panic.

The agriculture of this mountain zone was once much more prosperous. The retreat of our species can be traced in successive phases: here two or three courses of squared stones just below an exposed crest, the remains of a hilltop cottage abandoned perhaps three centuries ago, there on a hillside the roofless walls of a farm abandoned a hundred years ago, or lower down a still-roofed but rusty-padlocked dwelling in a valley. Occasionally one would meet peasants herding goats, gloomy men very unlike the village extroverts who figure in accounts of partisan warfare in 1944. A turn in the path might confront one with a view of the Mediterranean, shining like a vast diamond cupped between distant mountain sides: the Tyrrhenian Sea across which the Greeks came to this land in their oared galleys more than two and a half millennia ago, across which the British and the Americans came in their drab armada four years before my birth: a clean sea, when viewed in the perspective of history and mountain distances, not the septic broth resembling beer which I lived beside down on the coast.

On 4 June 1985 I hitchhiked to Acerno, which I had picked out some time earlier as a good starting point for a mountain walk. Acerno was not untypical of the small towns of the interior of Campania. It was approached by a single winding rising road enlivened by precipitous curves and panoramas reminiscent of Salvator Rosa. By the time one arrived there it felt as if one had completed the final stretch of the pilgrim path to Shangri-La, though in reality one was still near the edge of the coastal plain, and beyond the town the rugged landscape continued for at least another eighty kilometres. Entering Acerno one passed a couple of new but already neglected-looking villas, and small featureless apartment blocks with shops on the ground floor that suggested one of the less successful parts of Mexico. The older section of the town had a cathedral and other grand buildings, as if the place had once been more important; but in southern Italy buildings took on the appearance of decadence and economic decline as soon as they have been put up. The earthquake of five years previously had in any case laid half the town in ruins. Numbers of men, all looking like brothers and all aged either about 35 or about 65, loafed around the bars. Amongst the collapsing buildings, hollow façades and makeshift wooden props buttressing tottering walls, they had the appearance of troops occupying a front-line town, with greasy dark lounge suits by way of uniforms. Naked tawny mountain tops encircled the place.

I left the town along the road to Calabritto. This was an almost impassably pot-holed band of tarmac running along one side of a deep gorge and doubling back along the other side, coming out on a crag almost opposite the main square of Acerno but separated from the town by a steep ravine. Immediately below the roadway was some ragged grass where goats were feeding: above were naked rock faces and stunted awkwardly-angled trees. The whole gorge was so narrow that I have never once seen it with the sun shining into it, but only in the gloomiest shadow. Nevertheless, on that day there was a pleasant warm breeze and the company of fleecy white clouds in slow motion across the blue strip of sky visible above the enclosing cliffs.

A couple of kilometres from Acerno, shortly after skirting a farm with the inevitable barking dog, the road passed a queer watershed where two largish mountain torrents started from the ground within yards of each other and flowed in opposite directions, creating a pass into the next valley. I left the Calabritto road and followed a footpath through this pass, calculating that it would eventually lead me to the neighbourhood of Olevano, another hill town. Acerno was now on my right hand, but on the other side of the hill. After walking through a chestnut grove I found myself on the side of a long valley about two kilometres wide. It was difficult to be sure what was at the bottom of the valley because of the fall of the land: the opposite side was a succession of attractively wooded crests, quivering in the noon sunlight. One hill top seemed to have been cleared for cultivation, with only three or four pine trees left standing. It reminded me of English downland.

On my side of the valley it was open terrain: grass and a few bushes. There was a footpath worn on the turf just below the skyline on the side facing across the valley, with a sheer drop a little lower down, and I walked along this path, supposing it must lead somewhere. Over the previous few months I had developed the habit of striking out in whatever direction seemed most picturesque: sooner or later one would always come to a townlet or a road leading somewhere or other. On this particular day the track continued very distinctly for some hundreds of metres and then disappeared. This was not unusual. The footpaths in the mountains were in many cases centuries old, but with the contraction of the rural population they might not be visited for years. Torrential rains and, at this altitude, prolonged frosts from December to February, caused frequent minor landslips. In the warm weather plants grew unchecked. It was quite standard for footpaths to disappear into the middle of a bush, and to resume two or three boulders away to left or right. I thought this was what was happening here: I had forgotten that goats, whose only urgent business is to eat, often double back on their own tracks.

I was casting around for the continuation of the footpath, stumbling amongst boulders and rocky outcrops with a loose top-soil thinly covered with herbage, when I slipped and fell, slithering some distance downhill on my bottom towards the sheer drop down into the valley. I was only brought to a halt by a thin tree appearing providentially between my legs, just as used to happen in those cowboy serials they used to show at Saturday Morning Pictures. The tree, a juniper, grew horizontally from the point where the slope down into the valley became a precipice. I was at the very lip of an overhanging drop of something like fifteen metres. Behind me a loose shaley surface sloped up at 45 degrees towards a flatter area about four metres beyond my reach. There were no handholds, only a few tufts of leafy weed, which came away in my hands as I tugged at them.

Digging in my fingers I managed to scramble almost back up to the footpath, slid again, and was saved by another providentially placed tree. I tried again, reached even higher, slipped again, and was stopped from shooting over the precipice by the first tree. The pullover which I had been carrying knotted by its sleeves round my neck fell away out of sight below.

It was a warm sunny day. Glossy white clouds drifted overhead with ostentatious indifference to my plight, as if flaunting their denial of the Pathetic Fallacy of the French Romantics, who liked to think nature was disposed to echo human moods. Perhaps, I thought, it was just that I lacked Victor Hugo's world significance. I was very hot and very thirsty. The few birds that had survived the Easter massacre were rejoicing in the thickets below. I could hear a stream murmuring between concealing trees on the valley floor. It sounded like the music of Paradise, taunting me as I became thirstier and thirstier. The grassy meadow which had reminded me of English downland two kilometres away on the other side of the valley now seemed like a vision of the Elysian Fields, detailed in 3-D by the intense June light and seemingly almost within reach, yet separated from me by an uncrossable gulf. I imagined myself drinking from the fresh musical stream I could hear, stretching out luxuriously on the cool grassy slopes I could see, but all the while clinging to the dry dusty incline above the precipice with the sun beating down on my head. A dark glue-like scum began to form on my lips.

Be organized. I tried to think through every move as rationally as I could. Be calm. After my second attempt I gave up the idea of trying to regain the disappearing footpath above me. I had been saved by trees that were thin and insecurely rooted; I was heavy and my back-slidings towards the precipice had attained uncomfortable velocity. Statistical probability suggested that next time, even if I managed to grab a branch as I slipped I would nevertheless scoot out into the void with an uprooted tree in my hands. This time the cinematic model was *Tom and Jerry*, Tom the cat frantically treadmilling the air with a charred post or sawn-through pipe in his arms, hovering in space for a long moment only a yard from a third-floor ledge, before plummeting down like a runaway lift towards the open can of paint or vat of boiling pitch below. In my case, though, I lacked Tom's two-dimensional resilience. If I broke a leg in this wilderness, or otherwise injured myself in falling so that I could not move, I could count myself lucky if my bones were discovered while there was anything left about me sufficient for identification.

The alternative to scrambling upwards was to scramble downwards. To my left as I faced the Elysian Fields across the valley the cliff face had crumbled and sprouted shrubs and there seemed a possibility of sufficient toe and finger holds for a descent. I had been more than averagely cowardly about climbing trees as a boy, and I had no knowledge of mountaineering or rock-climbing techniques: but I did not have much choice. I managed to edge over towards the crumbled-away descent and found three or four easy holds. I succeeded finally in clambering down to within seven or eight metres of level ground. Then I ran out of finger-holds.

No doubt anyone with experience of mountaineering would have found further progress as easy as boarding a bus. For what seemed ages I considered my predicament. The sound of the stream hidden amongst the trees was nearer and louder and cooler and wetter. The sun continued to beat down on my head. I tried to decide whether to throw myself into a small spindly tree whose top was just below me, and count on it bending under my weight and lowering me gracefully to the ground, or whether to try and find more finger-holds in order to come down lower before jumping. Finally I made up my mind that it would be ridiculous to launch myself deliberately into space and then break a limb. I kept remembering my lack of daring when trying to climb trees as a child. I managed to descend a bit lower and was within two or three putative handgrips of a spot where I could stand when my feet slipped, and my hands were torn out of their holds. I fell: I remember only a sense of confusion as in any fall, a bang on my chest, surprise that I was still falling and that I bounced so easily.

I ended up in a huddle perhaps five or six metres below my last foothold, having rolled some way down the comparatively gentle slope at the foot of the cliff. My right foot looked as if it was somehow wearing my left shoe. It barely hurt but I supposed it was broken. For a moment I felt faint, as after even a much smaller fall, and lay waiting for the pain, but then I realized I was more or less all right. A circle of skin had been ripped off the tip of the big finger of my right hand as it had been torn away from the cliff face. I had great scratches on my hands and arms, on my left shoulder and over the area of my left kidney. My left knee and shin were bruised, and the front of my chest was beginning to swell: but nowhere was I bleeding. One of the scratches on my left arm has resulted in a permanent scar three inches long but it was never an open wound. There was a single round splash of bright blood on the rock beside me but I have no idea where it came from.

My first priority was to drink. I tried to stand and was startled at how promptly my right leg gave way under me. I was only able to move by dragging myself forward with my hands and slithering downhill through the undergrowth on my bottom. Beside the stream I found a barbed-wire fence. After drinking I had to decide which way to go: back along the fence in the general direction I had come from, or further into the unknown. In the direction of the Acerno-Calabritto road the fence ran uphill. For all I knew it might take on an impossibly steep gradient a little beyond the nearest curtain of trees. In that direction, moreover, I knew that the first human settlement I reached would be the farm I had skirted just before I had come to the watershed and the pass between the valleys. That would have been an hour's trek for someone with the use of both legs. For me it would be four or five hours. But what really decided me was the recollection of the barking dog: either an Alsatian or one of those gigantic, cream-coloured, completely fearless Abruzzi shepherds. It was likely that the farm people were off somewhere in the hills or in some remote corner of their scattered property. The dog was bound to go for me, and on my hands and knees I would be unable either to defend myself or run away. At that stage I was not thinking of life or death. My foot barely hurt and I was not sure it was even broken, but I was certain of being bitten if I managed to crawl up to the farm. In the other direction the barbed-wire fence sloped downhill. There was probably another farm there where the ground became flatter and perhaps the farmer would see me before his dog did. In any case it would probably be much closer. I headed downhill.

At first I hopped from fence-post to fence-post. Then I found a stick large enough to support me and hopped with that, but it soon broke. I used several sticks during my one-legged anabasis: most of them snapped under my weight after three or four strides, often causing me to fall quite heavily. It was like a variation of Russian roulette, trying to guess which step forward would drop me flat on my face. Though I was in the middle of a wood – mainly I think beech, lime, sycamore, ash and elder – there was no *mature* timber. There were plenty of saplings long and thick enough to support me but because they were still green and springy they were too tough to break with my bare hands. There were also quantities of dead branches lying amongst the undergrowth but I never saw one much thicker than my thumb, and at that thickness the dried-out wood quickly gave way under my weight. If I had been carrying a pen-knife I could have made a serviceable crutch out of a sapling in ten minutes: but I wasn't carrying a knife.

Part of the time I hopped, with or without a stick, falling frequently. At first I also tried crawling on my hands and knees but this was too painful. I don't know how small children manage but my knees could hardly bear it, especially on a hard stony surface. My foot could give me minimal support when standing but not enough to enable me to take a step. It seemed mainly the exterior swelling that ached, but even if the damage was only a sprain the foot was clearly useless for the time being. The most comfortable means of progress left to me was to slide forward on my bottom, facing backwards, pulling with my hands and pushing with my left foot.

Once in every ten minutes I could hear the neck bells of goats in the distance and after trying to guess how close they were I filled my lungs and yelled for help. *Ai-u-t-o!* I supposed that was what Italians shouted. I had never actually heard one calling for help. It was strange how feeble my shouting sounded in the open. The breeze which gently turned up the pale undersides of the leaves on the surrounding trees seemed to swallow up my voice completely. I felt I would have been inaudible a hundred metres away. The eventual clink from a neck bell came back too late to be any kind of response.

The track beside the fence became a surface wide enough for a tractor and began to rise, leaving the barbed-wire fence behind. As I hopped and slithered up the incline, the place where I had fallen began to come into view. While clinging above the cliff face I had thought that the impassable area was no more than a few metres wide. I now saw that I had been at the edge of a vast overhanging bluff which extended down one side of the valley for a couple of kilometres, a human-dwarfing rampart that seemed to belong to a virgin primeval continent, brooding and menacing even in the bright sunlight.

Little streams crossed the path every hundred yards or so and I could drink as much and as often as I wanted. Soon I was using the streams to punctuate my awkward progress: twenty yards of hopping and falling, eighty of slithering, then lap, slurp, splash. One might expect, if one had nothing else to sustain one but mountain streams, that at least they would taste like Perrier, but though cool and clean they were deficient in lime and rich in something like alum: at any rate, flat and insipid, and far below the standard of the landscape that provided the everlasting backdrop to the littleness of my now. To supplement the water there were occasional small patches of wild strawberries, some almost as large as a fingernail, but all virtually without flavour. Sometimes I would find as many as twenty in one patch. I suppose they contained fructose but obviously not very much. They were all I was to have to eat for three days.

By the time night fell I was beginning to think I might have made a mistake in my choice of direction. The path continued uphill. I tried to sleep, since it seemed inadvisable to move on a path which was too dark to see, but it was too cold for sleep. I would lie for twenty minutes, the flinty surface grinding into my hips and elbows, trying conscientiously to doze and then would have to continue my forward progress merely in order to stop shivering. I was at least a thousand feet above sea level and as it was still relatively early in the summer the drop in temperature at nightfall was considerable. It had not occurred to me, right after my fall, to scramble around looking for the pullover which had preceded me down the cliff.

About midnight – but really I had no idea what time precisely, for my pocket watch had stopped – I reached a point in the path where it rounded the side of a bluff and then began to descend. From this vantage point I expected to see lights from houses in the distance but there were none. I was now at least twelve hours away from the farm with the barking dog. I had no choice but to continue dragging myself forward along the lightless path.

It was a long night, and when dawn finally came it was still some hours before the sun rose high enough to provide warmth. I was supposed to be conducting an examination at the university from 9 a.m. onwards: it looked as if I was going to be late. I continued pulling myself along backwards with my hands, pushing with my one good foot, occasionally scrambling upright and hopping. When it became warmer I tried occasionally to doze, with my foot arranged where the sunlight was filtered through leaves, since the direct heat of the sun made it ache, but even with the wind in the trees as a lullaby I never quite managed to doze off. I tried once or twice to put my damaged foot on the ground, to test if the sprain was adjusting itself, but it would give way under me with a cautionary stab of pain. I was still not sure that it was broken, but the simple fact was I could not walk and I began to realize that if help was not fairly close I would not reach it before starvation brought me to a halt. The prospect of being killed, more or less, by a mere sprain was so demeaning as to seem all the more probable.

I was not especially worried by the idea of dying. I was thirty-eight. All the things I had wanted to do as a young man I had done, though none of them in the classic, consummate, triumphant way I had envisaged. Approximate achievement of ambition had brought me no sense of fulfilment but had made it clear that I would have felt little more content if I had achieved my programme in a more unambiguously perfect manner. I had a steady relationship with a girl I did not love enough. She would be sorrier to lose me than I would be to lose her, but I had long since given up hope of being really touched by anyone who wanted me, and did not think that death would cheat me of anything in the consuming passion line. I had a book, my fourth, nearing completion but knew that nobody would care enough about my ideas to add the finishing touches it needed and see to its publication: but my previous books had been failures professionally and commercially and this last one, because the best and most original so far, would probably founder in even greater apathy. Once I was dead none of this would matter. It was no such bad idea to leave the game while still one and a half points ahead. Death now meant that I would not die agonizingly and protractedly of cancer, or achieve brief public fame and be assassinated in front of the television cameras, or have a lonely and physically degraded old age.

I had only two worries. People in my predicament traditionally found God in their worst moments of danger and isolation and I did not want this to happen to me. I had been to a school where the chaplain was a former miner who had discovered God when lost and alone down a mineshaft. Just as he was giving up hope he had stumbled on the track of the underground railway used to move coal from the pit face to the bottom of the mineshaft. He had followed the rails to safety. This experience, he once claimed, had led to his taking Holy Orders. I had decided he was a charlatan some time before leaving this school. Now I found myself thinking not of the existence of God but of the humiliation of having to explain a conversion of this kind to my friends. As it turned out, God failed to manifest himself in my extremity. I was alone, totally alone, with the trees and the streams and the silent mountains but I never once felt the presence of God. However beautiful, however hostile and threatening to my mere existence, the woods and the mountains remained simply woods and mountains.

The second worry was my strength. Not that I was not strong enough, but that I was too strong. A diet of watery-tasting wild strawberries, cropped at the rate of two from this clump, five from that, three from the next one twenty minutes further on, was not going to sustain me indefinitely. The occasional ant or spider that crossed my path looked neither appetizing nor nourishing. Dragging myself along by my hands was heavy work, much more so than walking for all that it was so much slower. I knew that eventually I would be unable to drag myself any further: but I also calculated that from that point it would take at least a further six or seven days for me to die, and that I would be conscious almost till the end. I have never liked waiting and there was all the waiting I remembered in the prospect of that long, light-headed wait for death.

In other respects I was remarkably comfortable. My foot hurt only when the direct heat of the sun beat on the swelling. I also had a broken breast bone which did not subsequently show up in X-rays but which grated audibly when one pushed the midpoint of my chest. It continued to make a grating noise whenever I looked over my shoulder all through the ensuing summer but neither caused pain nor, now, interfered with the strenuous employment of my chest muscles involved in hauling myself backwards along the path. There was no risk of thirst, and I felt no hunger. Confronted by this challenge to its survival, my body was beginning to close down every function, every operation, that was not absolutely indispensable. My stomach did not rumble emptily or signal hunger pains. The digestion of the last meal I had before my accident slowed down so that it was to be more than a week before I had another bowel movement. My penis dwindled and retreated and lost the power of erection, which only came back slowly after six weeks, and my scrotum shrivelled up. My mind contracted. Mentally I felt perfectly alert, and while resting between bouts of dragging myself forward I would poke twigs inquisitively at passing creepy-crawlies, but though I kept telling myself that I could be using all this enforced quiet and solitude to do some hard, coherent thinking about whatever political, philosophical, historical, critical or aesthetic problem I ought to be working out, it was as if the tap supplying the energy for abstract thought had been turned off. I was not in pain, I was not preoccupied, I was able to focus my external senses, but my body was economizing on my powers of abstract ratiocination. Once the sun had risen I was warm, cheerful, neither anxious nor bored. It was like a picnic that had gone on too long, not disagreeable in itself but with the question of how one is going to get home always at the back of one's mind.

Shortly before nightfall the path joined a serviceable dirt roadway, wide enough for two vehicles to edge past each other. It was the sort of dirt track that one expects to join up with a main road a couple of corners further on. Near the junction was a capsized corrugated iron barn and a field of lush coarse grass. The latter seemed to offer a more comfortable bed than the flinty track of the previous night but I found it difficult to arrange myself.

A couple of elder bushes covered with sprays of white blossom gave the place the atmosphere of a long-abandoned garden. The wooded slopes where I had descended sprawled into a rolling woodland extending in the direction taken by the dirt roadway. The field where I lay was at the edge of a valley. On the far margin were mountains rising to bare peaks one after the other, like the backs of oxen. These became the merest crouching shadows in the dark. It was soon bitterly cold again. This time I lacked the energy to continue crawling and hopping through the night and lay on my fragrant but knotty couch, dozing fitfully, all through the hours of darkness. Once or twice I saw the headlights of cars about four kilometres away, on the other side of the valley and at a slightly higher level, but with the intervening ridges it would probably have taken a two hour walk to reach the road: and the whole point was I couldn't walk. After some hours I noticed a curious white light in a clump of trees about three hundred metres away. It was curious because it had a much whiter radiance than ordinary house lights and somehow suggested some sort of pre-war industrial lighting. I had not noticed any normal domestic lights in that direction earlier in the night. I would have to wait till daybreak before investigating in any case, as it would involve making a bee-line across broken terrain, away from the comparatively easy going of the dirt track. After a while however I realized that it was only the moon rising beyond the trees. This, incidentally, gives an idea of the contrast between my predicament at that moment and my customary style of life. I had gazed at the moon yearningly or speculatively hundreds of times in the past but only during the hours directly following the setting of the sun. I knew in theory that the moon sometimes rose later in the night but I had never seen this happen. I don't know why I hadn't observed it the previous night.

Dawn came eventually, and after another couple of hours a civilized degree of warmth returned. I still felt well, and there was still a plentiful supply of water, though now the insipid streams that trickled down between the trees were conducted under the roadway; but I felt much less capable of exertion, and made much slower progress. The road was descending in zig-zags, and in places I could slither through the undergrowth from one level down to where the road doubled back further down the hillside. Or perhaps that was what I had been doing the previous day: as my mental energy ran down, my perceptions made increasingly less impression on my memory, and the truth is that there were only a couple of occurrences which I am completely sure of pinning down to this, my third day in the wilderness.

The first occurrence was that, dragging myself round a bend, I saw a Fiat van parked further along the dirt track. On the far side of the track was a wooded descent, with a wooded ascent resuming right alongside the van: just a wooded hillside with a track running along its flank, and a van tidily parked on the track. I thought perhaps the driver was collecting mushrooms or looking for strayed goats. I shouted, but my voice seemed even more inadequate in the immense landscape than it had two days earlier. I dragged myself up to the van and found that it was rusting, the interior stripped. It had probably stood there for two or three years. I felt too lethargic to be disappointed: it proved at least that people *occasionally* came here.

The second occurrence was towards evening, when the road passed near a fair-sized mountain torrent just where it issued from a kind of miniature gorge. I crawled down to the water, on the principle that the larger the quantity of running water, the greater the likelihood of human settlement. Dragging myself along the bed of a stream was of course no more uncomfortable than dragging myself along a track, merely wetter. The gorge was small but spectacularly picturesque, with crags and tufts of vegetation arranged with almost Chinese elegance. I christened it the Caverns Measureless to Man, which indicates that as yet my mental activity had not completely ceased, though perhaps already moving in unwonted directions: of course the gorge was not really a cavern, and not so very big, but it had an authentically Kublai Khan-like atmosphere. And as I was slithering across the wet rocks of the torrent I heard voices.

I called out. There were three men a little further down the stream but when I shouted they promptly moved away and I had only the merest glimpse of them through the undergrowth. A minute later I saw a car moving off amongst the trees. I struggled on, and reached the junction of two quite broad though still unmetalled dirt roads. The tracks were scored out of a grey, almost cement-like sandstone, with short tough grass growing in streaks down the middle. A fair amount of rubbish was strewn along the verges: the Italian conception of a rural beauty spot is as a place where one goes to tip one's domestic trash. I was lying beside the road, feeling by now very much like the unfortunate traveller in the story of the Good Samaritan, when the men I had seen came by in their car. There were actually four of them, dressed in expensive casual gear, evidently from the city of Naples or Salerno, They had probably been fishing, though their appearance in the middle of nowhere at 6 p.m. on a working day may have betokened something more nefarious than merely poaching trout. The car passed me quite slowly and when I called for help the passenger next to the driver shouted back through the open window *Aspett* – wait. I waited, not being able to do much else, but they did not reappear.

I passed the third night on an uncomfortable bed of uprooted weeds, wrapped in dirty polythene sheeting. It was not much warmer than the previous nights. Before composing myself for sleep I wrote a good-bye note to my girl. Apart from the obvious reflection that I would have preferred to have been curled up in bed with her, I had not given her a lot of thought, but the last thing I could do for her now was to tell her that at least I had been thinking about her at the end.

In the morning, as I was hopping forward with the last of my rotten sticks, a peasant in a battered pale-blue Fiat passed me going in the direction of the Caverns Measureless to Man. I waved, and just after he passed me he slowed down and looked back, as if wondering whether I wanted a lift. He evidently decided I was heading in the opposite direction – of course he could not see that I was injured – because a moment later he accelerated and disappeared round a bend. It occurred to me that one of the dirt roads that joined up just after the Caverns probably led to a short-cut across the mountains.

On that day I made only about five hundred metres' progress. I had to rest much more frequently, and for longer periods. I passed an abandoned farm, and shortly afterwards encountered half a dozen cows grazing in the roadway. Again I had a moment of enervated hope: there would be a cow-herd. But there wasn't. The presence of the cows merely indicated that this was the kind of place people did *not* usually come to: otherwise it would have been unsafe to leave the cows unattended.

It crossed my mind that I could refresh myself by drinking directly from the largest cow's udders, but I knew nothing about milking cows, and thought that, even if I managed to manoeuvre myself under the beast, I would only manage to get shat on, or trodden on, and perhaps break a few more bones.

The dirt road ran parallel to, and about four metres from, a quite considerable river, about as broad as the Thames at Oxford but much faster, and with dense thickets growing down to the banks on either side. I think it must have been the Tusciano, and the streams I had drunk from previously must have flowed into it, for it had the same insipid taste. There was a constant swish and rumble from the river that made me think there was traffic passing only a little way ahead, but however much I strained my ears I could hear no sound of car horns or voices and I knew that if there was a road ahead it would be another two or three kilometres further on: and I was now simply too weak to drag myself that far.

I still felt well: simply incapable of effort. All the heroic narratives I had read of wounded soldiers dragging themselves along for days, in spite of gaping wounds and inconceivable pain, failed to inspire me with their example. Clearly I lacked the resilience and sheer animal will of the more memorable wounded heroes. Perhaps I didn't care enough about staying alive. Not life, not death, but the several days, probably disagreeable, that must elapse in my passage from one to the other, were the only subject of my foreboding. Having seen two cars already I thought I was as likely to be found where I was as two hundred metres further up the track, and I resolved to make myself comfortable, and at least be warm at night while I waited for rescue or release. A particularly lush roadside crop of cardboard and polythene bags suggested a good place to stop. I found an empty lemonade bottle. The river was close to the road but about a metre lower down and in my weakness I found this few feet of boulders and tree roots awkward to negotiate. One last effort would enable me at least to fill the bottle to supply me for some hours longer. I was rinsing this bottle, my feet up at road level, my face almost in the river, when a red pick-up truck passed me, heading in the direction of the Caverns Measureless to Man. The driver of course could not see me.

I noticed that the pick-up truck was loaded with bricks and rubble. It was probably the local builder on a fly-tipping expedition. I crawled back up to the road to wait for his return.

At about mid-day on 7 June the red pick-up came back down the dirt track.

And stopped.

And here I am.

(Written c. 1993)

The Last Days of Shakespeare

Keats died at 25: Shakespeare may have been 26 or 27 when he wrote the first of his surviving works. There are many cases of creative artists who, perhaps accumulating experience while in pursuit of false beginnings, make a slow start with their lives' work. Shakespeare's last known composition was written at the age of 48 or 49, at least three years before his death. He had apparently decided to abandon the London theatre world, but he is not known to have been in poor health, and his death was the result of a brief illness, brought on, according to legend, by an excess of socializing during a visit to London. His ceasing to write at 49 is much more remarkable than the slightly delayed commencement of his career as an author. It has been remarked that 'capacity for constant growth is among the surest indications of major creative power.' One should not think in this context of the etiolated second half of E. M. Forster's life but rather of Leonardo, Michelangelo, Titian, Milton, Goethe, Turner, Hugo, Tolstoy, Hardy: and yet during his productive years Shakespeare had been at least as prolific as any one of these. One might even suppose that the habit of dove-tailing themes, marshalling the poetry into verse, setting the magic down on paper, would have become necessary to him, as an addictive delight and as an indispensable means of organizing his solitary hours.

With the sudden termination of his writing career in view, one tends to see a coherent pattern in Shakespeare's dramas: the sound and fury of the history plays giving way to the agonized power of the great tragedies giving way to the ambivalence and cynicism of the problem plays (*Troilus and Cressida, Measure for Measure*) and this giving way in turn to the relaxed and reconciliatory mood of the final romances. What indeed should Shakespeare have written after *The Tempest?* – though it turns out that, a couple of years later, he collaborated with Fletcher on the confusing and somewhat objectless *Henry VIII*. The mere fact that Shakespeare then withdrew to Stratford proves that, after *Henry VIII*, he did not have it in him –

did not find the energy or the desire or the need – to write another play. But he was not simply a writer of plays, he had written narrative poems and sonnets in his time, was a master of prose as well as verse, and did not need to frequent London theatres if he was not proposing to write for the theatre. His transfer to Stratford evidently meant the end (or suspension) of his career as a dramatist: it did not necessarily mean a decision to stop writing.

Of course there is a version of Shakespeare which shows him as a long-headed businessman who took to writing plays merely to make money, and who ceased writing when he had made enough. This version of Shakespeare is little more than an elaboration of a literary agent's paradox ('If you can write better than Shakespeare, young man, you're probably smart enough to handle publishers yourself.') If Shakespeare had only been interested in the bread he could have made more – and with less uncertainty – as a lawyer or a businessman. The assumption that he acknowledged that even poets need to eat does not prove that he had no higher idea of poetry than the manager of a chop-house. There are many portrayals of the excesses of poetic imagination in his plays (Hotspur and Owen Glendower in *Henry IV* Part I for example, but perhaps even the protagonists of *Hamlet* and *Othello*) but however cynical his vision, he never fell back on the easy trick of reducing things to their lowest common denominator. His range of sympathy demands a similar effort of sympathy from us. Shakespeare the long-headed businessman may have co-existed with Shakespeare the author of *Hamlet*, but the one is not an adequate explanation of the other. And if, after all, Shakespeare's career as an author had no other guiding principle than desire for money, why should he have felt he had earned enough by the age of 49 when he was at the peak of his capacity to earn more?

It seems most likely that he retired to Stratford, not to escape from his career as a writer, but simply to put an end to his career as a writer for the theatre, a genre, after all, of no particular reputation or tradition. It seems most likely that he retired, not from writing, but in order to write: to write a work worthy of powers which he himself must have recognized as altogether exceptional.

The sonnet was essentially a minor genre, and one he had already explored. A long, philosophical poem without plot or action could never have been to his taste: 'The Growth of the Poet's Mind' might perhaps have been a theme worthy of Shakespeare but it belongs essentially to the *Zeitgeist* of Wordsworth's generation, two hundred years later. He may have thought of writing an epic: he would have known Samuel Daniel's *Civil Wars* of 1595 and Michael Drayton's *Mortimeriados* of 1596, and, less depressing and discouraging models, Spenser's *Faerie Queene* of 1590, Harrington's translation of *Orlando Furioso* and Chapman's translation of the *Iliad*. The capacity of epic poetry to attract would-be epic poets in this period is indicated by Toinet's *Quelques Recherches autour des Poèmes Héroïques-Épiques Français du Dix-Septième Siècle*. And yet how backward-looking the whole business of writing epic poems seems in retrospect. Milton's triumphant gesture at epic killed the genre for all practical purposes in English literature: his example was to inspire many imitators but none with the capacity to conceive and sustain such a literary effort, at the level required, and the achievement of *Paradise Lost* simply emphasizes the degree to which it was a literary dead end. Later Pope and Coleridge planned epic poems with which they found themselves incapable of proceeding. Perhaps Shakespeare did too: but he would have been at least as sensitive as Pope and Coleridge to the essential anachronism and irrelevance of such a project.

Epic poetry belonged to the past: the genre which was soon to replace drama as the focus of most European literatures was already taking shape in Shakespeare's time: the novel. *Gargantua and Pantagruel* belongs, indeed, to the generation before Shakespeare's birth: *Don Quixote* was published when Shakespeare was 41, and is approximately contemporary with *Othello*. *Pilgrim's Progress* was not to appear till 1678: it is slightly odd that the English should make such a slow beginning with an international genre which they were to dominate in the eighteenth and nineteenth centuries, and slightly humiliating that *Pilgrim's Progress*, England's first classic novel, is, in narrative concept and handling, markedly less sophisticated than the work of Cervantes almost three-quarters of a century earlier. The history of the novel would certainly look very different if Shakespeare were known to have written one.

One recalls that Sir Walter Scott – also a comparatively late starter as a writer –moved from poetry to the novel at the age of 43, and even with his much lesser talent shifted the whole genre into a new direction.

Looking at Shakespeare's plays, one is struck by how well-equipped he was to become a novelist. Though nearly all his plots were taken from older writers one may scarcely attribute this to lack of inventive faculty, and indeed, one cannot fail to notice his virtuosity in altering existing plots (as in *Measure for Measure*, where in the original story Isabella agrees to sleep with Angelo as the price of her brother's life, and is then presented with her brother's decapitated head) or in bringing out implications of the narrative and giving them an entirely new significance. Friedrich Schlegel acknowledged Shakespeare's contribution to the evolution of narrative when he noted, 'Ariosto, Cervantes and Shakespeare have each in different ways *poeticized* the *Novelle*.' Shakespeare was also a master of idiomatic prose: in fact, given the excellence of his prose it is odd that no work entirely in prose survives from his pen, though indeed *The Merry Wives of Windsor* and *Much Ado About Nothing* contain considerably more prose than verse.

It may be argued of course that it is one thing to write dramatic dialogue, quite another to write a sustained, architecturally structured, narrative. But the prose of Shakespeare's plays is often something quite different – and technically more accomplished – than what one normally understands by dramatic dialogue. In *Henry V* for example, the King discusses the limits of his moral responsibility in prose:

> So, if a son that is by his father sent about merchandise do sinfully miscarry upon the sea, the imputation of his wickedness, by your rule, should be imposed upon his father that sent him; or if a servant, under his master's command transporting a sum of money, be assailed by robbers and die in many irreconcil'd iniquities, you may call the business of the master the author of the servant's damnation. But this is not so: the King is not bound to answer the particular endings of his soldiers, the father of his son, nor the master of his servant; for they purpose not their death when they purpose their services. (Act IV sc.1.)

This is not dramatic dialogue: it is the prose of philosophical argument, though few sermons or theological texts of the period are as clear and straightforward. In *Hamlet* too the Prince speaks in prose when instructing the players:

> an excellent play, well digested in the scenes, set down with as much modesty as cunning. I remember one said there were not sallets in the lines to make the matter savoury, nor no matter in the phrase that might indict the author of affectation; but called it an honest method, as wholesome as sweet, and by very much more handsome than fine.
>
> (Act II sc. 2.)

This, and Hamlet's subsequent advice to the Players in Act III scene 2, belongs as much to the history of critical discourse as to the tradition of stage dialogue. Hamlet's speech to Rosencrantz and Guildenstern concerning his melancholy is also not dramatic in the narrower sense:

> What a piece of work is a man! How noble in reason! how infinite in faculty! in form, in moving, how express and admirable! in action how like an angel! in apprehension how like a god! the beauty of the world! the paragon of animals! And yet, to me, what is this quintessence of dust?
>
> (Act II sc. 2.)

This, surely, is a prose poem, and a clearer, more elegant example of the genre than any written by Lyly or his disciples at the time of Shakespeare's youth. And later in the play we find:

> Alas! poor Yorick. I knew him, Horatio; a fellow of infinite jest, of most excellent fancy; he hath borne me on his back a thousand times; and now, how abhorred in my imagination it is! my gorge rises at it. Here hung those lips I have kissed I know not how oft. Where be your gibes now? your gambols? your songs? your flashes of merriment, that were wont to set the table in a roar? Not one now, to mock your own grinning? quite chapfallen? Now get you to my lady's chamber, and tell her, let her paint an inch thick, to this favour she must come; make her laugh at that. (Act V sc.1.)

This surely is more than a demonstration that Shakespeare could pen a bravura passage as well in prose as in verse: in its expository technique and sensitivity to the sequencing of mental processes it looks forward to James Joyce.

Of course Shakespeare might have been adept in almost all varieties of prose, without being particularly proficient in narrative. There is relatively little verbal narrative in his plays, in which, in contrast to the plays of Racine, most of the important action takes place on-stage. And such formal narrative as there is is mostly in verse. But both in verse and prose Shakespeare showed his skill in pace, timing and climax. His excellence may be brought out by quoting a passage written by one of his contemporaries: a striking piece of writing that in many respects is typical and characteristic of the English prose of Shakespeare's time:

> In this distress it pleased God to send us rain in such plenty, as that we were well watered, and in good comfort to return. But after we came near unto the sun, our dried penguins began to corrupt, and there bred in them a most loathsome and ugly worm of an inch long. This worm did so mightily increase, and devour our victuals, that there was in reason no hope how we should avoid famine, but be devoured of these wicked creatures: there was nothing that they did not devour, only iron excepted: our clothes, boots, shoes, hats, shirts, stockings: and for the ship they did so eat the timbers, as that we greatly feared they would undo us, by gnawing through the ship's side. Great was the care and diligence of our captain, master, and company to consume these vermin, but the more we laboured to kill them, the more they increased; so that at the last we could not sleep for them, but they would eat our flesh, and bite like mosquitoes. In this woeful case, after we had passed the equinoctial toward the north, our men began to fall sick of such a monstrous disease, as I think the like was never heard of: for in their ankles it began to swell; from thence in two days it would be in their breasts, so that they could not draw their breath, and then fell into their cods; and

their cods and yards did swell most grievously, and most dreadfully to behold, so that they could neither stand, lie, nor go. Divers grew raging mad, and some died in most loathsome and furious pain. It were incredible to write our misery as it was: there was no man in perfect health, but the captain and one boy. To be short, all our men died, except 16, of which there were but 5 able to move.

This may be contrasted with the former Mistress Quickly's account of the death of Falstaff in *Henry V*:

'a parted ev'n just between twelve and one, ev'n at the turning o' th' tide; for after I saw him fumble with the sheets, and play with flowers, and smile upon his fingers' ends, I knew there was but one way; for his nose was sharp as a pen, and 'a babbl'd of green fields. 'How now, Sir John!' quoth I 'What, man, be o' good cheer'. So 'a cried out, 'God, God, God!' three or four times. Now I, to comfort him, bid him 'a should not think of God; I hop'd there was no need to trouble himself with any such thoughts yet. So 'a bade me lay more clothes on his feet; I put my hand into the bed and felt them, and they were as cold as any stone; then I felt to his knees, and so upward and upward, and all was as cold as any stone.
    (Act II sc. 3.)

The first passage achieves its effect by its total artlessness: the horrific details are inventoried, not with a view to how they will affect the reader, but simply because they have stamped themselves upon the memory: there is no attempt to heighten the effect by ordering or arrangement, by highlighting or building up to a climax: the simile of the worms biting 'like mosquitoes', which more than anything else brings the awfulness of this experience home to the reader, owes its force and impact mainly to the fact that it is so triumphantly and unself-consciously commonplace and anticlimactic. By comparison the description of the death of Falstaff is all art: the garrulous confusion of the narrator is only a pretence: in the reality everything is organized, timed for maximum effect and bent towards the climax, where the former Mistress Quickly reaches under the bed clothes and follows the remorseless onset of mortality from feet to knees 'and so upward and upward'. To write a novel would simply be to write like this on a larger scale.

Every writer's work is in a sense a work in progress, left uncompleted at his death, so that posterity is left to judge the direction it was taking from the point it had reached at the moment of the author's ceasing to write. This is true even of authors who outlive their talent; but it seems very unlikely that Shakespeare at 50 or 51 had outlived his talent. He retired to Stratford for a purpose, and he was interrupted in that purpose. The whereabouts of the manuscript he was working on at Stratford is of course a mystery. The literary undergrowth of the seventeenth century is rich in mysteriously lost manuscripts that come miraculously to light, but Shakespeare's manuscript was simply, irretrievably lost, disposed of, dispersed or destroyed without hope of recovery. One cannot discount the possibility that its destruction, deliberate or accidental, was in some way linked to the author's death. He died, apparently on his 52nd birthday, the greatest dramatist that had ever lived. What more he might have become, had he been given another dozen years, we will never know: but surely we can speculate.

Note

The quotation in the first paragraph is from an essay on Henry Moore by Sir John Rothenstein. Marie Joseph Raymond Toinet's *Quelques Recherches autour des Poèmes Héroïques-Épiques Français du Dix-Septième Siècle* was published in two volumes in 1899 and 1907: his discussion covers 115 epic poems, of which 32 have Biblical subjects. The quotation from Friedrich Schlegel is from his *Literary Notebooks 1797-1801*, note 1154. The passage of Elizabethan prose quoted for the purpose of comparison with Shakespeare is from Hakluyt's *The Last Voyage of Thomas Cavendish*.

Tess and Thomas Hardy

Virginia Woolf's father, Leslie Stephen, editor of *The Cornhill Magazine*, told Hardy, 'Remember the country parson's daughters. I have always to remember them!' But as the author of *Thomas Hardy's Minor Novels* has pointed out, of the English novelists of the Nineteenth Century it was Hardy who engaged most seriously with the problem of writing about sex *as sex*. In 1879 he was even offered membership of the Rabelais Club, 'as being the most virile writer of works of imagination then in London.' (Henry James had also been nominated, but was rejected.) A twenty-first-century reader will probably find Hardy's acknowledgement of the sexual side of human relationships in *Tess of the D'Urbervilles* and *Jude the Obscure* less striking than his coy allusiveness with regard to specific instances of physical intimacy, but no other main-stream English writer of Hardy's era published anything as erotically suggestive as Elfride Swancourt's taking off her dress (in *A Pair of Blue Eyes*) or Captain de Stancey's watching Paula Power through a spy hole as she goes through her gymnastic exercises with an 'absolute abandonment to every muscular whim,' (in *A Laodicean*). This aspect of Hardy's work was the subject of Leonard Burke's Ph.D thesis. He had been working on it for seven years. His problem – apart from the accidie, alienation, angst, anguish, anomie, apathy and whatever that is inseparable from the status of doctoral student – was that it was difficult to find anything new to say on the two key texts in the Hardy canon, *Tess of the D'Urbervilles* and *Jude the Obscure*. So much had already been written on these two books that his mind was paralysed merely by contemplating the task of sifting through all the various critiques and discovering a critical viewpoint which he could call his own and which would be consistent with his analysis of Hardy's earlier, minor novels.

Leonard Burke was, consequently, oppressed by a familiar combination of depression, confusion and uncertainty when he boarded a No.73 bus one morning, en route for the British Library. He found himself sitting next to a young girl who was reading a book that she had spread over her black-stockinged knees. He glanced idly at the text. The familiar names Alec and Angel and Tess seemed to spring at him from the page. He had a second look. It was a strikingly banal analysis of *Tess of the D'Urbervilles*, evidently aimed at the A-level and first year undergraduate market.

'You're doing *Tess of the D'Urbervilles* for A-level,' he announced: as this was likely to be the only intellectual discovery he would make that day he was reluctant to keep it to himself.

The girl looked up with a delighted grin. She was not only very young, but very pretty. Hardy would probably have described her as 'an exceptional young maiden who glowed amid the dullness like a single bright-red poppy in a field of brown stubble.' He would have probably gone on to say, 'Her face was exceedingly attractive, through artistically less perfect than her figure, which approached unusually near to the standard of faultlessness,' but Leonard could not confirm this comparison. The girl's face was certainly exceedingly attractive, and he detected 'small, tight, apple-like convexities' (as Hardy phrases it in *Jude the Obscure*), a change of direction in the hang of her necktie, between the lapels of her school blazer – yes, she was wearing a school blazer! – but he was going to remain unable to assess the rest of her figure till she stood up to get off the bus and leave his life for ever.

'Oh, have you read it?' she asked.

'Several times,' he said modestly. 'Do you like it?'

'In parts. The men are boring.'

'Well, they always say Alec and Angel are both cardboard characters. And in a sense it's true. George Eliot's male characters, always excepting Will Ladislaw in *Middlemarch*, and lots of the minor characters in Dickens always seem to be much more interesting than the situation they occupy in the novels. It doesn't necessarily help the plot but you keep thinking of them as interesting people you might meet in real life. Hardy's characters are never quite like that. Often they're ludicrously unconvincing, in fact. You must have known men who are good-looking, charming, successful with everything they did, who somehow had nothing to them after the first three minutes. Like Alec. If Alec had been a poet, or a political idealist, he might have been a more interesting literary characterization but he wouldn't have been Alec D'Urberville.'

The girl laughed again.

'And what about Angel Clare?'

'He's a bit more difficult. You haven't read *A Pair of Blue Eyes*? You ought to if you have time. It was published nearly twenty years before *Tess* but a lot of its themes are very similar. It's got a character like Angel Clare, called Harry Knight, who seems terrified by the idea of his girl having once placed herself in a compromising situation.'

'Well I've got A-levels in five weeks, so ....'

'So you're staying in every evening and all the week-ends reading and re-reading that wretched A-level primer you have in your hand.'

'Not exactly! I still go out some evenings.'

'How about tomorrow?'

She didn't hesitate: 'If you like,' she said, with a laugh almost of relief.

They arranged to meet at the *Robinson Crusoe*, in Green Lanes. (After seven years unconsummated research at least he had learnt that it was best to choose a rendezvous that was as close as possible to where one lived.)

Her stop came.

'What's your name?' he asked as he stood up to let her out of her seat.

She laughed once more.

'You won't believe this. It's Tess. Really and truly. Tess Mullett. And yours?'

He had a last good look at her as she moved down the aisle to get off the bus. She was not really the Tess type, not really the Junoesque dairy-maid of Hardy's novel: more Elfride Swancourt, for despite those 'small, tight, apple-like convexities' between the lapels of her blazer she was slimly built. Good legs, slender-knee'd and oval-calved: whereas Tess Durbeyfield had probably had fat legs, which wouldn't have shown under the long dresses of those times.

Wow! He thought. This brief encounter had left him effervescing with excitement and anticipation. She hadn't really said anything very interesting – at eighteen years of age she probably didn't have anything interesting to say – but she had been so pretty! And she seemed to like him! He recalled that Hardy had had a habit of becoming obsessed with young beauties whom had met briefly or glimpsed on buses, as his Journal shows:

May 29. That girl on the omnibus had one of those faces of marvellous beauty which are seen casually in the streets but never among one's friends. It was perfect in its softened classicality – a Greek face translated into English. Moreover, she was fair, and her hair pale chestnut. Where do these women come from? Who marries them? Who knows them?

July 9. Love lives on propinquity, but dies of contact.

July 23. Of the people I have met this summer, the lady whose mouth recalls more fully than any other beauty's the Elizabethan metaphor 'Her lips are roses full of snow' (or is it Lodge's?) is Mrs. Hamo Thorneycroft – whom I talked to at Gosse's dinner.

Leonard had sometimes thought that Hardy was much more successful – because much more interested? – in his description of the first meetings of his lovers than in their subsequent relationships. This is most obvious in the *Well-Beloved* where Jocelyn Pierston, at twenty year intervals, meets and falls in love with mother, daughter and grand-daughter, and this fickleness is apparently regarded as natural and normal by the women themselves, for as one of them confesses:

> I get tired of my lovers as soon as I get to know them well. What I see in one young man for a while soon leaves him and goes into another yonder, and I follow, and then what I admire fades out of him and springs up somewhere else; and so I follow on, and never fix to one.

But perhaps Hardy was right: beginnings were always best, because least adulterated by complications of personality and circumstance.

Somewhat to Leonard's surprise the real life Tess turned up for their date. (He had already observed that modern misses lacked the painful scrupulosity of a Tess Durbeyfield or a Sue Bridehead, at least with regard to keeping appointments.) She had changed into pink jeans and a T-shirt, and a nylon windcheater, which she slipped off in the pub, revealing slender teenage arms and the fact that her

bra was adjusted too high. After a lager and lime he felt bold enough
to confess his guilty secret: that he was more or less a professional
expert on Thomas Hardy, by virtue of his almost(?) completed doctoral
dissertation. Tess (looking prettier by the minute) expressed herself
positively thrilled by this discovery and was almost vehement in her
insistence on being permitted to view his inchoate masterpiece. 'I
mean, it could help me a lot with my A-level, couldn't it?'

His flat of course was nearby. He had even, with desperate
optimism, tidied it before leaving for the pub. The thesis, in various
drafts, was stacked with ostentatious neatness in three piles on the
sideboard, flanked by boxes of file cards.

'So there it is.'

Tess looked at it. She had evidently not seen an uncompleted
Ph.D thesis before. She touched it hesitantly, as if unsure whether it
was real, tentatively moved around one or two pages at the top of
the piles.

'I wish I had time to read it,' she said. 'You'll have to tell me
what's in it.'

They opened a couple of cans of lager and he began to explain
the central problem of *Tess of the D'Urbervilles*. Though the novel is
subtitled 'A Pure Woman' it seems that there was a degree of willing
participation in her original relationship with Alec D'Urberville. Even
if she was at the outset of their physical connection, literally raped –
and it's not at all clear that she was – she maintained some sort of
relationship with him, and when leaving him explained, 'My eyes
were dazed by you a little, and that was all.'

'Well, she was seduced,' said the latter-day Tess, curled up in
the corner of the sofa, can of lager in one hand.

'But that's the point. That's where Victorian convention
prevented Hardy even thinking straight about what happens in such
situations. What does seduction consist of? If rape is forcing someone
to have sex when she doesn't want to, is seduction *persuading* someone
to want to have sex when really she doesn't want to? If so, how do
you distinguish between what a girl has been persuaded she wants,
and what she really wants? Theoretically, of course, it might go in
stages. For example, if I kissed you – '

'I don't mind,' said Tess, leaning sideways to place her can of lager on the floor, out of the way.

He moved up beside her on the sofa. It was like in *A Pair of Blue Eyes* – 'before she suspected it his arm was round her waist, and the two sets of curls intermingled' – except that neither of them had curly hair: nor did Leonard feel either 'a momentary regret that his kiss should be spoilt by her confused receipt of it' or a 'pleasant perception that her awkwardness was her charm.' The fact was that Tess was alarmingly well-versed in what Hardy calls 'the art of tendering feminine lips for these amatory salutes': in other words she kissed as if competing in the heats of an inter-schools Snogging Championship. Leonard remembered the bit in *Desperate Remedies* where Cytherea Aldclyffe says after kissing Cytherea Graye, 'a minute ago and you seemed to me like a fresh spring meadow – now you seem a dusty highway,' but it occurred to him it might be more diplomatic not to mention dusty highways to Tess; which was a pity, as he had suddenly forgotten what else it was he had been about to say. And perhaps, on balance, Tess was more interested in what he had been saying: she had him in such a tight head-lock he could not manoeuvre himself into a more promising position, and she volunteered no indication that she was aware of the possibilities sex offered apart from reciprocatory gargling. He decided to continue his discourse.

'Well, supposing a girl was kissed, she might think she didn't mind being kissed, but didn't really want any more than that, but then, having gone so far, and feeling kind of warm and positive about the guy who's been kissing her, if he says to her, take your blouse off –'

'I don't mind.' Tess started undoing buttons.

He sat and watched her.

'There you are. You've got as far as getting my blouse off.'

'Do you want me to go on?'

'Yes, I really like the way you explain things. You don't know all about History and Sociology too, do you?'

'No.'

'Pity.'

He kissed her again, but when he tried to make her lie down on the sofa, she pushed him away.

'No, go on explaining.'

'Well, like I was saying, it might sort of go in stages. They've kissed, and then she's taken her blouse off, and then, once she's taken her blouse off, it's kind of easier psychologically to agree to take her bra off too.'

'This is better than strip poker,' said Tess.

She unfastened her bra and draped it over the back of a chair. Some modern writers make a habit of writing pen-portraits of naked breasts but Hardy tended to limit himself to phrases like 'magnificent resources in face and bosom', as in the case of Cytherea Graye in *Desperate Remedies*. Tess Mullet's resources were middle-sized, one palm sized, rather than magnificent, though no doubt perfectly classical in their position on chest, incipient droop and bulls-eye placing of nipples etc. – modest mangoes rather than magnificent melons.

'Well, as you see,' said Leonard. 'The point –'

'I might as well take everything else off,' said Tess, interrupting him. 'You take something off too. Where's your bedroom?'

For the next forty minutes they held an impromptu theatre workshop, complete with sound effects, on the theme of Alec D'Urberville bonks Tess Durbeyfield.

Afterwards she remarked, 'It's very physical isn't it?'

Leonard, for whom amassing foot-notes had become second nature, asked: 'How many men have you slept with before?'

'Oh God, you're not going to turn against me like Angel Clare because I'm not quite a virgin?'

'Of course not. I just kind of wondered.'

'Go on, admit it. The fact that I may have slept with the last two of my boyfriends, and so understand something about my own sexuality frightens you.'

'No. The whole business of Angel Clare being afraid of Tess's sexuality in the *Tess of the D'Urbervilles* and Harry Knight of Elfride Swancourt's in *A Pair of Blue Eyes* seems to me to have been totally misinterpreted. It's a good instance of how *A Pair of Blue Eyes* helps us understand *Tess of the D'Urbervilles*. Elfride goes to London to be with Stephen Smith but she changes her mind and doesn't sleep with him. Harry Knight, deeply conventional beneath his enlightened, politically Radical exterior, rejects Elfride not because he is afraid of her sexual experience, because he doesn't really know she has any, but because he cannot accept her defiance of a standard Victorian convention that even if nothing takes place between them, an unmarried woman's reputation is irretrievably compromised if she absents herself overnight from the parental home to meet her lover in secret. She never presented as being sexual in the normal sense, but innocent and naïve, and, when she has taken her underwear to make the rope with which she rescues Harry Knight on the cliff, she "seemed as small as an infant." '

'But I'm not very big, either' said Tess. 'Perhaps Hardy thought thin women were sexy.'

Well, Sue Bridehead in *Jude the Obscure* is also thin, more intellectual than physical. But *Tess of the D'Urbervilles* doesn't come across as thin at all.'

The latter-day Tess rolled over on to her tummy, presenting him with a view of peach-like buttocks, her least skinny bit, and making him wonder why they were discussing thin women.

'Hmm. I see I'll have to read *A Pair of Blue Eyes* after all,' she said.

'You'll find it much more ambiguous, in a way than *Tess of the D'Urbervilles*. Hardy hints that Elfride Swancourt has a kind of hereditary 'proneness to inconstancy' but elsewhere he suggests that the key to the tragedy is not Elfride's weakness but that of her lovers, but it all seems a little random and incoherent, and the tragedy is never perceived to be inevitable. In both *Tess of the D'Urbervilles* and *Jude the Obscure* on the other hand there seems to be a kind of fearful symmetry, a kind of fated harmony, almost a synchronization, of bad luck, momentary lapses of judgement, the irrevocableness of mistakes once committed, and –'

Tess cut him off in mid-sentence with a kiss. After a minute of necking, elbowing, fingering, sighing, and knee-between-thighing she announced, 'Oh goodie –' and Nature with a capital N once again took its course to the rhythm of groaning bed-springs.

During the course of proceedings she distracted him with

intelligent questions like 'Do breasts taste of anything in particular?' and 'Do you always kiss girls' armpits?'

When they were dressing, Leonard asked:

'What about tomorrow night?'

Tess frowned.

'Well, it's a bit like in Hardy, where the men always seem to look on the women merely as adjuncts to their own personalities, and in fact the essence of the women's tragic predicament is that their men are never prepared to see them as they really are. Thanks to you I feel reasonably confident as regards my English A-level, but you see, I want to read Law at University, so my English grade is the least important of the three.'

'But –'

'I mean Hardy's totally interesting and all that. Our teacher says it happens again and again in his novels that people change their minds, or some incident intervenes, so that they never settle down comfortably together in a stable relationship. It's as if, though he married twice, Hardy never really believe in relationships. Something was always happening to break them up. That's really true to life, isn't it?' She met his eyes with sudden determination. 'Anyway the long and the short of it is, I still need someone to help me with my Sociology and History revision.'

Doris Lessing's 'One off the Short List' and Leo Bellingham's 'In for the Kill.'

The practice of comparing works by different unrelated writers on ostensibly similar themes is open to fairly obvious objections, but will often serve to highlight characteristic peculiarities in the different way the subject is handled. Perhaps this will be especially so when the two writers are of different sexes and the common theme is an aspect of what used to be called the battle of sexes.[1]

Doris Lessing's 'One off the Short List' and Leo Bellingham's 'In for the Kill' are both short stories about a journalist who forces sex on a woman who does not want him and afterwards makes the humiliating discovery that he and his sexual attentions are of minimal importance in the woman's scheme of things.[2] Though the subject is what Germaine Greer has characterised as 'petty rape',[3] in both stories the women, without stooping to conscious retaliation, affirm their moral and intellectual superiority over a cocksure and intellectually manipulative male. Summarized briefly in these terms the two stories may seem rather too similar but the atmosphere, emphasis and handling of the two narratives could not be more disparate. According to an unofficial questionnaire which Leo Bellingham answered in 1987, 'I read most of Doris Lessing's short stories some years ago. At their best they draw attention to pretty common aspects of human behaviour. She doesn't own a copyright on these aspects even when she got at them first.'[4] In the present case, the theme of rape, and the unimpressed behaviour of the victim after the event, may be traced back at least as far as Samuel Richardson's novel *Clarissa* of 1747-48.[5] It is also arguable that much of Bellingham's fiction has a strong autobiographical element: in the questionnaire already referred to he says, 'I've done most of the things I write about. Or half done them. That's why I want to write about them.' [6] It seems therefore that 'In for the Kill' owes nothing to 'One off the Short List', except possibly the germ of an idea: certainly there is nothing in the way of verbal or symbolic parallels.

In 'One off the Short List' Graham Spence is a radio journalist, a failed writer, 'a member of that army of people who live by their wits on the fringes of the fine arts.' (OOSL, p. 8) Barbara Coles is a talented theatrical designer, moderately attractive physically but interesting to Graham Spence mainly because she has 'an assurance, a carelessness that he recognized as the signature of success' (OOSL, p. 8), and because his way of compensating for his failure as an artist is to demonstrate his flair for establishing intellectual rapport with intelligent, successful women: it is a question of 'an ironical dignity, a proving to himself not only: I can be honest about myself, but also: I have earned the best in *that* field whenever I want it.' (OOSL, p. 9) After a successful radio interview in Spence's best manner, he insists on sharing a taxi home with Barbara Coles, invites himself in for coffee, and after failing to make any positive impression on her by his conversation, grabs her when she stands up to show him out. For a while she merely submits passively to his kisses but eventually she agrees to go to bed with him:

> His body hove up against hers to start the pressure of a new embrace. Before it could, she said: 'Oh Lord, no, I'm not going through all that again. Right, then.'
> 'What do you mean, right, then?' he demanded.
> She said, 'You're going to sleep with me. OK. Anything rather than go through that again. Shall we get it over with?'
>
> (OOSL, p. 29)

As they are both aware, he does not really desire her and when they get into bed he loses his erection. Barbara Coles thinks, 'The only way to get this over with is to make him big again, otherwise I've got to put up with him all night.' (OOSL, pp. 29-30) She sets to work on him, 'Like a bored, skilled wife . . . or like a prostitute.' (OOSL, p. 30) He ejaculates prematurely and insists on staying the night: 'He said aloud: "I'm going to have you properly tonight". She said nothing, lay silent, yawned.' (OOSL, p. 30) In the morning she rises and dresses before he is awake, but he insists on accompanying her back to the theatre where she is currently engaged on the stage design:

> 'I'd prefer to go by myself,' she remarked. Then she smiled: 'However, you'll take me. Then you'll make a point of coming right in, so that James and everyone can see – that's what you want to take me for, isn't it?' (OOSL, p. 32)

He hates her for seeing through him; and at the theatre nobody is in the least interested by the fact that they are still in company after having left together fourteen hours previously:

> He walked off slowly, listening for what might be said. For instance 'Babs, for God's sake, what are you doing with him?' or she might say 'Are you wondering about Graham Spence? Let me explain.' Graham passed the stage-hands who, he could have sworn, didn't recognize him. Then at last he heard James's voice to Barbara: 'It's no good, Babs, I know you're enamoured of that particular shade of blue, but do have another look at it, there's a good girl . . . .'
> (OOSL, p. 33)

In Leo Bellingham's 'In for the Kill', Martin Walsh is even less of a literary figure than Graham Spence. He is a reporter on a local newspaper. Jennifer Manley is also a designer, but also at a much less prestigious level than Doris Lessing's Barbara Coles: of West Indian origin she is a partner in a 'style shop' in Camden Town, a boutique specialising in Black Consciousness and Black Style: she lives in a council flat and at 22 is only just beginning to make a living wage. Martin Walsh and Jennifer Manley meet at the bus stop at the corner of the street where they both live; later they occasionally run into each other when Jennifer Manley comes home late from work, as she has to pass Walsh's house on the way to the council flats.

Martin Walsh tries to engage Jennifer Manley's interest by talking of doing an article about her, but since her boutique is in a part of London not covered by his local paper this is patently only a chatting-up ploy. (Both stories are set in London and require at least an elementary knowledge of London topography; thus, in 'One off the

Short List', when Barbara Coles asks 'Where do you live?' Graham Spence answers: ' "Wimbledon". He lived in fact in Highgate; but she lived in Fulham.' (OOSL, p. 22) But the implications of such details, though possibly obscure to some readers, can fairly easily be understood, and in 'In for the Kill' it is even stated that, 'One of the reasons why life in London was so fruitfully anonymous was that, even at the hub, it functioned only as a conglomerate of overlapping market towns.' (IFK, p. 147)) As a journalist of the inner-city suburbs, Martin Walsh does not have any complexes about his failure as a literary genius and his marginality to the lives of the true creators; in any case, evidently younger than Doris Lessing's Graham Spence, he is unashamedly hungry for adventure and experience, cynically opportunist but also 'open and inquisitive, a little bored by life but still eager to be surprised by it.' (IFK, p. 148) After the first one or two accidental meetings with Jennifer Manley he begins to hang around waiting for her 'on those evenings when he had nothing better to do, when it was not raining and when there was nothing worth seeing on television.' (IFK, p. 148) When, at their fourth or fifth encounter, he asks Jennifer for a date, she says, 'I'm not trying to play hard to get but really I'm terribly busy at the moment, I *will* some time, but not just right now, right?' (IFK, p. 149) The more he sees of her the less interesting he finds her as a person:

> If she had any topics of conversation he was unable to discover them. She had left school with one A-level. She never read a book: 'Don't have time to.' She was always too busy to go to the cinema. 'Well, I do go out *sometimes*.' 'Where?' 'Well, sometimes I go to a club.' He scarcely dared ask what kind of a club. (IFK, p. 149)

On the other hand he finds himself becoming physically obsessed with her:

> Her little bun of hair on top of her head (like a young Sikh male's) . . . . her boyish figure [which] managed to seem leggy even though she was not very tall . . . . under her customary bomber jacket or windcheater all he could detect of her bosom was a suggestion, just above the level of her elbows, of convexity rather than concavity. All these details

seem to scream out for elucidation. Was her hair naturally
kinky and artificially straightened? – did she in fact have it
tied up in a bun to straighten it? – did she sleep in the bun?
– was her pubic hair straight or kinky? (IFK, pp. 149-50)

Finally, after walking her to the entrance of her apartment block 'for
about the twentieth time' he persuades her to ask him in for coffee:
' "It's only instant and I can't let you stay long." ' Once in the
apartment he closes 'in for the kill'; taking her in his arms and, ignoring
her protests, he 'progressively divested her, in that order, of her jeans,
her panties, her left sock, her T-shirt, her bra and her monthly sanitary
towel.' (IFK, pp. 151-2) After making love she 'submitted rigidly to
a final goodnight grope' (IFK, p. 152), and they fall asleep side by
side; but when he wakes in the middle of the night he discovers she
is no longer in bed beside him:

> She was probably in the kitchen, or even worse in the
> bathroom weeping her guts out, face ugly with tears, mouth
> ready with accusations, probably with threats. Oh God, he
> hated scenes.   (IFK, p. 153)

He searches the flat for her and finally discovers her at her work
table, 'deliciously naked (except for her remaining sock), perched on
a chair, bun of hair still perched erect on her head. Not crying at all.'
She is frowning, not with displeasure but with concentration:

> There was a pencil in her hand, fresh pencil shavings beside
> her exercise book.
>   'I had an idea,' she said distantly. 'I was working.'
>   'I thought –'
> The pencil, and the dark point of a droopy little caramel-
> coloured boob, hovered over the exercise book.
>   'Go on,' she said uninterestedly. 'Go back to bed.'
>   (IFK. p. 154)

Both stories deal with exploitative males who are eager to
impose their diminishing, degrading view of womankind on
individuals in whom they have no genuine interest. The socio-political
aspect of macho aggression is, as one might expect, more explicitly
stated in the Doris Lessing story, but 'One off the Short List' is

something more – perhaps one should say *less* – than the study of the archetypal predatory male in action. Parallel to Lessing's all too plausible man versus woman theme is a less convincingly handled journalist versus genuine artist theme:

> He understood that he was not going to make it: that he had become – not a hack, no one could call him that – but a member of that army of people who live by their wits on the fringes of the arts. (OOSL, p. 8)

> 'I've got to be interviewed,' she said to the group. 'Mr Spence is a journalist.'
> Graham allowed himself a small smile ironical of the word journalist, but she was not looking at him.
>
> (OOSL, p. 13)

> . . . in that pub there would be the stage-hands, and probably James, and he'd lose contact with her. He'd become a *journalist* again. (OOSL, p. 15)

> This comradeship was extraordinarily pleasant. It was balm to the wound he had not known he carried until that evening when he had had to accept the justice of the word *journalist*. (OOSL, p. 21)

Evidently Graham Spence is forced to make up for the inferiority of his status as a journalist by sleeping with women whose achievement is superior to mere journalism. He resents his exclusion from 'the democracy of respect for each other's work, a confidence in themselves and in each other' (OOSL, p. 13), which he recognizes amongst Barbara Coles's colleagues. The limitedness of Graham Spence's psychological horizons and the inescapability of his failure to achieve status as a true artist is underlined by the final sentence of the story:

> Luckily he had an excuse not to be home that day, for this evening he had to interview a young man (for television) about his new novel. (OOSL, p. 33)

Being for television this interview is of more importance than the interview with Barbara Coles for radio; on the other hand the young man with 'his new novel' is simply a reminder of his own former status as a 'poor youth with a great future as a writer' (OOSL, p. 8), back in the days before he became a mere journalist. The problem is that one cannot quite see why a career as a journalist is morally inferior to a career as a stage designer, or why appearing in 'some interviews in newspapers and on television' (OOSL, p. 12) is morally superior to being the regular interviewer. It is not as if, by Doris Lessing's account, Barbara Coles is a particularly interesting stage designer. The backdrop she is working on 'which had a design of blue and green spirals' (OOSL, p. 13) and the key role of 'Steven, the stage-hand' in criticizing and initiating decisions hardly seem in the mainstream tradition of Karl Friedrich Schinkel or Leon Bakst:[7] in fact the whole business seems to be largely a matter of choosing cloth, something which men have always tended to leave to women. It is not that the question of Barbara Coles's talent requires amplification in order completely to realize her 'character' in the story – the presentation of Barbara Coles is on the whole very effective – but it *is* necessary to establish the difference between what it is that she has and what it is that Graham Spence represents.

Evidently the point about Graham Spence's sexual quest after successful women is that he needs to revenge himself for *any* level of achievement by a female. His acceptance of the idea of the natural inferiority of women is almost instinctive. Having attempted to win over Barbara Coles by announcing his intention to 'get away from that old chestnut: Miss Coles, how extraordinary for a woman to be so versatile in her work,' he is unable to prevent himself from falling back on exactly that line, till Barbara Coles pulls him up: 'Do you mind if we get away from all that – my manifold talents, etc . . . .' (OOSL, p. 19) And when he sees her work room his first reaction is 'I wouldn't like it if my wife had a room like this.' (OOSL, p. 23) Even his notion of 'The thousand special women', chosen according to 'Whatever it is that makes them outstanding' (OOSL, p. 31), seems to have more to do with male ideas of bedworthiness than with genuine achievement by women: the women who have achieved most in the world are usually past the age of being prestigious sexual conquests by the time they have achieved real success status.[8] It is the meaninglessness of the concept of 'the thousand special women' which provokes Barbara Coles's obscure remark (which gives the title to the story) 'I hope at least there is a short list you can say I am on, for politeness' sake.' (OOSL, p. 31) It might even be that the sexual element in Graham Spence's competitiveness is only incidental. Only briefly does he experience 'desire for her, instead of the will to have her.' (OOSL, p. 28) The reassurance he seeks is essentially not physical, not erotic:

> He enjoyed the atmosphere he was able to set up between an intelligent woman and himself: a humorous complicity which had in it much that was unspoken, and which almost made sex irrelevant. (OOSL, p. 10)

It was a question of knowing 'I have earned the best in *that* field whenever I want it.' (OOSL, p. 9) It is not the wanting and the getting, but the knowing that he *can* get *if* he wants that is important: and this is related in the story to his objective failure to fulfil his original promise as a writer. His preying on women is a compensatory reflex deriving from his unacknowledged awareness of being a failure: but the implication of the story is that if he had not initially deceived himself in his estimate of his own creative potential, neither the sense of failure nor its reflex of sexual predatoriness would have manifested themselves. In the end, therefore, the story dwindles from a parable of the war between the sexes to a more limited study of the neuroses of the failed artist.

There is none of this diversion of focus in 'In for the Kill'. Even though Martin Walsh is involved in a much less prestigious form of journalism there is no indication of dissatisfaction with his own journalistic career. It is simply an agreeable way of making a living and has nothing to do with the way he holds his ego together. Not that Martin Walsh's career as a journalist is irrelevant to the story: it provides a neatly economical means of sketching in his character, in place of the five or six pages Doris Lessing principally devotes to explaining the phenomenon of Graham Spence:

> Martin Walsh was a journalist on the *Hackney Gazette*. He had done court reports, he had done flower shows, he had

done council politics, he had done cockroaches in the
maternity ward. He had avoided doing sport and scandals
in the local constabulary. On the whole he was not a bad
journalist, being open and inquisitive, a little bored by life
but still eager to be surprised by it. His special qualification
for being on the staff of a local paper was that he liked
local news and was bored by the kind of people who worked
for the big nationals. (IFK, p. 148)

If the last sentence in this passage refers to some deep-seated sense
of failure and resentment in the professional field, or a disposition to
envy success, the issue is not pursued. Nevertheless there is a hint
of a certain readiness to make dismissive judgements of other people,
singly or en masse, and this does have a role in the story. Graham
Spence is not interested in Barbara Coles or her ideas:

The ideas, he thought, were intelligent enough; and he
would agree with them, with her, if he believed it mattered
a damn one way or another, if any of these enthusiasms
mattered a damn. (OOSL, p. 20)

For Graham Spence, Barbara Coles is simply one more means of
proving a point. Martin Walsh *is* interested in Jennifer Manley: one
has the impression of someone who, with a journalist's instincts and
habits, enjoys hanging around, snooping around, pursuing whatever
fancy attracts his attention: the problem is that, being fairly
experienced in evaluating situations and not having any particular
mental block about admitting the truth about himself to himself, he
has no difficulty in seeing that, as far as he is concerned, Jennifer
Manley is not interesting *as a person*. She is interesting as a body, as a
sex object, as an aesthetic experience divorced from the complications
of personality:

. . . . she made him think of fresh breezes, of clear thrilling
drafts of sweetly chilled spring water taken on a hot
afternoon, pure poignant sensation without consequence
or comeback . . . . (IFK, p. 149)

He is also interested in her because she is black:

> He had never had a coloured girl before. As the Regent
> d'Orléans is said to have remarked, all cats are grey in the
> dark, but not all girls were as neatly and exquisitely put
> together as this one, and her trim athletic body had an
> additional allure from being associated in his mind with
> burly West Indian youths attending weight training classes
> and exercizing in Clissold Park, as if keeping themselves
> in training for the coming race-war . . . . (IFK, p. 150)

This is close to being racist, as is:

> She was evidently one of the up and coming generation of
> black businessmen – sorry, businesspersons – which seemed
> to exist mainly in the reciprocating fantasies of liberals and
> black primary school teachers: the archetypal Miss Young
> Gifted and Black. (IFK, p. 150)

His sexual interest in her has an added piquancy from the colour of
her skin: her status as prey, is underlined by the fact that she is a
black woman. Walsh's sexism and his racism are of a piece. Whereas
Barbara Coles's alleged talents cut across the simplicity of 'One off
the Short List's' depiction of sexual exploitation, Jennifer Manley's
undoubted blackness, 'or rather coffee-colouredness' (IFK, p. 149),
simply emphasizes the principle of exploitation which is at stake,[9]
At the same time, while Doris Lessing fumbles in the attempt to
make Barbara Coles's talent convincing, the question of whether
Jennifer Manley is really as dim as Martin Walsh assumes is not really
at issue: one can accept Martin Walsh's estimate conditionally because
he is not, like Graham Spence, trying to prove himself a more
considerable person *as a person* than the woman he is pursuing: he is
simply 'on the look out for a screw' (IFK, p. 148).

It is at this point that one confronts the issue of the different
genders of the two authors, and their different sexual ideologies. 'One
off the Short List' is a story by a woman who has written movingly
about the psychological, moral and sexual exploitation of women by
men: this story itself has an important position in her contribution
on this theme.[10] 'In for the Kill' is written by a man who clearly
enjoys writing about males pursuing females and who, though clearly
very much aware of the exploitative aspect, does not regard this as

an axe to grind.[11] 'One off the Short List' is characteristic of an *oeuvre* which if anything is over-explicit, even inartistic, in its moral and ideological emphases; 'In for the Kill' is no less typical of an *oeuvre* (admittedly a much smaller one as yet) that is meticulously ambiguous in its revelation of authorial point of view. Even the status of what one might call the key fact in both stories is much more fully elucidated in 'One off the Short List':

> He let her go, but said: 'I'm going to sleep with you tonight, you know that, don't you?' . . . .
>
> She said: 'What am I supposed to do? Telephone for the police, or what?' He was hurt that she still addressed the man who had ground her into sulky apathy; she was not addressing *him* at all.
>
> She said: 'Or scream for the neighbours, is that what you want?'
>
> The gold-fringed eyes were almost black, because of the depth of the shadow of boredom over them. She was bored and weary to the point of falling to the floor, he could see that. (OOSL, pp. 27-8)

Finally she capitulates: 'Shall we get it over with?' (OOSL, p. 29) Jennifer Manley resists for a shorter period, but never officially capitulates:

> . . . . she struggled with decreasing conviction and an increasing solicitude to avoid having her clothes torn as he pulled them off her. 'Mind my T-shirt – it's a souvenir from St Vincent,' she expostulated, raising sharp-elbowed arms cooperatively, ballerina-like, to enable him to pull it off her more easily, and even half acknowledging the kiss he gave her mouth as soon as it emerged from the folds of the garment. (IFK, p. 152)

As he tries to make love to her, Barbara Coles shrinks from Graham Spence: 'He saw that she gritted her teeth against his touch' (OOSL, p. 29), 'he could feel the distaste of her flesh for his.' (OOSL, p. 30) Jennifer Manley is scarcely more enthusiastic, though 'disposing her arms and legs apparently more out of inexperience than opposition'

(IFK, p. 152), but the degree of her rejection of Martin Walsh is never as unambiguous as Barbara Coles's repudiation of Graham Spence. If Martin Walsh is a less explicitly dreary specimen than Graham Spence it does not mean that the author portrays him as acting any better, but the author so to speak *collaborates* in his sexual abuse of Jennifer Manley partly by hinting that she may have been essentially compliant in her submission but also, more importantly, by describing her rape, or seduction, or whatever it is to be called, with enthusiastically graphic flourishes. It is not simply that by comparison with Leo Bellingham, Doris Lessing often seems a grey, colourless, understated prose-stylist. Their points of view are totally different. When Doris Lessing writes:

> He lay on his side by her, secretly at work on himself, while
> he supported himself across her body on his elbow, using
> his free hand to manipulate her breasts. (OOSL, p. 29)

whether one thinks of grey prose style, classical restraint, clinical detachment, even hinted disgust, it is indisputable that Doris Lessing does not seem to find the picture she presents titillating. When Leo Bellingham writes of 'delightful memories of pointy little titties and spread thighs' and 'an adorable little bum, each succulent buttock . . . as rounded and brown as farmhouse eggs, and as smooth, except down where little twists of black hair were to be glimpsed straying back from her pubic fuzz' (IFK, p. 152), one supposes that this almost voyeuristic lyricism has the aim of making the narrative seem as sexy as Jennifer Manley seems to Martin Walsh: that is, sexy from an uncompromisingly male, macho, even sexist point of view.[12] At the same time the eventual repudiation of Martin Walsh's evaluation of Jennifer Manley is as emphatic as anything in 'One off the Short List', but less heavy-handed. This rejection is highlighted by the insistence right to the very end on Jennifer Manley as a sex-object:

> The pencil, and the dark point of a droopy little caramel-
> coloured boob, hovered over the exercise book. (IFK, p.
> 154)

The final line of the story is deceptively simple: 'Go on,' she said uninterestedly, 'Go back to bed'. The implications of what has happened have already been accepted even though their consideration in detail has been postponed on account of more important concerns. 'Bed' is where they sleep together, make love: the fact that this is their first night together and that he has forced the situation on her is less important, less interesting, than an idea she has had for her work. Yet throughout the story it has never been hinted or assumed that Jennifer Manley's work is of any objective artistic value: rather the opposite. She is presented as a boring and commonplace young woman pursuing a not untypical inner-city career: far from being interviewed in national newspapers and on television like Barbara Coles, the best she rates is being tempted half-heartedly by a philanderer with the talk of a possible feature in a local paper. Barbara Coles's home has the elegance one expects from the residence of a professional designer, with 'a little bright, intimate hall', and 'a white door' leading to 'a long, very tidy white room.' (OOSL, p. 23) Jennifer Manley's flat, inherited from parents who have returned to the West Indies, is simply 'Vintage 1959 Council Flat, with touches of post-Bob Marley teenager, the overall stylistic concept less Upper Neo-Black than Lower Paleo-Inner City Eclectic.' (IFK, p. 151) Barbara Coles has 'a table covered with drawings, sketching's, pencils' and walls concealed by 'swatches of coloured stuffs' (OOSL, p. 23); Jennifer Manley has an angle-poise lamp and an exercise book. But the point is that the quality and importance of Jennifer Manley's work is not at issue: what matters is simply that it is *hers*, it is what *she* regards as important in her life, it is an area in which *she* has chosen to invest her personality. If she is as boring an individual as Martin Walsh is inclined to suppose, it is entirely consistent that her work should be as mediocre as he suspects; but it remains her right, by virtue of her autonomy as an individual, to choose her own order of priorities, her own scale of values, and it is on this subjective scale – irrespective of any supposedly objective assessment of their comparative value as human beings – that Martin Walsh finds himself so shockingly of little account in her eyes. His seduction, or rape, of her is an intrusion in her life that is insufficiently important to derange its rhythm. (The story can also be read as suggesting that their sexual encounter had given her an idea for her work, but even in this reading the idea remains more urgent than the man who was simply the accidental occasion for having it.) If anyone it is Martin Walsh who is thrown off balance:

> If it had been up to him he would have sneaked out and left her weeping in the loo or wherever she had hidden herself. But he couldn't quite escape from a lifetime's conditioning with out-moded notions of chivalry: after all, a word or two from him might make her feel better and *then* he would sneak off. It was mean of her, really: what should have been a pleasant uncomplicated shag was being fouled up: there was always going to be the ugly contracted face and the sense of being (once again) a classic shit and cad superimposed on which should have been delightful memories of pointy little titties and spread thighs. (IFK, p. 152)

This provides a build-up sufficient to make the reader surprised that Jennifer Manley is discovered not weeping but working: Martin Walsh's surprise requires no more exposition than the strangled sentence 'I thought –'; the reader's surprise is transferred to the character and in this process the reader's whole understanding of the point of the story is transformed. It is not a twist in the plot in the classic O. Henry sense: it is an ultimatum to the reader to reassess his moral and aesthetic judgement of what has gone before.

Nevertheless the story in some senses ends in the middle. What does Martin do next? Does Jennifer come back to bed eventually? Do they make love again? Do they part friends? In a way 'In for the Kill' is less a complete narrative than a vignette, focusing on one situation in a series of situations.[13] The story ends with Martin Walsh experiencing a moment of truth. Perhaps something positive will come of it.

There is no moment of truth at the end of 'One off the Short List', only the preparation of more lies:

> Graham left the stage, went past the office where the stage-door man sat reading a newspaper. He looked up, nodded, went back to his paper. Graham went to find a taxi, thinking: I'd better think up something convincing, then I'll telephone my wife. (OOSL, p. 33)

An unattractive episode is closed: now everyone is in a hurry to forget about it as soon as possible.

But at least Doris Lessing has made her point: or perhaps half-made two separate points. In the end the chief difference between the two stories is that one is trying to make points: the other is simply written with a somewhat elusive point of view, and with a stronger faith in the power of circumstances to speak for themselves. Perhaps a man could not have had the bitterness to write 'One off the Short List', and perhaps a woman would not have had the slyness to write 'In for the Kill', but ultimately it is not gender, or ideology, or underlying preoccupation but two different styles of narrative which distinguish the two stories: not a female writer's narrative manner and a male writer's narrative manner, but simply a point-making manner and a point-hinting manner: the different narrative manners of two very different writers who have happened to illustrate their difference by tackling a similar theme.

Notes

1   This question is handled (from a somewhat different per-spective) in two forthcoming articles: A. D. Harvey's 'Living Together and Writing Apart – Richard Aldington and H. D.' and Graham Headley's 'Marrying for Position in *Jane Eyre*, *Wuthering Heights* and *Agnes Grey*'. The authors dealt with in the latter piece are not of course unrelated but the general theoretical issue is illuminatingly discussed in the introduc-tory section.

   I am grateful to Ludovico Parra, who is currently working on a full-length study of Bellingham, for advice and access to unpublished materials relevant to this essay.

2   Doris Lessing's 'One off the Short List' was originally published in *Kenyon Review* (1963), vol. 25, no. 2, pp. 217-44 and appeared in her collection *A Man and Two Women* (Lon-don, 1963). This article quotes page references from the 1965 Granada paperback edition which has been frequently reprinted. The story also appears in Doris Lessing, *Stories* (New York, 1978) and other collections of twentieth-

century short stories, e.g. James H. Pickering (ed.), *Fiction 100; an anthology of short stories* (London, 1974).

The following are useful articles on Doris Lessing's short fiction:

Clare Hanson, 'Each Other: Images of Otherness in the Short Fiction of Doris Lessing, Jean Rhys and Angela Carter', *Journal of the Short Story in English* (Spring 1988), vol.10, pp. 67-82.

Virginia Pruitt, 'The Crucial Balance: A Theme in Lessing's Short Fiction', *Studies in Short Fiction* (Summer 1981), vol. 18, no. 3, pp. 281-5.

Helen J. Millar, 'Don's Lessing's Short Stories: A Woman's Right to Choose?', *Literature in North Queensland* (1978), vol.6, no.1, pp. 24-38.

Helen J. Millar, 'Doris Lessing's Short Stories: the Male's Point of View', *Literature in North Queensland* (1978), vol.6 no.2, pp. 42-52.

Leo Bellingham's 'In for the Kill' was originally published in *New Beginning* (1986), vol.5, no.2, pp. 147-54, which is the edition quoted in this article: the story has also been published in Italian.

3   Germaine Greer, *The Madwoman's Underclothes: Essays and Occasional Writings 1968-85* (London, 1986), pp. 152-68, 'Seduction is a four letter word' at p. 159ff. This essay was first published in *Playboy* in January 1973.

4   From a typescript communicated by Ludovico Parra.

5   Samuel Richardson, *Clarissa*, 7 vols (London 1747-8), especially vol. 5, letter xlviii.

6   From a typescript communicated by Ludovico Parra, cf. Juan Luis Borges, 'The Approach to Al-Mu'tasim', in *Fictions* (London, 1965), where Mir Bahadur Ali says, with regard to the suggestion that his narrative has a resemblance to Kipling's story 'On the City Wall', 'it would be most abnormal if two paintings depicting the tenth night of Muharram did not coincide in some way.'

7   Schinkel (1781-1841) is more famous as an architect but also produced some astonishingly romantic stage designs in the 1800s; Bakst (1886-1924) was, amongst other things, the most innovative of the designers working for Diaghilev.

8   Perhaps one might adduce in this context Catherine the Great at the height of her power, Golda Meir, Margaret Thatcher, or Margaret Mead and Marie Curie. Perhaps significantly, women holding political power are generally characterized either as totally sexless, even anaphrodisiac (Thatcher) or else as insatiable sexual predators (Catherine the Great).

9   A. D. Harvey, *Literature into History* (London, 1988), pp. 31-2 discusses, in connection with Richardson's *Pamela*, the analogous process whereby class oppression fuses with sexual oppression.

10   Doris Lessing's best-known book, and the classic statement on this topic, is *The Golden Notebook* which was written during the period that also produced 'One off the Short List'. First published in 1962 and reprinted three times during the next decade, *The Golden Notebook* was issued in a new edition in 1972 and thereafter became a key text in the Women's Movement.

11   Leo Bellingham's only novel to date, *Oxford: the Novel* (London, 1981) [reissued under my own name in 2012], may even be described as a set of variations on the theme of men pursuing women, though in a couple of chapters the experience is convincingly described from the woman's point of view. See Ludovico Parra, 'Oxford: the Novel come romanzo storico', *Annuario dell'Università degli Studi di Bari* (1983), vol.2, pp. 215-38, at pp. 220-2.

One notes that Thomas Hardy showed himself, from *A Pair of Blue Eyes* onwards, almost as sensitive as George Eliot to the way in which contemporary society limited women to type-cast roles and psychologically hemmed in their strivings towards selfhood, but that, having completed his classic study of sexual exploitation in *Tess of the D'Urbervilles*, he went on to produce *The Well-Beloved* in which, at twenty-year intervals, a man evidently incapable of forming an adult relationship pursues a series of claustrophobic flirtations with girls belonging to three generations of the same family, it being clearly implied that women are only interesting as young girls to be picked up.

12   Something similar may be seen in Vladimir Nabokov's *Lolita* (1955), a work which arguably has had considerable influence on Bellingham. Despite his notorious fondness for technicolor prose, and despite the claim made on its first appearance that *Lolita* was simply pornographic, Nabokov's lyrical descriptions of young girls in his novel have a key function in communicating Humbert's personality and in developing the novel's theme of lost, displaced or wasted beauty. Note also the use of titillating description (with a more obvious sense of pastiche) in Nabokov's earlier *Kamera Obskura* (1933), translated by the author as *Laughter in the Dark* (1938), and his remark in *The Real Life of Sebastian Knight* (1941), 'he used parody as a kind of springboard for leaping into the highest region of serious emotion' (Penguin, 1964 edn. p. 76). The way in which Nabokov's apparent self-indulgence is always kept in check by an ironic framework is one of the elements of his influence on Bellingham that can be most readily identified in e.g. *Oxford: the Novel*.

13   For a discussion of different categories of short narrative, see Johannes Klein, *Geschichte der Deutschen Novelle: von Goethe bis zur Gegenwart* (Wiesbaden, 1956), pp. 8-27.

Dickens's Villains: A Confession and a Suggestion

Since Edmund Wilson's essay 'Dickens: The Two Scrooges', published in *The Wound and the Bow* in 1941, it has been something of a commonplace that Dickens drew on what he suspected about his own character and disposition for his villains, even the most theatrical and extravagant of them.[1] For Christopher Hibbert, writing in the 1960s, James Carker in *Dombey and Son* was 'the type of character in which Dickens puts much of his fears about himself, the sort of man he dreads to think he might have been, or might even yet become.'[2] For John Carey in the 1990s, Ralph Nickleby in *Nicholas Nickleby* 'reveals a real uncertainty in Dickens about what ideals are acceptable. He represents a relentless drive to succeed – and in this respect he is much more like Dickens than Nicholas is. . . . Ralph, like Dickens, would laugh scathingly at people who lay claim to over much sensitivity such as Mrs Wititterly.'[3]

This view of Dickens finds unexpected confirmation in a letter which the Russian novelist Fyodor Dostoyevsky wrote to his friend Stepan Dmitriyevich Yanovsky in 1878: the relevant passage of this letter – translated here for the first time into English – is as follows:

> Obviously a writer cannot escape from what he has seen and felt in his own life. It is his own senses that tell him that the sky is blue in summer, that rain is wet, that ice is cold. The characters in his books speak or are silent like people he has met. The person he sees most of, most often, actually every day, is himself. When it comes to a question of why a man does something else, it's the author's own actions which make him understand, or fail to understand, the sources of human action. Dickens told me the same thing when I met him at the office of his magazine 'All Through The Year' [*All The Year Round*] in 1862. He told

me that all the good simple people in his novels, Little Nell, even the holy simpletons like Barnaby Rudge, are what he wanted to have been, and his villains were what he was (or rather, what he found in himself), his cruelty, his attacks of causeless enmity towards those who were helpless and looked to him for comfort, his shrinking from those whom he ought to love, being used up in what he wrote. There were two people in him, he told me: one who feels as he ought to feel and one who feels the opposite. From the one who feels the opposite I make my evil characters, from the one who feels as a man ought to feel I try to live my life. Only two people? I asked.[4]

Dostoyevsky was in London for eight days in the summer of 1862, but though he later published an interesting account of the tour in western Europe which he made in that year,[5] and though he mentions Dickens's books elsewhere in his correspondence, his letter to Yanovsky is the only reference he ever made to meeting with Dickens: there seems to be no record of this encounter in Dickens's own papers.[6]

Particularly intriguing is Dickens's allusion to 'attacks of causeless enmity towards those who were helpless and looked to him for comfort'. It is a truism that Dickens, product of a dysfunctional family, filled his novels with dysfunctional families, but it is worth asking whether Dickens's frequent recurrence to this theme originates in the traumas he experienced as a child or in the accumulating pressures of being himself a head of a family. Mr Micawber, in *David Copperfield*, evidently owes much to Dickens's improvident father but is essentially a minor – and comic – character. Apart from the parasitic Dorrit, the frozen Dombey and the equally frigid Gradgrind – the latter two seemingly lay figures necessitated by the author's agenda rather than drawn from life – fathers are not as important in the plots of Dickens's novels as father-substitutes such as an uncle or an older brother, or possibly an uncle who seems like an older brother. In *Nicholas Nickleby* the villainous uncle, Ralph Nickleby, actually hangs himself when he discovers that he is a father.

One may argue that the melodramatic family relationships of

Dickens's fiction belong to a well-established literary tradition. In *Oliver Twist* the actions of Monks, Oliver's unknown half-brother, are reminiscent of the persecution of the poet Richard Savage by his mother (as recorded by Savage's first biographer, the great Dr Johnson) and of Falkland's harrying of the eponymous hero of Godwin's novel *Caleb Williams*. Dickens could hardly have been unaware of the parallels. In 1835 he had sent his future wife 'the volume [of Johnson's *Lives of the Poets*] which contains the Life of Savage. I have turned down the leaf. Now *do* read it attentively'.[7] A couple of years later he was trying to interest publishers in a novel about Savage written by an acquaintance named Charles Whitehead.[8] As for *Caleb Williams*, in 1842 he referred, in a letter to Edgar Allan Poe, to Godwin's claim that he had written his most famous novel backwards, dénouement first, a matter that would hardly have interested Dickens if he had never read the book.[9] Yet it is difficult to believe that Dickens would have so consistently returned, over a period of more than thirty years, to a theme that derived primarily from other writers: on the contrary it seems more plausible that his interest in Johnson's 'Life of Savage' and *Caleb Williams* was at least partly to be accounted for by their consonance with his own preoccupations. Yet however painful the experiences of Dickens's adolescence, he had never been the victim of a cold-bloodedly unrelenting persecution such as experienced by Savage, Caleb Williams, or Oliver Twist, etc. That his insight into persecution came at least to some extent from a guilty conscience is suggested by a passage in Chapter XLIX of *Barnaby Rudge* where he describes the older Rudge's attitude towards his half-witted son Barnaby:

> In the intense selfishness which the constant presence before him of his great crimes. . . . engendered, every thought of Barnaby, as his son, was swallowed up and lost. Still, his presence was a torture and a reproach . . . . with his unearthly aspect, and half-formed mind, he seemed to the murderer a creature who had sprung into existence from his victim's blood.

When he wrote that, Dickens already had a wife and three small children and was perhaps already a connoisseur of the mingled impatience and delight, frustration and enchantment, that are part and parcel of sharing a home with a trio of noisy toddlers. Always a man of especially intense feelings, and unusually ardent in his self-absorption, Dickens may well have been astonished by the bitterness of the vexation his wife and off-spring must occasionally – perhaps more than just occasionally – have caused him. Or perhaps it was less his children than his irritatingly useless father, whose debts he was seeking to repudiate at about the time he was writing *Barnaby Rudge*; perhaps it was a combination of his parent and his children, squeezing him, as it were, between the older and the younger generation. By the time Dostoyevsky met Dickens, the latter's father was dead, his wife had been abandoned, his older children were adults, and all but two of his novels had been written and published to great acclaim, but Dostoyevsky's reminiscence of Dickens's words indicates that, even after two decades, some sort of conflict of feeling regarding family obligations was still vivid in Dickens's memory.

1   Edmund Wilson, *The Wound and the Bow* (Cambridge Mass. 1941) pp. 1-104, especially pp. 102-3

2   Christopher Hibbert, *The Making of Charles Dickens* (London 1967) p. 199 – see too p. 232 for the suggestion that Quilp's 'wild vitality' and 'wonderful command of vivid language' in *The Old Curiosity Shop* is also reminiscent of Dickens.

3   Charles Dickens, *Nicholas Nickleby*, Everyman Edition with Introduction by John Carey (London 1993) p. xxviii.

4   'F. M. Dostoyevskii: Dva Pis'ma 1878', ed. K. K. Shayakhmetov, *Vedomosti Akademii Nauk Kazakhskoi* SSR: *Institut Istorii, Filologii i Filosofii* vol. 45 (Alma Ata 1987) pp. 49-55 at p. 53-4. This letter, dated from Staraya Russa 18 July O.S. 1878, is not in A. S. Dolinin's standard edition of *F. M. Dostoyevskii: Pis'ma* (4 vols. Moscow 1928-1959) or in Joseph Frank and David I. Goldstein eds. *Selected Letters of Fyodor Dostoyevsky* (New Brunswick 1987).

5   Fyodor Dostoyevsky, *Winter Notes on Summer Impressions* ed. Kyril FitzLyon (London 1985) espec. pp.43-7.

6   Cf. Madeline House, Graham Storey, Kathleen Tillotson eds. *The Pilgrim Edition: The Letters of Charles Dickens* (12 vols.

Oxford 1965-2002) vol. 10 passim.

7   Ibid. vol. 1 p. 85, Dickens to Catherine Hogarth, ?29 Oct 1835.

8   Ibid. vol. 1 p. 250, Dickens to Richard Bentley, ?21 April 1837.

9   Ibid. vol. 3 p. 107, Dickens to Edgar Allan Poe, 6 March 1842.

The Emperor's New Clothes: Hans Christian Andersen's Alternative Ending

When Hans Christian Andersen published his story 'The Emperor's New Clothes' ('Keyserens nye Klaeder') in the third instalment of his *Eventyr* in 1837 it had the ending which ever since has been familiar to generations of young readers. As the Emperor, proud of his amazing light-weight new robes, parades through the town, a little child cries, 'He hasn't anything on!' The cry is taken up by the crowd, but the Emperor thinks, 'The procession has to go on,' and walks on more proudly than ever, while his noblemen hold high the train that isn't actually there. In fact this ending was added to the story at the printers: originally the narrative ended with the crowd admiring the amazing new robes.(Jackie Wullschlager, *Hans Christian Andersen: the Life of a Storyteller*, published in 2000, p.170-171) And there is another, even more ironical, version which Hans Christian Andersen apparently confided to the first of his English translators, Mary Howitt, when he visited her in Clapton, in what is now the London Borough of Hackney, in July 1847. (For this meeting see Elias Bredsdorff, *H.C. Andersen og England.* published in 1954, p.60)

The first edition of Mary Howitt's rendering of Andersen's fairy stories, published in 1846, did not include 'The Emperor's New Clothes'. She seems to have prepared a second, enlarged, edition that included the story, but this was not published in her lifetime because the first edition was a commercial failure: according to her autobiography it 'did not pay the cost of printing'. (*Autobiography*, edited by her daughter Margaret Howitt, published in two volumes 1889, vol.2 p.30) By the time this second edition was issued, in 1897, nine years after Howitt's death, numerous rival translations had popularized what had become the standard ending of 'The Emperor's New Clothes', and the publisher, W. & R. Chambers, evidently thought it best to go along with the usual version of the ending instead of the one found in her papers.

Mary Howitt's papers are now in the archives of the London Borough of Hackney. Her draft translation of 'The Emperor's New Clothes', which she called 'The Invisible Robe', is headed 'Mr. Andersen gave me this. He told me the people in Copenhagen objected to it.' The text is identical to the rather wooden rendering of Andersen's story in the 1897 edition of *Wonderful Stories: for Children* till the final paragraphs. In the Hackney manuscript version the narrative concludes:

> 'But he has no robes on at all!', a little child cried out.
> 'That rude child wants to spoil the procession,' said a bystander.
> 'He's trying to spoil the procession,' said all the people.
> And so they beat the child with their walking sticks, and those who had no walking sticks threw mud at him.
> But the Emperor thought within himself, 'I must go through with the procession,' and so he held himself a little higher, and the chamberlains held on tighter than ever, and carried the train that was not there at all. (Hackney Archives L/15)

One can see why this version seemed a little too strong for the Danes. A satirical handling of the vanity of the high and mighty makes a safer political point than a satirical handling of ordinary people who might buy Andersen's books.

About My Writing

Ninety-nine per cent — over one million words — of the non-fiction I have had published has been under my own name. Inevitably it has contained errors and even 'howlers', but as far as has been humanly possible, despite the demoralizing conditions in which I usually had to work, it has been checked and rechecked for accuracy and clarity. The bulk of the remaining one per cent has also involved no sort of scam, other than the use of a pseudonym, a ploy adopted by any number of well-known writers. Unlike certain members of the British Academy I have never published under my own name things I have invented to back up a scholarly thesis.

I was originally a political historian, and began with a Ph.D. thesis, a couple of articles in scholarly quarterlies and a book on the politics of party in early nineteenth-century Britain. I also became interested in the relationship of literature and society, thinking that a study of changing styles and fashions in literature might provide an accessible route to a clearer understanding of the mechanisms of social change generally. I even hoped it might be possible to achieve a bringing together of the disciplines of history and literary studies, something much talked of at that period. Over the next twenty-five years, I wrote three books on different aspects of the history/literature overlap (or four books if one includes my *Sex in Georgian England*, in which the sources cited include poetry and novels). Even more predominant than literature as a cultural form is war. I wrote two books about war (three if one includes my book on war literature), plus one on political violence, and the equivalent of a book in journal articles. In my work on the history of warfare, as with my work on the relationship of literature and society, I explored the parallels and divergences of developments in different countries, regarding comparative analysis of this kind as a precondition of any attempt at placing investigation of these subjects on a scientific basis. My growing recognition that we simply do not know enough about the details of what happened in the past sidetracked me into bibliographical work in a number of neglected areas and into archival research that resulted in the publication of previously unknown texts by Lord Byron, Rudyard Kipling, E. M. Forster, Ezra Pound, T.S. Eliot and other writers.

One's published work should stand on its own, speak for itself. In Britain however a number of organizations have made it their business to try and prevent this happening. In 1978 the Historical Association's *Annual Bulletin of Historical Literature* mentioned me six times, noting for example that my first book, *Britain in the Early Nineteenth Century*, 'has been widely praised'. The same publication, in its 1992 to 1995 issues, mentioned me not once, though during this period I published *Collision of Empires: Britain in Three World Wars 1793 –1945*, which according to *The Times*, showed 'astounding erudition', and *Sex in Georgian England*, which *The New Statesman* thought 'magnificently researched', and co-edited an edition of the prison diary of the political reformer John Horne Tooke which was praised in *The Times Literary Supplement*. *The Annual Bulletin of Historical Literature* is on the open shelves of quite a number of larger libraries: readers don't need to ask anyone's permission to check for themselves. One review of *Sex in Georgian England* in the national daily press described me as an 'adroit deployer of the precious scrap of hard fact', and many of these facts had not appeared in print since the early nineteenth century, but the book is not referred to in the voluminous footnotes of most of the supposedly scholarly works covering the same topic published since the appearance of the hard-back edition of my book twenty-five years ago. Ph.D. students at London University are routinely advised not to include any of my publications in the bibliographies of their dissertations: especially in cases where I have produced archival evidence contradicting the surmises or outright fabrications of earlier scholars. In effect I have been air-brushed out of the picture, like a liquidated ex-colleague in a group photo of communist leaders.

Since this sort of thing is regarded as legitimate scholarly behaviour in Britain it is perhaps not surprising that 700 or so applications for lecturing posts in this country were unsuccessful (though it certainly surprised senior academics at the Italian, French and German universities where I did find temporary employment). Having always wanted to be a novelist in any case I utilized some of my unwanted leisure to write experiments in fiction, three of which were published as novels and others as short stories: some of the latter also appeared in Italian, German and Japanese translation. In my late forties I also began to have my poems posted up on London buses, and some of these poems later appeared in magazines. Like other writers in the second half of the twentieth century I experimented with mixing fact and fiction, and had the idea of producing a short story that existed only in the summaries and short extracts appearing in a scholarly article about it (see *Critical Survey* vol.5 no.1, 1993). My now famous Dostoyevsky-meets-Dickens piece in *The Dickensian* (vol.98 part 3, 2002), like the more recent Hans Christian Andersen spoof in *The Times Literary Supplement* (21 February 2014) were a variation on this theme, though these two pieces may also be regarded as *hommages* to the writers in question. Of course, if I had found somewhere to publish these *hommages* under my own name, the immediate response would have been that they were nothing at all like Dickens or Hans Christian Andersen and that they would not fool anyone for an instant.

I might say here that the Hans Christian Andersen *hommage* was in no sense conceived as revenge on *The Times Literary Supplement* for printing a hatchet job on me by Eric Naiman in 2013. The latter might have been seen as a standing invitation to respond in an appropriate manner, especially as it inspired the *Journal of the Society for Army Historical Research* to pull an article of mine after I had completely rewritten it according to their requirements, and corrected the proofs, but as one of Elmore Leonard's characters says 'Revenge is for losers, guys that got nothing else to do.' In fact I only sent the Hans Christian Andersen skit to *The Times Literary Supplement* after half a dozen publications with larger circulations had shown no interest. As for the notion that my occasional spoofs undermine scholarship, well, that rather depends on whether or not one regards the concepts 'scholarship' and 'ganging up on someone with a better publication record' as synonymous.

Envoi:
I Want to Make Something With You

I want to make something with you
So the magic in what you do
The vibe that goes from your bones to your work
Becomes my magic too.

I want to put the best of me
In a shared design that gives the key
To the dreams and the hopes and the loves of the world
Till at least the Twenty-second Century.

But even more I want to see
New existences take shape
That come from your eyes and your will and your hands
In some way because of me.

Lightning Source UK Ltd.
Milton Keynes UK
UKHW022139030120
356337UK00001B/10/P